FEEDING THE URGE

REMASTERED

JEFFREY KOSH

FEEDING THE URGE
Fourth Edition
Copyright © 2017 Jeffrey Kosh
All rights reserved.
Edited by Natalie G. Owens
Introduction by Kat Yares
Published by Optimus Maximus Publishing
Cover by Jeffrey Kosh Graphics
First Edition published on January 31st 2012

ISBN-10: 1-944732-26-8
ISBN-13: 978-1-944732-26-4

KUDOS TO THESE PEOPLE

During the creation of this novel, I received help and encouragement from Cheri Kimmi, Simona Rossetti, and Pamela Nihiser.

A special thank you goes to Natalie G. Owens for keeping Axel J. Hyde's voice intact in her wonderful edits, to Kat Yares for moving my soul, to Billie Sue Mosiman and Franklin E. Wales for believing in me, and to Suzi M for her constructive critics. Special mentions go to Jaime Johnesee for being my little sister in the written world, Vix Kirkpatrick for pointing me to the right way, and Jennifer Thomas for loving Axel so much.

INTRODUCTION

by Kat Yares

I was first introduced to the remarkable Jeffrey Kosh's writing back in February of 2012 with the First Edition of the book you are now holding in your hands (or reading on your eReader), *Feeding the Urge*. I remember opening it on my brand new Kindle and being lost for two days in the wonder and imagery his words brought to what I thought was going to be 'just another serial killer' story. In that thought, I was wrong, so very, very wrong.

Since that time, I've gotten to know Jeffrey Kosh's work well and have read just about-if not all-of everything he has written since the original release of this book. Each story he crafts has the same magic as this and I've yet not to enjoy each and every one.

Yet, *Feeding the Urge* will always be my favorite. Not because it was my first, but more because the story opened up the English language to me in ways I had not encountered in a very long time. *Feeding the Urge* was both literary and horrifying at the same time and other than Shirley Jackson and a few others, that was rare and wonderful.

The characters in this story will have you questioning what is good, what is evil and if, in the end, it is your own perceptions that make that choice for you. Nothing here is black and white – the shades of gray at times are overpowering and yet, you will keep turning the pages.

Since I read the first edition of this book, I have gotten to know Jeffrey Kosh as a person also. As friends on Facebook and other social networking sites, he and I have chatted, ranted and raved about this and that, and simply enjoyed each other's company and opinions. Part of me is very jealous of his 'digital nomad' status – while the other part is simply and thoroughly happy that his nomadic path crossed past my hermitized door.

Not only is Jeffrey a brilliant writer, he is also an amazing artist. The cover of the book you hold in your hands was designed by him. In fact, Jeffrey has done all of his book covers, as well as the covers decorating the books of many Indie authors. The man has more talent in his pinky than I have in my entire brain.

So kick back and read this new edition of *Feeding the Urge*. I can almost guarantee you that this will not be the last Jeffrey Kosh book you read – it's only the first in a long adventure through the mind of a brilliant writer.

FEEDING

THE URGE

REMASTERED

A Novel by
JEFFREY KOSH

JEFFREY KOSH

When you came in the air went out.
And every shadow filled up with doubt.
I don't know who you think you are,
But before the night is through,
I wanna do bad things with you.

BAD THINGS – Jace Everett

PROLOGUE

THE MONSTER I AM

Hello, my fellow traveler, my name is Axel Jeffrey Hyde. I'm Assistant Medical Examiner at the Prosperity County Morgue – here in south-central Florida. Hope this does not upset you. Well, actually it's too late for that; I don't think you ever dreamed of ending up down here, at least, not intentionally. Yes, buddy, you are now laying on one of my autopsy slabs, waiting for me to cut you open and find out what caused your actual condition.

That means ... you're dead.

Sorry about that.

State Trooper Danforth Wallace found you by the side of Route 78. Nobody knows who you are, and I'm here for that—to discover your identity.

Do you mind if we chat while I'm doing my job? I'm sure this does not disturb you too much, but it helps me focus. Would you like to know something about me?

Well, here we go.

I was born in Phoenix, Arizona, from Randolph Hyde—a self-made man and not-so- honest cop   and Janc Thewlis, a good nurse with a frail nervous system. I was a good boy, you know? Calm, I never caused troubles. Neat; I always kept my room tidy.

Just wait a minute … cutting your sternum requires strength.

CRACK!

What was I saying? Oh yes, my infancy.

Nothing special, I do not want to bore you to death ... oh, sorry! I didn't mean to be rude. Stupid pun. Really stupid pun.

Anyway, I had an almost plain infancy. The usual—schooling, games, going to church on Sundays. Except friends. Those I had not. You see, I was the silent guy, the one other kids avoid because of his weirdness. Not a nerd, neither the most popular; I was just like a keepsake, you know: one of those things you do not have a use for, but you find among your stuff nonetheless. As for bullies, no, they never tried to pick me up, being big for my age, with a strong body and a no-shit face. Being raised on my grandparents' farm provided to that. So, they simply ignored me.

Girls?

None—too scary for them, they called me 'Spooky'— behind my back. I knew about it, but simply, I didn't give a rat's ass. Well, after all, they had been right. I *was* spooky. I was like a disturbing black spot on the wallpaper; you know it's there, but you don't remember how it came to be, and mostly, you don't know what it's made of; you try to rub it off, but it never goes away, until you just give up and decide to ignore its existence. But it's still there.

I liked weird things, dead animals the most. I could spend a whole day looking inside a recent road kill, especially armadillos—those freaky animals are very interesting.

But, except for that, nothing traumatic happened in my infancy. I was not mistreated or molested by my parents, I was well-fed, and no queer relative filled my mind with scary, shocking stuff.

Until ... 1978, when everything changed, giving birth to this strange guy who's extracting your stomach right now.

I was reborn in a terrible night of August in a place called Kamp Koko, on the shores of Lake Okeechobee, right here, in Prosperity Glades. My father had lost his job six months before—still do not know why, but I do suspect he was thrown out of the force for unconventional behavior for a cop. As for my mother, well, she had a final break and was recovering from a bad attack of hysteria. My dad had an older brother here, Deputy Sergeant Angus M. Hyde—a big piece of shit in my opinion, if you ask me. And you are not.

Uncle Angus offered my family a new start.

'Come over here,' he said. *'You can work with me; we're brothers,'* and a load of crap like that. You see, it was just good old Angus' way to kill two birds with one stone: first, having his little

4

bro again under control (something he really enjoyed); second, well, my mother. I do not know all the details—and do not want to, but my dear mom used to be Angus' girlfriend a long time ago, but not in a galaxy so far away, if you know what I mean.

Here now, I'm sorry, but I have to turn you facedown.

THUMP!

Good boy.

To make a long story short, we ended down here. Oh, it was amazing for a ten-year rascal raised in the desert.

You got it all here. Alligators (I love them), plenty of snakes, birds, frogs, fishes, wonderful colorful plants, mosquitoes, beautiful flowers, mosquitoes, lakes, mosquitoes, and the ocean.

Did I mention the mosquitoes?

They're widespread here; have to get used to them or you'll go nuts by the end of the month.

It didn't take me too long to adapt.

However, that summer of '78, my parents sent me to have a wonderful outdoor experience in the swamps.

'A Marvelous place for a marvelous fun'—so said the commercial. Circus-themed bunks, clown-like camp counselors, funny excursions in the wilds, and...

… forceful sexual encounters with *Kurmudgeon*—Mr. Russell Floyd's *'comic'* alter ego.

That bastard—I still hate him after all these years—had put the place up because he cared for kids. No, he loved kids. Too much for my tastes.

A plump guy, who liked to dress up as a clown – for he'd been one back in the '60s – Floyd was everything except a caring person. He was like a lone wolf scanning the herd before the strike. He probed, selected, probed again, teased, until he was certain he'd found his perfect playmate. Problematic kids were his ground because nobody would believe them, mostly their parents.

And, guess what? He decided I fitted, so got the luck of being among the chosen—beaten, bitten, terrorized, and violated in all possible ways for almost two weeks, until things went from bad to worse.

I saw Floyd kill Arnold Rothstein, a seven-year old brat. And the man saw me, too.

It had been by accident; the creep had no interest in killing kids, just scaring them and ...

Well, you know.

Poor Arnie had been hit so hard by one of Kurmy's love-slaps that he had tumbled, his head had hit a table's corner and that had left him as cold as stone on the spot. Floyd, of course, had panicked. He didn't know what to do, and had frantically looked for a way out of the big mess he had just fallen into.

Unfortunately, I was hiding in the same damn room in which the murder had just happened, and—here comes the bad news—I let out a loud sigh, revealing my presence to the fiend.

Nice tattoo, this one you have here, right below the shoulder blade. Is it a star or a pentagram? Not responding, huh? Not yet?

You'll think I'm nuts; a lunatic speaking to dead people. Maybe it's true, maybe I am mad and that would surely be the way people would call me should they find out about my 'real' activities. However, this doesn't change what I am.

I'm some kind of monster.

I don't know what kind, exactly, but one, stay sure.

For sometimes, dead people—like you—speak to me.

Not with words or full sentences, but on an instinctual level, a spiritual one if you prefer. To be honest, they do not speak right to me; to be more precise, they speak to my *Rider*.

What's a Rider?

Oh, here comes the nice part of the story. I don't know what it is, or what it really looks like—besides, I just had a glimpse of it. I only felt its urges and some suggestions came to my mind. You know, sometimes, if the Rider considered one like you interesting (meaning a dead body) it would send a name, an image maybe, of a place where I could find something helpful to identify the dead person, and—most of all—the murderer.

Nevertheless, you are still not talking, and my friend, that is good news for me. That could mean that the damn thing is finally gone. Bad news for you: we'll have to hold you here in the freezer for some time.

Sorry for doing that to you, but I have to probe the anus.

Time to go on with my story.

My hellish rebirth happened that night. I tried to hide everywhere as the bastard came after me with an ax. You know how it works: first kill is a mountain, next one is a slope. So, the bastard pedophile decided that one dead kid or two wouldn't make any difference.

That night, the darn campground appeared scarier than it really was, while I looked for a way out, a safe place to hide.

Anything.

The only place I managed to find was inside a half-submerged, abandoned concrete pipe, which jutted out of the marshy waters by the lake. Deep darkness clouded its depths, and I was clearly afraid of going in there, but the stalking pig – who kept calling my name, promising no hurt yet brandishing an ax – convinced me otherwise. So I gathered courage and crawled inside, feetfirst, then slid backward. Had I descended headfirst I'd have faced the trouble of being unable to turn on myself—the pipe was too tight for my size—and mostly I didn't want to get stuck inside there with a pedo-clown bearing on my ass. You can't imagine the awfulness of being there alone in that claustrophobic darkness, with the knowledge of my tormentor being outside, maybe enjoying my fear—or worse, just waiting in ambush. Hell! I was ten years old! I didn't want to die.

I can't remember how much time I spent inside that pipe; it felt like eternity to me.

Outside, I could hear no movements, no sounds. Once, I was tempted to get a peek, but couldn't gather enough bravery, having spent all I had. Then, the wind carried the stench of his terrible cheap cologne down the tube. He was close, right out there. Maybe he'd found my hiding place and was standing still, close to the entrance, waiting for me to stick out my head and...

I retreated further down the tube like a snail taking refuge into its shell, my heart playing a deafening tune into my ears.

And that was when something strange, unnatural, happened.

I remember hearing a voice, coming out of nowhere, whispering my name. At first, I believed it came from him. I was sure it was his voice taunting me, letting me know he knew where my hiding place was. Then, I realized the murmuring came from behind me, right from the pitch darkness beyond my own feet! I had to turn my head to scan into that blackness, but saw nothing. Yet, I heard it again...

And peed into my pants.

After that, the thing from below began to chuckle, not in an evil way, as one of them monsters in horror flicks, but it was the hearty chuckling of a benevolent granny. And, I do not know how—or why—but I was no longer afraid. Not of the thing, at least. I was still worried about Kurmudgeon, yet I felt different.

My fear was replaced by hate.

If hate does have a taste, buddy, I assure you I sampled it, because that phantom inside the pipe handed me a first dose, in the same way a pusher does with the soon-to-be drug-addicted client, and then put me on the string for the rest of my life.

Somehow, I retrieved a yard-long iron spike inside the tube and clutched it with both hands. And Russell Floyd became my Rider's first victim as I sprang like a jack-in-a-box from the tube and plunged the metal rod inside man's left eye. He squealed—as the pig he was—trashing on the ground, while dark blood, mixed with yellowish optic fluid, oozed through his trembling fingers. Then, I quickly retrieved his ax and had it find its way into his balding skull, ending his screams once for all.

After that, I lost consciousness.

You're clean, boy. Nothing inside. Just a pause, I need to change my gloves.

I do not remember how I was cleared of the murder, or what

happened next. I only know I'd changed. A Rider, a spirit of murder if you like, lived inside me from that night on, urging me to kill, spill blood, and revel in morbid stuff. Oh, I had no control over it. You see, the thing only came out at certain times, such as when, with my job as Assistant Medical Examiner, I stumbled on crimes of sexual nature. As you can imagine, dude, I can't stand pedophiles, rapists, and their sort. No, absolutely.

So, I convinced myself the thing was using my rage—my *urge*, if you prefer—to clean up the world from such useless scum.

What a douche! I didn't know the spirit's true purposes, and believe me, I still ignore it, but of one thing I'm certain: there's nothing noble in its needs.

I wasn't a vigilante, a Bat-Man-like avenger of the dark, far from it; I liked to play with my victims.

Didn't I say I'm a monster?

For, even if I finally got rid of its dark influence, I can't erase the memories of my gory games. And I can't deny my enjoyment. I am as guilty as charged.

After that, I became even more detached from humanity—living among them, but not being one of them. You see, I did not understand feelings. I emulated them. I had no relationships; I simulated a social life with my co-workers, relatives, and acquaintances, because the thing that made me the way I am left me hollow and unable to feel. I faked my everyday human contact, mimicking all of it, because I had no feelings for the living. I understood only dead things. I liked my work, I liked dead people.

Until I met her. My savior, my 'Angel of Darkness'.

Oh, I almost forgot! Another weirdness happened to me: I gained, somehow, a 'Mind Diary'. I had already an eidetic memory; recalling minute details, just like they were happening again in front of my eyes (I can still access long stored memories, such as remembering my phone number when I lived in Phoenix), but the joining with this Rider has enhanced it. Do not know why, but I assure you it works. It's just like having a personal log inside the head. I figure it being like a long hall, full of mirrors, each one reflecting images from my past. Sometimes, I like to stroll in that darkened corridor, stopping by to relive some of my experiences, withdrawing into myself, shutting out the outside world. Yet, some of the mirrors appear missing, like the one regarding the first encounter with my Rider. For that, I have access only to my fog-laden basic memory.

But I was talking about my 'Angel', sorry; I'm sure you're curious about that part of the story.

Lately, someone has changed my life; the last days having been particularly devastating … for bad or good, I haven't decided.

Now I do *feel*.

Yes. I have feelings. I discovered them, right inside me, hidden somewhere all these years, but they were still there. Do you want to know what happened, buddy? Let's just say the said events played such an important role in my future decisions, that you'll most likely be my last client. To tell you what happened, I have to access my Hall of Memories

So, let's begin. I have a long story to tell.

CHAPTER 1

CHAINSAW DANCE

(FROM AXEL'S HALL OF MEMORIES)

"Where the fuck am I?" That was the first thing Richard Solomon said once he popped his eyes open. I had just revived him on my autopsy slab, and the fucker was clearly scared, disoriented, and still confused by the effect of the tranquilliser I had injected him. I did not reply as I never give that kind of information to my victims. I just stared at him, from the darkness.

He began to whine and beg, after he realized he was strapped – naked – on a cold metallic table, the only light in the room coming from the appliance over him. For the rest, the room was in complete darkness.

I knew what he was going to do—they all behave in the same manner. At first, they call for someone's help, and then they begin to yell. Until they see me.

I've learned from previous experiences that is better for me to wear a mask when I do these things. I didn't like it, for I felt stupid – *come on, Axel, you are acting like Jason or Michael Myers! You look like a fool* – however, after one of my *playmates* nearly escaped, well ... I felt uneasy. What if, somehow, one of my victims fled and I wasn't able to stop it? I could get into real trouble. No, stupid or not I needed to cover my face. So, I used this old gas mask I'd found at the swap meet last year in Moore Haven. Yep, it made me look like *Henry Warden* from *My Bloody Valentine*, but at least it was practical—I even used a pickax, once!

As for my voice ... well, I didn't need a disguise for that. When I was on the '*Hunt*', somehow, my Rider's voice took hold, as if my vocal chords were pulled by an invisible hand, like the strings of a cello. In these situations, I did not speak—I whispered.

Or, *it* whispered.

"Hey! You! I saw you moving there! Come over here, help

11

me," Richard growled after taking in my hulky shadow.

I allowed him to see me.

And he understood.

****

It had all begun two weeks ago, after my autopsy of Mr. Benjamin Graham, beloved father of one, old fart, retired army vet, and respected member of our little community. Ben was returning home after a long night of drinks, old stories-swapping, drinks, laughs, drinks, sharing of memories with vets comrades, and more drinking. He had left the Roughhouse, a seedy pub attended by bikers, ne'er-do-wells, and other less savory types, when he had confused the Seward Channel for Route 78, resulting in his *Hummer* going straight into the swampy waters, and he going straight to Valhalla—or wherever old warriors go when they die. Bud Gopher had fished his body out of the car and loaded it down here for autopsy. I had just finished recomposing his body when I heard the sad voice of Cameron, the nineteen-year-old only daughter of the drinking-too-much Ben. She was sobbing for her loss, obviously, but there was something else hidden beneath the surface. She was afraid, I could feel it. I offered her some cool water and a clean napkin—things I'd learned from TV. You always see people handing those things to crying girls in those shows. I did not understand, but I simulated it.

She told me she was alone in the world now, her father being the only person who took care of her after Mitch, her older brother, had died in Afghanistan. She felt cursed, some way. Her mommy had gone first, swept away by cancer, then Mitch, now her daddy. It was like Death herself had taken a liking to her family.

I tried to comfort her, in my awkward ways, hoping that someone more human than me would show up soon in the morgue to give her some authentic warmness.

Then, it happened.

I wasn't listening to her mournful sobs - just making up

appearances - when she said that thing about her *stalker*. My interest was immediately buzzed by that word, and my Rider, who had been asleep for a long time, reawakened from its deep slumber with wolfish eyes and a grumbling stomach.

"What stalker?" I asked while releasing my hold. "What are you talking about, Miss Graham?"

She looked at me with tear-streaked eyes; her black make-up having her look like *Erik Draven* in *The Crow*, and her soul locked its gaze with my tainted one.

When this happens, I do not know why, they say everything; I know they are not talking to me, but to my Rider, revealing to it all their fears, all their doubts.

She did just that, and revealed to me that a guy—Richard Solomon was his name—had stalked her for more than two years. He was not just following wherever she went, but he was scaring the hell out of her almost every day with threatening phone calls, weird emails, posts on her social media, etc. The guy had an obsession of sorts about her, but he was smart, being good at not leaving enough evidence to attract the attention of a judge willing to elevate restrictions. She also said her father had told the sheriff's office about this stalker, but they could do nothing because of lack of proof.

And, of course, my Rider had stirred like an awakened cat.

****

"What do you want from me? Money? Dope? Tell me," droned Richard, now with a hint of hope on his face.

Been there, done that, I thought, being another of the things they do. I call it ... *'Dealing Time'*.

I did not respond—just wanted him to understand that I was not here for a deal, and to help him understand better I started to gather my autopsy tools. Oh, it was just a show. Having a fixation for order, I always keep my tools in neat perfection. I just made that scene to have him have a clear look at my scalpels, surgical saws, and knives. That's the moment they realize their very life is in jeopardy. The fact that they're strapped on a mortuary table with a masked guy bent on dissecting them alive helps, too. You can bet their irises do get wide.

"What do you ... want to do ... to me?" Richard gasped, his voice broken by fear.

Used to that, too.

How strange; these guys live on others' fear, yet can't stand it happening to them. I replaced my scalpels, showing him the special tool I had reserved for him. He released his bladder in his pants at the sight of it.

Tah-Dah! My brand-new vanadium-reinforced chainsaw.

I presented it with all my joy, being my first time with such an instrument. He should have felt honored. Well, who was I kidding; I knew he wouldn't appreciate.

Now, he changed mood again, starting to shout, crying out for help, begging me not to hurt him, asking why I was doing this to him, and all the usual repertoire.

Finally, he surprised me: he started laughing.

I lowered the chainsaw, watching him closely. Had he gone nuts?

"Oh, boy! Now ... I understand!" Solomon exclaimed, amid nervous laughter, "It's a joke! I've been selected for one of them shows ... like ... like *Fear Factor*, right?" He looked at me, "Tim? Is that you?" He kept laughing, becoming almost contagious; I felt the need to laugh back myself, and in fact I did, but the sound that came out of the rubber mask was the glassy and creepy chuckle of the Rider.

"Good joke, Tim, really!"

Everything became clear to me: people nowadays cannot separate reality from fiction.

So, I started the chainsaw and applied it to his left leg, separating knee from ankle.

Reality shows are really fucking up this country.

FEEDING THE URGE

****

After Cameron's long confession about her dark Romeo, I went to her house where she showed me some of the emails the guy had sent her the past six months. She also allowed me to see the photos he'd sent, showing he could follow her everywhere. She was living in terror.

One of the deputies she'd talked to had suggested her to get a good lawyer and sue Solomon for good. But he had also added that, even if they obtained mandate to arrest the guy, the heaviest sentence he risked was one year and six months for stalking. After that, he would be right back, more dangerous than before. Deputy Lane suggested the better if she could find proof he'd invaded her property—the more Salomon could be accused of, the longer he was going to spend time in jail.

No, she wasn't going to get out of this easily. Unless ...

Unless Richard Solomon won first prize at my special '*Dark Lottery*'!

Because I promised never to hurt innocents, I had to find proof Richard was a bastard maniac, one feeding on the fear he created in Cameron. Therefore, two weeks later I went inside Solomon's house.

And I did not find one piece of evidence.

I found thousands of them.

This guy was obsessed with the young woman, owning something like a hundred stolen pictures of her, including poster-sized enlargements, a small altar with a lock of her hair, and a whole library of DVDs showing Cameron going to bed, undressing herself, having breakfast ... even one of her at a public toilet!

Plus, one had to see his book collection. Books on rape, real crime stories about men doing bad things to women, and best of all, a personal diary full of notes in which he wrote how he felt good about stalking the girl, how he intended to raise the risk-level by penetrating her house and take pictures of her while she was asleep. He was still unsure whether he was going to kill her or not.

15

Not for now—he needed her alive to feel himself in power.

I was disgusted, but my Rider was alive and kicking, urging me to get this one—now.

I am familiar with Edmond Locard's theory. A French forensic scientist from the early half of the twentieth century, he believed that every contact leaves a trace. A criminal will always take something away from the scene of his crime and leave something behind. Therefore, when I'm on the hunt, I always match the same clothes my victim usually wears, or has in his closet. I try to study my soon-to-be playmate, following him in his shopping errands, watching him play golf, bowling, or whatever. Any stray fibers I leave behind will inevitably be ascribed to the victim's own wardrobe. Strong latex gloves also help.

That night, I wore a pair of dark blue jeans of the same brand I'd seen Richard wear so often. I'd outfitted them with the exact double of the hooded jacket I had watched him buy at *Animalize*, a sportswear joint inside Osceola Mall. I had no intent to get Richard immediately, but later, with a good laid out plan. It happened by pure chance.

Richard decided to get back home early from his errands around Cameron's house. So I had to neutralize him with 10 cc of *Betathanazine*. When in action, I always carry with me a full shot of that stuff; it being fast acting and able to knock off a rhino.

The bad part was, I had come to Richard's house by my own car, not with the morgue van (the meat wagon, we call it). So, I went outside, watched the road for eventual passersby, and ran straight for my car, then parked it right in front of Solomon's house and loaded him fast in the passenger seat. I locked the door to his house and drove slowly to the morgue, hoping no one had seen me loading the unconscious body of the bastard inside the vehicle. Everything went well until I turned on to Jefferson Avenue, two blocks from the morgue. Deputy Espinoza, my fiancée, at that time, was right there, watching me straight from her duty car with a pouting face.

It's over! I thought.

She got off her vehicle and marched toward me, still that unnerving expression on her face. I stopped the car. Morena—that's her first name—knocked on my window with her baton. I had no choices left. I was done. I didn't want to be arrested, yet my Rider kept urging me to off her. However, I could not. So, I lowered the window.

"You told me you could not come at the Bowlarama with me because you had a special stiff at the meat house tonight," she said. Her words were icy and distant, as if coming from another dimension. "I traded my off day with Peter Tipple, so as to be free next Monday, when it will be your next day off," she kept trailing on with that annoying cold voice. Then, she glanced off to my side taking in the presence of my sleeping passenger. "And you lied to me to get out with that ... wino?" She concluded, with such spurn in her question that had she spat she would've creased a hole in the pavement.

"It's ... it's ..." I always stutter when I'm scared or distressed—a gift from Rusty Floyd's treatments at the camp in '78. "It's complicated, Morena; it's not ... the www ... way you ..."

She didn't allow me a defense. "I know what I see, Axel Hyde. I see you're so freaky, preferring to spend free time with a *maricon* of a smelly boozer, rather than go out with me!"

I felt relief rushing all over. She didn't know the guy!

"Yes, Morena ... I mean, no. I'm just driving this guy back to his house. He is ... so ... so drunk ... he cannot drive. Not after what happened to poor Graham ..." I mentioned Ben to have her mind get back to last week's funeral, decoying attention away from my companion. "I did not cheat on you. ... I ... I didn't lie. I promise I'll be all yours next Monday!" I added immediately.

That had to work. I had to get away as soon as possible before Richard got back to his senses.

"No, Axel. We aren't going anywhere," she interrupted me again with that ice-cold voice. "I'm off with you. You know what I was into before coming here to Prosperity." And she began rambling about her past marriage, her troubles with alcohol, and so

17

on. I wasn't paying attention; I had to keep my eyes on 'Stalky Solomon', for any telling signals of him coming to his senses. Had he moved a finger? Or was that just my imagination?

No, he was still under the drug's effect.

"I should check that *pendejo* for drugs," said Morena, shocking me off.

Was she starting to read my thoughts, too?

"Nah! Go away, I do not want to see you again," she said with disgust.

I happily obliged.

****

After I finished with both legs, Richard 'Stalky' Solomon looked like a broken doll. He screamed a lot, and lost his senses, too. However, I wasn't going to have him die of blood loss, so I cauterized his stumps with a welder, reawakened him, and produced even more screams. Then, I stopped. I wanted him to know why he was going to die, so for the first time I allowed my Rider to speak.

"You know why you are here, Richie?" it whispered out of my mouth. Solomon was too feeble to talk, he just shook his head. "You feed off Cameron, darling ... your obsession, your dark passion."

Richard watched me with half-closed eyes, but he couldn't talk, being too weak by now.

"Do not be afraid, Richie, nobody will know," it added, having me wink my eye to Solomon. "I'm not a vigilante. I'm a predator, like you; however, a bigger one."

He seemed to see the Rider; he was looking at me with pure terror in his eyes, no more holding a shadow of doubt regarding what I was.

That was the moment for me to begin the Chainsaw Dance.

CHAPTER 2

BURNT BONES

She felt his lewd hands on her, followed by his foul, stale breath on her face—and instinctively reacted. Fast, very fast. With her left hand, she struck the man's neck at the Adam's apple, sending him backward with pain and surprise. The punch was followed by a kick with the point of her right boot between Jay's legs, and a lightning elbow strike to his nose. In less than five seconds, Jay Fraser was down, his face a mix of running blood, dead leaves, dirt, and mucus.

****

She came slowly, but resolute, toward him, her beautiful hips moving with the grace of a wild animal on the hunt, her blue-green eyes fixed on him, shining like gems in the darkness of the abandoned campground. For the first time in his life, Jay was really scared by a woman. She could feel it, and she smirked.

"Look what you did to me!" Jay cried out, trying to convey a sense of threat in his words, but in the end sounding more like a scared little boy.

What the hell was this woman up to? What did she want from him?

He had met her at the Roughhouse, the biker's watering hole of the town. She had appeared suddenly from nothing, turning the heads of local customers, distracting them from their beverages for the first time in the evening. An angel out of Hell, the woman was tall, sporting a wonderful developed body under her tight denim clothes. Skin as pale as the moonlight, eyes the color of the sea, Jay could not believe himself when she came straight to his table with a smiling face.

She had beautiful flowing night-black hair running down to

19

her waist, which seemed to have a life of its own, sweeping left and right at her shoulders as she sat down. Black jeans, black duster with silver medallions, black cowboy boots and hat. Except for the silver highlights of her accessories and her skin, everything was black on that woman. The body moved with arrogant grace, swinging an ass you could bounce a quarter off, yet something about her was oddly chilling. Maybe it was her smile, or her jewel-like eyes.

She said she was looking for company, and she had chosen him. They had had some rounds of beer, Jay could not remember how many, then she had been on him—never too close, never too far, teasing him in a way Jay Fraser, the leader of the local Aryan Brotherhood Bikers, had never experienced with a mysterious chick like that.

Jay was fifty-five years old. Originally sent down for grand theft auto, he had quickly established himself as a force to be reckoned with. Having taken an early beating upon entering prison society, he'd had his revenge by slipping ground glass into his would-be oppressor's food in the cafeteria. As the prisoner choked out, coughing up blood, all eyes had turned to Jay who calmly drank a toast to the dying con. From that point on, no one wanted to mess with him. Jay was then quickly accepted into the Aryan Brotherhood gang in the prison, rising through its ranks through a process of political deals and violent takeovers. When he had finished his stretch, he was considered one of the gang's rising stars. The reason the gang was in town was that the senior members of the Aryan Brotherhood had spotted the chance to capture new market for drugs that opened with the construction of the prison.

And the task of smuggling in narcotics and looking after the interests of the cons had been given to Jay. He was ideally suited for this job. Unlike most of the Brotherhood's members, he relied on brain rather than raw brawn.

However, that night, he had fallen in the trap of this predatory woman like a sixteen-year-old boy in the clutches of an expert hooker.

"Look at me, Jay," she whispered, while extracting a wicked blade from under her jacket. Jay saw the gleaming of metal in the moonlight and reacted in the only way he knew—by entering combat mode. An adrenaline surge flowed throughout his body, subduing the pain and giving him the strength to regain his feet.

Too late!

The she-devil was already on him, aiming the knife sharp point toward his neck. Jay instinctively raised his left arm, trying to deflect the lethal strike, but the blade carved into the top of his shoulder in a downward stabbing motion, catching between the bones of his shoulder and arm and wrenching it out of alignment. Blood flowed profusely from the deep wound, bathing the swampy, putrid, overgrown ground. He reacted with blind fury mixed with fear, and swung a balled up fist into her lip, crushing it against her teeth. Her meaty lower lip split open and the woman drooled blood. Jay smiled despite his aching bloodied face, enjoying the small victory while preparing for a second strike.

Nobody was going to off him; especially a broad!

Reversed, the blade stabbed up into his stomach and carved up toward his sternum before being pulled free. Jay's entrails were exposed to the air as blood coursed down into his lap.

Fraser couldn't believe it; the girl had acted fast, allowing herself to be hit, and then luring him again into a trap as a way to gain a clear spot to slice into his abdomen.

He staggered backward, gazing with shock at his dark blood that flowed copiously from the jagged, irregular slash in his belly. Then, he lifted his gaze in time to see the smiling monster, which to him had seemed a gorgeous woman just hours earlier, lift her left leg and smash it into the side of his jaw. The act ground Jay's teeth against each other and snapped his head violently to one side. He staggered again, spitting out splintered fragments of a shattered tooth. A second blow, so fast Jay believed someone else had struck him out of nowhere, caught him in the knee, dislocating it with a crunch and sending him to kiss the ground.

Somewhere, a night bird cried out a haunting shriek.

There was stillness in the air as, caught in an infinite spiral of pain, Jay tried desperately to regain his feet. He pooled enough strength to rise prone, but nothing more; his shaking arms abandoned him and fell again in the muck.

A pale hand with black-lacquered nails reached for his lapel, turned him and laid him spread-eagled onto his back. Through blooded eyes, Jay could see only the trees and the indifferent stars. Painfully, he trained his eyes to her. She was still grinning, her pale face stained by spattered blood. She was about to sit on him, in a lethal parody of what Jay had pictured in his mind from the moment he had first rested eyes on her at the pub.

"Who the fuck are you, whore?" he spat through the ruin of his mouth.

Something different passed inside the woman's eyes, blinking like the taillight of a landing aircraft. Just before she plunged the blade into Jay's side in a powerful strike—piercing right between his ribs and stabbing deep into his lungs and heart. Blood ripped free and splinters of bone splashed out.

"Never ... never call me that!" She roared, her face twisted by a sneer, pure hate in her eyes.

"You ... you're ... crazy," whispered Fraser in his last breaths.

She smiled wickedly. "I'm not crazy, I get even."

Life left Jay's body with that last meaningful message.

And that was exactly when he remembered who this woman was.

****

A bonfire lit up the clearing in the abandoned summer camp, casting weird shadows over the faded wooden totems and crumbled longhouses. The woman, who had been the sexy but deadly cowgirl, was now changing her clothes, reverting to the icon of living pain she actually was.

Her pale skin was tracked by dozens of old scars.

She removed the raven-black wig, revealing a shorter, more practical haircut—the better to disguise herself when needed. She neatly replaced her clothes inside a bag in the pick-up truck, and instead slid on a handy worker outfit complete with a tool belt full of equipment. A baseball cap covered her short, chocolate brown hair.

She returned for a last gaze at the burning remains of Jay Fraser, her face no longer smiling. Instead, she wore a static expression of emptiness. Her fury spent, she felt nothing now: no sense of remorse, fear, or satisfaction.

Just nothing.

Jay Fraser's mangled body was burning in the improvised bonfire, his dead flesh melting like wax, his blood tissues and charred flesh blackening his exposed bones.

She felt nothing.

However, somewhere inside her, her own Rider felt elation.

CHAPTER 3

SURPRISE AT THE DUMPING SPOT
(FROM AXEL'S HALL OF MEMORIES)

At 5.16 AM, I finished my wetwork on Richard Solomon. I felt tired but happy inside. With my Rider asleep like a sated alligator, I placed all the bags inside the meat wagon, and then slowly drove to my usual disposal site, the place where I was reborn in '78. Now an abandoned ruin, Kamp Koko was my favored place to get rid of what was left of my 'playmates'—after the games. A part of me, that side that froze when I was a ten-year-old boy, still feared the place. That part could still see Russell Floyd's ghost running around empty longhouses, the overgrown archery range, and those rotten docking pontoons. Nevertheless, I felt the need to come over here. It was part of the "urge"; it was what the Rider wanted. I know it may sound ritualistic—and maybe it is—just like being part of a primal sacrificial ceremony, but I couldn't help it. It had to be done that way.

I kept driving past the Lakeview Motel, one of the most dismal and fetid sleeping holes in all of Florida. How much I hate that place. Bear in mind, I have nothing against sex. I just do not understand the way people get into all the laborious affair of courtship, dating, calling, and dating again, just for some intimate activity. I see sex only as a natural drive, a mechanism developed by nature to lead species to procreate. What does that have to do with love or pleasure? Mechanics are always the same, so ... you could do-it-yourself.

Anyway, I don't feel that need. No, seriously, it has never happened to me.

Maybe just once, to be honest.

I was sixteen and some of my pals at Prosperity High convinced me to help get a look inside the girls' dressing room. Being already tall for my age, they needed me as some kind of ladder. For the rest, they never cared about me. I was just 'Spooky', the weird, silent guy of the class. It was in that instance that I saw the first and only member of the opposite sex that moved something inside me: she was a beautiful Asian girl with pale skin, nice legs....

But, that's another story.

I had to get down the van to remove the big chain with the county seal warning passersby about impounded private property. It had to take just a min—

What the heck!

The chain was already down. No: it had been cut with truncheons, or similar instruments.

Someone was here.

I rushed up aboard the van to cut the lights off, when I noticed the telling tire tracks heading both in and out of the property. Whoever had been here was also gone. Some kind of heavy truck, maybe a pick-up.

Again, I drove slowly—this time with the lights off—looking around. I have a good night vision and can usually spot a black cat in a darkened alley.

Oh my, my....

There was a dying fire straight in front of me, its last flames sending a deep gray smoke from something as big as a man right under that creepy fake Seminole totem. No, I correct myself, it *was* a man, or had been one.

I switched off the engine and dismounted, watching in alertness for signs of any living activity. The charred corpse was still ablaze, with small blue flames covering most of it—their futile battle to keep the oxygen burning out. From the shape of the hipbone and the size of the cranium, I could surely identify it as belonging to a male, but nothing more.

What could I do? Extinguish the flames, give a close cursory exam on the spot, and then bury it to avoid the Department ending up combing this place? I was not used at covering someone else's job. Plus, it sounded unfair. On the other hand, if I didn't allow it to disappear, Prosperity's finest and bravest would all converge here to place yards of yellow plastic tape around the place and investigate for clues.

And worse: they could stumble upon some of my previous playmates' remains.

But if I covered up the murder that would make me the unwilling accomplice of whoever did this. Not that I cared ... yes, I do not care about justice. I work for it, not really understanding the meanings behind laws and regulations. I just try to find the facts in a clear, scientific, perhaps pragmatic way.

I had to act quickly, before dawn came. Someone could have spotted smoke lifting out of the cedar forest. My brain was at a loss, yet my instincts took over. So, I found myself quickly smothering the flames on the sizzling corpse by helping myself with some buckets of water and a wet blanket. I worked on all gears, without knowing how or why I did it. I suppose, deep inside me I was just curious to understand what had happened here.

****

By 5.44 AM I had completely doused the fire. I took one of the body bags, loaded the charred bones and melted flesh into the van, and then remembered why I was here.

Richard Solomon.

Yessir.

I had to get free of those damned body parts.

"No more games, Richie. You're broken," I chided.

I left the van as close to the water's edge as possible, then I started to unload the plastic bags. As if responding to the Rider—as they always did—a couple of gators swam closer to the dock. They knew me; hell, I was almost their zookeeper. I did not feed them regularly, but somehow they always came when they heard my van's engine. I suspected it was all because of my Rider's magic. I was like a dark version of St. Francis ... with alligators. I didn't talk to the reptiles; I just allowed them to feed on the neatly sliced remains of my playmates.

As I've told you already, I do not have empathy of any sort; not for humans, not for animals. In fact, most of the animals I met in my life feared me. Well, not me, but the Rider. Somehow, they sensed it.

The gators swam closer, eager, hungry; they knew I had something for them. I almost looked like one of those old grannies out of Town Square Park, feeding pigeons in the morning.

However, you couldn't hear me piping: *Here, here, here!*

Alligators cannot chew, so they eat by tearing chunks off their prey and then swallowing these whole. They dismember larger prey by biting and then spinning about on their own axis, or thrashing to tear the meat apart. Unless, of course, someone clearly sliced food for them. They may attack people, and those that have been regularly hand-fed are the most dangerous since they come to associate humans with food. Poking an alligator in the eyes with a stick or other sharp object can help at deterring an attacking alligator. But I never had to do that. None ever attacked me.

I had to act fast, couldn't spend too much time watching them cleaning my dirty job as I had an urgent, if unexpected, duty. Therefore, I emptied the bloody content of my bags into the waters, allowing the reptiles to help themselves, and then rushed back to the improvised cremation site. I had to clean up the place, remove all traces I could about the body.

I was very good at that—I could allow myself to be messy in my private games, but I needed to tidy up afterwards. That comes natural to me, having been tidy most of my life. I was the kid who always made up his own room, putting the toys back in the box after an afternoon of games. It was just me, not the Rider. The Rider didn't give a fart about the tidy work; it loved the messy one, full of screams, blood, and pain.

A rosy dawn rose on the horizon, so I had to get out of there in a hurry. I just stopped at the chain to fix it up with some iron thread and put it back again, allowing it to dangle its dirty and faded county warning in the wind.

A light rain came down, adding water to water. I drove my van down one of those never-used picnic spots around the lake and parked it behind a convenient large bush, hiding it from the main trail, scaring a couple of raccoons in the process. They looked like a pair of burglars returning for their nightly errands.

"Do not be afraid, we're accomplices tonight. I saw nothing, you saw nothing," I said in my best mafia goon's imitation. Which is quite lame, if you ask me.

I opened the body bag to get a closer look at the charred remains. The smell was strong, acrid. Not a big problem in this kind of van, as you can imagine. I have to clean it up myself almost all days, so the smell would not linger.

To be honest, getting this job as a medical examiner was a boon for my hidden activities, and working for old Abigail Zimmerman helped a lot. As Coroner, it is her responsibility to sign death certificates and to establish the cause of death. If the cause is unclear or a consequence of criminal action, Zimmerman can insist that the sheriff's office conducts a criminal investigation. After serving three years as a pathologist, she was promoted to Chief Medical Examiner for the county. As her assistant, I had the opportunity to work often with her, and somehow, gain her trust. She even allowed me to act as a guardian of the morgue. I can work there at night, and given it is not one of the happiest spots in town, nobody pays a visit. I still had to be careful, never committing mistakes, just like earlier with my... how would you call her?

Girlfriend.

Abigail is smart, very smart, with a bright, inquisitive mind. I couldn't add this body to those in the stacks. Somebody would surely notice.

I sent away my thoughts and concentrated on the remains I'd found. From what was left I could clearly see the burning had happened after death, the smell of industrial kerosene still discernible. The guy had been stabbed at least three times, and his jaw had been dislocated by a powerful blow from a blunt instrument or a well-assessed kick. Whoever had done this was a pro; no doubt, someone who knew how to kill. I felt something akin to admiration while looking at the precise deep wounds, just like watching the work of a comrade. However, I was totally disappointed when I saw the killer's mistake.

Among the burned bones, across the ashes of some of the victim's clothes, I retrieved what was left of a jacket's inner pocket with a half-burned wallet inside it.

My, my, how could you make such a gross mistake?

I almost smirked at the thought of me leaving around such a clue. The wallet contents were clearly damaged by fire, yet I could still discern the top corner of a 100 dollar bill, some scraps of paper—maybe personal notes—and most of all, a half melted plastic ID!

I was able to decipher his name out of the mess of soot and fused plastic: Jay R. Fraser.

Hey! I knew the guy.

Not a personal acquaintance, but he was a familiar face at the sheriff's office. An ex-con working at the warehouse of the local Shop N' Save Mart, down at the Bend Outlet, he'd been suspected by Deputy Peter Tipple of smuggling drugs inside prison, but no evidence had ever been found. Still, Tipple did not trust the guy, and kept watching the man from the shadows, sure he would commit a mistake at some point.

And, obviously, now he had.

This Fraser was a tough one; not large, but he could handle a fight. Whoever had killed the man must have been quite skilled at combat, because he was not ambushed, or made inoffensive for later work—as I usually do with my victims—he was faced square on. Maybe it had been an act of revenge in the local underworld, or Jay must have stepped on someone's toes, a bigger fish in the lake. Still, there was something inside me that kept telling me this was not the case. This seemed personal, like an avenging act—too much passion in the strokes, if you know what I mean. The person who did it hated this man. And as I said, I know hate.

Then, I got it.

The wallet wasn't a mistake. The broken chain link, the pick-up's tracks, all the mess clearly spelled out that the killer didn't care if we found the body or not. They didn't care if we could identify the remains. There was only rage and destruction. I could feel it.

And so did the Rider.

CHAPTER 4

DARK DREAMIN' GIRL

The girl was falling again. Falling into the darkness. And she was afraid of that darkness—at the same time feeling safety in it, safety from the monsters outside.

She stopped falling and began to float in absolute blackness, as if immersed in an oily liquid.

In that darkness, she saw a light. It looked like a distant fire. By instinct, she moved closer, attracted by it, as the moth that cannot avoid the light's charming spell.

She found herself back to her teen years, sitting around a campfire with her uncle. He was still alive—here. She felt better, warmed by the flames and the companionship. The smell of burned cedar and old tobacco reached her nostrils, so she breathed it heavily in, as if that were the first time she'd smelled those aromas, and that wasn't the case.

"The spirits lived in the Lands beyond on the Other Side for many seasons, and became bored, so they created magic," Uncle Johnny said, then paused to poke the fire with a stick, then adding more cedar leaves.

"After many more seasons, they tired of their new toy and, using their magic, they created the This Side World with the heavens and the stars," he continued. The girl had heard it dozens of times, but never got tired of listening to her beloved uncle, her savior.

Around the two figures, brightened by the fire, the blackness became thinner, like a dark misty haze, allowing the girl to take in her surroundings.

She was again on the Devil's Backbone, a sharp ridge due south of the Old Stone Fort, a sacred place for her ancestor's tribe. Laurel, holly, iris, fern, honeysuckle, sage orange, huckleberry and similar water-loving plants nestled among trees of walnut, oak,

31

locust and sourwood. She was again nineteen, enthralled by Uncle Johnny's old stories, enjoying his warm voice, feeling safe again, away from the monsters of 'This Side'.

"This was good. But they became bored again, so they created the animals and the Human Beings. After many more seasons, the spirits again turned their faces to the This Side World and, not being bored and being in a good mood, created the other Indians," continued Uncle Johnny, staring intently at the flickering flames.

"But the spirits became bored again. They turned to one another and remarked, 'The This Side World we have created with our magic is boring. We must play a joke on our creations, so we will never be bored again.'"

The pale-skinned girl smiled, liking that part of the tale, the part explaining the coming of the Whites.

"Thus it was that the spirits played their joke upon us, upon all the Human Beings and the Indians. The spirits created the White People and put them across the Stinking Waters, and filled them with the desire to move." Uncle Johnny opened his medicine bundle, casually taking out some mixed raven and owl feathers. How much she loved that Cherokee craftwork made of tanned wolf hide, and decorated with beadwork and porcupine quills.

"And this is how it has been told to us by our Fathers, and their Fathers, and their Fathers' Fathers," he concluded as he rose and reached for more firewood.

She felt happy again, safe again, but it didn't last.

Darkness returned, embraced her, filled with visions of the horrible visage of her monsters; those monsters that walk as men.

The monsters that violated *gaktv'ta,* an area under ceremonial taboo.

The monsters that had violated *her* gaktv'ta.

The pale-skinned girl found herself falling again, in the black. She screamed her rage, unwilling to lose her uncle again, her only anchor in this cruel world, her guardian against the *Ada'wehi*, the Moon-Eyed People—the ones who lived underground. Yet, it was all for nothing.

No one was there to hear her screams; no one was there to protect her.

Around her, music played loud from the nothingness, a music she knew well and didn't like. The kind of music she'd been forced to listen and dance to for more than ten years.

"Here, now!" The familiar cold voice of her invisible companion spoke in her mind. The *Sunnayi Edahi*—The Night Goer. The hidden Rider, her dark partner in these late nights, the one who filled her with purpose.

The pale-skinned girl relaxed; she didn't trust the Night Goer, yet she had no choice.

"We have a job to finish," it whispered. Her thoughts ran again to her long lost uncle, desperately seeking a way to summon him back, but knowing deep inside, it was impossible. Uncle Johnny died back in 1996, when a five ton block fell on him down at the Hurst Concrete Company, killing the man on the spot. She had cried for months after his death, as she was alone in the world again. Then, she'd fallen into depression, lost her job, and only memories about her mother's heroin addiction had kept her away from the lure of artificial joy. With time, she had found a new job, one she did not like, but she had no other choice. With her wonderful pale-skinned body, athletic build, and graceful movements, she was a natural born dancer.

And she danced. She had danced for months, years, until both music and time had meant nothing anymore, becoming one with her sorrow.

Then came that night, when the monsters-who-walked-as-men showed up at the Dancing Coyote. And now, they were again here, all over her, those dirty hands touching her, grabbing, hurting…

Cheri screamed, and in doing so, got out of the nightmare. Pearly cold watery drops of sweat streamed down her high cheekbones.

"It was a dream," she whispered to the empty room.

However, she knew it was not.

They were memories about her past, haunting her every night

like ancient ghosts in the English countryside. Cheri rose from the bed and went to wash herself in the bathroom. She gazed at her reflection in the mirror, looking for her true self and finding none. The mirror sent back the now too familiar image of what she had become: her short brown hair, practically cut to help her at her job, but also to hide her true identity, spoke of what she had been, and what she was now. She had always loved her long flowing hair. Her body was no longer that of a dancer, but the strong and muscled one of a construction worker. Only her green-blue eyes had not changed. They still shone with light, even if a phony one, a mask for those around her.

Cheri looked deeper inside her eyes. And found what she was looking for.

The Night Goer was still there, gazing back.

CHAPTER 5

A FAILED DELIVERY

Three miles to the south of the town center stood the Prosperity Men's Correctional Facility. A rather grim, newly built prison, which acted as an overflow complex for the overstretched prisons system in Florida, it was originally designed to cope with low risk prisoners. Since then, it had been upgraded to cope with more dangerous ones. The Men's Correctional was completed in 2004 to house the overspill from other prisons. Former mayor Frank Eugene Hall campaigned hard to have it built near town. Rumors of favors and back-scratching abounded and there were several stories in the press about shady deals. The prison currently held only two hundred out of a maximum possible three hundred inmates, and had a staff of one hundred. The majority of the prison warders, secretarial staff, and administrators lived nearby. Many other people in the town of Prosperity Glades worked for ancillary businesses connected to the prison, such as supplying government contracts for food, stationery, and so on. Unfortunately, however, the crime rate in the town had risen because of it. The demand for narcotics and contraband within the prison had brought former 'associates' into the area and made local bad boys rich. The population of the prison divided itself along strictly racial lines, with Asians, Afro-Americans, Hispanics, and Whites keeping themselves to themselves. Many members of the nastier prison gangs were held at PMCF. Like the Aryan Brotherhood, the Mexican Mafia, and the Blood gangs.

This grim place also spawned another of the blights of the area: the South Glade Trailer Park. Originally built to house the workers who constructed the prison, the trailer park was now home to many new families who had moved to Prosperity Glades. They wanted either to take advantage of cheap accommodation, or to stay near their loved ones while they served time in the prison. It was just a matter of time that the place would become a meeting point for the town's shady deals.

One of these deals was going on between Frank E. Hall and Robert Doyle.

They were both sitting, facing each other, at one of those wooden impromptu barbecue tables that littered the densely overgrown area around the park.

Frank was a tall, slender individual with proportioned extremities. His hair was dark and wavy with a trace of gray at the temples; his blue eyes, small and penetrating, resembled those of a raptor bird. He dressed in conservative clothes—a well-tailored gray suit over an immaculate white shirt. A regimental tie and expensive Italian shoes completed his statement about being in one of the top classes.

Robert Doyle was quite the opposite. A large, hulky individual, with arms shaped like tree-trunks, he sported a blond military cut over a heavy-boned face. An old scar ran from below his right eye socket to the corner of his small mouth. A hispid, but well-trimmed, beard surrounded his lower face. His eyes were also blue, but of a lighter shade. He dressed casually in a yellow t-shirt with a surfing alligator print, over a pair of dark blue jeans, abused *Nike* sneakers and a gold chain at his thick neck. His clothes were tight to show off his street-fighter body.

"I hope it is important, Doyle," said Frank, looking straight in the man's eyes, then adding, "You know how much I dislike this place."

"Yes, sir. I know, but it is." Doyle didn't flinch but kept a straight look.

Two different kinds of predators they were—needing, but despising, each other.

Frank checked his cell phone for messages. "Go ahead; I do not have much time."

"Well, it's … it's about Fraser. He did not deliver this morning. And I'm quite pissed 'bout that."

"Why?"

"I'm asking you, sir. Two days ago, he said was going to deliver the stuff at the usual place. That means this morning."

Frank ignored the cell and raised his raptor gaze back to Doyle. "Did you try to contact him? Maybe he is dozing off a hangover after one of his nights."

Hall sent away that thought immediately. Had it been Billy or Marvin … maybe … but Jay? No, he was professional about this stuff, never failing in a deal.

Doyle plucked out a *Marlboro* from his packet, flipped it on the side and stuck it into his mouth. Then, he reached for his penis-shaped lighter. But, Hall was faster and clumped Rob's hand. "Listen. Something is fishy about this. I know Jay by a long time. He might be rude, shrewd, and cocky, but I know one thing about him: he is serious on the job. He has to be. His seniors are people you can't mess with. They want the business going on smoothly."

"The point is," Doyle remarked, freeing his hand and grabbing the obscene lighter, "he did not show up. Period!"

Frank watched him, disgust on his face, while the brawny man set fire to the cig with that bad taste thing. How could a grown-up man buy such a lewd device?!

"Look. I suggest you get back to work. Take some time. I'll take care of this–"

"Not so easy, sir." Doyle interrupted. "Deals are deals. I cannot just get back and tell the Aryans there's going to be no stuff. I may be tough, but I can't always watch my back."

Frank rose, dusted off his pants, and regained his usual stance—that of the master over his vassal—stating the conversation was over. "I said: I'll take care of this, Doyle." Icy words came out of his unflinching mouth. "And when I say I'll take care of something, I mean it."

"But how can I calm down the waters back at the jig?"

Frank kept his gaze on him, like an owl transfixing his prey. A natural for Hall, that gaze had nailed down bigger rats than prison warden Doyle, back in his heyday years as town mayor.

"You just do *your* job, Robert. Just do that. I have *my* role in this, you have *yours*. I can't be there to dry up your nose when you sneeze."

"But sir…" Doyle was backing off, knowing he had lost the confrontation.

"No, Doyle," Frank stopped him. "It's not my part in it. Period." He smirked.

Frank Eugene Hall, former mayor of Prosperity Glades, construction baron of the area, inheritor of the Hall fortunes, and owner of at least half of the local properties, had said no. And when he said that simple word, everybody in the area knew there was no turning point.

He went back to his car—a blue *BMW*—and backed it out of the cul-de-sac into which he'd parked it. Then, he drove up to the Hall Activity Center, the only decent building in the whole area, a structure he had donated to the poorer inhabitants of the trailer park, a place to show off his generosity—and his power. He had to show up there, a way to explain his presence down here, among the town's outsiders, as a courtesy visit to his favored future re-electors. He intended to run again in next year's campaign and would regain his rightful place as mayor of Prosperity Glades. This was his town, it had always been. His family had run it in one way or the other for generations. The personal scandal about his relationship with a prostitute in Moore Haven was outdated by now. Sheep forget easily if you bring them to good grazing fields, regularly. So, he was just that, an able shepherd who'd led his flock well in the past management. He had created job opportunities for at least half of the locals, especially with the prison construction. However, that snoopy journalist, that Nate Harding, that asshole, was surely paid by his opponents. He had ruined it all, with photos, details, articles. But, he had paid him back; oh, if he had. Back in 2007, Jay Fraser and Ray Lombardi had taken care, sending him sleeping with the fishes in Lake Okeechobee, not before having some of their usual fun with the guy.

You can't play with Frank Eugene Hall, oh no!

And, if you really want to play, prepare for a long fight.

****

The Hall Activity Center was a two-story concrete building, decorated with crushed seashell stucco, and painted with pink flamingos and palm motifs over a sandy background. The murals were the work of local artist, Warwick Nodds, who had mysteriously left the town in 2006, after a harsh argument with his sister Cynthia, a former deputy in the local sheriff's department. Warwick had a warped creativity. In fact, if you watched closely to the various silhouetted figures of birds and plants, you would notice that each shape reproduced, in some way, a stylized sexual motif. Nodds was also suspected of being a voyeur, and had even been sued by Lisa Bellevue, the beautiful manager of the Central Glades Bank, for stalking her. However, nothing serious was ever found about him, so he'd been a natural choice for Frank Hall when he'd handpicked him for the decorating job. Besides, he had signed the contract for a nickel!

Frank, after all, really liked those alluring subliminal undertones; they added some spice to the big box of cement and wood.

Hall spent some of his time there, mostly shaking hands with locals, self-appointed neighborhood committee representatives, and people who simply were in the need to shine with his starlight. They offered him orange juice, some coffee (bleak and tasteless), the 'renowned' *Grandma Stewart's Kookies* (tasted like baked sea sand), and talked a lot. About themselves, mostly. Used to being a public figure from the age of eleven, when his father, the late Johnston Hall, was town mayor, Frank simulated his interest in everything they said, making promises, and rallying against the current administration. Yet, he was not listening; his mind kept going back to the unpleasant conversation he'd had with Warden Robert Doyle.

Why had Jay Fraser missed a delivery? And, why was he not

answering his messages? Had the newcomers ambushed him? Had they scared him?

Unlikely. Fraser was not the guy to be scared easily, not by Mexican Mafia's goons. Besides, the Mexicans delivered 'Downers' to the Hispanic prisoners, while the Aryans smuggled 'Uppers' to the white ones. The interests of the two gangs would rarely clash.

No. There was something different going on here, something unexpected.

"Do you agree on that?" said a plump old woman in an obscene pink and white jumpsuit.

"Yes, I do, ma'am. I surely do," he responded automatically, no matter what that bulldog-ape hybrid had just asked him—be it the death penalty for teenage wall scribblers, or the legalization of cocaine in the whole county.

He sent yet another message to Fraser, unnerved.

"But that would change several things. I think the best solution, you know," ranted another guy on his left, convinced that he cared about everything they proposed to him.

I have to get away from here…

He checked his cell phone.

Nothing.

Respond! You bastard, respond!

Then, the final nail into his personal coffin's lid—they escorted him outside, to the back of the building. An ugly crafty deck, completed with tasteless ceramic figures (donated by the South Glade community), potted plants, and unsafe-looking wooden benches revealed itself in its full ingloriousness. The constant prattling continued, out there, to enumerate the values of community works, social awareness, and love for God. His head was about to explode.

So, he pulled out his .45 auto from under his jacket, and blew off the head of each one of his interlopers.

Bulldog-Ape was the first; her head exploded like a ripe melon and showered the area with blood and gray matter. Then it was Concerned Citizen Number One's turn. He shot him right in the forehead, creating a perfect new hole into his still chattering head. One after the other, they fell, leaving a bloodbath on the woodwork of their precious 'Community Deck', filling it with splintered cranium bones, teeth, and yellowish fluids …

"Do you want another cookie, sir?" said Bulldog-Ape, interrupting his daydreaming fantasy.

"No, thank you. Really." He smirked. "I'm on a diet. If you want your next-to-be-mayor in health and shape, please do not tempt me." Then inserted a phony laugh to break tension.

However, Bulldog-Ape had caught his smirk; she was watching him with different eyes now.

Christ! I'm getting paranoid!

He allowed the 'Committee' to lead him on a tour of the carpentry masterpiece of the glades, and even listened to some of their requests.

Then, a light switched on in his pain-wracked brain.

Just call Billy Gamble.

Yeah! That was the right thing to do.

CHAPTER 6

FEELINGS AND MONSTERS
(FROM AXEL'S HALL OF MEMORIES)

I took my decision at dawn's first rays. I buried Jay R. Fraser's remains in the black soil of Lake Okeechobee's shores. Not a good or neatly job, if you ask me. However, I was in hurry; no time to be prissy as I had to get back to the morgue, clean myself and the van before the beginning of the day shift. Interring someone in marshy terrain is easier, but can leave traces, too. But, this had happened so fast, unexpectedly. Anyway, I did all in the right way, leaving as few clues I could.

I was just dressing myself back with my spare clothes when I heard her voice.

"Axel? Are you in there?"

Dr. Abigail Zimmerman, Chief Medical Examiner for the county. My boss.

I finished buttoning up my clean shirt and yelled a 'Yes'.

I heard her moving around in the other room; a metallic sound revealed to me she'd just thrown her car keys inside the glass bowl. A rustle of clothes—she was taking off her overcoat. I hastily grabbed my dirty clothes sack and rushed out of the examination room. She was there, sitting at the desk, absently reading some forms.

Abigail Zimmerman is a black woman with crispy hairs that have started to get some streaks of white by age. She always wears huge specs – of which she is so fond of, but make her look older than she is. Still agile, even if a bit thin on the frame, Abby moves with elegance, and her slender, but firm hands, clearly show practice in fine work. In fact, she is an accomplished pathologist and a surgeon, too.

"Hey, Big Boy!" she welcomed me with her pearly smile.

"Hey, Big Mama," I answered back, in our own usual change

of the guard pantomime.

I tried to go straight for the exit, but she halted me in my tracks. "Did you find anything interesting tonight?"

I froze. I knew her acute mind; she must have noticed something about me. I was sure.

"Axel?"

I did not know what to answer. I just stood there, like a potted plant.

"What about our new resident, the J.D.?" she finally said.

I felt the need let loose a sigh of relief, but did not. My muscles relaxed, my mind calmed down. *Oh, that!*

"N...o"

Stop that! Stop that stutter, now!

I regained my usual composure and turned to face her right back. My coldness returned.

"No, Abby. I made a report about my exam. You can find it in your office. This J.D., this unidentified body, sports some interesting marks. Maybe Clewiston can help us." I blew it out all in a single breath, to hide my sense of relief.

Abigail stacked away the papers, took off her glasses and cleaned the lenses with a rag. "Well. Never mind, Axel. Get home; you surely need some rest, Big Boy."

I could get away, but something unusual happened to me. A question surfaced to my mind, and before I could even realize it, I fired it to her: "Are you feeling well, Abby?"

What the fuck was that?

Feeling.

What about feelings? I did not feel, so from where had that question come? My Rider? No, certainly not.

She lifted her eyes to me. I could clearly see she had some worries on her face. "No, Axel, I'm not feeling well. Nothing serious, just some dizziness." She paused, her face creased in a quizzed look, then she smiled. "But ... thank ... thank you for asking."

"You're welcome!" I exclaimed, but it was not my usual

voice; it was a new me responding. I immediately caught the opportunity of her silent stupor to get away. Behind me, I could still *feel* her eyes on me.

****

After climbing into my bed that morning, I was unable to fall asleep. I had to—my body ached, fatigued after all my hard work. Invading Solomon's house was one thing; everything that had happened later was another brand of soup. Was I getting clumsy in my hunts? Was I turning toward the theoretical phase, in which all serial killers become overconfident and make gross mistakes, as though in some unconscious way they want to be caught, to be stopped? I stared at the white ceiling of my bedroom, searching for my answer.

Do I want to be stopped?

I did not know.

Why did I ask that thing about Abby's health?

I didn't care about others' feelings. Hell, I didn't care about others, period.

Maybe, just maybe, I was simply scared. Morena first, then the poaching of my dumping grounds, Abby later.

What scared me most was Abby. And with good reasons. It was just as if she could feel something about me being wrong.

I met her for the first time in 1995, after a four-year stint as junior pathologist in Moore Haven. She picked me up as her assistant at the Hall Memorial Hospital. She had been looking for new blood in her staff, and she liked my devotion for the job. However, after a year, she got worried. I was always alone—never went out with friends—with a home-job-home routine, and spending more time with the dead than the living. I had some obsession with death, and she noticed it; therefore, she investigated my past life, probed me, and made inquiries with those locals who knew me better, so to say.

One day she approached me directly, while I was performing a comparative test.

"You have quite an obsession with death, boy. Don't you?" she asked—but it wasn't really a question. "Really, I'm not talking about a workaholic compulsion, but a real obsessive disorder in there," she continued, pointing one of her bony fingers to my head. "I think you should get an appointment with Dr. Hart." Her tone indicated she was not taking no for an answer.

"I never went into psychoanalysis, ma'am. I do not think I need that stuff," I gently protested.

Yet, she didn't flinch. "Axel, I know what happened when you were just ten years old. You never faced that, you're still keeping it inside. It's not safe for your health." She had then grabbed my arm. "Look, you are what ... twenty-eight, by now?" Her smile tried to assure me there was nothing wrong, that she just cared about me. "You have no friends, only acquaintances. You never date women—or even men for that matter. You just come here, do your job—excellently—and then go back home. You are not living, Axel. You just exist." She raised her tone in that last line, to put emphasis on the meat of her statement.

I just stared back, not understanding what she was saying. I couldn't tell her I didn't care about friends or dates. I couldn't tell her that my interests were ... somewhat different.

"Listen, boy. I'm going to arrange a visit with Dr. Hart. I cannot help you in any other way, yet I do not like you wasting your life away," she pressed.

"I'm *not* wasting my life!" I reacted abruptly, my cold voice sounding too much like that of my dark companion for my taste.

Her deep brown eyes studied my expression, as she always did when feeling something unnerving about me.

This woman can see me.

She did not go back to the issue.

****

Five days later, I had my first session with Dr. Henry Hart. I had no choice if I wanted to dispel Dr. Zimmerman's doubts about me.

Dr. Hart was an attractive man in his mid-to-late forties, with ruddy skin, permanently tanned for the time he spent outdoors. He was five foot ten with a stocky build. Easygoing and casual, he enjoyed wearing loose cotton shirts, always left unbuttoned to show his vast collection of t-shirts with funny slogans or images on them. That day, he sported the one printed with: 'Got Mind?'

His office reflected his relaxed and humoristic personality, packed as it was with colorful keepsakes, travel mementos, and funny postcards from his patients.

After the usual conventional to keep me at ease, Hart went straight to the point.

"So, before we start to understand where your obsession with death stems from, it is better for me to explain what a real obsession is." He stressed the word 'real' with the quotation marks hand sign. "Real obsessions develop from neurosis. Neurotic individuals often cultivate a very intense, exaggerated concern about some danger or problem. For example, it may be necessary for a person to get out countless times to check his car's locks. Or, in extreme cases, someone may be so concerned about bacteria that he is compelled to constantly wash his hands or to become a recluse."

I was sincerely interested in his lecture about obsessions, but out of curiosity, because I felt I had none. I just had an 'alien' thing inside me, and no one would ever believe that.

"Neurotic obsessions are believed to hide some wish, often of a destructive or sexual nature. This obscure desire—or need—is usually concealed in symbolic distortion," he continued.

Need. Yes, the 'Need', I felt it every time my Rider awakened. Was he going to explain to me what a Rider was?

I noticed he had a jagged scar on his lower left arm. Another memento from an outdoor experience?

"Human obsession with death is called thanatophilia, while a person who extremely fears death is termed a thanatophobe," Hart concluded, after which he sipped some orange juice from his tall glass. He was expecting for me to talk, to add something to his statement, but I was simply staring at the scar, wondering how he had gained it, musing about the object that had caused the slash.

Because I was not talking, Dr. Hart continued his probing, but took notice of my behavior toward his distinctive mark. "Let's talk about your thoughts, Axel. What are you thinking right now?"

I diverted my gaze from the scar to his piercing gray eyes. "Nothing. I'm just listening to you," I lied.

However, he did not surrender. "That is impossible, Axel. We are constantly besieged by thoughts. Our mind can't conceive emptiness, so it fills itself with anything ... a song, an unrelated memory, an idea."

"I don't know, doctor. Really. Nothing comes to my mind right now," I said defensively.

Henry Hart got silent for a moment, then rose from his armchair and went to the window. It was a typical Floridian midsummer day, overcast and sunny at the same time, with large streaks of light coming through south-marching banks of clouds.

"Some thoughts originate from complexes...." he said suddenly, without turning. He was watching something out there, but I could not see it from my position on the couch.

"Have you ever heard someone saying that man has an inferiority complex ... or that he's got an Oedipus complex, Axel?"

Hey! I never dreamed about fucking my own mother!

"But, what is a complex?" he continued without waiting for my response, his eyes still locked on a spot outside the window.

Curious, I had the urge to stand and rush to the window to have a peek. In addition, I was scared, because urges are never a good thing for me. Was that my need, or was it coming from the Rider?

"A complex is a group of ideas that tend to dominate your thoughts and moods, your way of experiencing life, to the point of leading you to see everything in relation to those ideas. If you hate, for example, the slightest thing, like a fleeting smell, will bring

47

immediately to mind all the ideas and sensations that make up your hate complex." He went on in his litany, yet something had changed. He was talking about himself now. I sensed it.

On the other hand, was he right? Did I have some kind of obsession?

"What happens when a peculiar complex is for some reason out of harmony with the rest of the conscious? Maybe its group of ideas is unbearably chained to pain. Maybe it comes from a sexual nature incompatible with the person's rigid principles..."

No. I was sure he was talking about something personal, something that was right out there.

"A conflict arises, just like two incompatible programs inside the same processing system in a computer—a struggle between the rebel complex and the rest of the personality ensues. Maybe the complex can be made compatible, or the mind consciously chooses to abandon one in favor of the other."

He paused, turned to face me and evaluated me, as if he sensed I had been doing the same from the moment I had come inside his office.

And, he was right. I had checked his background before coming to his office.

I always do that, as I do not like surprises.

He had a stint at Florida State Hospital in Chattahoochee, but had fallen out of grace for a minor incident, having experienced an emotional breakdown after his divorce with Courtney Barnes. She had left him for 'irreparable relationship conflicts'—whatever that meant. Hart became depressed, and his work got under low standards, so he was convinced by Administration to get some rest and straighten himself. Henry wandered from town to town in the state, practicing as a consultant, assistant to research groups, and even going as low as getting some underpaid jobs as a bartender in Jacksonville. Then, he'd sprung up here, in Prosperity Glades, last year, at the time when I was taking care of one Bradley Washington of South Bay—a serial rapist who had been terrorizing the area for months.

"Or perhaps this results impossible for some minds and a final battle begins," he droned on, his eyes never straying from me, not for a second.

He was tense now. Nonetheless, it wasn't about me. He felt shaken by something he had just seen out of that window and was struggling to send away those feelings.

"The usual method used by the human mind to resolve such a conflict is repression. In repression, conflict is avoided by banishing one of the opponents to a dark subconscious place of the mind—picture it as a dungeon. The winner gets it all, and is left in control of the conscious personality."

"So, you are trying to say that I chained a complex, developed in my infancy, down into an obscure cellar of my unconscious. And that's why I'm a workaholic?" I interrupted, trying to get him back on track.

He ignored me, and kept blathering about this theory. "The unfunny part comes next. Though the complex is chained in the dark downstairs, denied its normal expression, it is far from being annihilated. It continues to exist down there, although prevented from coming to the surface by the mind's force of repression—the Warden." He leaned backward into the window and rubbed his temple with visibly shaking hands. "The repressed complex can only influence the conscious indirectly, because the Warden is standing watch at the dungeon's door. Therefore, it finds subtle ways to resurface. The uglier the monster, the more twisted its trail."

Now, that was interesting. Was he trying to psychoanalyze my Rider?

"Let's just presume, something happened which caused remorse inside your mind. Let's say this remorse is too painful to you to bear. Something about someone's death."

Yes, many of them, but I feel no remorse, doc.

"The complex still needs to manifest itself. So, it uses some circuitous routes. It disguises itself." He returned to his seat in the armchair, taking advantage of the roof fan to refresh his heated body. It was a humid day, but he was also sweating for something personal.

A 'need', maybe?

"The mind can use symbolism to express the dissociated ideas. It develops a delusion—say, the man who thinks he is God's gift to women. Or it can use projection. The complex is visualized into other people, or a group of people, like homophobes or racists do." He sipped again from the glass of juice. "If the complex is projected onto an imaginary person, or one who has died, the repressed complex may appear in the form of hallucination; the patient sees ghosts from his past or hears voices in his mind commanding him what to do. If, on the contrary, the monster is projected onto real people, then a persecution delusion may develop. And in a state of anxiety, the sufferer may try to attack or kill those offending persons."

"Are you saying I'm dangerous, Dr. Hart?" I interrupted, frowning.

He smiled, and raised his palms, in a halting gesture. I was starting to like the guy.

"No, no, no, Axel! I'm just saying that in extreme cases the mind can react in such a way. That's why you're here. I just want to warn you about the dangers of repressed memories," he said. "I just want you to ask yourself: 'Do I have a monster lurking in my mind's dungeon?'"

I feigned a smile, but inside me, something laughed for sure. *Yes, I do harbor such a thing, doctor.*

"But it is not so simple, Axel. For if you do involuntarily chain it in the dark, it has been repressed, and you won't even know you harbor such beast." He paused, then glanced back instinctively at the window. "Until it breaks free."

Yes, there was definitely something personal out there.

And my Rider was urging me to discover what it was.

After that first session with Dr. Hart, I found it easier to accept therapy. This made Abigail happy and no longer worried about me.

50

Also, I had the opportunity to understand my Rider better. Besides, Dr. Henry Hart was a funny and pleasant person to talk with.

It was a pity that I had to kill him six months later.

****

I was still awake. I could not really sleep that morning. Abigail could see something was wrong about me, just like back in 1995. What about that stupid behavior I had?

Relax, Axel Hyde, relax. Try to concentrate on something else. Try to understand who violated your dumping spot, who killed and burned Jay Fraser with so much hate.

A gang war it couldn't be; they would've simply shot him in the head.

A personal grudge, maybe?

Focus, Axel!

Jay had been killed the same night I was having my way with Richard Solomon at the morgue. Who could lure such a man in a secluded spot like abandoned Kamp Koko?

A deal?

No. There were better places for that.

The promise of sex?

A light switched on suddenly in my mind.

A woman! My, my!

A woman could have lured him to the spot. I was not very used to sexual attraction or things of that nature, such as hooking techniques, myself not being a 'Charmer'. Ted Bundy was like that. Charmers kill with trust. One has to be impeccably polite, sympathetic, well spoken, and knowledgeable. One must be selfless, a superb listener and have a voice that makes a person hang on to every word from one's mouth. Clearly, I couldn't be one of them. I was too scary, too distant from other people. Not all Charmers are males. A female Charmer could get at victims more easily and more frequently; men are more willing to run off with an unknown woman than vice versa. So, the killer could have been a woman.

Besides, looking back at the angle and depth of the wounds, the struggle signs, and most of all the small size of some of the boot footprints in the muck, everything pointed to that solution.

She had to be very attractive—or easygoing— and possess good social skills. She could've hooked him in some place, like a bar, a pub, or a dancing spot. All I had to do was go out and make some queries about Jay Fraser at the right places. The closest spot that came to my mind was the Lakeview Motel, but I discarded it immediately. That's one place you go to for intercourse, not to look for a partner.

Then, while someone honked the car's horn out in the street, I realized that the best spot was right on the same trail: The Roughhouse.

I would've started investigations right from there. Maybe someone had seen Jay getting away with an unknown woman.

Maybe...

CHAPTER 7

WEIRD GIRL

"Ridge, what the heck are you doing in here?" Paul Carling stood in the doorway of the tool's shed and stared at the girl rummaging through the construction equipment. She turned to face him, showing her beautiful face.

"Nothing. I was just having a look at your selection."

Carling knew the young woman was weird from the moment he had first met her at the hiring office. A drifter, as there were many these days, the woman had surprised him with her skillful knowledge in carpentry, and most of all, an athletic sense of balance.

"Well, babe, your week's off. Doncha have a life outta here?"

She straightened her back, allowing Supervisor Carling to notice her alluring, shapely body, even hidden inside that baggy working suit she was so fond of. "Good Lord! I'm going, Paul. Gimme a break."

She had the build of a dancer, one of those girls you could imagine rolling around a pole or in a cage, in a strip joint or topless bar. How could such a beautiful young woman work in construction, a predominantly male field?

"May I ask you a simple question, Ridge?"

The pale girl dusted off her hands on the sides of her suit, then raised green-blue eyes on him. "Yup. But I warn you: ain't answering to personal or intimate ones." She grinned.

"No. Nothing like that, Ridge," Carling replied, smiling back amicably. "I was wondering, why are you doing this? I mean, you are clearly an attractive woman, you're young, you could've very different opportunities out—"

"Are you gonna fire me, Chief?" Cheri interrupted him, a cold stare sending an uneasy chill down the man's spine.

"No," he rushed up. "I was just musing about your choice.

53

You're a good worker; you're always on time and—"

"So? Can't see any problem 'bout that. Or do you?" she interrupted him again, moving closer.

Paul Carling was a tall man, a bit overweight, but with strong muscles and meaty hands. Still, he felt something akin to awe when she came closer, something primal. Just like wolves and dogs; canines form packs, which are led by a dominant 'alpha male'. This dominance is settled by fighting from very early in their life. Weaker dogs or wolves can instinctively perceive the alpha in their pack. Paul was feeling like that, sensing Cheri's intimidating presence.

"It's not about performance, Ridge." He tried to regain his usual coolness. "I was just trying to say that—"

Again, she halted him in his tracks. "I like the job, Carling. I'm skilled with tools. Father raised me as a tomboy, praise him. Is that okay?"

He stared at her gorgeous eyes; it was like gazing into refreshing pools of water. "Okay." He felt could not ask for more.

"Have a nice day, Chief," Cheri said, striding past him, straight to the changing shed.

Carling could not deny he was attracted by the woman's mysterious attitude, but he was also scared by her unnatural coldness. He kept staring at her back while she went away, wondering how good the chick would look naked, then sent those thoughts off with disgust.

He was fifty-two with a caring and sweet wife at home, a promising son in a law firm down in Miami, and two lovable grandkids.

For God's sake, the girl could've been his daughter!

He was a good man; he had never cheated on his wife, and never felt the need to. Nonetheless, there was something inside this young woman that lured him like the gar was lured by the angler's bait.

Was it those hypnotic eyes? Those wonderful eyes …

Still, he felt something was wrong inside the girl, something about her past was stuck down her soul, having her appear cold, distant, and uneasy to talk to.

On a subconscious level, he knew a gator swam in the depths of those pools.

****

After a brief stop at her rented trailer in South Glade to have a shower and change her clothes, Cheri Ridge jumped aboard her battered Toyota pick-up. She went straight to West Bend, a rough neighborhood full of run-down homes, unkempt lawns, rusted vehicles, and generally, a bad attitude. West Bend had fallen on hard times back in the '70s, and had never recovered. Most of the inhabitants were low income and some of them were on welfare, after the forcible closure of the Stone Packing Plant five years prior. Mayor Duval Fallon had worked hard for the betterment of the area in the last years by having the Bend Outlet, one of the largest in the county, built there. However, things had not gone better; the streets were riddled with potholes, and many streetlamps were constantly out of order. Crime was also on the rise over the last six years, especially serious crime such as violent assaults and arson. Litter filled the streets and sidewalks. Losing lottery tickets, crumpled cigarette packages and beer cans gathered at curbsides. Most of the duplex homes were badly in need of a new paintjob. This was the place where no one took notice if a man inflicted a savage beating on a woman attired as a low-rent prostitute, and no one moved to stop him. Pawnshops, sleazy bars, used car dealerships, liquor stores, and some porn shops flanked Wear Street, the neighborhood's main thoroughfare.

A small drove of teenagers wandered past, talking far too loudly, and making rude commentary at the sight of Cheri. She ignored them and entered a dilapidated parking lot, also pockmarked by potholes and buckled asphalt. Most of the cars here looked abandoned, and various bits of debris cluttered up the area. She parked her truck between a rusted Chevy and an old

Winnebago Camper with flat tires. Then, Cheri lowered her black cowboy hat on her eyes, relaxed in the driver's seat, and waited.

It was late afternoon now, with a pinkish dusk casting long shadows among the vehicles, and the sound of birds, frenetic in their search for a roosting spot to spend the approaching night, filled the air. The place brought back memories of a faraway place, a place she had left two years ago. The same faces, the same bleakness, the same decay.

In those times, she had worked as an entertainer at the Dancing Coyote, in Manchester, Tennessee. The club was typical of the genre, a watering hole catering to cowpokes, construction workers, and truckers. Decorated in the style of an old west saloon with modern addenda, such as the central walkway stage with vertical poles, the place had seen better times. The wooden furnishing was marked and riddled with holes; the subdued club lighting brightened with warm red hues only half of the customers. The bar lacked in stock, offering a limited choice in alcoholics. Nevertheless, clients kept coming, and they came for her—and her Moon Dance. Cheri had developed a dance of her own—a mixture of traditional gyrating and writhing movements of lap performance with the sensual, animalistic steps of a primordial dance, long forgotten by modern natives. Her uncle Johnny had taught her how to dance with the Moon. The dance symbolized the battle of the Spirit of the Moon against the coming of Windigo. It was a difficult stunt, yet Cheri was exceptional in her performance. The fact that she'd added it to the usual sexy moves of lap dancing would've put shame in her uncle, yet...

Yet, Uncle Johnny was no more; he was just dust and ashes.

A movement to her left swept away those memories, projecting her attention back to the present, like a bucket of chilly water poured on a sleepy drunkard. A lone figure came out of the shadows from a garbage-strewn alley, while a cross breeze stirred up a tiny vortex of discarded newspaper and plastic bags.

Somewhere at the end of the alley, a dog barked.

A white male in his late thirties, with a whole bald head and numerous piercing and studs on his face, shuffled out of the alley, kicking away an empty soda can. He wore a faded black biker jacket, which seemed a bit too large on his skinny body, a pair of baggy and torn jeans kept on by a heavy buckled belt, and some dirty and consumed sneakers.

Cheri's eyes became slits, concentrating on the figure, trying to focalize on the detail she was looking for.

She found it.

On the boy's right temple was a half-sun tattoo.

Here comes the signal!

He was the man she was waiting for.

****

Marvin Wilson crossed the parking lot, skulking among the vehicles like a rummaging skunk. A thin man, concealing his skeletal body—which looked like it hadn't been fed in a month—under piles of loose clothing; Marvin was the epitome of the methamphetamine junkie. He moved around with a twitchy and nervous demeanor, and had a thin mouth with perennial parched lips and full of rotting teeth, and a paranoid attitude. The cook for the Aryan Brotherhood chapter in Prosperity, he used as many drugs as he passed on. He was an expert in the matter; he knew how to fix and mix narcotics, or to cut them with all kinds of shit to make a profit. He was also proficient in cooking synthetic dope, like crystal meth and PCP, down at the little chemistry lab Jay Fraser had set up for him in a cabin around the lake. He packaged and dosed the stuff in the right way, so it could be slipped inside the Correctional. However, Marvin was also an addict user himself. And this was a problem as he could not indulge too much on the stuff. Jay had found out once and he had received a severe beating from Ray and Billy—as a first warning. Fraser and Billy delivered raw drugs to him, once a month. Wilson knew they had a deal with another chapter house of the Brotherhood down in Belle Glade, but he suspected the chemicals were smuggled there by runners from Miami. Not that he cared much about the provenience; all he wanted was to find a way to fix himself when in a low.

Like now, when he had found another way to get some good stuff—Shannon Cooper.

Shannon was a part-time lap dancer and part-time whore with a serious dependence on cocaine, an expensive dependence. She had no problems getting a high with other junk, such as meth or pills, but she made business mainly with the Mexicans. Marvin had hooked her two months ago, while he was testing his skills as a pusher at the Banshee's Cry, a strip club in West Bend. He did not intend to spend his whole life under the orders of Jay and his goons. He would soon move out of the place to lease his cooking abilities and knowledge for better-organized gangs, like the Mexican Mafia, having already tested ground in South Glade where he knew the Mexicans were setting up shop.

Wilson had discovered that two brothers, Benicio and Pedro Núñez, currently ran the operation. A cousin, Charlie Escalera, acted as enforcer. The powerful trio was ruthless and violent; they had forced out some minor dealers who traded marijuana in the public school with a sudden coup. Arriving in the middle of the night, they caught them unawares, bundling them into the trunks of their cars and bringing them down at Billy Ortega's Alligator Farm. The farm had been established twenty years ago by Billy's late father, Ernesto, and had grown steadily since. Billy raised the alligators for zoos, local restaurants, and for the handbag and shoe trade. On average, he had some sixty alligators in residence at any one time. Nevertheless, he also made affairs with the criminal underground, and he and his nephew, Joe Cárdenas, were more than eager to help the Núñez brothers in their trade.

In the middle of the alligator pool stood a large island with a retractable bridge leading out to it; this was where the alligators were fed. After some beating and general mistreatment, the three pushers had been roped and suspended for more than thirty minutes above the alligator's gaping jaws. Not surprisingly, the dealers left town without looking back.

The newcomers had then set up business in the trailer park, in the area the local South Gladers had christened, 'Cubaland'.

The Núñez brothers and Escalera were extremely dangerous cocaine nuts. Their peaceful appearance belied the fact that they would protect their business with whatever means they could. Their connections were such that, should someone speak too much about their dealings, they would find the moocher and inflict brutal vengeance upon them and their family. The problem was, Marvin wasn't Hispanic, and his only contact with the gang had been through Joe Cárdenas, who used to spend his weekly wage on Shannon's intimate performances at the Banshee.

Marvin was going there now, to get some soft junk from Joe and maybe spend some of his bucks for a quickie with Shannon.

This evening, all she wore were ankle-strapped, high-heeled leather boots and a studded G-string. Her tits were bare already. She danced to the canned music coming from the big speakers that hung above the stage. While Marvin Wilson scanned the customers' faces looking out for Joe Cárdenas or one of his friends, Shannon danced to the edge of the stage and squatted down in front of a solitary balding guy in a business suit with his tie undone and collar open. Spreading her legs wide, she pulled aside the G-string to expose her pussy to him. Whistles and hooting filled the room, while the businessman stared at her genitals and the girl pursed her lips. Then, leaning backwards and supporting her body on her hands and feet, she began to thrust her pelvis towards the man's face, pumping and rocking her hips.

Marvin couldn't help laughing at the scene. Shannon was such a good showoff.

He didn't notice the pale-skinned cowgirl who had just entered the place behind him and took a seat in one of the darkened booths.

****

From her booth's shadows, Cheri stared at the scene onstage, and couldn't avoid going back to her memories, to the Dancing Coyote. Before the coming of the Ada'wehi.

Adam Doohan, the bartender, had been serving Coors all-night, spilling it from the old-west-styled tap at his back. That Saturday, the place crawled with tourists, habitués, and hoppers. Shania Twain sang 'That Don't Impress Me Much' out of the speakers, while Candice, dressed as a bare-assed biker, shook her buttocks on the center stage.

Cheri had just finished applying her make-up over her Moon Lady outfit—a mixture of a cowgirl and a succubus. She was next. The hoots and cheers from the club's main room were the signal that Candice had just finished her show in the usual way. Once she had stripped herself completely, the girl had the habit of sliding all over the catwalk, her biker's boots screeching on the waxed wood, and ending down, wide-legged, with her pussy exposed for all to see.

Gross and vulgar, for Cheri's taste.

She had no problems with undressing herself, but had a different approach to lap dance. Cheri liked to tease, allure, and show off some parts of her body, then put the clothes back on. You never knew when, or if, she was going to unveil her beautiful body completely.

A rush of air and the smell of French perfume warned her of the passage of Candice returning from the stage. Cheri rose from her stool when Brett, the Coyote's DJ, announced her performance to the crowd. 'Dark Night' began to play, while the lights were dimmed further, a silvery full moon prop was lowered down, and a synthetic mist filled the scenery. Cheri appeared suddenly on stage after removing her black hood, which had kept her hidden among similarly colored curtains, and provoked a series of hoots from the public. Her black leather corset glimmered like satin in the silver light reflected by the moon prop, while her whitish legs, clad in dark cowboy boots, moved in time with the tune. Her long, flowing hair, streaked in mercurial hues, seemed to possess a life of its own, as Cheri left it free to swing wildly from side to side. As the music rose in rhythm, so the pale woman moved her body with even more daring stunts, rolling around one of the poles, lifting herself with just the aid of her strong legs, and partly revealing some of the juiciest parts, but only fleetingly. She vaulted, played with her cowgal hat, rocked, and squatted. The silent crowd watched hypnotized, as if they were at a circus stage-act, not a nightclub strip dance. At her stunt's apex, Cheri climbed the pole, clasped her legs tightly around it, and allowed her body to fall downward, head down, at the same time removing her corset and casting it aside. Her boobs bounced down, the shiny silver rings that pierced her nipples sending blinking reflexes.

Upside down, Cheri noticed for the first time the five monsters seated at the front table next to the stage. She did not know what they were at that moment, but she could feel their ugly stare.

They were all different—one an elegant man in an expensive suit, another like a boxer in street wear. A skeletally thin figure wore a Miami Dolphins t-shirt, a well-dressed guy had the body of a bouncer, and a squat individual possessed an ex-con face.

However, every one of them sported the same eyes—those of wolves stalking prey.

Cheri sent away those memories of what she later discovered were Ada'wehi monsters, and turned her attention back to the boy with the shaved head. He now sat at a table with a younger looking Hispanic guy. They smiled at each other, exchanging puns and lewd jokes at the expense of the overexcited executive down by the stage. Aroused by her intimate performance on his plump face, the man had tried to touch one of the dancers' legs, causing one of the bouncers to intervene. He was now making a scene, protesting with the threatening goon, denying his tentative, and yelling for a chat with the owner.

What an asshole! One of the many.

The crowd in the room vociferously urged the bouncer to throw the man outside. Meanwhile, the junkie dancer—Cheri could tell she was a drug-addict by the signs on her armpits and the sunken eyes—had retreated backstage at once. She returned some minutes later wearing a fishnet top over a black bra, a ruffled miniskirt above knee-length stretch leggings, and an infinite number of bracelets and charms covering both her arms. Cheri heard the bald-headed man call the dancer. "Hey, Shannon! Come over here!"

The girl's features were long, angular and sharp; she had frame narrow green eyes. Carefully styled, short black hair crowned her face, knife-sharp locks fell across her forehead. She joined the pair at the table and sipped from one of the men's glasses. Yet her eyes stayed on the executive, who was now on the point of being escorted out by the bouncer. Cherie could not hear what they were telling one another, but she did not care.

She was here to stalk the man with the shaved head—one of the Moon-Eyed People. She was sure he was one of them, an Ada'wehi, hiding in human clothes.

The Night Goer had recognized him.

CHAPTER 8

MASTER AND MINION

More than a home, the mansion is a status symbol. Its exterior is kept perfectly groomed, its grounds well-manicured and lush. Inside, one finds antique furnishings, state-of-the-art electronics, and art pieces worth thousands of dollars. The garage holds numerous expensive vehicles, from classics to modern sports cars and limousines. The cost of buying and maintaining such a mansion is simply beyond the reach of most people. This is the home of the extremely fortunate.

Frank Eugene Hall was one of them.

Actually, he had not built the neoclassical revival style manor of which he was so proud—he had inherited it from his father, along with half of the town's land.

Hall Mansion was a large structure with a two-story, columned front porch, topped with a Greco-Roman pediment. A large, hip-style roof, with no dormers, surmounted a symmetrical layout, both on the exterior and interior. The walls had smooth and white surfaces. Silhouetted against the reddening sky, the three-story mansion crouched behind an iron fence, surrounded by beautiful vegetation and orchard trees. A white marble statue of an old mariner, complete with a ship's wheel, stood halfway between the imposing house and the decorated main gate. To the right side was a large garage of design similar to the mansion. The grounds were extensive and crisscrossed by many cobbled paths, each leading to one of the marvels of the property, such as the beautiful pool and barbecue area—one of Frank's favored places—or the raised gazebo.

It was here that Frank stood now, his arms resting on the summerhouse's parapet, staring at his grounds. The dangling lamp under the roof illuminated the rattan furniture—a coffee table, four armchairs, and a love seat.

It also lit up a second figure, which was relaxing on the love seat, smoking a cigar.

Billy Gamble wasn't the kind of man you could expect to be a guest in such premises. A white male, six foot two and weighing close to two hundred twenty-five pounds, his toned, muscular body revealed how much time he spent at the gym. He kept his blonde hair in a military buzz cut and his face clean-shaven. The man wore army boots, fatigue pants, and an army green tank top, exposing his wide chest.

"So, you're saying J.F. is a ghost, right?" he said, puffing out a cloud of Cuban smoke from the side of his mouth.

Frank did not turn to answer; he just kept his stance and sipped some red wine from his fine crystal chalice. "Yes, Billy. That's exactly what I said. This is not normal of him, you know. He may be stubborn, shady, and moody too, but he's a pro on the job."

"And you want me to find out what happened to this jerk, right?" Gamble continued.

"Yes. Go around, snoop into his usual places."

Billy changed position on the couch, pulling some more from the cigar. "I oughta know a lot of places this joke wastes money into, but they're not my usual digs, mister."

"Listen, Billy, I have neither the time nor the patience today to spend in unnecessary conversation about what is your *usual* part in our organization." Hall raised his voice, revealing his bad mood. It had been a stressful day from the moment he met Doyle to the terrible tour of the Community Center. Then he'd had a full day down at the construction yard, meeting some Russian investors, and now this. Though Gamble was good at what he did, Frank could not stand to stay close to him more than necessary. He was cocky, arrogant, and cheap.

"Calm down, sir! Didn't say ain't going to find the asshole. I just want to spell it clear I'm not a hound o'sort," replied Gamble, smothering the cigar's butt in a pewter ashtray.

Frank turned to face him, staring right into the man's hazelnut eyes, then grabbed the wine bottle and poured some more into his empty glass. "What I am asking, Bill, is simple. Jay disappeared by a whole day, now. I'm not going to warn Sheriff Andrews about it. I just want to know what happened to him. Because I smell rotten fish in this story."

"Think the rooster has fled the nest?"

Frank shook his head. "No. I'm sure something happened to him. Find someone who last saw him yesterday."

Billy rose from his seat and went for the wine bottle, helping himself. "Do you think the brownies took him off?"

'Brownies'—that was Billy's favored derogatory term for Hispanics. He had quite a repertory for all ethnicities—Blacks were 'Mungoes', Italians were 'Pizzamen', Natives got 'Manitous', and Russians had 'Vodkas'. No doubt, a wretched dictionary he had learned while doing time in prison. How much Frank hated it. Couldn't he call them just Spics, like anyone else?

"Maybe, Bill, maybe. At the present time there is a truce between the Mexican Mafia and Aryan Brotherhood nationwide, though that may change at any moment, you know."

"Do you suspect the newcomers, that worthless scum down there at Cubaland?"

"Do not underestimate them, Billy," Frank said.

"Come on boss, they are just a pair of kittens trying to look like cougars—"

"No! Stop that, you idiot!" Hall exploded. "I want professionals here; I have no use for showoffs, boasting around how much they are tough, but then getting swept off by a couple of low-profile muggers!" He added the last line voluntarily, knowing how much the Fisher's Bay fiasco still burned into Billy's ego.

Gamble stared at him with brazen eyes, not being the kind of man who accepted a scolding easily, but he also knew when to shut up and let the bigger dog bark. "Okay. Listen, sir. I'm gonna check the *Caveman* first, then the *Happy Gator* and the *Moola*. These are all the bars J.F. usually attends. Oh, and the *Roughhouse*, too," Billy said in a cold tone, eyeing him with a challenging grin which said: *Calm down, old dog, you know what I'm made of, and how much you owe me.*

"Good," said Hall, returning to his previous position at the banister, uneasy.

Gamble took another Cuban cigar from the box on the coffee table, plucked it inside one of his Army pants' pockets, and started down the gazebo steps.

"Just one more thing," Hall said. "Once you find whoever was last seen going away with him," he paused. "You have free reign, Gamble. Do as you like. The meat is like this: I want to know what happened to Jay Fraser. Understood?"

Gamble did not turn to answer Frank; he kept walking, heading for the main entrance, where his bike waited like a faithful horse. He decided to add to the tension inside the old man, just for kicks.

Understood?" Hall repeated, this time in a louder tone.

"Yeah, Master. As you wish," he finally scoffed.

CHAPTER 9

QUESTIONS AND VEHICLES
(FROM AXEL'S HALL OF MEMORIES)

I took my car out of the garage late in the afternoon, heading straight to the Roughhouse, keeping low speed among Elm Street, past the little houses with low hedges and white fences. I paid attention to a couple of kids playing football on their front lawn, but threatening to get on the street at any moment. Looking at my town with different eyes, I watched out for new faces among the usual crowd.

In Town Square, I witnessed the change of the community's fauna—for day life is very different from nightlife in a hamlet.

There was the 'Constant Jogger'—three more miles to go tonight and four more pounds to go in the long-term. And the 'Inattentive Commuter'—on his way back home, but with his nose so deeply buried in his paperback that he wasn't watching where he was going. The 'Bluetooth Maniac' ambled down the streets, seemingly talking to himself. And the 'Righteous Cyclist' traveled around on her bicycle, scrupulously observing traffic-safety laws, getting agitated when others did not. Finally, the 'Future Champion', who dribbled his basketball down the street in his oversized jersey and shorts while gulping down a sports drink.

I have nicknames for all types of humanity. Yet, I have no nickname for me, except Spooky, but that was so long ago.

Rain had started to pour down from the early evening sky. It was getting dark, and the water splashed on the pavement, forming puddles that reflected beams from passing cars. A thunder boomed overhead; a storm was coming. I passed Johnston Hall Estates just in time to avoid crashing into a stupid biker on his Harley Davidson. He came out of nowhere from the community's main gate. Not happy enough for the scare he'd caused me, the man raised his right hand to show me the finger.

You are one lucky asshole, man.

I kept driving down Route 78, passing Austerity Field Fairground on my left, and then turned right to get on Lakeview Parkway. While driving southward, I met Jerry Meeks' pickup. He flashed his headlights in sign of salute. I flashed back.

Jerry Meeks. The other weird guy in town.

People wondered if the bland little man had any interests besides fishing. Customers who frequented his bait-and-tackle shop wondered instead of how he stayed in business, with such a dingy store.

Jerry likes me. I don't know why, but he does, or so I think.

Jerry is all soft, with a sagging body, rumpled clothes, and the drooping face of an elkhound. Everything about him says *non-threatening*, starting from his receding hairline, to his beer-belly gut and pudgy face. Every time I see him, he wears the same style of clothes—a hook-studded hat and an angler's vest. The man is considered weird by the townsfolk because he is a workaholic, like me. He loves his job at the Fish & Tackle Shack, and when he is off-duty, he likes to go on fishing expeditions on the lake. He collects everything about that hobby: from Norwegian hooks to Canadian lures. He has no friends, family, or whatever. Like me, he is a lonely man.

Maybe he has his kind of Rider, too.

I am one of his usual customers. I visit his shop from time to time to buy some useful stuff for my own version of fishing. Nylon cords and fishing hooks, strong gloves, and hip-waders can be useful for my trips to the swamp. Besides, having a hobby helps me a lot in my daily masquerade.

Dr. Hart had suggested it to me some time ago—hunting and fishing.

I practice both.

I saw the neon sign of the Roughhouse, with that big ugly pointing arrow, coming out suddenly through the rain-soaked windshield. Turning my car on the left, I parked it near a group of motorcycles, but had to run to the pub's front entrance, for the rain was falling down so heavily that it almost whipped me.

The Roughhouse is a typical, one-story roadside pub of ordinary construction and appearance from the outside. Inside, it features ordinary decor too, with cheap, imitation knotty-wood walls, a bar, and a dozen round tables. In a side room there is a pool table, a gaming area for darts, and sports memorabilia. The main seating area has a giant video screen – usually showing NFL games, like that night – an empty disk jockey booth, and a small stage for local bands that never seems to get any use.

Half dozen customers lingered there now. I looked at the faces in the property. A couple of bikers, a lonely drunkard seated in a corner talking to his glass of beer, and three local road workers enjoying an evening out together. I knew some of them. The two bikers I didn't recognize—they were oblivious to me and chatted about some trip they had down on the Tamiami Trail last week. The drunkard I knew; he was Dan Mantz, the burly owner of the Grassy Swamp Boat Rentals, and local boozer. He could get violent sometimes, but usually he just spent his nights standing in a pool of his own vomit outside one of the town's watering holes. Mantz isn't bad. He had fallen this way two years ago, after his wife had run away with a half-Seminole broker from Brighton. After the 'incident', as he referred to it, he had no respect for anyone, except Deputy Espinoza—my soon to be ex-girlfriend—who had laid him out in a brawl at the Moola months ago. Being bested by a woman wasn't a problem to him; he did not consider her a female.

The three men were employed by Hall Constructions, the main contractor for civic works and maintenance in town.

I had a glance at the bar. There, cleaning glasses with a rag, was Mark Scarlett, the manager and owner of the place. Mark was a big man, a bit overweight, but with strong, tattooed forearms, a barrel chest, and long, unkempt whitish hair topping a wrinkled face and framed by a short—also whitening—goatee. "Look what the cat dragged in," he said when noticing me.

I'm not exactly famous for being a barfly in town. Not at all.

69

"What are you doing here, Doc?" he asked, still cleaning glasses.

I moved to the bar, took a seat on one of the stools, and tried to be as natural as I could. That was the hardest part for me. I'm not good at socializing; might be good at my practice, but talking with other people, well....

"Some of your cold companions in need of a beer?" he joked, letting out a sharp laugh with the result of getting me even more nervous.

No, Mr. Scarlett. I'm here to meet a person. But I'm not sure if she will get here tonight".

"A *she*?" Mark almost fumbled the glass he was holding when hearing that word.

Mr. Spook's having a date? I could hear him think. Well, I am not renowned for dating, either.

"Who's the lucky one?"

"Oh, nothing so special. She's just a person who could help me identify a John Doe down at the morgue," I lied.

Scarlett replaced the glass on the overhead holder, then looked back at me, while the three road workers cried out in protest when the video screen went blank due to some glitch in broadcasting transmission.

"Do you want something to drink while you wait, Doc?" Scarlett asked me, directing his attention to what was happening in the main room.

"Yes, please. I'll have a draft beer." I do not make use of alcohol, usually, but I didn't want to appear too much out of place. I had to get information from the man, to get his sympathy, or so I thought.

The game returned on screen, letting the sports lovers yell out their approval, but it was soon followed by moans of disappointment when they found out their team was losing.

"Mr. Fraser should introduce me to this woman," I bluffed, while Scarlett drafted the beer from the tap.

He turned and placed the tall glass, filled with golden liquid, on the bar. "Fraser? Do you mean Jay Fraser?" he said, a concerned look on his face.

Gotcha!

"Yes," I said, gulping a sip down.

"I think you're late," he said.

I raised my eyes to him. "What do you mean?"

He stared back, cold gray eyes looking out for something on my face. "I mean, last night I saw the man in the company of quite a hottie right here. They had some shots, then went away."

"Can you describe her?"

Mark Scarlett changed expression, and suddenly looked like he regretted what he had just let slip out of his mouth. "Well ... she was a bombshell. Not one to get away unnoticed, if you know what I mean."

I didn't know what he was meaning, that was for sure, but I needed him to talk because I'd been right; a woman lured Fraser down at the campground.

"She packed one of the nicest asses I've ever seen—" he continued.

"I don't need to know if she was like some kind of stripper, Mr. Scarlett. I need to know her hair color, and what she was wearing, just that," I interrupted, then forced a social smile on my face, that I was sure resulted in a dreadful grin.

Mark looked at me with a dumb face, as if he'd been trying to explain football to an alien from another world. "Oh, yes. I could never forget that. She dressed like a cowgirl, or something similar."

I gulped down another draught.

Bingo! I was right.

"Black jeans, black denim jacket, black cowboy boots and hat. Everything was black."

Cowboy boots. Like the tracks I'd found at the murder scene. Had to be her.

"Long, black hair, pale skin, that bouncy swinging ass..." He trailed on, until I stopped him again. That fixation about the woman's butt was getting on my nerves.

"So, you are saying that Miss Picket came here *last night*," I objected, as if disappointed by the news, "with Mr. Fraser?"

Mark looked at me with a quizzing look. "Yeah, that's what I'm telling you, Doc," he said, then backtracked. "No. I mean, they didn't come together. Jay was here first. She arrived after."

I poured the last sip from the glass down my throat. "And went away together? At what time?"

The crowd of three let out another series of protests and less polite epithets when the screen went blank again. The bikers came over to the bar, paid their checks, and went out, revealing to me that it was still downpouring.

Mark Scarlett cashed bucks, then returned to me, his face showing he was trying to focalize. "I think it must have been almost four in the morning when they went out."

"Are you sure about that?"

For a moment, but just for a moment, I saw a feeling of worry crossing his face, as if he had perceived something wrong about our conversation. Maybe I was getting too inquisitive; maybe I was acting too much like a police officer for his tastes. I diverted the gaze to my empty glass, playing my index finger on the border.

"Well, I'm not so sure," he said, shaking his head. "But I know it was very late because Jay popped up here around three and twenty. I remember that, because that's the time I usually start switching off the TV screen and lock the game room."

I rose from the stool, compulsively cleaning my back with the hands, as if to not let anything from that place come with me, just like when a cat scratches the ground to communicate its discomfort about an unpleasant smell. Scarlett looked at me in a wrong way for that gesture, interpreting it as a remark that his place was not clean.

"My, my! Better for me to leave," I said, not even attempting a smile this time.

"Hey! Maybe they'll be back tonight. Jay may not be called a regular, but he comes here one or two nights a week. Now, if he was going to introduce you to the gal, you can bet he'll be here."

No, dear bartender, I wouldn't bet on that.

"Look, I can't wait more. Here's my office phone number." I reached for a paper napkin and wrote a series of numbers on it, while the three rowdy men shouted their approval for a touchdown. "Should Mr. Fraser pop up tonight, let him have it," Then, I left the place.

Outside, the rain had turned into a tropical storm, with strong winds sweeping the parking lot. Leaves and twigs were flying wildly on the air, while lukewarm water soaked me in a few seconds. I reached my car and relaxed on the seat.

I was right; an attractive woman had lured Jay Fraser like an angler lures a fish to its doom. She had hooked him in this place, and then had surely convinced the man to follow her on her pickup. However, something felt wrong about the story.

If Jay Fraser had come to the Roughhouse on his own, how had he come here? On foot?

Unlikely. He must have had a vehicle of some sort.

A car? Nope. The bartender would've noticed it still parked here.

A bike?

That could be loaded on a big truck. If I remembered well, Deputy Peter Tipple had said something about a *Yamaha* and Fraser some time ago. Perhaps the killer had come back here to hide the bike.

I opened my car door and got out in the lashing, rain-soaked wind. A drainage channel opened on the right side of the pub's parking lot. I couldn't be sure the woman was the killer I was looking for, however, inside me, the Rider was awakening. It had no doubts.

I went over there and inspected it, using my torchlight to scan the place. The drainage was cluttered with dead vegetation and litter and the waters moved slowly, too slowly. Should the thunderstorm last enough, soon it would fill up and overflow. Something big was blocking its course at the junction with the

Lakeview Drain. I moved further down, the unceasing rain cluttering my vision, to frantically reach the junction point. The Rider pointed me like a compass.

Cold, warm, lukewarm ... hot...

Fire!

Amid the cluttered foliage, the shining chrome of a *Yamaha* motorcycle told me I was on the right track.

CHAPTER 10

JUNK AND FUNK

A quivering thunder roared over the West Bend's parking lot, while slashing rain fell on the young couple leaving the Banshee's Cry. Marvin and Shannon took refuge inside the dancer's Chevy. They didn't take notice of the dark figure following them from the nightclub, being too eager to share some of the stuff inside's Shannon's purse.

After some minutes, the car's windows fogged and the pungent smell of marijuana filled the vehicle as Marvin puffed on the joint, drawing with passion to fill his lungs. Then, he released a vaporous cloud of smoke from his mouth, designing little rings in the air.

"Over here, you selfish bastard!" Shannon exclaimed, breaking the silence of the craving.

"I'm not selfish," he protested, moving toward her and squeezing her right breast with the free hand. She chuckled, then removed the joint from the boy's hand and took a long drag from it.

"This is really good shit, hun. The real stuff, I mean," he said, his voice cluttered by smoke. "Is this what your Mexican friends sell?"

"Yes. Absolutely. And you can't figure out where they grow it up!" she said, releasing smoke and giggles at the same time.

Marvin stole again the smoldering joint from the woman's hand, puffing some more, while a thunder shook the car's windows, and an alarm began to blare in the distance. The bald headed boy took a glance at the dancer's breasts, and then offered her the marijuana. He reached out with both hands to grab her bosom. Shannon mishandled the joint and let it fall down on her gown, causing it to scorch her left leg. She let out a cry of pain, pushed away Marvin' probing hands, and thrashed about, causing the burning cinders to fall off. Marvin laughed at the scene, so much that she took offense at the boy's lack of sensibility.

A lightning bolt lit up the outskirts of the lot, and the downpour assumed the strength of a tropical storm, with strong winds sweeping away the litter in droves.

"You bastard!" Shannon pouted; while Marvin reached down to retrieve the still burning joint from under her seat.

Marvin could not stop laughing, partly because of the intoxicating effects of the grass. This irritated the girl even more. She slapped him on his back, while he finally took hold of the cigarette.

"Easy, gal," he said, trying to get back serious.

"I got burned and shit and all you do is laugh?" she rebuked

He stopped her pouts by kissing her, the joint still in his hand. She responded with desire as he grabbed her head and let his tongue roll around hers. Shannon halted her tirade and returned the advance, reaching out for his groin, palming the already turgid penis through the pants' cloth. Marvin grunted softly, then removed in a hurry his biker jacket, allowing her a better grasp of his manhood. She squeezed it, then, suddenly, let it go, leaving Marvin with a deluded face.

"What the fuck?"

"Pay first," she said stubbornly.

Marvin quickly reached into his baggy pant's left pocket, in a nervous search of a roll of dollars he kept there. He offered her fifty bucks.

"Just fifty fucking clams … for me?" She smirked.

"Come on baby, how much d'ya think ya're worth?"

"I make that just in tips for shaking my tits, dude!"

Marvin did not intend to lift the offer; he knew she fucked for even less in a crisis. "Yes. But you are getting more here. You're going to get stuffed by my big cock, hon."

She glanced at him sideways, with a queasy expression. "*That?*" she said, pointing a finger to his groin. "You consider *that* a big one?" Shannon cracked a laugh.

It was Marvin's turn to take offense. His face turned red, while his neck's muscles tensed in rage. His left hand sprung up and grabbed the stripper's top. "Fifty bucks are more than enough to suck my rod, bitch!"

Shannon saw the wild expression in the boy's eyes and flinched. She knew the man could get dangerous. Also, she had already experienced some punishment by one of his 'brothers. She wasn't so much scared of him, but of Billy Gamble. That fucked up scum had raped her—two months ago—and she didn't have the guts to report the incident at the sheriff's office. She was a well-known hooker, and a junkie. No way out.

"Okay. Calm down, Marv. I'll blow you for fifty."

Marvin relaxed, eased himself on the seat, opened his jeans zipper and plucked out his penis. Still scared by the boy's reaction, Shannon grabbed the stiff organ with her right hand and caressed it with soft strokes. Then, she lowered her head and took it into her mouth.

Outside, the storm began to quell. The wind had a last, strong, lash, then ceased completely. A late thunder roared in the distance, signaling the passage of the perturbation, now heading northward. In the car, Shannon continued her mouth-job, while Marvin grabbed her head, pushed her harder, thrust his hips toward her lips.

A heron cried out from the swamp, while the storm turned into light raining, intermittent drops ticking on the car's windshield.

Inside her truck, the dark cowgirl kept her eyes focused on the vehicle, patiently waiting for the right moment to strike.

****

Marvin shot his load inside the woman's mouth, at the same time yelling out his satisfaction. Shannon left his relaxing penis immediately, lowered the car's window and spat the man's fluid on the concrete.

"Hey! You had to swallow it, for fifty!" protested the boy.

"Nope. Sorry, that's not included in the service."

The skeletal boy replaced his organ inside his pants and frowned, but decided he had had enough. He was sated and had no intention spending the rest of the night bickering with a whore inside that fucking parking lot.

"What are you doing now?" Shannon asked him, drying her lips with a napkin.

"What do you mean? I'm just relaxing, baby. What do you want from me? Just ease my ass off your car?"

"Exactly! I want to go home. Ain't gonna let you use my car for a nap!"

Marvin shot daggers at her, then raised his medium and got off the car. "See you soon, sweetie," he mocked.

Shannon closed the door and ignored him, starting the engine. Marvin raised his jogging suit's hood to cover his bald head and slipped on his biker jacket, then headed back to the garbage-filled alley.

****

From inside her truck, Cheri followed him with her gaze and waited for him to get far enough before starting her engine. Then, she drove her vehicle out of the lot, allowing Shannon's car to induct first on Wear Street. On her right, she spotted the man on a motorcycle; he came out from another alley and turned eastward, two blocks away from her. Cheri tailed him at a distance, with two or three cars between her truck and the bike. She noticed him turning on his left, and followed suit.

A while later, to avoid attracting attention, she widened the distance because the road out of town was deserted. The man continued down South Glade, crossed the trailer park's main thoroughfare, then headed straight for the wooded area of Grassy Swamp. Once, he seemed to spot her and lowered his speed. Cheri noticed him glancing back, so she took decision to let him go for a while, turning northward in the direction of the Independence Field

Golf Course, yet effectuating a U-turn after less than a mile. Back on Okeechobee Drive, she switched off her headlights and resumed the trail.

The bike was nowhere to be seen, but she kept going eastward, until her guts told her—or was that the Night Goer?—that she had lost him. She pulled her truck to the side of the road, and then scoured the landscape. The area was rich in vegetation and little light filtered down from the now starry night. Everything was wet and drenched, the only sound coming from the dripping on the leaves.

Then, she spotted the light amid the wilds.

A close by trail headed straight into the tropical forest, a barely visible dirt road. She turned the engine on, then took the truck onto the trail, driving it slowly, headlights off. The road ran for almost half a mile, twisting at different times, through saw grass and trees, deep into the swamp and ending into a clearing. The illumination came from a wooden shack, one of those used by hunters and vacationers in the wilds. Cheri heard the distinct hum of a power generator and moved closer, then killed the engine, got out of the car and stealthily advanced to the cabin. She spotted the man's bike parked in front of the shack.

He was there.

And he was alone.

CHAPTER 11

WHAT MONSTERS ARE MADE OF
(FROM AXEL'S HALL OF MEMORIES)

The storm had stopped by twenty minutes when I entered my working place. Thomas Michaels, the morgue's caretaker, hailed me with a smile, while I removed my wet clothes and left them in the dryer. There was silence in the air. People were all huddled inside their homes, watching TV or minding to daily chores. I slipped on my lab coat, went to the main desk to check about any notes from the CME, found none, so I decided to retreat into my office. The place was not a real office but more a small side room, once used as storage—it still contained spare materials and some registers. However, it also hosted a small desk and wooden chair. I eased on it and relaxed my aching shoulders.

My mind, on the contrary, was very active.

What do we have here?

The alluring woman had hooked J.F.—the ex-con—at the Roughhouse, in the late hours of the night. Then, she had convinced the man to get in her truck and had carried him down to Kamp Koko. Once there, the mask had fallen off and she had killed Fraser with extreme brutality. Afterward, she had burned his remains with kerosene and backtracked to the roadside pub to push the man's bike inside the drainage ditch, using some fallen vegetation to cover it up. This pointed to one thing: her job was not over. She had no intent to cover her tracks from the police—no, she didn't care about details. Probably, she just didn't want to put on alert someone close to her victim.

This was a passionate murder, something similar to when I killed my own uncle in 1986. Mine was a murder of revenge, and this one, I felt, was no different.

All my past victims—thirty-two of them, counting Solomon—had been the product of my Rider's urge, except one: retired

Sheriff Angus M. Hyde.

For none of them I felt regret, for I had no feelings, but I was close to being sorry when I had to kill Dr. Henry Hart. He was such a funny and brilliant man, even a friend for some time, and it was a pity that he'd wasted that mind of his to devise terrible ways to haunt and torment his ex-wife. I could clearly recall my last session at his office, on Hall Memorial Hospital's third floor.

****

It had been a clear spring day in 1996. The sun shone bright through the windows, casting orange light over the doctor's memorabilia, playing with airborne dust. By now, I had been meeting with Hart for over five months, and he knew a lot about my past traumas and my workaholic obsession. He knew about the horrible things I had experienced at the damned camp at the hands of Russell Floyd, of my unnatural calm reaction at my father's death, and my contrasting relationship with my uncle. Henry and I were not proper friends, but he had been the person who knew the most about me.

We even went to the *Bowlarama* inauguration together. That evening, he had introduced me to Katherine Adler, an attractive blonde nurse with dissociation disorders—one of his patients. I dated her only twice, and then had ceased all contact when I discovered she was much more interested in what lay inside my pants, than what was inside my mind. And, I had not been ready for sex, yet. She comforted herself easily two days after we broke up. With Nelson Brooks, the Prosperity Cougars' quarterback. She likes big men.

Henry and I had just returned from an excursion to my uncle's house.

He'd called it 'Primal Therapy', a form of psychotherapy in which patients are encouraged to relive past traumatic events by achieving catharsis and lowering psychological defenses. It had not been funny. However, it helped me remember some details about my uncle's and mother's tormented relationship and how much I hated it.

"As a simple pathologist, I feel inferior to you, Henry," I said, while sipping some of the orange juice he used to prepare by himself. It was very good.

He laughed. "There is a joke we use to share in psychiatry: I have at last isolated the cause of your inferiority complex..." He paused, expecting me to ask for the rest of the joke, which I didn't.

"You *are* inferior!" he finished.

We laughed together. Mine was simulated, of course. I still don't get that joke.

I let myself fall on the couch, relaxing after that enduring experience inside the old house's basement. Henry Hart removed his jean jacket, revealing yet another t-shirt with the print: *I have an Obsessive Disorder: You!* He took a seat at his desk and casually flipped through his notebook.

Was he looking for another blind date?

He was a fanatic of that stuff, once admitting to being quite a lustful guy. Blondes, brunettes, redheads, Blacks, Asians, Hispanics—he had a vast conquests collection. I had almost believed it was part of his job.

He lifted his head toward me with a serious expression; eyes showing a hint of sudden sadness. "So, Axel, we have to talk again about what happened inside your uncle's cellar. I've noticed your reticence in getting down there."

I shifted my gaze away, instinctively. I had told him—well, I had shouted to him, to be exact—what had happened there in 1986.

So much for 'Primal Therapy'.

"However, I feel there is more down there that you're still hiding."

I could not tell him that that same night, after I surprised my dear uncle Angus beating the hell out of my mother and forcing his way on her, I'd killed him on the spot, with primal rage—and a little help from my Rider. I was eighteen at the time and he was my fourth victim already.

"Axel, a shrink is like a religious confessor, or your tax accountant. You have to tell him everything, even your darkest secrets," he said.

He knew!

He knew I had murdered former Sheriff Hyde.

****

I must admit it hadn't been one of my best performances, but no one had ever suspected me. It had been a pure murder of passion. After beating and forcing my mother to have sex with him, the bastard had gone to his favored watering hole, the *Happy Gator*, where he had indulged in all kinds of booze; a retired sheriff could drink as much as he liked in a small town like ours. My mother had closed herself inside her room. She didn't know I had been home, believing me to be out on one of my frequent, solitary trips to the swamp collecting dead animals for my studies. A seething rage had burned inside me, and it had been mine, mine alone. Four years before, my father—the late Vice Sheriff Randolph Hyde—had been killed in a stakeout, while helping the State Troopers in the capture of two dangerous armed-robbers from Belle Glade. The following year, we had transferred inside my uncle's home, after my mother had finally accepted his incessant offers.

I never got along with him.

More, I hated him; the guy was a jackal, an arrogant and selfish man, who saw me as a retarded boy, as somehow, he could feel something was wrong with me. Also, he had cleared me from the death of Russell Floyd, but he knew I had murdered the clown—in self-defense, but a violent murder, nonetheless.

In a way, he'd been right.

Because of this, he had kept going around town, telling people I was beyond repair, having been forever touched by those terrible events; however, I was his brother's only son, so...

Life with him was a continuous hardship. He had decided I had to be straightened up, that he had to get a 'real man' out of me—or get me in an institution.

Damn bastard!

In 1984, I finally discovered my mother had surrendered to Angus' unceasing advances. They had worked hard to keep it secret from me, but I had found out, nonetheless. I wasn't happy about it, but it was none of my concern—worried as I was about my third victim, Liam Seese, a rapist I dismembered with an ax right at Kamp Koko, and whose chopped body parts I fed to the alligators.

The following year I had yet another displeasure—during an outdoor excursion, I'd surprised 'Dear Uncle Angus' partying out his retirement in a Waynesford brothel.

I never told my mom, but she found out by herself when he passed her some kind of sexual disease.

I laid a simple plan to get rid of him once for all. My uncle's home was an old style brick suburban cottage in Northside's outskirts; a two-story affair, with a large cellar that could be used as a refuge in case of a hurricane warning. It had a large double set of storm doors. My uncle hated when I left them open, so when he came back from his nightly booze, the first thing he would check would be those goddamned doors. That night he came back at four in the morning, parked his car behind the house and took notice of the open doors. Craving to administer a scolding to his odious nephew, he came down the stairs, his legs barely holding him up.

And I was there, waiting in darkness.

I strangled him with a rope, using all my repressed fury as strength; my pure hate concentrated in that final act. Then, I loaded his limp body inside the car and sent it down the reservoir. I watched his *Chevy* slowly sink into the waters, unable to move, still feeling hate inside me and uncaring about my future. I knew I would've been charged for his murder. The rope signs on his neck would've revealed he'd been killed before his body displacement in the mire. However, I got lucky. Next day, his car was found, the body recovered and sent to the morgue for examination by the coroner. I stood with my mother all day, waiting for the deputies to come to arrest me.

It never happened.

In those times, the Chief Medical Examiner was Arthur Finnegan, a lazy and corrupt son of a bitch. Sheriff Bob 'Good Ole Boy' Kiley had been a close friend of my uncle, and suspected him drinking too much in those last days, so he believed old Angus ended inside the reservoir after one of his usual nights. He paid Dr. Finnegan to skip autopsy, deliver the man to Mr. Howard Finley's Funeral Parlor, place him into a coffin, and close the case as a bad road accident.

I was shocked.

However, I also learned something about small communities. They're like family; my uncle was a respected man, no matter how ornery he was, so the thing had to stay in the family.

His funeral took place two days later. I was there, my face impassive, lacking any hint of sadness or uneasiness, but people had been used to that.

****

"So, Axel, what else happened inside that basement?" Henry's question swept away my memories.

I looked at him, something inside me—not the Rider—feeling the need to tell the truth, confess my murder, tell him I had to kill the bastard. However, I just kept silent, my face a blank slate.

"Did you kill your uncle?"

My face showed no emotions at that unexpected question, but my mind was in panic.

"What do you mean? Are you implying I'm a killer?" I said, still no emotions on my face, but my heart pumping faster.

He came closer to me, taking a seat on the couch. "Look, Axel. We all do have secrets. We try to hide them from the others, we keep them down, in a dark cellar of our mind, hoping they will never come back to haunt us," he said in a lower tone. "You were eighteen years old. You hated your uncle. And you loved your mother. You saw him abusing her."

"Yes. But that doesn't mean I killed him."

He stood silent for a moment, then rose from the couch and went straight for the window. He closed it and returned to the couch. "Axel, if this helps you, I've killed a man once," he said suddenly, in an ushered voice, almost whispering.

I couldn't believe what he was saying. The funny, easygoing Dr. Hart was confessing a crime. *To me?*

"Do you recall that guy, Stanley Terwilliger?"

Yes, I remembered him. He had been brought at the morgue two weeks before, in really bad shape, after his *Pinto* had crashed into a truck on US 27. His life had ended with the sounds of shattering glass and spinning wheels. He had left behind a mourning wife, Courtney, and a three-year old girl, Nancy. He had been also a successful executive and left a fortune to his family.

"I tampered with his brakes," Henry said.

I didn't flinch—just kept my eyes on his. "Why did you do it?"

"I had to, Axel." Henry left the couch and went to a side cabinet he had never opened in my presence, but I already knew what it contained. You see, I had been there, inside his office, alone, two months before, to check out his secrets. I had found nothing special, except that he stocked a large quantity of alcohol for a doctor. He returned with two glasses and a bottle of Kentucky Bourbon.

"He ... that bastard, I mean. He stole my wife," he whispered.

Everything became clear inside my mind. His divorce, his depression, his wandering from a town to another; Henry had been following his ex-wife because of his obsession with her. My mind rushed back to our first meeting. The scar on his lower left arm, the window. He had been watching her, out there.

"She left me for that asshole! Would you believe that? A pitiful, insignificant insurance agent," he went on.

I was no longer listening to him; my memories were running at high-speed, trying to recall all the clues. The places we had visited together, even that night at the *Bowlarama*, when I'd surprised him spending more time peeking at a couple than listening to his date.

Those people were Courtney and Stanley.

"She always said she was not ready for kids, then, after she left me, well, not even after a year of marriage with that son of a bitch, she got pregnant!" He was on the verge of shouting, but kept his temper.

"So, you killed him," I said, still not a trace of visible emotions in my voice, just a statement.

"Yes, Axel. I killed him, I hated him. Couldn't suffer his ... happiness ... with my Courtney." He poured a second shot of bourbon, without realizing I had not yet touched mine.

"This will not change things, Henry. Your wife was in love with that man. She is not coming back to you because of his death."

"I know. But, I just could not accept the situation. I've solved my inner conflict; I allowed the monster out," he said. Then he smiled, mostly to himself, turning attention to my glass. "Aren't you drinking with me?"

I took the glass and allowed some of the liquid to burn my throat. As you already know, I'm not an alcohol enthusiast; it does no good for my practices. However, I felt sympathy for him—he was confessing a murder.

Nevertheless, there was something wrong about that because he had killed an innocent man.

"So, tell me, Axel J. Hyde. ... Did you kill your uncle?"

A long silence fell between us before I answered back.

"Yes, I did."

****

I told him the entire story—omitting my other victims—with precise details. I felt relief in doing so, not knowing why. Henry listened to my story in silence, never interrupting me, never questioning. He had just been there, so he watched me as a matching dark companion, a long lost sibling in the mists of secrecy. When I stopped talking, he poured some more brown liquid and proposed a toast: to secrets!

Then, he hugged me, as if we had been family in our deeds. I returned the embrace with less emphasis.

"Thank you for sharing your pain, Axel," Henry said.

I said nothing.

He rose from the couch, retrieved his jean jacket, and slipped it on. His reddened face slowly regained his usual hue. We went away together.

Two weeks later, he was lying on my autopsy slab, where I performed my special work on him.

CHAPTER 12

DRILL

Shhhrewww...

The first arrow struck into Marvin's right shoulder, sinking deep as the razor-head forged its way through the skinny flesh and blood spurted from the rounded muscle. He did not realize immediately what had just happened; his face froze in a comical expression of disbelief. He staggered backward more for the shock than for the impact force of the weapon. Then, he screamed in pain, his shrill voice quivering in the wooden cabin.

Shhhrewww...

Another arrow flew out of nowhere, piercing the man's flesh just above the left knee, and puncturing down through the back of it, wrenching the kneecap, and crippling the leg.

"Ohwwwwww!" Marvin's yelp sounded like that of howling dog, a pitiful cry that echoed off the swamp, but only nocturnal wildlife could hear it.

Fu—

That thought never completed inside his mind, attention being caught by the shadowy figure leaping through the shack's open window. He watched with disbelief as the dark-clad woman revealed herself in the yellowish light produced by the lone bulb in the one-room cabin. Dressed up as a cowgirl, the pale-skinned woman moved with feline grace and looked straight into his terror-stricken eyes. She held a bow in her right hand. Instinctively, Marvin's hands went down to clutch the arrow's shaft, as if that would ease his pain.

"Please…," he stuttered in fear.

The woman said nothing. She just flashed a weird smile, then glanced around, looking for something and finding it in a rusted mallet. With a terrible slam and crunch, Marvin' nose was flattened by the blow. Blood welled, his whole face suddenly felt swollen and tears spilled from his eyes. He saw stars and then blackness.

****

Marvin was wrenched back to consciousness by the splashing of an oily liquid on his face. His head ached with pulsating pain, unable to focus on one of his many wounds. He did notice the light was dimmer now, no longer coming from the single bulb, but from a flickering candle—one of those he used in his chemistry lab—placed on a small coffee dish near his face. For the rest, the room was in complete darkness, the only sounds produced by the continuous drippings of the drying foliage outside, the haunting cry of some nocturnal bird, and the shuffling of clothes above him. He found himself gagged and hog-tied inside the cabin, lying on his side on the floor, covered with the smelly and pungent odor of urine mixed with blood. His eyes darted about, looking for his assailant. She was standing above him, her features hidden in darkness, but the white of her eyes clearly visible under the shadow of her cowboy hat. She still sported that wicked smile.

Marvin shuddered.

"Hello, my dear. Welcome back to the light," said the woman in a whispering voice, something that Marvin would have found erotic in another situation, but that was not the case then.

She knelt down, showing beautiful features in the candlelight. Her long flowing hair shuffled on the cloth of her black jean jacket. His eyes widened. "Do you remember me, Ada'wehi?"

Marvin frowned. What was she talking about?

Who the fuck knew this murderous bitch?

His mind ran frantically to past memories—could she be a member of the Núñez brothers' gang? Or one of those weirdos hanging around Billy Gamble?

Gamble was a passionate survivalist, who often drilled with some other fucks deep in the wilds. He and his friends had even set up a stockade identical to one of those cavalry forts portrayed in movies about the Old West. Standing on some acres of—illegally—cleared land, the fort boasted two guard posts on either side of the front gate, and was built with tanned pine logs. Billy and his idiot followers spent the weekends at the fort, practicing their survival skills and playing war-games. The common bond of the group was that though civilization was deservedly doomed, its fall could be survived and something simpler may be built from its ashes.

"I'm the Moon Dancer, Ada'wehi," she said in that soothing tone.

The Moon Dancer? What the fuck she was talking about. This bitch was outright crazy! Who's this 'Ada-something' she kept talking of?

"Don't you recognize me, Ada'wehi? Are you sure?" She moved her face closer to his, watching him like a snake does with a mouse.

Then, she took off her hat. The cracking candle cast strange shadows on her pale face, playing with high cheekbones, black-painted lips. Indeed, there was something familiar about her, but Marvin could not yet remember who she was. He shook his head to show his denial, provoking a shooting pain to explode in his injured head.

"Do you remember Manchester, Ada'wehi? Do you remember the Old Stone Fort?" The pale-faced woman was no longer smiling now. She grabbed his neck, causing even more pain, forcing his eyes to meet hers.

And he remembered her.

He remembered what he and his four friends had done to *that* woman. But, she was supposed to be dead! How in Hell had she survived?! Marvin gazed inside her blue-green irises ... and saw something.

He saw the 'Sunnayi Edahi', the Night Goer.

Everything went black again.

****

91

He came back to his senses, awakened by a buzzing sound. At first, he did not remember where he was or what had happened to him—he only felt the pain in the head. Then, his recent memories kicked in—the woman! He was now lying on his back, still roped like a wild animal.

Buzzz ... Buzzz ... Buzzz...

The whirling sound continued, somewhere in the dark. Then, he saw her again, coming into the light of the candle, holding something in her hand.

Oh, my God! She's got a gun, she's gonna kill me!

However, he soon realized that no gun produces a buzzing sound. Marvin relaxed just for a moment before the woman—who was also a monster—clearly showed to him what she was carrying.

A power drill.

He released his bladder into his pants, the pungent smell of urine again mixed with the iron-like odor of spilled blood.

The pale-faced girl smiled again, and then lowered her tool on the wooden floor. Relief washed over Marvin; cold sweat dripped from his brow into his eyes.

The woman—the monster—handled some pliers and used them to remove the razor-headed arrow from his right shoulder. Blood flew copiously from the gaping hole, but he was surprised by the fact he felt less pain than expected. She did the same to the shaft protruding from his left knee. More black blood. Not much pain. It spread on the floor like petroleum spilled from a tanker, mixing with his urine. It marched downward, out of the circle of light produced by the candle.

A white hand with long black nails showed him something—a blue pill.

Meth! The fucker has given that to me to endure the pain! She wants for me to last longer!

When he saw the woman retrieve the power drill, he understood why.

The power tool's bit tore down next to his head, narrowly missing it as he ducked aside and instead it drove down into his left side, whirring through Marvin' flesh and biting deep down between the collarbone and shoulder right into the meat. He yelped like a wounded dog through the gag. Spittle fell from his mouth, wetting his already blood-drenched ragged t-shirt.

The black-clad woman removed the tool from the wound; strips of wet flesh dangled from the still whirling bit.

Then, she was on him again. The motor in the drill screamed deafeningly as the bit embedded into his thigh. A smoky stink came from the motor as the metal skipped and grinded against the bone. Blood flooded back up the hole.

Marvin started to convulse. Vomit rushed up into his throat, so she loosened the gag enough to avoid him suffocating with his own fluids. He regurgitated violently, adding the remains of his dinner to the already smelly mess. However, the woman didn't flinch. She allowed him time to take a deep breath, and then resumed her work.

The bloodied bit whirled in front of his exhausted face, making him sway back and then plunged down into Marvin' groin. His gorge rose in his throat as flesh was pulped and raw nerves were severed and burned by the heat of the steel; his genitals destroyed in the process. A shrilling scream, filtered by the gag, rose high up in the night's air, and then Marvin collapsed. He shivered and convulsed like a rattle in the hands of a toddler.

"And now, Ada'wehi, return to the Other Side," she said. "You already told me everything I needed to know. Thanks for sharing the Windigo's hiding place. I'm not crazy, I get even!"

Then, she placed the power tool to the left side of his head and slammed into it, biting into the bone and drilling on through, scattering splinters. The wet gray tissue was churned liquid that welled up around the burrowing drill head as it scrambled the frontal lobes like two beaten eggs. The motor shrieked one last time, while Marvin Wilson's body vibrated with its rotation, and then ceased completely when it became clogged with brainy matter and gore.

****

After the work was done, Cheri poured the content of two gasoline tanks all over the place, adding even some of the cabin's chemicals as fuel, and created a starting trail outside. She returned to her truck, lit a match and sent it flying to the awaiting fuel. A blue-red flame developed, running faster toward the shack, and setting it ablaze in seconds. Cheri removed her hat and black wig, placed them below the passenger seat, and drove away from the raging fire.

"*Just two more to go*" whispered the Night Goer, "*just two more.*"

CHAPTER 13

FIRE

Pa-hay-okee—Grass River. His ancestors used that name for that vast expanse of marshy waters. The Everglades. That was the name chosen by the White Man. Some believed it came from the ancient English word 'Glaed', meaning clear, bright, or shining. Other historians traced the origins to the warping of the term, 'River Glades'. High-sounding designations were wasted for the place: from World Heritage Site to International Biosphere Reserve.

For William 'Tukosee' Powell, the place had just one name: Refuge.

Refuge from his boring job, from his large family, his duties. He liked those rare moments of solitude, deep in the wilds where he enjoyed the company of his own thoughts. William lived in Brighton, inside the Seminole Reservation, and worked as a clerk in a casino, surrounded by the deafening sound of hundreds of slot machines, yelling winners, and rowdy customers. It was natural for him to seek out peace in the backwoods, away from cars, cheap souvenirs, discount attraction tokens, and all-you-can-eat restaurants.

Today's Seminoles were scattered among the various reservations in Tampa, Immokalee, Hollywood, Brighton, and Big Cypress. Their main activities ranged from stock farming to speculation in the stock exchange; however, their major incomes came from the casinos and the sale of duty-free tobacco. His people still spoke the Creek language and kept their traditions, like the June's Green Corn Dance, when the tribe's males went with the Medicine Man to renovate the ancient rites, perform bold quests, and to feel like true Indians—even if just for a day. However, the people's determination to conserve the old heritage was not enough to avoid modern life's illnesses. As in all reservations in the U.S., alcoholism and obesity reaped victims yearly, due to the fact that many preferred 'fast-food' to the original fish-based diet. Suicide, caused by social unfitness and tediousness, was on the rise, too.

William was different. He had found his own way to fight off the dangers of modern life. By escaping into the wilds, setting up his chikee—the traditional Seminole tent—and living off the land for a couple of days, hunting with his crossbow and spearing fishes in the murky waters. He wandered in the dense vegetation, stalking a buck he had spotted before dusk had settled down over Grassy Swamp's south bend.

Hunting was another of his passions. His father had been a skilled hunter himself and by the age of ten, William "Tukosee" was able to take out a possum with a .220 SWIFT at almost one hundred yards. Army camouflage, completed with heavy, high-treading boots, covered his outdoor clothes. At thirty-seven, he stood tall with square shoulders, a muscular body, and strong legs. His face looked like pockmarked stone, but he'd been told his high cheekbones, sharp nose, and jet-black hair gave him a noble savage look.

He stopped his advance abruptly behind the tall trunk of a tree and pushed his back against it, enjoying the rush of adrenaline, while he moved stealthily to avoid scaring off the deer. The young beast, a female, was feeding off the wet shoots growing around a large rock in the clearing. A low mist rose out of the humid terrain due to the heavy rain, which had kept falling for more than an hour. A bright limey-green tree frog, streaked with yellow and orange, rested on a nearby frond, covered by drops of water, its tiny, unblinking black eyes, warily watching the hunter. Then, a mournful cry—a night bird, maybe—echoed in the forest, northward, causing the deer to raise its head in alarm. However, no more like sounds followed and the beast relaxed, albeit with up-strung ears, ready to flee at the sign of any incoming danger. William stood still, keeping his breath low and his heartbeat at a reduced pulse. The frog jumped away, disappearing in the tall foliage, as if it knew better than to stay there watching a hunter stalk prey.

The hooting of a small owl resumed in the distance, soon followed by a chorus of bullfrogs from the swamp. William peeked out from his hiding place to have a clear look at the deer. It was still there, showing its flank to him, grazing on the short grasses around the stone. He cocked the steel-capped arrow on the crossbow, and without producing the slightest sound, kept his slit-eyes on the prey.

BOOOMMM!!

A loud explosion erupted northward, causing the buck to flee in the opposite direction. William almost stuck his right foot with the arrow when he involuntarily gripped the trigger, releasing the projectile in the tree's upturned root.

What the hell was that?

Ignoring the now fleeing prey, William unstuck the arrow from the wooden appendage, and directed his eyes in direction of the booming. Reddish light shined through the dense vegetation, flickering and faltering, but getting brighter every second. William rushed toward the growing brightness, splashing through the mud and the muck, setting aside interfering branches, jumping over unearthed roots. He reached a clearing and finally saw what had originated the red light.

A cabin was on fire.

CHAPTER 14

HOT BODIES

The call ringed into the sheriff's office when Agatha Kiley was about to leave. Agatha had been at the reception the whole day, as she had done for too many years to remember, leaving only at noon for a quick lunch. The reception was located at the front of the building, just off the public parking lot. Two doors—one on each side of the desk—led into the main office. Here, an untidy mixture of outdated PCs, half covered by newspaper clippings, notes, charts, and post-its, stood side-by-side with stacks of files, markers, half-finished coffee cups and ashtrays. Safety billboards, informational posters, district maps, wanted posters, and new regulations covered the walls. This room was used to investigate any crime requiring detective work rather than mere policing to solve. Agatha had done her best to carry the station house up-to-date, but bad habits never died, so yesteryear records were still here, stored in piles of dusty boxes. She was sixty-eight years old with strong health and a sharp mind, but could not compete with the chaos left by Sheriff Andrews and his four officers. The current sheriff, Roger T. Andrews, had recruited her in 2006, after her husband, Robert "Good Ole Boy" Kiley, still one of the most beloved sheriffs of the county, had left her after a bad stroke while repairing the roof's shingles a year before. She had helped her husband in paperwork for fourteen years during his three consecutive mandates, gaining much experience in police procedure and dealing with crises. She had also campaigned hard for Andrews's election and gained the support of many in the community. Therefore, it was natural for Roger to offer her the position, to allow the woman to keep the paperwork in order, process the payroll, and manage the front desk. A job she did efficiently, together with handling tourists' inquiries, emergency medical attention, and lost pets.

Agatha inspected the two secure rooms on the first floor, checking for lights left on and misplaced stationery. The first one was the evidence room, in which all seized goods—contraband, narcotics, and weapons—were bagged, tagged, and stored. It also doubled as storage for emergency equipment that had been heaped over the years, like specialty chemical hazard suits and crime scene tape. Agatha had noticed the office's safe had been left open, so she'd locked it as Deputy Espinoza would always complained about that with the other men. Deputy Espinoza came from a 'real' police department in Miami; things were different down there.

The other room had two small holding cells, each one hosting a pair of bunks and a toilet. They were mostly used as sobering tanks, rather than for holding real criminals. Agatha worked hard to keep the cells clean, but the smell of vomit and urine clung to that area like a haunting ghost. They were empty now; however, the lights had been left on. As always, Agatha had switched them off then went upstairs to warn Tipple and Espinoza she was leaving. A set of stairs led to the common area, also used by the night shift officers as a recreation room.

Peter Tipple relaxed on one of the two battered sofas, reading a paperback novel, while Morena Espinoza was changing into her civil clothes in the locker room because she had finished her duty. A pot of stale coffee stood next to the old TV set, often used by visiting officers from State or Federal agencies for visual briefings on important cases. However, it had seen much more use as the source of many common entertainment shows, such as serials or the latest NBA game.

"Hey, Pete, I'm going," she said to him, waving her hand.

Peter raised his eyes from the book and waved back with a nod of his square-jawed head. He was thirty-two and six feet tall, with broad muscled shoulders and a large bone structure. A former quarterback in the local football team, the Prosperity Cougars, he kept his body in shape by practicing fitness and a healthy diet. His fair skin was freckled around steel-gray eyes. His hair, of a dark blonde hue, was always kept short in an army cut.

"All right, Agatha. Thank you," Morena called out from the locker room, then came out to join them.

The sight of her left Peter Tipple with an 'oh' expression on his face. He had never seen her like that. And Agatha, too.

Morena Espinoza was an attractive Hispanic woman, five foot five tall with long brown hair and light brown eyes. Usually, she kept her hair pulled back in a bun, but tonight she had decided to show off her sultry and luscious looks. Her slender figure belied a significant strength and she also packed a powerful punch, as many drunkards in town had learned at their expense. She never dressed provocatively, by no means using her attractiveness to help in her career. However, tonight she wore a figure-hugging, low-rise pair of jeans that emphasized perfectly flat abdominals, and a white, ruffled, top that exposed much of her generous cleavage. Big oval-shaped, earrings dangled from her small ears, tingling in time with the charms on her left wrist. She looked astounding and hot as hell.

"Wow! Do you have a special date, Morena?" Agatha asked her, amused, while wondering why that woman had always hidden her amazing figure under voluminous clothes and baggy trousers.

She smiled, and then turned attention to Peter who still held that stupid expression. "Maybe ..."

Something was clearly going on here. However, Agatha had decided it was none of her business. She left them with a 'Take care' and headed back to the first floor, where she recovered her purse from the front desk, and finally opened the front door.

That was when the telephone rang.

****

Peter Tipple was the town's gentle giant. Once a skilled local sports hero, he had to renounce his dreams of going pro when is dad died of cancer at an early age. Not willing to leave his mom alone, he decided to stay in the small town, choosing service in the local fire department at first, and then joining the force. Mommy had taught him to be always polite, to do his schoolwork, and to follow the word of God. As a result, Peter could come across as quiet, naive, and shy. He still lived at home with his mother and always attended church services, even if it meant rescheduling the duty roster for the entire station house. However, Peter was a good cop, believing a police officer's duty was one of the most important jobs in the whole world: to make sure the hometown's streets were safe and to be the thin line between civilization and barbarism. He really cared about his town. But at thirty-two, he was still single. Although he was an attractive man, his shyness kept the opposite sex away, deeming him too stupid or else. He had experienced some short-lived relationships in the past, ending regularly when Norma Tipple—his mom and owner of the Vistana Boarding House on Central Avenue—stuck her nose and unwanted opinions into the affairs.

His latest sweetheart had been a Joan Blakely, server at the *Moola*, who had moved into Prosperity Glades to stay close to her husband while he spent time at PMCF. Once released on parole, her husband did not waste time to abuse her and ended on the wrong side of Tipple. Peter arrested him and sent him back to prison, and passed the night at the Hall Memorial Hospital, waiting for her to be discharged, and got her home safely. He had envisioned her as a delicate woman in need of help. She had seen in him a gentle old-times knight, the only good man Joan had ever met. The relationship lasted only one month, after Norma had made Joan's life so poor as to force her to leave Prosperity Glades forever. To ensure the 'Trashy Girl' would leave her big boy alone, Norma had paid three thousand dollars to Blakely. Peter had never found the real motives of Joan's sudden escape, but had suspected that his mother, and some of her friends, had induced her to leave.

After this last bad experience, Deputy Tipple concentrated on his job, paying less attention to girls. Until that night, when his steel-grey eyes rose from the paperback he was reading, and met the sight of the all-new Deputy Espinoza. He'd known she was hiding her prettiness under those shapeless clothes she usually wore, but he had never dreamed the woman could look so gorgeous and sexy.

Espinoza had showed up in Prosperity Glades two years ago, after responding to Sheriff Andrews' request for hiring an experienced city cop to replace the retiring Deputy Rupert Olsen. Born in Miami, Morena Espinoza had graduated at the Police Academy after getting her high school diploma. She had walked the tough streets of Overtown and Liberty City, going from a wet-behind-the-ears rookie into a seasoned cop in just two years. After a failed marriage, which had ended at the sound of crashing furniture out of a second floor apartment, a police summoning for domestic violence, and her suspension for pointing a gun at a violent husband, Morena had fallen into alcohol abuse. Until she had sobered up, after a particular bad incident she never liked to talk about, she had packed her belongings, and decided to start a new life from zero in the small town community where everyone knew everyone else.

The first time Peter saw her he had thought she was one of those crazy feminist cops from the big city. He had tried to be polite in the manner his mother had raised him up to be, by doing things like keeping open the door and allowing her to go first. However, she had always viewed these old-fashioned manners as 'sexist' and 'patronizing'.

Whatever those two words meant.

With time, they began to get along as colleagues, nothing more. Six months ago, Espinoza started dating that creepy guy from the morgue, Dr. Axel Hyde. From what Peter knew, it was not a real relationship, in the true sense of the word; their association looked more like two close friends enjoying each other's company than a true couple. They went bowling, to the fair, or shared a dinner at some greasy spoon restaurant out of town.

Tipple had always wondered what they had found in each other. They were both grim, true, but at least Deputy Espinoza could pull some good pranks. In the rare event she enjoyed an evening out with the squad at the *Happy Gator* pub, she had always demonstrated the ability for merriment and camaraderie.

Dr. Hyde had none. He was a creepy individual, spending more time with the dead than the living. Also, he seemed incapable of understanding a joke, a remark on some cutie, or similar things. He was one of the most asocial men Peter had ever met. Nonetheless, the two went steady for almost six months. Yet, last night, something had broken the couple. Espinoza returned from her patrol with a darkened face. When he asked her about their shift's exchange, she told him there was no need for that as she did not intend to go out with 'Dr. Weird' (so she'd called him) anymore. Tipple abandoned the issue, knowing better than to irritate his hot-tempered partner with personal questions about her off-duty life.

And now she came out of the changing room looking like one of those hot models Peter had only seen on magazine's covers. The opposite of the masculine-looking cop he'd known, Peter had not resisted the urge to get a clear look at her beautiful ass as she knelt to retrieve something from the bookcase's lower shelf. Her too tight jeans showcased the perfect rotundity of the buttocks, fueling his lust. He felt shame for that, but he could not help it.

Another thing that aroused his testosterone was her perfume— an exotic mixture of warm and spicy scents—and her long, shiny brown hair. Tipple's shame for himself grew even more once she'd turned to him to ask something about a frayed paperback novel she was holding. He hadn't heard a word she said because his concentration was caught by her revealed bronze cleavage.

****

People who knew Morena Espinoza when she was a kid figured she would grow up like her older brothers and sisters—drop out of high school at an early age, accept some low-wage job, maybe even get pregnant too young. Should she keep her good looks, she could hope for a modeling career and get a rich husband in the process. But Morena had ideas of her own. She did not want to spend her whole life in Little Havana; she dreamed about traveling, doing many interesting things, and having money. Therefore, she studied English hard, knowing she would not get all those things just by speaking Spanish. She was an attentive student and got good results, but this was not enough to raise her above her peers. Her family was poor, could not afford to pay the huge sums needed by expensive colleges, and her good grades were not good enough to allow a scholarship. This had turned her to modeling for aspiring photographers and shops. It had also frustrated her to the point that she developed a drinking habit. At twenty-one, Morena spent whole nights out with her friends, becoming a real barfly. One night, she got pulled over for speeding in South Beach. The cop who arrested her was a Latina, just like her. While spending the night among the boozers in the precinct's drunk tank, a thought hit her.

The police academy.

You just need a high school diploma and pass a test to join the force, and being a cop was a better job than wasting her life with alcohol. Exercising an iron will, Morena worked hard and gained excellent results at the Academy; in a short time, she got out of her drinking problem. She was assigned to patrol tough beats, such as Overtown and Liberty City. In that area of Miami, almost eighty-eight percent of the population lived in a condition of extreme poverty, their only evasion from a hopeless existence being the use of drugs, especially cocaine, cut and altered in all possible ways. It was not Disneyland.

Officer Espinoza's dream was to progress to Detective or enlist in the FBI. However, dreams die at dawn. After eight years as a patrol officer, after finding herself in some hard situations, she lost her drive again and fell into chronic depression. Only her chance meeting with Dr. Angelo Chavez, a charming chiropractor, rescued her from the dark hole she had fallen into. He was a generous and sensible man as a boyfriend. However, he turned into a liar, a cheater, and a violent husband. After five years of marriage, their relationship ended abruptly when Morena surprised him riding his assistant, Keira Martinez, right in the apartment's Morena shared with him. Things went from bad to worse when he'd reacted to her fury by slapping her and yelling it was her fault if he felt the need to bed other women—because she was never home and spent more time in her dreams of getting a shield, ignoring his drives. A terrible fight had erupted, with crashing furniture, many insults, and a severe beating from her husband. Blinded by rage against a man who'd showed his true nature for the first time, Morena had overreacted. She pointed her gun at him, threatening to kill, lost in her desperation. Everything had been a lie—her marriage was a lie, and her life was a lie. Fortunately, someone had called 911 after hearing too many shouts and crashes coming from their apartment. She was suspended.

Her life reduced into wreckage, Morena had returned to Little Havana to live with her parents for six months, experiencing humiliating monthly talks with a district shrink. With time, she fell again into drinking. Even after her readmission into service, she kept drinking, hiding her dependence with skillfulness. Then, three years ago, she had sobered up once and for all. Police officers often claim to hate domestic disturbance calls because of the unpredictable and violent emotions of those involved in the situation. A sudden reversal of perspective can occur as when a beaten wife realizes that her partner could go into jail for real, and turns against the arresting officers. In the middle of one of such calls, Morena Espinoza had cracked out. Having drunk a little too much just before going to work, she had overreacted against insults from a battered spouse who had suddenly had switched sides, fearing her violent hubby was going to spend some time in the correctional. In that woman, she had seen herself, a life ruined by a lying bastard. How many times had she believed her man? How many times had she acted like that stupid gal who was now shouting against her to protect her unfaithful mate?

She had kicked the woman hard in her stomach, sending her crashing onto a wall, and leaving her partner—Agent Rodrigo Jimenez—with a shocked expression on his face. She was lucky Jimenez fixed the thing by forcefully carrying her out and settling the incident with the couple. He never reported it. However, he counseled her to have a break, to find a way to get even with her bad temper. Morena accepted his suggestions and left the force and Miami, too.

Leaving her stormy past back, she had showed up in Prosperity Glades and applied to fill the vacant deputy position. Unfortunately, the small town attitude of Prosperity had backfired on her and it was a shock to the system to discover how the other deputies felt about her. Just because she did not know everybody's name, where they lived, and what their grandparents did—it did not mean she was not good at her job. In the beginning, she was assigned only to minor cases, such as finding lost cats or dogs, something which irritated her the most. However, when she displayed her fighting skills by sending a local drunken misogynist, renowned for being a tough customer, to kiss the floor of one of the small town's watering holes, she gained the respect of her squad. Her professional life had then improved, but her personal one had not. She had never been one of those women who liked to show their attractiveness, preferring to be reckoned for her skills rather than her good looks. Nonetheless, she knew she was considered one of the most beautiful officers in her precinct down in Overtown. Yet, after her failed marriage, she had become distant from the opposed sex, seeing all males as pigs and sexists. She no longer wore tight-fitting clothes or feminine articles such as miniskirts or high heels, and applied a minimum of make-up just to look healthy.

Then, she met Axel Hyde.

The assistant medical examiner was a strange guy, but she could feel he was a good man. He had that innocent way of looking at the world, which was reassuring to her. He had never pressed her, never talked about sex, and she had to kiss him first before he had even allowed himself to touch her hand. That was good, because Morena had still been too traumatized by her broken relationship to feel safe with a man. They frequented each other for six months, behaving as two frightened kids living their first love story. Axel was attractive, but also scary, somehow. Sometimes he could prattle on for hours about the dissection of a corpse before realizing he was making her sick. Well, Morena had seen her share of dead bodies in her days down in Miami, but the minute descriptions of the pathologist were too much even for a cop. However, she had skipped over this side of his character, seeing in him an overgrown kid who needed some real human, and warm, company to get out of his creepy world. Just like she had needed some company to get social again. Therefore, Axel was just the right guy—sensible, gentle, and one who favored talking above intimacy. He had been the perfect mate for practicing sports on weekdays, hiking in the countryside—something in which he was a real expert—or jogging early in the morning. Despite it all, though, she had to admit something was weird about him, like the fact he remembered all the birthdays of his colleagues and acquaintances, and would punctually send the person some stupid Hallmark card on that day.

Unusual in a grown up man.

Morena had endured his strange habits—from renouncing a date with her to be at the morgue when a new stiff showed up, to him strolling around at four in the morning in the most dangerous areas of town. One night he told her to meet him at that damn place he'd almost died in when he was ten years old, and another day she discovered his unnerving habit of asking strange questions about people he did not even know. In addition, he had that strange way of changing his look. He did not show a favored style. Had a thousand—classic, trendy, outsider, country, sportsman, grungy, urban, professional … all were his kind. Except the most extreme of fashions, he wore everything, from frayed jeans to executive suits. However, when he lied to her, telling her he could not go bowling because had a special corpse at the morgue, while he was going around with a boozer, something snapped inside her head. The spell was broken.

What am I doing to my life? she thought then.

She realized she was no longer Morena Espinoza, the most attractive female officer of Overtown, the hot Latina that had turned men's heads at the precinct. The girl who was so determined and strong that she fought her alcohol dependence not once, but twice! She had looked into the mirror and seen what she had become. A grim, unsmiling bitchy cop, who dated lunatics because she couldn't be so bold as to date real people. Morena hit the mirror so that it shook, close to cracking.

The next day she had made a trip up to the Heights Shopping Center and dropped four hundred dollars in new clothes and accessories. She returned home, emptied the contents of her wardrobe in some large plastic sacks and donated them to the Church of St. Michael in Northside. Then she spent the whole day trying on her new, sexy clothes and looking at herself in the mirror. She felt like a real woman again—not the old Morena who had denied her femininity.

Packing the last outfit she tried inside her sports bag, she wore her duty uniform and headed to the station house. That night, after three years of sexual abstinence, she had the purpose of hooking a man. It was like quitting the drinking habit, only in the reverse.

She had always suspected that Peter Tipple had a soft spot for her, even after all those terrible things she had accused him about—things the poor country boy did not even understand. He was so old-style, with that entire Southerner chivalrous attitude; the old Morena could not stand one like him—she could not believe he was gentle. In her mind, he was sexist. However, the new Morena realized he was just a good man, raised by an overbearing mother. Also, there had been that night at the Happy Gator pub.

On a night off, she, Peter, and Amber Willis, had gone partying with Vice Sheriff James Lane. There was a country fair in town, and Tipple had showed up dressed like a cowpoke out of an old Marlboro spot. She had instinctively laughed, but the others stared at her with quizzical expressions. Later, Amber had explained to her that Peter Tipple was dressed like that because he always made an appearance at the annual local rodeo. He had also won some prizes.

Surprised, Morena realized that the gentle giant had a wild side. Lane and Willis delivered endless praise about Tipple's bravery and skills, until they had forced him to show the newcomer how a real 'Glader' rode the mechanical bull. Espinoza had to admit that she had felt some hotness returning that night, as she watched Peter clutch the mechanical beast with his strong legs, showing his prowess with shyness.

Yes, that night she wanted—craved—to be that beast. Just for a moment that thought had crossed her mind on a primal sexual level, but she had sent it away, turning her eyes somewhere else.

However, she had changed her mind today.

Today, she was going to tease the man, to show him that she could be the sexy woman he had dreamed about when he had seen her the first time. She had purposely allowed him a clear look at her behind when she reached out to recover that insignificant paperback in the bookcase. Then she straightened slowly and turned around with an innocent look on her face to catch him turn away quickly, his face red as a beetroot. When she asked him if the book she held was an interesting novel, she noticed, with a sense of pride, that he had been staring at her generous bosom. She looked straight into his eyes, those charming steel-grey eyes, enjoying his embarrassment, feeling again a desired woman.

"Aren't you ... going ... home?" he stuttered, unable to remove his eyes from her cleavage.

She smiled, then remarked softly, "Why? Would you escort me like an old-fashioned shining knight?"

"No," he immediately answered back, probably fearing to appear like one of those 'sexist' things she always talked about. Morena giggled. Putting back the paperback in the bookcase, she allowed him a lingering second glimpse of her backside. She knew she'd acted like a slut, yet it also was what she needed. Peter had no idea how to deal with this new woman she was showing him— but she knew the effect she had on his libido.

Then, the spell was broken by the ringing of the phone, soon followed by the shrill voice of Agatha Kiley yelling from below that someone had found a body in the woods.

****

Prosperity Glades has eight full-time firefighters and two full-time paramedics on the duty roster. The De Soto Avenue station holds two fire engines, both more than fifteen years old, a brand-new hook and ladder truck, and an updated Emergency Response vehicle for small, nonfire emergencies. Four firefighters and at least one paramedic are on duty at all hours on two rotating shifts. On duty personnel usually sleeps on the upper floor.

Not that night.

They had been summoned by a man who reported a shack was on fire in the depths of Grassy Swamp's south bend. The four firemen worked hard to first stop the fire from spreading to the surrounding woods, then concentrating on the cabin itself. The flames had been clearly caused by chemicals, which had acted as accelerants, but there were clear signs of 'streamers'—substances such as kerosene used to spread a fire fast—indicating that the blaze originated from a deliberate act of arson.

Amateurs splash accelerants, such as petroleum fuel, around a scene and throw a lit match on it. Burn patterns for this type of fire are fairly easy to detect. Professional arsonists often create short-circuited electrical wiring to disguise their activities, many of them developing a personal preference for a specific technique—a particular ignition device or accelerant, for example—and these become the fire setter's signature trademark. Detecting the point of origin is the key to determining the cause of a fire, because it can rule out natural or accidental causes. If there are two or more points of origin, a lingering smell of fuel, or unexplainable burn patterns, arson is highly probable.

When the firefighters had finally defeated the raging blue-orange flames, indicating alcoholic chemicals had fueled them, they found a surprise inside the cooling shack.

The smoldering body of a man.

CHAPTER 15

DISSECTION OF THE SOUL
(FROM AXEL'S HALL OF MEMORIES)

I relaxed in my chair, trying to awake my Rider, feeding it with my sensations about the murder of Jay Fraser; in a remote hope that it would work its magic by revealing to me some missed insight. It had worked that way with many of my victims—the Rider urging me toward the truth, stopping monsters that were worse than I was. It had happened even with my friend, Dr. Hart, back in 1996...

****

After my last visit to his office, and his revelation about the murder of Terwilliger, something already familiar to me had begun to take form inside my mind. The Rider had warned me, right from the first time I'd met Henry, when it urged me to raise my ass from that couch and go looking out of that window. It had filled my mind with doubts, curiosity, and a general bad feeling. Two weeks later, I could not resist its urges anymore, so I left the driving wheel to it, allowing the being to take control and bring me wherever it needed.

I had found myself breaking and entering his office, my flashlight brightening the deserted room, my eyes darting around like fishes in a bowl. I had searched the whole place with attention to details, being careful to leave no traces of my passage. Papers, files, personal pictures, notebooks, everything that could point me in the right direction—I searched for that one indisputable clue about him to deserve my work.

I had found none. Just piles of notes about his patients, contacts, and his outdoor trips. Then, I had gone to that window, pulled away the simple curtains, and had a peek for the first time,

111

to see what was so important for my Rider to see. The window loomed above a small playground with freshly painted slides, a rope ladder leading into a wooden hut on a large tree, some plastic benches, and a couple of drinking fountains.

Nothing special.

It was one of those small town parks where you could find young moms chatting about their daily troubles to one another, while keeping an eye on their socializing kids. To the other side you could see the back of the Saltonstall Retirement Home and Finley's Funeral Parlor. I could not see anything that captured my attention about Hart.

Until I saw her, a blonde woman in her thirties, her hair combed in a ponytail, wearing an old pair of torn and paint-marked jeans with a white t-shirt under a loose, checkered male shirt, sleeves rolled up. She was not attractive; her sides were too ample, her shoulders v-shaped, and she was a bit overweight. The woman caught my attention because she had been kneeling down to tie her little daughter's shoe. It had been late for a stroll in the park for a kid her age. I was just wondering about that when both figures had dissolved in thin air.

They had not been real.

They had been ghostly images projected over my eyes by the Rider, showing me what Henry Hart had watched that day. I felt rage, that then turned into hate, hate directed toward...

... the little girl!

I immediately left the window, retreated into the darkness of the office as the last moonbeams cast silvery hues on the furniture until the curtains walled them off. The emotions had left me. Those were not mine. They were his.

Dr. Henry Hart hated that kid; he wished her dead. No, it could not have been; he was just an obsessive man, still in love with his former wife. He had killed her new husband.

However, could he really kill that innocent creature?

Inside me, the Rider had chuckled, as if mocking my naiveté.

In those times, I had not completely trusted my dark

companion. You see, my first victim, Russell Floyd, I had killed in self-defense. My second one, Hank Lumley, a seventeen-year-old bully, had practically forced me to kill him, after his many torments.

Liam Seese, a rapist I'd surprised having his way with a young girl after beating her boyfriend nearly to death in Grassy Swamp, had been a chance meeting. I used to enjoy the solitude of the swamp and I had practically stumbled upon him. As for my uncle, well, that had been planned, but it had been a murder out of personal revenge.

Professor Jenkins I had killed because I'd overheard some girls talking about his bad habit of molesting young female students in exchange for high grades at the School of Medicine.

James Marsh was a guy who liked to vent his daily frustrations on his poor wife by beating her like a drum every odd day. However, that I had discovered by myself, while being a frequent customer in the bar where she worked.

Jerry Sanford and his accomplice in rape, Lukas Hood, I had met in another chance encounter in one of the worst parts of Clewiston.

Father Peter O'Reilly, a disgusting pedophile, I had murdered because some kids had told me the ugly truth back in 1992.

However, the last two victims—Lenny Vaughn and Bradley Washington—I had actively looked out for, at the urging of my Rider. The first one had been a child molester. I had discovered it in horror when I saw his ugly face in a dream after meeting Charlie Rhodes, a six-year old boy, while working as an intern at the Moore Haven Morgue. Back then, I had also doubled as a paramedic at the public hospital's emergency room. I had become so obsessed in finding the man—urged by the Rider—that I had to go to West Palm Beach to get him.

Washington was a serial rapist; he was terrorizing the area around the US 27 in 1994. I had to treat some of his victims, all young and beautiful black women, at the emergency. Every one of these women had projected into me the real face of the perpetrator, even if all of them had been unable to give a right description to the State Troopers. I had finally found him living in South Bay.

There he had died, too.

However, after these weird experiences, I'd learned my Rider was able to see the face of those who poison the world with their existence, those filthy beings using their brawn or guile to get at their vile needs. Couldn't understand how it worked, but it was for real.

Later, I discovered it worked with dead people, too.

Therefore, I feared for the life of young Nancy Terwilliger, but at the same time, it had looked to me like a preventive strike against someone who had not yet committed the crime. I couldn't slay a man because he had been thinking about killing a kid; he could have had a change of mind, could have abandoned his purpose. Yet, something inside me had kept yelling that poor Nancy was on the verge of losing her life.

****

With a mind full of doubts, I had left the office and had gone back to the morgue, passing through the ER section of the Hall Memorial Hospital. And I had seen her. That same woman I had watched tying the shoes of her daughter down at the park, the same woman at the Bowlarama, the woman who had probably been Courtney Terwilliger—Henry's former wife. She sat in the waiting room, desperate, clasping her face with both hands, wearing the same clothes I had seen her with in the ghostly image. To her side stood an old woman wrapped in a dressing gown, her wrinkly face showing an expression of worriment. She held her left hand on the woman's right shoulder.

Inside my head, the Rider chuckled again.

I froze in terror at the thought that poor little Nancy had been killed by Henry, not realizing that I was in the Emergency Treatment Unit and not yet at the Morgue. Nonetheless, she could have already been carried over there, her small body laid out on one of my slabs, waiting for me....

Then, I saw Noreen Nichols, one of the paramedics, walk toward the blonde woman. I checked her face, looking for the telltale body language signs that she was reporting some bad news to the shocked mother. I saw none. Noreen was smiling, and in a short time the woman was smiling, too, along with the distressed oldster.

I also heard the paramedic's words. "Nancy is out of danger, Mrs. Terwilliger."

Henry's ex-wife said nothing; she just rose and hugged the paramedic like a bear, crying out in relief—her face ruined by streaks of pain for the loss of her husband first, and then worriment for her only daughter.

My clenched jaw relaxed. Still, this meant nothing. Maybe the kid had just injured herself in some way that only children are able to. On the other hand, an accident had occurred. I felt the need to know.

What had happened to little Nancy?

Noreen and Mrs. Terwilliger moved inside the Intensive Care Unit, the paramedic sustaining the worn out, but relieved, woman. I took opportunity to approach the old lady, who had finally sat down to sip some warm coffee, alone. I'd been so taken by the shock of seeing Courtney Terwilliger here, my mind had failed to recognize the older woman as Maggie Jackson, owner of JFF, a grocery store that specialized in the sale of southern Floridian produce at fair prices. I had bought oranges from her.

"Excuse me, Mrs. Jackson," I said, causing her to raise her absent looking eyes to me. "Is there something wrong? Are you well?" I feigned my most sincere concern about her health.

As you know, I didn't feel anything for other people. It was not that I was uncaring; on the contrary, I could be a helpful and kind man, yet I did not understand emotion. Sometimes, the world looked to me like a *holodeck* out of *Star Trek*, filled with holographic people, with only me being real.

She immediately recognized me.

"Yes, Dr. Hyde. A terrible thing happened," she said. "A terrible thing happened." She stared down at her half-empty coffee cup. "The daughter of my dear neighbor ... suffered some kind of poisoning accident. I do not know how it happened, I only know that I heard Courtney screaming and calling for help..."

She was reliving the scene inside her mind, clearly still shocked by the thought of it.

"I was reading a book under the porch—something I like to do after dark before going to bed. As you can see, I didn't get time to dress properly."

"Is she ... well, now?" I asked.

She nodded. "Yes, but you had to see the poor little cutie was salivating and foaming so much ... the first thing that came to my mind was that she was rabid!"

Maggie paused, then, looked up at me and seized my hand, clutching it as if that would help her regain strength. The woman was weary from the emotional effort, and as I'd read on some psychology text at university, she would need human contact. Someone who could ease the burden.

I forced my hand to return the clench but exaggerated my reaction. When she grimaced in pain at my too tight grasp, I let her hand go.

"Do you suspect she was deliberately poisoned ... by someone?" I hazarded, still worried by my ineptitude.

She looked into my eyes with a sense of disgust, not directed at me, but at the mere thought that someone would do such a horrible thing to a kid.

"No! I believe something was wrong in her food. Accidents like these happen at all times, all around the world, doctor." She gestured to stress her point, "One month ago, eighteen French kids were infected with some bacteria inside burger meat."

"Does the child suffer from some peculiar nervous system affliction? There are some that cause severe spasms and convulsions, in a way similar to those you described," I said, but she immediately shook her head.

"No, Doctor. I know what you are talking about, but no, she does not suffer from any of that. She was poisoned. Something was inside her food, I am sure."

I looked again straight inside her hazelnut eyes, but the only thing I saw was sincere concern for Nancy's health.

Our chat was interrupted by the return of Noreen Nichols, who acknowledged me with a smile.

"Mrs. Jackson, please, can you come with me to release a statement. We need your help to identify some of the symptoms the girl suffered before being carried here."

I smiled back awkwardly, and then asked, "Do you suspect some poison?"

"Yes. Nancy's skin has assumed a dark scarlet color and parts of the stomach suffered corrosion. We were lucky to save her. But more I can't disclose, sir,"

Cyanide!

That poison had become infamous in recent years when some deranged individuals had killed people by putting it in Tylenol, Kool-Aid, and other products. It has been also extensively used in spy-movies, particularly the 'suicide capsules' carried by spies. Cyanide has two distinctive features, which make it easy to find if looked for. First, to some people it smells like almonds: forty percent of the population has genes that allow the person to smell cyanide. Second, cyanide turns the blood and skin a dark scarlet color and corrodes parts of the stomach, effects that can be easily detected.

The Rider laughed again.

There are many different varieties of poison, with many different effects. Poisons are often difficult to detect and can be overlooked in an autopsy, unless specifically tested for. That is not the case for cyanide poisoning. Dr. Hart had been careless; somehow he'd slipped the substance inside Nancy's food, uncaring that the hospital staff—or better, my autopsy—would discover the use of the toxic medium.

It was far worse than that, as I discovered later.

****

That same night I invited Henry for a meeting at the morgue, telling him I had some important news about the death of Nancy Terwilliger. I lied, obviously. When he showed up—it was about two in the morning—I had already prepared myself.

With one hand, I gripped his hair and with the other, I applied a chloroform pad to his mouth and nose. He struggled and a clump of his hair ended in my hand before he subsided into unconsciousness. After that, I removed his clothes, strapped him on my autopsy slab, gagging his mouth, and waited for him to get back to his senses.

In the dark.

When muffled sounds came from behind the tape on his mouth, I switched on the big lamp over the working area. His eyes flashed angry daggers at me; deluded, not surprised. I was not wearing a mask so he could clearly see me. I got closer and gazed deeply into his angry eyes.

"No need to fight, no need to shout," I whispered.

He nodded, and then growled something unintelligible, signaling down towards the gag with his eyes. I understood, and he, too.

I loomed over him and removed the surgical tape in one swift movement. It is less painful that way, believe me. Henry moved his jaw and licked his dry lips. He glared at me. "That's better ... at least we can talk," he grunted with a shaky voice.

"Do you know why you are here, Henry?" I asked him, as I always did to my victims. My voice was starting to turn into that of the Rider.

Henry looked at me with a worried face, his mind probably running frantically through all his experience and knowledge of neurological disorders. "Because you do not trust me, Axel? Because you confessed the murder of your uncle?" he snapped back.

I remember myself staring back at him, expressionless. "No. I do not care about that," I explained. "You're here because you tried to kill an innocent kid. And I can't allow you to do that."

He looked at me with disbelief, as if he would not accept what I had said, as if that was not something he was expecting from me. "For Heaven's sake, what are you talking about, Ax?" he snapped again, but I immediately interrupted his useless denial by placing my big hand on his mouth.

"Shh ... do not waste your last breath in telling lies, Henry. We're friends, remember? We shared some secrets. You told me you killed Terwilliger and I confessed my murder of Angus Hyde. We are even, do not worry about that." I took a pause, still staring at him, waiting for my Rider to come out, but it had taken to staying in the background for unfathomable motives, as if it was waiting for something. "I'm afraid you are going to die because you can no longer stop. Your obsession toward Courtney is beyond salvation, Henry."

"So, do you intend to kill me?" Henry asked calmly, keeping his professional temper.

"Sadly yes, my friend," I responded. "But, you must tell me one thing first."

Henry nodded under the heavy belt blocking his head at the table.

"Did you expect me to cover up your poisoning of a five-year old girl?"

He lowered his eyes like a shy kid, and then whispered something.

"I can't hear you," I said.

"Yes ... I mean, you are my friend! Christ, I know you killed your uncle, and you also know I would never betray you! Please, release me!" he shouted.

He'd been using me, using our friendship and my position—and dire secrets—to have his way with Courtney.

"No. This is different, Henry," I said.

"It is no different! We are kindred souls, Axel. I do understand your pain ... the monster hiding in the dark cellar. We both have one!" he rebuked.

"I would never kill a kid!" I raised my voice to spell it clearly, as if I really cared about others.

That surprised me.

"Look, Axel ... I understand you still live there ... in that camp. You're still that ten-year-old boy who hates those who cause suffering to children. It is called a transfer. But, this is different. See, the girl has to die! She's what stands between me and my Courtney!"

"*You* are what stands between the two of you! Killing little Nancy will change nothing!"

Henry looked at me, but could not understand, too taken with his personal vision of the world—taken with his *obsession*.

"Listen, Axel ... just let me go. We will never talk again about ... this. Just let me go!"

"No," I said, calmly this time.

At that, Hart lost his temper. No longer trying to make a deal with me, he started to cry out for help. I placed my hand on his mouth; the other going to my lips, motioning for him to shut up.

"No need to fight, no need to shout," I repeated.

Once coming out of his rage, he nodded.

"Good. Should that happen again, I'll cut your tongue off." I meant it, and he knew it. Deep inside his soul, I was aware he'd begun to realize that it was not the first time I had a man tied on this very slab. Once I removed the hand from his mouth he remained silent, just watching me with wide-open eyes.

"As you can see, I'm quite used to killing people, Henry. I just do not like the idea of killing you."

"So, do not do it! We can deal this out, Axel. I can help you ... please."

"I said I do not like the idea, but I can't help myself. It's not only me you are dealing with, Henry."

The psychiatrist frowned as if trying to understand the meaning of my last affirmation, but failing. Then, I felt the Rider leave the dungeon, come up to the surface, and send my true self down, in that dark spot of my *Id*.

"Do you remember that stuff about Neurotic Obsession you talked about the first time we met, Dr. Hart?" it said, allowing me to listen to its voice from the obscure cellar my personality had been secluded in.

He nodded, but there was something different on his face, something I recognized as terror.

"They hide a *need*. Yes. And I have ... a need," the Rider continued. "I'm not a complex, chained inside some dark dungeon of yours. I'm real, Dr. Hart. Maybe, I am an *obsession*—maybe I'm made of it—but I do assure you, I'm here right now!"

Henry began to straddle the fasteners, completely maddened by fear. He was seeing the Rider.

"I have no remorse, because I'm not made of it. I have no chains, because I am free. I do not project myself into others, because I am only one thing..."

The Rider stopped talking and turned toward the closest mirror in the room, allowing it to be seen by me for the first time. My eyes had changed; they were black, like those of a shark, but more alive, as if they had been made of liquid darkness, flowing and swiveling like unholy mists. And, from my obscure prison, I cried like a madman left inside one those ancient asylums of the past, because for the first time I realized that I was really harboring a monster inside, not an imaginary transfer.

Henry Hart had almost convinced me that it was all about some psychological problem, that my monster had been a metaphysical one, not a living, alien being.

He had been wrong.

Once the Rider finished its job, it left me back in command, retreating down to its living place, not a prison as I had thought. That had been reserved for me. I worked hard to clean the place, placing all his bloody body pieces inside my transport bag. As usual, I went down to Kamp Koko, no longer sure whether it was my idea or the Rider's. I disposed of Henry's remains in the lake from the docking pontoon where I had done the same with the dismembered bodies of Liam Seese, Lenny Vaughn, and Bradley Washington.

The alligators came, as always.

As for the Rider, it had gone sleeping again.

****

I was still remembering my first vision of the Rider when the phone rang in the main room. I hurried over there and answered. Morena's voice greeted me. "Axel we need your services," she said. There was no trace of the usual cold tone she used with me after our break up. She sounded professional and concerned.

I did not like it.

"Deputy Tipple has just found a burned body down at the lake," she continued, while my blood began to freeze inside my veins.

They had found it! Damn, I should have buried him in another place ... that was a bad spot!

"Bring your meatwagon down to Okeechobee Drive; five miles past the junction with the Sycamore you'll spot Sheriff Andrews' four-by-four. He will point you to the burned shack in which the body was found." She closed the conversation without expecting me to reply.

They hadn't found JF.

This was another one!

CHAPTER 18

BILLY ALWAYS GETS HIS MAN

Billy Gamble had been flipping from bar to bar that night. The first one on his list was *The Caveman*, in Uptown. Situated at the end of Everglades Street, it was a shabby, dark, smelly, and smoky place. The owner-manager was Leonid Nikitin, a Russian immigrant with a shady past. He had been suspected of everything, from being an ex-GRU agent, to being the leader of a satanic cult. In truth, Nikitin had come to the U.S. back in the eighties during one of the times when the KGB exploited loose emigration restrictions to cleanse Soviet prisons. After membership with the New York chapter of the Pagans motorcycle gang, he retired to the status of Honorary Member and opened a bar here in Prosperity Glades to cater to motorists and rowdy types. The Pagans are rated among the fiercest and baddest outlaw bikers in the country. They are around nine hundred strong in membership, spread over forty-four chapters between New York and Florida. They are the only major gang without international chapters, although they have links to gangs in Canada. Most chapters are concentrated in the eastern United States with the states of New Jersey, Pennsylvania, Delaware and Maryland having high proportions of bikers. They are heavily into the prostitution racket. Many of the Pagan girlfriends or female associates generate money for the club by selling themselves. The Pagans also put to work as prostitutes any runaways they pick up hitchhiking off the highways, or the street. The bikers often gang rape them as a form of training, and sometimes the Pagans photograph them for blackmail. The Pagans' inclination toward violence and reputation for ruthlessness have earned them the respect of the Mafia. The close proximity to mob turf in New York, Cleveland, Philadelphia and New Jersey has gained the club the best connection with traditional organized crime syndicates. Pagans are often employed as drug couriers, enforcers, bodyguards, and hit men for the mob. They associate with the Genovese and Gambino Families of New York, with which they cooperate in schemes of extortion, counterfeiting, carjacking and drug trafficking. They also have close relations with the Aryan Brotherhood, or other alt right wing neo-Nazis with white supremacist ideologies.

The Caveman had a bar, a few battered long tables, reflecting its communal attitude, three pool tables, video-pokers and a small stage, where a stripper performed twice on Saturday nights. On the walls were motorists' mementos, uncouth pictures and stains of various origins. Being the leader of the local Aryan Brotherhood gang, Jay Fraser often came here to chat with Leo Nikitin, gaining news of a national scale, and eavesdropping on the movers and shakers of the Underworld. However, Leo had not seen him by a week.

The Happy Gator was completely different. First, it was a country-themed pub, catering to rodeo enthusiasts, rednecks and local farmers. Second, it was one of the oldest fixtures in town, centrally located, and with a less rowdy atmosphere than the others. The place was also the favorite spot for local cops, including Sheriff Andrews, so it used to be tame and placid. No brawls, please. The Gator was a bit larger than the Caveman, offering to its customers a bar and a series of round tables arranged around half of the main floor. The other was occupied by two pool tables, a mechanical bull, some slot machines, and a medium-sized dancing floor. Decorated with mounted bullhorns, old west wagon wheels, and framed pictures of local rodeo heroes, it was also the place to be when the town celebrated some important event. The owner was Rita 'White Dove' Logan, a half-Seminole woman who had bought the place from the previous proprietor ten years ago. Jay used to come here sometimes, just for the sake of listening to country music, which he loved, but since it was frequented by the county's cops, it was one of his less favorite ones. Even here, Billy had found no useful info about Fraser. Ray Henderson, the barkeeper, said he had not spotted the man in more than a month.

Next on the list was the *Moola*, more a small casino than a pub; it was one of those cheap places where you could find 99 cents shrimp cocktails rubbing elbows with discount sushi plates. As for the décor, plastic iguanas shared space with Rolex replicas—a real kingdom in bad taste. Billy hated that place. He hated it even more when he was forced to stay there longer than needed because of the heavy downpour that had hit the town. Another failure.

After the storm subsided, Gamble finally left the *Moola* and directed himself down to the *Roughhouse*. Lakeview Drive was covered with fallen leaves and other vegetable matter and he had to be careful to avoid losing control of his bike and skidding out of the road.

He reached the place and approached Mark Scarlett, who was busy trying to fix the notoriously faulty TV cable of the large screen. "Hey, Scarlett, do you have a couple of minutes?"

Mark turned to face him with a pissed off attitude, as if ready to tell him how to get lost for disturbing while he was so fucking busy with the wrecking box, but his face paled when he saw Billy. "Hey ... look what the storm brought in," he said, quickly hiding his emotions.

Gamble took a seat in the closest booth by climbing over the back of it and letting himself fall down on the worn out fake leather cushion below.

"Fixing again that can of worms?" he asked, not really expecting an answer.

"Yeah, but next week I'm gonna buy a new one. I'm tired of it, you see. These kinds of—"

"Mark, I'm not here to talk about your shopping list," Billy interrupted him before he started blathering about the differences about buying American products versus Chinese ones, his next favorite issue after bikes and whores. "Have you seen Jay? Lately, I mean?"

Scarlett let out a grin. "What do you boys have tonight? Are you all in love with old J.F.?"

Gamble did not grin back; his face turned as cold as stone. "What do you mean with that, Marky? Who else asked about him?"

The bartender's smile died on his face. He knew Billy was not the guy you could play with. He was a dangerous man; affiliated with the local Aryan Brotherhood gang, and he had contacts in and out of the Correctional. Former enforcer for a minor chapter of the Pagans out of Norfolk, Virginia, some gossiped that he was still inside that stuff. He was not one who liked to start a brawl, but was one who always finished it. *Stay by his side and you are in danger, stay in his way and you're dead meat*—this is what people thought of him.

"Well ... you are not the first one asking me about Jay tonight."

"Cut the bullshit, please. Go straight to the point, Scarlett." Billy said this while pulling out his switch knife from his bomber jacket. He sprung the blade out and used it to clean dirt from under his nails.

"The morgue's guy asked me about Jay's doings almost an hour ago, I think. That fucking creep came here to meet him, but he had it wrong ... the doc, I mean,"

"Are you telling me that ghoul had a date with Jay?"

"Yes, but not with him. He said that J.F. had to introduce a gal, one from out of town."

Gamble stuck the blade on the already pockmarked tabletop.

"A girl? Why? Jay does not deal in pimping, usually. I can't remember him having a stable."

Mark eyed the knife that stuck out of his table like a sprouted sapling, but said nothing about it.

"I do not know, Bill. He just said the chick was an important witness for one of the stiffs down at the body dump. You know how strange the dude is."

Billy retrieved the tool and switched it off, the blade making a dry click while retreating inside the mechanism. "And you said he had it wrong. What do you mean by that?"

The bartender climbed down the ladder he was standing on and took a seat in front of him. "Listen, I don't know anything about the story. All I know is that yesterday night Jay was here. He had a couple of beers alone, until that saucy pussy showed up and joined him."

"Do you think Jay knew the gal already?"

"No. She just approached him. She looked like some kind of professional whore, you know. I mean, Jay doesn't look like George Clooney, man."

Gamble reached out with his right hand, grabbed a half-empty beer bottle, and drank from it.

"She was something to be seen, man. All dark, cowboy clothes. An ass so firm you'll like to ride it for days. Nice boobs. Moved like a cat."

"And she went straight for Jay?" Billy asked, incredulous.

"No. She first went for the jukebox, played a song, and started shaking her ass in rhythm with the music. She made quite a show, I assure you."

"This implies you recall her well. But, don't you know her name, huh?"

"First time I saw her. But I can tell you a thing or two about the broad. First, she has a Tennessee swag. I heard her talking with Jay. Second, she has Indian blood in her veins. Although she has very pale skin, she sports the typical high cheekbones of them people."

Billy stared at him, while leaving the now empty bottle on the table.

"You're saying the gal teased him, then moved to his booth and hooked him. Did they go away together?" he asked.

"Yes. After some rounds, they started palming each other, then they went out. I recall the two getting aboard a truck of sorts. Black or dark blue pick-up, I think."

"And did you see Jay coming back to get his bike?"

"No. I don't remember if he'd come here to straddle that wreck of his."

"So, you did not see him again. What about the doc?"

"As I said, he came over here an hour ago asking about Jay and the woman."

"Did you tell him the same you told me about last night?"

"Yes. Then he said he had to get back to his job..." Mark stopped in mid-sentence then fished in his breast pocket. "Here! The ghoul left me this contact..." He passed him a paper napkin with the number on it.

Gamble grabbed it with a puzzled face. "He asked you to give it to Jay, should he show up tonight?"

"Yes".

"Go fetch me a beer, Mark. I'll park my ass here for a while."

Scarlett moved to the bar and poured some from the tap, while Billy relaxed on the seat. He leaned back and placed his feet on the rough table.

Jay Fraser had been hooked by a gal, then he had disappeared, failing to deliver the stuff to the mules. However, the most interesting thing was that the creepy doctor from the coroner's office had been looking for Jay and the girl. Maybe he could not find the whore, now. However, he knew where the doc lived, and where he worked. But he had better ideas.

Time for him to have a chat with this guy.

CHAPTER 17

SUPERNATURAL FORENSICS
(FROM AXEL'S HALL OF MEMORIES)

It is extremely difficult to burn an entire body, even if the outside is charred; the inner organs are usually undamaged. Severely burned bodies may have split skin, exposing the muscle beneath. Bones exposed to extreme heat display distinctive fractures, which shows by their pattern whether or not the skin had flesh on it when it was burned. Sometimes even what type of bone was burned is revealed as different bones fracture in different ways based on their thickness and shape. Furthermore, unless bones are pulverized after being burned—as they are in a crematorium—it is often still possible to determine certain facts about the skeleton, such as its age and gender, despite the damage caused by the flames. Teeth are also highly resistant to heat, and are often used to identify burned bodies. Accurate identification can be made with as little as one tooth. Burns from fire or heat are ranked by degrees: first (superficial, no blisters); second (burns of part of the thickness of the skin, usually with a red, moist, and blistered outer appearance); third (burns of the full thickness of the skin, with a leathery white outer appearance and no blisters), and fourth (incinerating burns extending beneath the skin). For the most part, examiners cannot distinguish between pre-death and post-mortem burns. Blistering does occur after death. Victims who die in a fire often die not of burns, but of carbon monoxide inhalation, which turns the skin bright red in color.

Such was not the case with the body in the burned shack. This victim had no carbon particles in his larynx and lungs; therefore, he had been killed before the fire, which could have been set in an attempt to destroy the body.

After working on the remains for less than one hour, I had already identified him as a male of medium stature with a light bone-frame, and not in good health at the moment of his demise.

The sheriff's men—Tipple, Willis, Lane, and Andrews himself—had set up flares to mark out the scene of the crime, but it was still dark within the woods.

The men from the Prosperity Glades Fire Department were still there, with their chief releasing a statement to Sheriff Andrews, while the others relaxed a little by passing one another plastic cups of coffee. Tipple cordoned off the area with yellow tape, while Sergeant Deputy Lane talked with the man who had called the firefighters in the first place—a Seminole hunter, who was now seated on the loading bay of the emergency ambulance with a thermal blanket wrapped around his body. Amber Willis was busy snapping photos of the scene.

Crime scenes like these were rare in Prosperity Glades. Well, mostly because I was good at not leaving traces of my wet work.

In addition, they were particularly hated by Sheriff Andrews, who prided himself on Prosperity Glades being one of the safest towns in Florida. Murder crimes always made him nervous. He had been elected for a first term in 2006, under the auspices of Mayor Duval Fallon. He'd done his best to satisfy the simple people of the area, making the roads safe at night, keeping the town clean, and generally lowering the crime rates in West Bend. Now, he was serving his second term of office, and things had gone fairly straight, the only major accident being the death of young Bruce Davis at Camp Osceola last summer, when the boy had drowned in the lake. Bruce's family had sued the camp owner, Mr. Justin Pearce, for good, and now the camp was closed until further notice.

Weren't lucky with summer camps here.

More, Andrews was worried because crimes like these attracted journalists and curiosity of all kinds like maggots to dead meat. I knew exactly what he was wishing for inside his mind: *Let's hope it has been an accident, please!*

Murder in a rural community was always bad news for law enforcement.

Prosperity Glades forensic investigators were different from those *CSI* types on TV. Forensic experts often complain that books, films, and television shows are full of inaccuracies about the scientific nature of their work. I'm one of them. Moreover, to be correct, I was the only one—except Dr. Zimmerman, and maybe Deputy Espinoza—with enough experience on homicide scenes.

Forensic investigators have to collect evidence as soon as possible after a crime is discovered, while it is still fresh, even if the area is unsafe and they have to work under armed guard. This was not the case here, obviously, but I'd been in some dangerous situations in the past, such as when someone had dumped a dead body inside Billy Ortega's Alligator Farm. I had nothing to do with that. I only fed gators at Kamp Koko for two motives. First, disposing of whole dead bodies by feeding them to alligators is unsafe. Although the beasts can be quite voracious, often they leave parts; some even store the meat under fallen trees to have it rot. Bones can be discarded by the reptiles.

That's why I only fed them with neatly sliced parts. Sliced and diced.

In a farm, which is a closed pool affair, bones and other parts could be easily found by the managers, or be spotted by visitors, or worse, inspectors. Second, I did not know why, but the gators at Kamp Koko belonged to a strange variety; they never discarded a single little piece. I was almost sure they lived in some kind of supernatural symbiosis with the Rider.

In the past, police officers would walk around the scene of a crime and handle evidence with their bare hands. This did not matter much, since the simple forensic techniques available could not detect the effects of their actions on the evidence itself. Today, with the enormous advances in forensic science, the situation is very different.

When a serious crime occurs, the forensic specialist has to turn the whole scene into an area resembling a lab. I did this by placing an isolating tent over the body, recording all the names of those present at the scene, taking DNA and blood samples from each one—except those we had already filed in the past, such as the deputies—and working directly on the spot for the preliminary exam. Speed was essential: physical evidence had to be preserved before it was altered by time or weather conditions. This precious window of opportunity is known as the 'golden hour'.

After establishing that burning had happened post-mortem, I took notice of all irregularities on the body' structure, checking for blunt traumas or indentures. Blunt trauma means injuries caused by impact—beatings, collisions, and similar incidents. Victims of beatings sometimes display blunt trauma 'defense wounds' on the arms and hands, indicating that they were trying to fend off the blows. There are four types of blunt trauma: abrasions, contusions, lacerations, and skeletal fractures. I could check only for the last type right on the spot, the other varieties requiring the use of my full lab down at the morgue. Skeletal fractures are injuries to the victim's bones. I found a severe one on the cranium; the nasal socket had suffered a strong blow from a blunt instrument, which had fractured and splintered. It also told me the direction of the impact and the amount of force employed, and that it had occurred when the victim was alive. Some instruments leave a distinctive shape on bone, and in short time I found a probable culprit among the many implements scattered around the wrecked cabin—a rusted hammer. I matched it against the v-shaped indenture on the skull, calculating the former presence of skin, muscles, cartilage, and fat deposits.

Yes, the poor bastard had been hit hard with that tool, so I placed it inside a plastic bag, and stitched an adhesive tag on it.

However, there were more interesting things on the charred body.

Apart, from various strange holes in some of the bones, including the one on the cranium that clearly could have been the victim's cause of death, there were clear signs of torture. Wounds from torture could look just like wounds received during a struggle.

However, if the victim was still alive for a while after wounds were inflicted, certain blood traces and biochemicals, such as leucocytes or serotonin, would be found in the edges of the wound or in increased levels in the body. That I could not discern. I needed more time and some tests at the lab.

Oh, but there were other signs pointing me in the right direction. Although, the flames had consumed the ropes that were used to tie this man like a lamb, I spotted ligature marks on the withered skin around the wrists and legs. Between this and the location and type of wound, I determined the victim was tortured, rather than mutilated after death. Then, there were two special wounds, both of the same type—stabbing cavities.

Stab wounds are sharp traumas where the depth of the wound is greater than the length of the wound. The edges of the wound are usually distinct, without abrasions or contusions, although this may vary depending upon how sharp the stabbing object is.

The first one I found above the left knee. It had dislodged the kneecap, perforating the cartilage between the hipbone and the lower leg and leaving a distinctive mark. The second was a bit vaguer, and had caused a deep cavity in the victim's right shoulder. The weapon, which had caused these deep and precise wounds, had been removed from the flesh of the victim. It was nowhere to be found, and I did not even try to look for it. I was almost sure the man had been pinned by arrows.

I heard someone come closer to the tent, move cautiously among the debris.

"Axel, may I come in?" said Dr. Zimmermann's voice.

I sighed. What the hell she was doing here, so late, and out of her turn of service?

Then, it happened—unexpected and almost having me gasp in shock. My vision blurred for an instant, replacing the burned figure of my charred companion with a face so scary and beautiful at the same time. The face of a woman, pale as the Moon, with black make-up and sparkling eyes, her long, dark hair flowing around her head like snakes. Her mouth whispered something I couldn't hear.

The sound of the tent's zipper being opened dispelled the

'ghost' in an instant, leaving an afterimage on my eyes. Abigail entered the portable isolation chamber.

"What do we have here, Axel? Was it a murder or not?" she asked.

I could not respond. I was too enthralled by the vision the Rider had sent me. A vision of the same woman that had killed Jay Fraser down at Kamp Koko last night.

I had seen her.

And the Rider was urging me to find this woman.

CHAPTER 18

WINDIGO

Cheri fell again in the darkness. However, this time, she swam in it like a shark in the ocean, moving her body sinuously toward a pinpoint of light on her left. Eager to reach the light-source, she swam faster, beating her feet, using her arms as flippers—filled with the need to come out of the pitch-blackness surrounding her.

The more she moved toward the luminosity, the more it grew, until it became a beacon, and like a moth, she fell into it, burning herself. The white light hurt her skin, and her eyes were blinded by the brilliant whiteness. She instinctively closed her eyes, but it was useless; the brightness reached through her lids.

Then, she found herself watching her uncle. In one hand he held a lamp, in the other he grasped a white oak staff, straight and with no knots, the spearhead made of obsidian. Below the head were stitched five tail feathers; two from raven and three from owl. Also, from the stitch departed three ribbons—one dark red, one dark blue, and one made of three colors (red, white and blue). A length of buffalo skin covered the staff itself. It was a Windigo Staff. Her uncle Johnny had assembled it the night before to 'Shorten the Windigo on This Side'.

Johnny led her inside Copperas Cave, a place her ancestors believed to be a passage to the Spirit World.

"Things have gotten bad on the Other Side. Manitous prey on the spirits and departed souls, which inhabit the Hunting Grounds. The strong preys on the weak in the next world, and the weak becomes food. The Hunting Grounds aren't so happy anymore," he said, while illuminating small green crystals of ferrous sulfate, or copperas, that streaked some of the shale surfaces of the cave, giving it its name.

Cheri followed him, as she had done when she was twenty-one, past events repeating in this dream. The darkness of the caves seemed to soak up the light from the lantern, which was only able to brighten small portions of their trail, and only dimly. Darkness surrounded them on all sides; complete, unrelieved darkness. Ominous shadows fluttered at the edges of the lamp's beam. Cheri caught glimpses of movement out of the corners of her eyes.

Was something out there, or was it just a shadow?

"Our ancestors believed that every tribe—even the white tribes and the black tribes and all the other tribes from across the great waters—had its own place in the Hunting Grounds," the man continued, while removing a large patch of spider webs between the wall and a large column, allowing Cheri to pass freely. His voice reverberated in an ominous and strangely distorted echo. The cool air had a stale and musty smell, chilling Cheri's skin with moisture. The couple rounded a corner on slippery terrain. A steady dripping sound revealed the presence of water coming from the roof of the cave.

"They believed these places were in turn merely branches on a great tree that stretched from the deepest depths of evil up to the celestial resting place of revered ancestors. This was the Tree of Life," droned on Johnny's voice.

The cave walls were cold and damp in that spot, feeling clammy to the touch. Cheri felt, again, the same chilling fear she had felt so long a time ago. She remembered where they were going.

The Moon Gate.

The passage from This Side to the Other Side. The places from where the Ada'wehi came forth. The Moon-eyed people lived close to that portal. These evil spirits were human only in form, and lived on the suffering of Man. They were created by the Windigo to serve as its minions, to protect its underground dwelling from intruders. Over the years, they were overcome with a wish to cross to This Side and pass themselves off as true humans. They could see extremely well in the dark, and could be rendered immobile by bright lights, so they ventured forth only after the sun had set, or when the sky was overcast and cloudy.

136

Uncle Johnny came here every time his Vision Quest had revealed to him that something was wrong at the Moon Gate. He said that, sometimes, the White Man attracted the Spirit of the Windigo, causing it to come to This Side—but only a part of it, because the Windigo could not be summoned or bound by humans. It always came out on its own when it sensed a similar spirit.

Uncle Johnny 'Bead Eyes' Dancer was a White Faction Shaman. That meant he could not take lives. In the Cherokee nation, Shamans were divided into two groups, or *Factions*. The Red Faction was the war faction, while the White Faction could be paired with peace. Death and Life, Killing and Healing, Male and Female; the two aspects of the Universe.

As a White Faction Shaman, Johnny was allowed to cure illnesses, turn away evil spells, block the entry of spirits, or return them to the Other Side. One of the last true believers of the Ancient Ways, Johnny Dancer Ridge was respected by many people of Cherokee ancestry in the area.

A skilled carpenter and an able mechanic, Johnny had taught his niece many crafts. Construction working, fixing a car, electrical jobs, herbalism, and how to survive in the wilds. He taught her how to fish, but never how to hunt.

Cheri had run away from her drug addict mother when she was sixteen, managing to avoid a life of prostitution to help her get the daily fix. Her father, Jason "Soaring Hawk" Ridge, had died when she was eleven years old, and after some time her mother had fallen into the clutches of a bastard, who had turned her into a junkie and a whore. The young girl remembered that her father had mentioned to her an older brother, Johnny, a weird man who lived in Hoodoo, a crossroad town north of Manchester. It took her almost a year to find him. However, he had accepted her as if she had been his own daughter—which is why he took her with him on this expedition.

They reached the area called Avenue of the Virgins. It was named that way because in the long stony corridor were two huge stalagmites, each one stark white and vaguely feminine in shape, referred to as The Virgin Twins. The breeze that blew from north to south carried an odd odor, as well as some disturbing sounds to Cheri's ears. Once, they seemed like creaks or groans. At other times, they sounded much like whistles or sighs.

"We're almost there, Cheri," Johnny said, pointing to an opening on his right while illuminating it with the lamp.

Strange chitterings could be heard in the darkness just beyond the lights' beam. A foul stench of corruption, the smell of death and decay, reached her nose. Beyond that tight opening stood the Moon Gate, the place Johnny was looking for to perform his ritual to 'shorten' the Windigo on This Side.

Johnny Dancer entered the caving first. The light from the lamp died suddenly when he disappeared behind a corner. Cheri panicked. She felt alone, in that living darkness, full of horrible odors and scary sounds.

She hurried in the same direction her uncle had disappeared into, to get back in the light, but found none of it. She could not see anything, and when she reached out to touch her surroundings, she discovered that everything seemed out of reach.

"Uncle?" she cried out.

However, only her echo answered back, surrounding her with her own voice, mocking her like a living being.

"Unnnncleeee!!!" she shouted, on the verge of crying, because she felt, inside, that he was no longer there. That he had been taken by the Windigo.

She tried to get back from where she had come, but it was impossible. The obscurity was impenetrable, with no walls to lean on; only her feet stood on unidentifiable solid ground.

"UNNNCLEEEEE!!!" Again, she shouted, this time with desperation in her voice and tears in her sightless eyes. No echo responded to her this time. Only silence.

Then, she saw them.

Two huge yellow eyes opening in the dark, filled with hate and rage.

"Come here," whispered the *Thing in the Dark*.

She began to scream...
...and awakened inside her bed in the trailer.

CHAPTER 19

ON THE RECORDS

Deputy Espinoza was falling asleep. Her turn of duty had been over six hours ago, but she had to stay at the station house to wait for the return of the others from the woods. She was still angry at destiny. That night she had decided to release herself, to get out of the misery she had turned into in these last years. She remembered the days when she was a minor model in Miami, before the ways of the rich and beautiful had driven her toward alcoholism. She wasn't a slut, but she'd had much fun with men she liked. Maybe, too much fun. Anyway, she was young, gorgeous, and single. Men drooled around her, like worker bees with a queen-bee. Then, she had realized how empty all of that felt. Life cannot be all fun, easy money, and booze. She had straightened up. However, her failed marriage had carried away that cheering girl, her charming smile replaced by a sarcastic smirk. In some ways, she had to be grateful to Axel Hyde. Chumming out with him had helped her see how dark and grim her life had become. Spending a whole night meditating on why she had been dating such a weird individual for almost six months had forced her to come out of the spell.

Come on, Axel, you are not normal. Tu esta loco en la cabeza, chico!

How'd it happen? How on Earth had she ever thought of dating him? She searched her mind for reasons.

****

Morena Espinoza had caught a glimpse of Dr. Hyde on various occasions, but she had never deigned him of a second glance. He was the big man down at the morgue, nothing more. The silent guy who filed reports and consigned them always personally at the station.

140

Until that night at the County Fair. She had been forced by her colleague and only friend in town, Amber Willis, to go to the fair, just to do something different. After some mild protesting, she had accepted, and begrudgingly wore one of those long dresses that only an Amish woman would wear. Amber broke into laughter the moment she saw her getup.

"It's a County Fair, not a *Country* Fair!" she had exclaimed, pushing her back into her house.

Amber had messed up her wardrobe to find some decent clothes, but the only stuff she had found was an old pair of everyday jeans, of the kind only a technician or a mom would wear, and a blue t-shirt more suited to a vacationer than a woman trying to look good.

They had strolled together among the booths and tents, having a look around, not wanting anything to buy, just enjoying the company and the crowd. They had played at some of the Midway games, enjoyed a stage-magician show, and laughed as kids at the poor performance of a deluded singer, who had sung a repertory of Madonna's greatest hits—from *Like a Virgin* to *Vogue*—with attempts at sexy moves ... except he had a fat, lard ass wrapped in rodeo clothes.

After that, they had tried some of the food court cuisine, loading their big plastic plates with everything from fried alligator wings to Cajun chicken, to spring rolls and chimichangas. They had found a seat in the common area set aside for hungry visitors—a series of long tables and benches distanced enough from the main attractions, but close to the dance area.

The music had been so loud that conversation was impossible, the food awful and the rowdy company of four drunken male revelers had worsened her mood.

Amber Willis knew about Morena's infamous temper and lack of patience with annoying men, and had done her best to steer clear of trouble. Twice they moved tables to avoid the attentions of the boozers, but the guys kept tailing, making comments, and churning out a loud chorus of dumb laughter.

Finally, when they had reached the Funhouse, the three men had let them go; their attention diverted by the 'Madonna Cowboy' who was doing his best to look as ridiculous as he could, singing *Material Girl*.

Yet one of the men, a burly and brawny type, such as those you could find working in a foundry, had not resigned his purpose, and went from annoying to dangerous when he tried to slap Morena's butt.

Fortunately for Amber, his hand had never reached the target, because it had been stopped by the grasp of Dr. Hyde.

The drunkard had turned with disbelief and anger toward the big doctor, ready to retaliate. However, something strange had happened. He had locked his eyes with those of Dr. Hyde, then had started screaming like a pig. He had pulled out of the man's grip and had run away in panic.

Alcohol.

Morena remembered then why she had quit drinking that stuff.

"Thank you, sir," she had said, "but there was no need for that. I'm perfectly able to defend myself from such scum."

"I wasn't helping you," he had remarked, shrugging his shoulders "I was helping *him*."

Amber Willis had laughed to break the tension, and it had worked because Morena followed suit. Axel Hyde, instead, had looked confused; sure that he had not said anything funny.

This had intrigued Morena. "Are you saying you knew I could have hurt him very bad? If that punk even tried to touch me…"

"No," he had interrupted her. "I just said I was helping him from … himself."

Then, he had fixed his chocolate brown eyes on Morena's, sending a shiver up her back. She couldn't understand why. Cautiously, like a shy kid, he had offered her his hand for a shake. "I think it is a good thing I introduce myself at this point. I'm Axel Hyde, the Assistant Medical Examiner for Prosperity County."

"Morena Espinoza, Sheriff's Deputy. And I think I already know you, doc."

"Sure! I come to your office, sometimes. However, it's the first time I see you not wearing the uniform."

Morena had found that man different. He did not try to press himself on her, but appeared like a kindred soul, someone so detached from the rest of humanity that he could barely exist within it.

In a short time, the three had joined company; a companionship of off-duty county officers, exchanging news and old stories about their jobs. By the end of the evening, Morena had found many things in common with the big man from the morgue.

He was a lonely type, full of doubts and loneliness. She had even found him attractive. He was tall and well-built, with a muscular body more suited to a wrestler than a medic. Short, black hair, cut in a neat, but not so ordinary style, covered his head above a square-jaw. His skin was fair and freckled around the nose, with strong but appealing features. All in all, he looked more like a heavy metal singer than a pathologist. Gene Simmons—when *Kiss* were big—with short hair. Scary, but charming.

They had spent the rest of the evening together, until Amber had spotted a cousin of hers and had said goodnight to both, leaving them alone.

Axel had walked Morena back to her house.

Morena had been shocked when she had realized they had walked all the way down from the fairgrounds. Time had flown while they chatted as they had strolled among the deserted streets of the town, occasionally stopping by some local feature, like Town Square, where the good doctor, who had been living there from the age of ten, had acted like a tour guide for her, but of the morbid kind. He had a weird story for every corner of the town.

In the middle of Town Square, amid the fig trees and marble benches, stood the statue of the community's founder: John Walker Murchison. That's what everyone thought—but Axel said it wasn't true.

He told her the statue actually depicted General Thomas S. Jessup, the man made notorious for the massacre of numerous native villages and camps in 1836, at the peak of the Second Seminole War. According to Axel, Mayor Jonathan McAllister had bought the art piece in 1898 to replace an ugly slab of greenish stone that had been on display since before the coming of the White Man. To add insult to injury, the original rock had been carried off somewhere into the depths of North Grassy Swamp, the inhabitants considering it cursed and unwilling to break it up. In truth, the slab had marked a taboo place for the original population, a long lost tribal offshoot of the Calusa.

The local tribe, which Patricia Moore—the Curator of the Prosperity Heritage Society—had unofficially christened Pahayokeeni, had been wiped out by Spaniards in the 1750s, and the land had not seen human encroachment until the beginnings of the new century when Georgian Creek natives took refuge in the Everglades to escape the White invaders. These Seminole (a word which in Creek has many meanings, like 'fugitive', 'indomitable', or 'pioneer') settled along the shores of the lake's west bend, but even they stood at large from the greenish standing rock. Axel had also added that the rock had finally been blown to pieces by Maddox Chemicals, a large pharmaceutical company with several branches around the country, when they were building their facility in Grassy Swamp in 1966.

On Central Avenue was the Vistana Boarding House, where Morena's colleague, Peter, still lived with his mom. Dr. Hyde told her the place had been a speakeasy in the Roaring Twenties, which had become a bloodbath on July 4, 1938, when men from the Torrecone clan of Miami had wiped out Vito Morini and his family—along with his bodyguards.

He had then showed her a shabby mansion at the corner of Cortez Street. Between 1942 and 1955 there had been six double-murders, all honeymooners staying at the now defunct Glades Grand Hotel. After years of investigation, police had finally obtained enough evidence to convict Albert Dunning, the owner of that ugly mansion, who had done seasonal ground-works at the hotel. The sheriff's men stumbled upon glass jars holding preserved eyes, fingers, and ears from each of the twelve victims. Dunning was convicted in 1957; his house had been impounded and put on the market, and was still property of the County because no one had ever bought it.

And so on.

Axel Hyde had a story for every street, house, and nook. With time, they began to frequent each other, never going beyond friendship, just spending free time together. He continued to be her local spooky guide into the darkest secrets of Prosperity Glades and its environs.

Then, after three months, while they were enjoying a nightly excursion on the Okeechobee aboard Axel's airboat, he had asked her—nervous and stuttering—to become his girlfriend. She had accepted and they had kissed each other under the full moon's bright light over the lake. That kiss had tasted empty, unreal, as there was no passion, something due, like a date stamp on a dossier.

They had never repeated the experience.

They'd just gone on as a couple of teens, not yet ready for sex, but eager for the opposite sex's company. Until she had watched herself in the mirror last night and seen, finally, what she had become.

****

Morena was just playing back those memories when Vice Sheriff Lane and Peter Tipple returned to the station. It was just after 3:50 AM and the storm had left the lights of Town Square sparkling like gems. As Espinoza opened the front doors to allow the two officers to get in, a waft of crisp air reached her lungs and the freshness of the night slapped her awake. Lane looked at her new clothes and released a whistle of admiration, gaining a dour grimace from Morena as a response. "Wow! What happened here? Is the world going to an end?"

"Stop that, James, please. And just tell me what kept you

down there all this time, justifying my loss of sleep."

Peter opened his mouth first. "Something big, Espinoza. We have a murder and arson in our hands."

"In a drug lab, too!" added Lane.

"A drug lab? What are you saying? Wasn't that a fishing shack?" Morena mused.

Lane went immediately to the office room, ignoring her questions, while Peter placed his cowboy hat on the reception desk. "Espinoza, as I said the case is big. Someone was using that place to cook up drugs. But he left his skin right there. He was murdered. No, tortured and murdered, then the whole place was set on fire."

Morena noticed his tired face; he looked even more attractive with that serious expression. "Andrews? What does he think?"

"He is as dark as this night. He is sure some rival gang is responsible for the mess," he replied, letting himself fall on the reception's couch, releasing a grunt as if his aching bones had sent an electrical-like jolt up his spine.

"Are you okay?" Morena asked, with sincere concern.

He looked at her with a quizzing look, then turned away from her cleavage, where his eyes had lingered again. "Yes, thank you ... just a bit wrecked. I spent too much time in those damn woods, combing the place."

"Would you like some hot coffee? I've made some..."

"Oh, that would be nice! Yes, please. It will do nothing for my back, but at least it will keep me awake."

Morena went upstairs, retrieved her bag, poured some coffee into a clean mug, and came down, offering the warm beverage to Peter.

Meanwhile, Vice Lane returned from the back-office, noticed the woman handing the mug, and could not avoid rolling his eyes. He knew Tipple had a crush on her, but also knew that Morena was one of the bitchiest female officers he had ever served with. "Okay, you bulls listen. I've checked our records and found the name of the cabin's owner. We already know the man: he is Jerry Meeks—the Fishman, as we call him."

146

"Meeks? You mean that funny guy owning that fish and tackle shop down at the lake?" Tipple said.

"Yes, that's him. However, the charred body can't be his. Not matching with his physique. Jerry is overweight, while this guy was as thin as a skeleton."

Axel Hyde chose that moment to come in, a brown envelope in his hands. Morena could not avoid glimpsing Peter's eyes narrowing when they turned to face him. He did not like that guy, especially since she'd started dating him.

She liked that.

"Here are the results of our examinations, officers," he said, handing the envelope to Lane. He glanced at her sideways, as if trying to avoid her gaze, like a kid caught in the act of stealing some jelly from his mom's pantry.

She liked that, too.

"Thank you, Doctor. You were very fast," said Lane.

"We have already identified the body. We had his dental records down at the lab. ... Name's Marvin Wilson, and I'm sure you already know him as a small-time pusher," continued Hyde.

Tipple sipped some of the coffee and kept gazing at the medical examiner, while Morena rushed to the desk to match the name with past records. She found him. He had been arrested once for dealing drugs in the Osceola Mall's parking lot. He also had various precedents for minor assault, rowdy behavior, and speeding. When Espinoza raised her eyes, Axel had already gone away.

Typical of him.

"So, this confirms our theory," said Lane.

"However, this does not explain why he was cooking drugs inside Mr. Meeks' shack, why he was killed, and overall ... who killed him."

Morena checked on the rents records and found something interesting. Peter noticed her raised eyebrow. "What's up? Is there something wrong?"

Morena swayed her attention from the screen and looked at

both men. "Here. There's a regular rental agreement registered at the County Hall of Records. It is between Jerry Meeks and another man ... not Marvin Wilson," she said.

"What's the name?" Lane frowned.

She stared at Peter. He had spoken often about that guy—how he was sure that the man was behind many of the traffics here in the county.

"Jay Fraser," she said.

Tipple's face darkened. "I knew it!" he cried out as he sprinted from the couch, almost splashing his pants with some of the coffee.

"What's the story?" Lane asked.

"Simple. That scum is a dealer. I was sure about it by months..."

"Just calm down, Peter! We have no proof he's responsible for what went down there. We can stop and question him, but we need more clues to nail him for drugs."

"Bullshit! We have a cabin full of it! This is the right time to nab him once for all..."

"I said, calm down! We'll do this by the book. Now, you two, the turn's over. Just get some rest. I'll wait for Andrews. Tomorrow you get the night shift. Me and the sheriff will go looking for Fraser and Meeks." Lane glared sternly at Peter. He was not expecting a refusal.

"Okay," the younger officer replied, then turned to Morena.

"Are you going with me? I can give you a hitch back home ... if you like."

She looked at him, smiled, and then grabbed her bag. "Why not? Hell, I'm too tired to walk over to my house as I usually do. Thank you, Peter."

The two officers went out, allowing a waft of warm Floridian air to invade the station.

****

Once alone, Vice Sheriff James Lane rushed to the door, locked it, and went upstairs. He scrambled frantically inside one of the drawers, where he retrieved a cell phone and made a call.

A name appeared on the display:

JAY.

CHAPTER 20

PARTNERS

Peter Tipple was fond of his *Cherokee Grand Chief*. He loved the car. Every time he was at the wheel he had no eyes but for his vehicle. Not that morning. He could not stop glancing sideways on the passenger's side. Because seated next to him was the most beautiful woman he had even seen. Oh, he had seen her many times—she was a partner, after all—but this instance was different. She looked like a cover model out of one of those magazines Mama bought. At 4.30 in the morning, the streets were empty, but Peter made a huge effort to keep his attention on the road, not on his colleague.

They went along Central Avenue, northward, directed to the Uptown neighborhood, when Morena Espinoza exclaimed something in Spanish. "Mierda! Que asco!"

Peter was surprised by her sudden expression; she had not said a word from the moment they had left the station, and now she was swearing profanities in her language.

What've I done, now?

Then, he noticed her usual bronze-skinned face was now pale, and a disgusted look creased the corners of her mouth. "What happened?"

"Didn't you see it?"

"See what?"

"On the stop sign, back at the corner of Cortez Street?"

He backtracked until the car reached the spot. Tipple did not immediately realize what he was seeing, then it finally hit him.

For on the stop sign, someone had nailed a dead animal.

"What the f..." he began, then, remembering he was in company of a woman—Mom had taught him never to swear in the presence of one—he stopped.

Morena stared at him, a knowing smile reaching her eyes.

"I meant ... what's happening to this town?" Peter corrected himself, blushing.

He got out the car and approached the traffic signal, shining his flashlight on it. The beam revealed the rotten carcass of a dead raccoon, still dripping blood from its half-open mouth. The animal's belly had been opened, its bristling interiors exposed. A pool of black blood had taken form on the concrete, under the pole. Behind it, a dark and broken-down house standing loomed with, its empty windows like skull's orbits, black and unnerving.

"Peter, isn't that Dunning's house? The one where that serial killer lived back in the fifties?"

Still gazing at the mauled raccoon, Peter nodded.

"Yeah, maybe it's a morbid kid's joke. That house has a bad repute, you know." The light clearly showed the poor beast had been nailed with rusty iron spikes driven into all its paws, in a macabre parody of the crucifixion. "I do not want to remove it right now. It's a disgusting job! Sheesh!" he said.

"Do not, please!" she yelled, and then added, "I do not want you to drive me back home smelling like a pathologist."

"You dated one for six months. You are used to the smell." Peter turned toward her, smiling.

"I know. That's why I'm telling you," she replied.

He gave one last look at the crucified animal, switched the flashlight off, then got back to the vehicle. "Don't worry; I'll come back later to remove it before some old lady sees it tomorrow morning."

****

Morena realized how blind she had been all these years. She had accused him of being sexist, superficial, and even a little dumb. Now, she understood Peter was just a good country boy, maybe a bit old-style, but well-mannered and concerned about his peers.

"Yeah, I know you'll do it. You're such a friendly neighbor, *Peter*." She envisioned him wearing a Spiderman costume, but he did not get the pun.

"I just do my duty, Morena. I care about the safety of our citizens. And something like that ... in front of that house ... gonna cause a lot o' mayhem around here. Speculations about Dunning's ghost returning from the grave, Satanists or worse. This is a small country town," he replied seriously.

Morena let her eyes run all over him. His white shirt clung on him with the night's humidity. Unbuttoned at the collar, it outlined the strong, flexing muscles of his chest. His sturdy, quarterback legs fit snugly inside a pair of faded jeans, and while he was seated at the wheel, the fabric tightened at the groin, revealing a bulge large enough to attract attention. Immediately, she looked away from the spot, feeling dirty.

I'm acting like a bitch in heat!

Yet, it had been an eternity since she had felt a drive like that, sex having been out of her life for more than two years.

"Everything's fine, Morena?" he asked suddenly, shaking her off from those erotic thoughts.

"Oh ... yes. I was just thinking about the murder," she lied.

"Yep, really bad news! I'm sure this is an act of vengeance between drug smugglers. Man, I can't stand that scum!" He turned the car leftward on Orange Avenue. The road was empty and silent, the flashing traffic lights the only witnesses of their presence.

"May I ask you something personal, Morena?" he said without taking his eyes from the road.

"Yes, go on."

Peter cleared his throat, as if trying to find the right words, along with his courage. "Considering that you look very gorgeous in these new clothes ... I was just wondering ... I mean, I'm not used in seeing you dressed like that..."

"Are you are asking why I changed my way of dress?" she interrupted, causing him to shut up and blush. "I tell you what, Peter. Before I came here, I was a very different woman. Would you believe I modeled in my youth?"

Peter nodded, while swerving the car to avoid running over a crossing cat.

"It's true. I was a model in my early twenties. Not a famous one—in fact I modeled bathing suits and clothes for some local stores—but a model nonetheless."

They had almost reached her home, however Morena became aware that Tipple was slowing down, in a way to prolong their time together. Who could have figured such a scene just three weeks before, when they had spent their whole patrol shift trying to stay out of each other's nerves?

Not Peter's fault.

"After my failed marriage ... and that still burns at me ... I changed. However, yesterday I grasped couldn't go on that way. Look Peter, you said you find me attractive, right?"

"Yes," he said, then rushed to add, "Not that you weren't before."

She smiled. "But, I wasn't anymore. I mean, it's not just how I look outside, Peter. ... It's about how I feel inside."

Peter stopped the car once they reached her house.

"All these years you have known the worst side of me, Peter. I acted bitchy because I was bitchy. I didn't trust men. They were all pigs in my eyes. I was so blinded by my past that I could not see my present," she continued, sadness in her eyes. "I always messed with you because I couldn't believe you were different and sincere in your behavior..."

"Oh, forget about it. I can be so dumb, sometimes," he interrupted her.

Morena stared at him. Even now, he was acting like one of those ancient knights out of fairy tales, courteous and gallant in that old Southerner way. "No, Peter, you're not. It was my entire fault. You were just the undeserving victim of my bitchiness. And ... I would like to apologize to you."

Peter shifted, uneasy on his seat, as if it had turned hot in that very moment. "I ... took no offense, Morena. We're partners. Partners can fight, but they have to trust each other on duty.

Besides, I always trusted you. You are such a good officer, with more experience than our whole department—"

He could not end his speech, because Morena reached out, grabbed his face, and forcing it down to hers. She kissed him softly on the lips, taking him off-guard. The kiss lasted only a second, but replayed inside her mind for hours.

Then, she got out of the car and rushed to her door, like a schoolchild who had just received her first kiss, unwilling to let her emotions run wild. She probed inside her purse for her keys, fumbling them, along with some lipsticks, and the lot fell on the doorstep. She stooped down to gather all her stuff, however, in doing so, caused even more personal items to pour out of the open zipper.

Tipple quickly got out of the *Cherokee*, at once coming to her side, and knelt to help her. Still feeling stupid for what she had done, Morena smiled in embarrassment. "Here ... do not worry, we'll find all the stuff," he said.

"Thanks Peter," she whispered.

"You're welcome," he answered back, in that droning tone she had always hated, nevertheless finding it pleasant now.

Once all her items were back into the bag, she opened her door and went inside. However, she stopped on the threshold, turned toward the man, and smiled again. "Good night, Peter. You're a good man. See you tomorrow."

Peter made a step forward, as if trying to get inside, taken by the passion of the moment, but Morena hastily closed the door, unwilling to rush things more than she already had. She heard him still standing outside and could not avoid going to the side window to have a last glance at him.

"Good night, Morena. Take care," he said, then backed to his car.

She found herself unable to take her eyes off of him. She waited until he was out of her sight, figuring he was probably going to remove that horrible decoration down in Cortez Street.

That night she dreamed about him, but not in the way she

would have wanted.

She dreamed about him being crucified on a road sign ... by Axel Hyde.

CHAPTER 21

GONE FISHING

It was 8:45 in the morning when Jerry Meeks came back from his early fishing expedition on Lake Okeechobee. He was upset because it had not been a good one. First, he had lost a large bass—and a good *Oregon Black* fishing rod—in the jaws of a big gator, which had been hiding under the opaque waters to pounce at the right time and carry everything, fish and tool away. Then, his airboat's rotor had stalled, forcing him to spend half of his time fixing it up. Last, he had returned almost empty-handed.

What else was going to spoil his day further?

Nothing.

The sheriff's car parked in front of his shop told him otherwise.

Jerry parked his vehicle, his small porcine-like eyes glancing nervously to the cop's 4x4. That had to be Andrews himself. In fact, the man descended from the car, his left hand reaching inside to catch the black Stetson he was so fond of, and push it down on his head.

Sheriff Roger Thornton Andrews was in his late fifties now, and he still looked pretty trim compared to many men his age, although obviously a little bit pudgier than he was a decade or two ago. His once-black hair had now mostly gone gray, but his deep blue eyes kept the same fire and sparkle as ever, particularly when he was going to squeeze someone. His features were a cross between Robert Mitchum and Lee Marvin.

Jerry Meek hated that man. Oh, to be honest, Jerry hated all men, and women, too. He hated kids, dogs, old people, and youngsters. In fact, Jerry Meeks hated the whole world.

Only, the world did not know about it. Nobody knew he was so full of hate and bitterness. Jerry had a jolly attitude—and face, too—that made people at ease. He had been a nobody for much of his life; the kid who was always the target of the schoolyard bullies, the teen who never got a dancing partner at prom night, the employee who never got a promotion.

His only luck had been a small fortune he'd inherited from his aunt Mary ten years ago—a couple of properties here in Prosperity.

However, things had not changed. He was still an outsider, considered by many only as the weird jolly man down at the lake. Nobody hated him. Nobody loved him. He was just that. Nobody.

As for bullies, well, they still picked on him. *Bullies can smell prey a mile away* – he always said. Mostly to himself. *But intelligent prey run if they may* - he also said. To himself, too.

Sheriff Andrews was one of them. Jerry knew it.

Firstly, he was a law enforcement officer. All cops are bullies. Secondly, he was a sheriff, politically elected, so he was also a politician. All politicians are bullies.

Thirdly, he kept himself in shape for his age. He practiced fitness. All fitness fanatics are bullies.

His frantic thoughts about bullies were swept away by Andrews.

"Good morning, Mr. Meeks. May I have a word with you?"

Blood pressure rushed up his veins.

"Yes, Sheriff. Have I been tackled?" he said, showing his best sales agent's smile, while thinking, *What the fuck do you want from me now, asshole?*

"No, Mr. Meeks. However, I do have bad news for you."

Inside his mind, Jerry paled, scared as hell; outside he kept his jovial face.

"I'm sorry to inform you that your shack, down Okeechobee Drive, is no more. It was burned down to cinders ... last night," added Andrews without looking into his eyes, but gazing in the distance, in that cool, detached way that all bullies do.

"Wh ... what?" he burbled.

"Yes. Sorry about that. Hope you had insurance on it," the sheriff continued.

"How? How on earth did it happen, sir?" Jerry was getting

pale out of his brain, too.

"Ain't better if we discuss this inside your shop, Meeks?" Andrews said.

"Y...es," stuttered Jerry, as he fumbled with his keys, unable to focus on the right one until, with a gasp of relief, he found it.

The Fish & Tackle shop was a log cabin turned into a commercial activity catering to anglers and weekend explorers. Full of stuff and junk, it was difficult to find a place to step in without bumping into something or knocking it down. The place smelled of fish and worse things, with an earthen undertone. Badly illuminated with only one side window, it was dark and shadowy.

Jerry went directly behind his counter, removed something from its surface, and placed it inside a drawer. Andrews's eyes drifted to his erotic magazines a split second before he put them away.

"So, tell me, Sheriff, how'd it happen?" Meeks flushed with embarrassment.

Andrews did not respond immediately; he glanced around the shop, focusing his gaze on a small red kayak, and then fixed his eyes on Jerry. "Quite a mess you've got here. You should do something about it. Someone could get hurt,"

Fuck you! It's my shop and my mess! I keep it as I like it. Just stop talking about bullshit and tell me what happened to my shack!

"Yes," Jerry said.

The sheriff moved around, knocking off an inflatable gator from one of the shelves in the process. He replaced it. "See? That's what I was talking about," he said with a wicked smile.

Stay cool, Jerry, stay cool. He is provoking you; you know it, that's what bullies do!

"All right, Meeks, let's go straight to the facts," Andrews said. "Last night the shack was burned down by unknown arsonists. It was a piece o' cake to do it for how much it was stuffed with chemicals. Anyway, someone died inside the place—"

"Someone got killed inside my cabin?" interrupted Jerry, the blood draining from his face.

"Yes, Meeks. Name's Marvin Wilson. Did you know him?"

"Yes ... I mean no. I mean not personally. He was a friend of my lodger..."

"And your lodger's name is?"

Jerry lowered his eyes, his lips in a pout.

"The answer doesn't lie in your shoes, Meeks," Andrews said.

"Fraser. Jay Fraser, sir."

Andrews faked a smile then shifted his gaze back at the inflatable gator. "I already knew that," he said.

Jerry stared at his back with angry eyes. How much he hated that man. He'd like to hang him with hundreds of fishing hooks, and then open his belly like a trout. If only he had the balls to do it ...

Andrews turned again, the smile gone from his face, his thumbs plucked into his belt. "Meeks. How'd it happen that you turned to dealing drugs?"

If Jerry could get even more unnerved than he was, it happened now. "Drugs! I do not deal in drugs, Sheriff! I'm an honest citizen, I pay my taxes, and I'm respectful of the law," he shouted.

"Stop that, please!" Andrews interrupted him. "I'm not accusing you of anything. What I want to state is that you could get into a really dirty mess for renting your shack to a guy like Fraser. Look, Meeks, the place was used as a chemistry lab to cut drugs. Things like meth and PCP, you know?"

Jerry lowered his eyes back to his shoes, this time really looking for a way out in his footwear.

"Meeks, I know you're a good guy. We never received a complaint about your business. You're a fine member of our community. That's why this thing took me out of the blue," said Andrews, this time in a confidential tone.

"I swear. I knew nothing about the drugs..."

"You knew it, Jerry. I would bet my left *huevo* on it. Like I'm sure you weren't part of the deal," Andrews rebuked.

"What do you mean?"

"I mean, Jerry, that you were forced to rent the shack to Fraser. Innit?"

Jerry blushed, still avoiding the sheriff's eyes. The man was like a cobra, using them to cow him into submission.

"As I thought," the sheriff nodded to himself, then advanced toward Jerry, ignoring the mess he made by bumping and stomping on all the merchandise. "Look Jerry, I do not want you to get into something bigger than you. Whoever killed Wilson is a brutal torturer, not a pissed off tourist. Just tell me the facts, and I'll place you under protection, understood?"

"Do you think my life can be in danger?"

"It depends. It depends on your part in the story. Were you in or not?"

"No! I swear it, sir! That guy, Fraser, he is a member of the Aryan Brotherhood, you know? I'm scared of him!" Jerry was on the point of crying, but did not want that to happen in front of such a macho man like Mr. Andrews.

The Mexicans? Could it have been the Mexicans? Oh, my!

"Fraser is an Aryan 'hood's member? He told you so?" asked Andrews.

Jerry regained his composure, then passed a hand over his face to clean away the cold sweat from his brows. "Yes. He came here some time ago, along with that bald guy, Wilson. He told me I had to rent it to him, or he would make my life a misery. At first I refused, but after they threatened me ... in a serious way, I gave in,"

"You could come over to the office and report. We could have charged them for threat and assault. Why did you not?"

"I was too frightened, sir. You can't trifle with those monsters. I know it. Besides, they never hurt me, they just scared me. I had no way to prove it. It would have been my words against theirs."

"Fraser is an ex-con, Meeks. I would've believed you. When will you learn you got rights, people?" Andrews said that last statement as if addressing the whole of Prosperity.

"You are right, sir. But when scary guys like that point a knife at your belly..."

"Are you telling me they threatened with a weapon? That's an increase in charges!" Andrews interrupted him, raising his voice.

Meeks turned again his gaze to the shoes.

"All right, Jerry. What's done is done. However, you can help me now in sending that scum back to where he belongs. Here now. You're going to sign a statement declaring that Fraser and Wilson forced you to rent them the shack under threat of your own life. Understood?"

Jerry said nothing, just kept staring at his shoes, shaking.

"Meeks? I'm serious; if you do not collaborate, I can charge you for accessory with those bastards. Start looking for a good lawyer, Jerry," Andrews stated.

"No. No need for that! I'll release a statement, Sheriff. Just give me the time for a glass of water, please."

Andrews smiled. "Of course, Jerry. I have the whole morning, don't worry. I'll stay here until we make this thing clear. Now relax and focus. And, I'll have a glass too, if you don't mind. Hot as hell in here!"

Jerry went in the backroom and opened the refrigerator unit. It was full of ice, frozen fishes, and other food. He searched into the cold ice and retrieved a can of beer. Then he passed some of the granular ice over his face, as if that would send away the terror that was getting at him. He placed the can on a nearby shelf, close to a dirty and cracked mirror that reflected his upset face. Then he smiled.

Wilson had been killed! Maybe even Fraser would get punishment. The newcomers, the Mexicans, were starting a gang-war. He was sure about that. He was free!

Bullies versus bullies.

That's the right way. In a lake, there are many bullies. There is the snapper and there is the gar. There's the pike and there's the catfish. Everyone knows its place. However, sometimes, they overstep each other's territories, and only the stronger survives. Too much predators inside a lake and they end up eating one another.

Yes, everything will be fine.

However, Jerry was forgetting one thing.

In Florida, there are alligators.

CHAPTER 22

TERRITORIES

Frank Hall relaxed under a big cypress tree watching his adversary's back with dagger eyes. *Come on, old man; let's put an end to this!*

Hall's rival had a leonine head of gray hair and a precise, rigid posture. He was sixty-eight years old, but looked younger. He turned toward Frank, showing a knowing smile, as he knew it was over. He savored the taste of victory on his full lips.

Are you waiting for the apocalypse, Sheppard?

Sheppard lifted the club high above his head, finally ready to strike, then with a swift and elegant movement, struck down. The golf ball flew high, making a nearly perfect descending arch in the air, and finally went to rest close to a lonely little banner, several yards from its starting point.

"Yes!" Sheppard exclaimed, bending on his knees and shaking the left fist.

"Excellent shot, Albert!" Hall said, smiling only with his mouth, while he drew closer.

Judge Albert Sheppard was an extraordinary golf player, but also a courageous and stern man of law, reckoned for his black and white view of the world—there was right and there was wrong; the latter could not be the former; and the wrongs needed to be punished or corrected. Once he decided which was which, he disliked being contradicted, or argued with, as more than a lawyer had learned to his regret. The same he did in everything, from going to a restaurant and not being served exactly what he had in mind, to playing golf and having to argue about the score.

Frank disliked the man; however, he was another of those he had to hang around, not for pleasure, but for convenience. Just like Vince Lucci.

Hall had spotted the entrepreneur down at the Clubhouse. He

had been having a cup of coffee with Mrs. Helen Sanders, Maddox's public relations officer. Vince was the owner and manager of the Rainbow Glade in Northside, a classy gentlemen's nightclub catering to discriminating palates. Part strip-joint, part dance club, the Rainbow was not for everybody. You had to be a member to get in, and becoming one was not an easy affair. Vince was also suspected of being a Caporegime of the Gambino family of New York, taking care of their interests down in Miami. The Mafia considered that city a "free place", open to anyone who wants to make money. However, everyone must play by the rules, and rules were made by two families—the Gambino and the Genovese.

"Are you well, Frank?" Sheppard asked, suddenly shaking away Hall's thoughts.

They walked over the green, pacing to reach the last hole, and Albert noticed his pounding expression. Frank turned his head toward the judge and smiled faintly. "Huh? Oh, yes, I was just thinking about some stuff down at the office."

"Stop it immediately! You know the rules; what happens at the office stays at the office!"

Frank nodded, but could not avoid thinking about Fraser's disappearance.

"If you want to talk about your personal problems, you'll have to wait until we're back at the Clubhouse. Now ... it's playtime," Sheppard added with his jolliest voice.

"Yeah. Do not worry Albert. Besides, you already won, the game's over."

"Correct. However, the game is not over until I send that ball into the hole and you do the same with yours."

"Oh, no. I'm off. I don't see the point at doing that. I do not want to lower my score even more. I quit."

The judge halted his pacing and turned toward him, hands at his sides, with that odious stern face. "No way, Frank. We are going to end this. You can't quit..."

"Albert, I'm not in the mood for a lesson about rules right

now," he interrupted him.

Sheppard's face turned even more stone like. "This must be serious! You never quit before. Anyway, just let me finish my game."

"Of course, Albert."

Where the fuck are you, Jay?

****

Later, the two men sat at the Clubhouse, enjoying a light meal of canapés, fruits, and cheese, bathed by freshly squeezed orange juice and hot coffee. The sky was turning into a gray hue and a new storm threatened to hit the town. Frank sipped some orange juice, while keeping an eye on Vince Lucci, who sat on the balcony perching over the swimming pool, still in Helen Sanders' company.

Vince was the man who supplied Phencyclidine and Amphetamine to Hall. The deal was simple. Frank bought large quantities of pharmaceuticals from Lucci—they made their transactions right here at the Prosperity Field Golf Club—then, after the Mafioso received payment for the stuff, two of his goons shipped the meds by airboat, docking at a hidden pier in north Grassy Swamp, where Billy Gamble took care by sheltering the substances in his survivalist camp.

Jay Fraser's duty was to load some and carry it down to the chemistry lab, where Marvin Wilson cooked Angel Dust (PCP) from Phencyclidine and Speed, Crystal, and Ice from Methamphetamine. Once they were made into pill or liquid form, Jay delivered the final product to Doyle. The warden paid for the stuff with money gained from the sale of narcotics to the Aryan Brotherhood members inside the PMCF. Finally, Jay paid Billy and Marvin their parts, took his own, and the rest went to Hall.

Lucci sold Phencyclidine as a powder, easily soluble in water, to Hall for eight thousand dollars per kilo. Doyle bought it by the gram for twenty bucks, then resold it at forty to the Aryans. Hall bought Methamphetamine at nine thousand per kilo, and once processed into pill form by Marvin, Doyle paid as much as three hundred per ounce, bagged it up into one-gram deals, and sold it at twenty-five bucks.

However, Lucci's main interests were prostitution and cocaine, though he did not deal them in Prosperity for motives of his own. He supplied wholesale *snow* only in the Brighton Seminole Reservation. Frank suspected the substances came direct from Maddox, it being the company involved in the manufacture of prescription medical drugs, although they also produced chemical fertilizers and pesticides. Vince was often seen going around with Helen Sanders, Maddox's PR in Prosperity Glades, a beautiful woman in her late thirties and a shark to deal with. Nonetheless, Hall had never stuck his nose into the matter; the lesser he knew, the better.

Things went smoothly for almost two years. Until Jay Fraser failed to deliver the last batch to Doyle. There were two possible explanations. Either he'd fled town with some of the stuff—a risky business, he would be marked by the rest of the Brotherhood as a traitor and his life would be worth less than a dime in a month—or he had been killed. Frank suspected the second one to be true.

"Do you think it's going to rain again?" Sheppard said, disturbing him from these thoughts.

"Sure. We got lucky this morning, but by the end of the day I'm expecting another shower," he answered back absently, his attention still drawn by the couple on the deck.

Vince was pouring some coffee for the brown-haired woman who had on a fashionable white suit, open at the front just enough to reveal the border of expensive lingerie. She smiled under her sunglasses, while scrutinizing the pleasant countryside of the club. Frank had to talk to the man, but he could not do it in the presence of that woman, and overall, that of Judge Sheppard. Then, he spotted movement on his left. An employee was coming straight for him—a Hispanic boy, who appeared to be sweating not just for the temperature, but also for the long walk he had endured to reach the Clubhouse. From the color of the uniform, Frank guessed he came from the Main Reception Office.

"Excuse me, Mr. Hall, may I disturb you?" the young man asked.

Frank looked back at him with a puzzled expression. "Yes. No problem. What's the matter?"

The Hispanic waiter straightened up, then took something out of his pocket—a small piece a paper with something written on it in cursive handwriting. "This is for you, sir. A man at the Reception told me to give it to you."

Hall tipped the boy and took the message.

"What's that?" Sheppard inquired.

Frank gave the message a quick glance, enough to be aware of it coming from someone he did not want to reveal to the judge. "Oh, nothing important, Albert. Just someone who owns me a favor. Do you mind if I leave for twenty minutes?"

Albert Sheppard stared at him with those terrible inquisitive eyes, which had sent more than a shiver to many who had been sentenced by him in the last twenty-five years. He did not have to say anything.

"Come on! I'll be back. This will not spoil your day off. Just twenty minutes," Hall said.

"Okay. However, do not be too late," the judge finally answered.

Yes. Ugly bastard of a pompous old fart, I'll be back so you can gloat over me about your great skills as a golf player!

"It will take a moment. Do not worry," he said.

Then, he went to the golf cart to meet Billy Gamble at the Club's reception. The message had said:

'We need to talk. Now!'

****

Billy tried to escape the heat of the day by sitting under the reception's large ceiling fan, and although he wore a green tank top and fatigue pants, he still sweated copiously. As soon as he spotted Frank Hall crossing the sliding glass doors, he rose to his feet, eager to make his report to the man. However, the executive ignored him and went straight for the bar. Gamble followed and took a seat on a stool next to him. At this hour of the morning the place was empty, in fact it usually opened for business only after 11.00 AM

"Good morning. I have some bad news for you," he started immediately, but Hall interrupted him with a raised hand, then glanced back and forth, to be sure no one was hanging around. Only when he was satisfied about their privacy did he turn his attention to Billy.

"Be fast, Gamble. I'm in the company of Judge Sheppard, and I do not want him to see you here," he said.

"Well ... I'm going to start with some really bad news. Tonight someone killed Wilson..."

"WHAT?"

Now Billy had the man's complete consideration.

"Yes. There's been action down at the lab. Firemen everywhere. The place has been torched to a crisp. We lost everything down there..."

Frank grabbed Gamble's tank top, his face a mask of rage. "What the fuck are you saying?"

Billy stared deeply into Hall's eyes, his gaze suggesting that the man release his clothes, which he did. "Calm down, okay? It's a mess down there. However, I have may have a lead."

"Tell me."

"Let's start with the facts. Firstly, I haven't found J.F.; but we aren't the only ones looking for the jerk."

"Who else?" Frank asked, glancing nervously toward the main room.

"The owner of the Roughhouse, Mark Scarlett, says he saw Jay the night before. The dick had some drinks with an unknown chick, then they went away together. I've checked the Lakeview Motel, because I thought they went there for the sweat business.

But, they did not take a room."

A crashing sound came from the main hall, causing Frank to jump from his seat. Someone had fumbled a glass over there.

"Scarlett also says that Dr. Hyde, the coroner's assistant, inquired about the man a couple of hours before. He said he had to meet Jay and a woman. Something about the identification of a corpse," continued Billy.

"And what happened to Marvin? An accident, an explosion?"

"No. He's dead, that's for sure, but details are still kept hidden by the sheriff. I'm sure it was not an accident. The place was intentionally burned down. But save this for later, let's focus on Hyde and the woman," stated Gamble.

"Okay. Go on."

"Scarlett reckons the woman is a country gal of some kind: very attractive, long black hair, pale skinned, dressed in black denim and cowboy boots. She hooked Jay right at the Roughhouse. They had some rounds of beer, then went away in her truck. No one has seen him again. Funny thing is that Dr. Hyde shows up at the Roughhouse the following night, saying he's looking for J.F. He also says the man had to introduce him to a girl ... a Miss Picket, he said, but the name could be bogus."

"Why is that dude looking for Jay? I don't think he knows Fraser," said Hall.

"This I do not know, but intend to find out. I just think Jay's been iced by the bitch and the doc knows something about it."

"Do you suspect she's a hitter?" Frank asked.

"Yes. A pro. And a damn good one, too. She was contracted by the Núñez guys to disrupt our business, I can feel it. I do not trust the Brownies; it's not the first time they break the rules. I've told you a zillion times, we must teach 'em to behave."

"What about Marvin? Do you think he was killed by the same woman?"

"It could be. I want to have a look at the place, but ain't easy. The pigs are watching it close – they have found the drugs. However, I have a better idea..." Billy trailed off.

169

"What? Do not do stupid things. I can't help you this time should you get into a jam."

"I intend to bring the dear doc at the Fort. Have a chat with him ... my way," Gamble said.

"Run the thing as smoothly as you can, Billy. We can't afford another mess. I've enough problems already. You know, with the place blown up, two men down, and a loss of God only knows how much stuff..."

"Yeah, I know. We have to find a new cook as soon as possible. But I've told you from the start the cabin idea was a wrong one. Next time, we cook directly at the Fort. The secret room is ready now," Billy interrupted.

"Forget about the chemist now. We have to clean up the mess and find out who fingered us. Do you think your survivalist friends are ready to step in?"

"Not yet. However, now that I think about it ... this could be the right occasion for a drill. You know what? I'm going to check their moxie with the pathologist," Billy said.

"Fine. You take care of this snooping doc. I'll look out for the bitch. Have some contacts I can use to find her."

Frank left his seat, straightened his back, and gave another peek to the reception hall, afraid he'd spot Sheppard right there.

"What about the Núñez? We have to do something about that."

Frank returned his eyes to Gamble. "No. Not now. Just take care of Dr. Hyde, find out everything he knows—if he works as an intermediary for someone else, why he was looking for this woman, etc. That's your assignment, Billy, nothing more. For now."

"What happens if the Mexicans are trying to intrude?" Billy asked.

"Do not worry. We are not alone in this. Bigger walls protect our backs. If they are stepping into our territory, we'll treat them like the roaches they are. We'll step on them. Now, lemme go."

Frank was about to leave the vacant bar when he changed his

mind, stopped in his tracks, and turned back to face Gamble. "Ah, one last thing, Billy. Do not go close to the shack. It is better to leave the place alone for now. Besides, I have a way or two to know what happened there. Understood?"

Billy rose from the stool. "Okay. I'll take care of Hyde tonight. Do not call me. I'll inform you when everything's over."

Hall proceeded to the reception, leaving Gamble alone in the bar. Frank had a couple of cards he could play to sort out the matter.

The first was Vince Lucci.

The second was James Lane.

He knew the Vice Sheriff was on Fraser's payroll, closing an eye on Jay's traffics in town. Lane was a small-minded and petty man who had joined the sheriff's office in 2001, transferring from West Palm Beach Police Department. He saw Prosperity Glades as a place to make a name for himself. However, ten years taking orders, from Sheriff Ford first and Andrews later, had started to chafe on him. Now he felt his life was wasting away. Despite all the good work he had done for the small community he had not gained enough support to win an election, or even try to run for it. The man had become disillusioned and spiteful toward Prosperity. Frank had discovered that James had intercepted Jay Fraser's car while he was doing one of his first errands to deliver drugs to Warden Doyle. Fraser had made an offer to cut him into his operation—all he had to do was to let him go. He did even more. He informed Fraser about the patrol movements in the area, warned him about the wrong nights to make deliveries, and generally covered all tracks. Hall had not wanted the cop to know he was into this business, but now things had changed. There was an investigation ongoing down at the shack and he was sure as hell that Lane was trying to contact Fraser.

Well, maybe the time had come for Frank to reveal himself to Lane.

CHAPTER 23

THE SCENT OF DEATH

It had been a wonderful trip, before Prosperity Glades. They had left Miami for the Everglades in a *'Funtastical Road Adventure'*—that was the appellative Derek Bigelow had used to convince his family of this vacation plan—seven days before. Final destination: the Brighton Seminole Indian Reservation. Once there, they would camp on the shores of Lake Okeechobee for another week, then back again to the big city. His family had not been so eager at the start. Karen, his wife, had been dreaming of something more exotic, like a cruise to the Antilles or a trip to Mexico. But at last, she'd agreed with him, after he had explained how a camping trip would allow them to stay closer, to show the kids they were still a family.

Derek and Karen had been through some difficulties in their relationship in the last six months, their once solid marriage was teetering on the verge of separation. However, lately, things had changed, for the better. Karen had become more understanding of his needs, of his desire for space. Like the weekly 'Pals Night' on Friday's nights when he, Dave and Lenny would go bar hopping without their spouses for an innocent, all-male, *'Funtastical'* booze time.

Life as an assistant bank manager wasn't easy. It kept him busy and gave him heavy headaches. He needed that wild release once in a while. However, after they had that stupid incident where Dave had crashed his Lincoln against a public mailbox, and they had spent the whole night in a police station, Karen started to harp about his irresponsibility and selfishness. He had promised it would not happen twice, but she had not changed her attitude, starting a war at home, which had lasted months with daily fights, until she finally realized she was going to lose him.

He was a good father and looked after the family, caring about their needs. She could not afford to let him go. So, things had settled down. Moreen, his sixteen years old daughter, was coming along only because she had no other choice. She had been complaining all over, about this and about that. Derek understood she was too old now for a happy camping vacation with family, but she was also too young for that darn journey to New York her best friend Janeesha—the one with the nice pair of oversized boobs and a slut attitude—had in mind.

Moreen pouted throughout the trip, but he was sure, once the real outdoor experience began, she would relax and enjoy the beauty of the wilds. Dwight had been tamer. He was fourteen, also a difficult client, but Derek had allowed him to bring along his best friend, Justin. Derek did not like the boy much, too uncouth and coming from a family of hippie-like dorks. Nonetheless, this was a small sacrifice for two weeks of unspoiled refuge. Justin Wythe, also fourteen, was one of those kids who liked to act as an adult and was a bad influence on his son. Derek suspected he also smoked pot. However, he had behaved, been collaborative and soft-spoken, to Derek's surprise.

Troubles had emerged from unsuspected waters.

Worf, their six-year-old golden retriever, usually calm and obedient, had revealed a darker side from the moment they entered Prosperity Glades' city limits. The dog had been respectful all through the ride, ignoring raccoons, squirrels, and wildlife in general. He had stopped barking when ordered to do so, had compliantly waited out of shopping premises without making a scene.

But this morning he was getting on Derek's nerves. The dog bayed at every shadow and nervously paced back and forth in the rear of the station wagon. Derek had shouted for it to shut up a zillion times by now, to no avail. Moreen tried to calm it down by stroking and whispering inside its ears those mysterious sweet words she used to soothe. Even that worked for a minute or two, then the beast resumed growling in a low key, sending shivers up Derek's spine. He feared the retriever had caught some kind of illness in the swamp.

Bad news for a *'Funtastical Road Adventure'*.

At last, Derek decided to make a stop to have the dog—and his family—get out of the car, hoping that the pet would tire a little by playing with the kids. This unexpected pause would cost him a delay on his well-planned schedule; however he would recover the wasted time by skipping the visit to the Osceola Mall. He spotted a nice picnic area near a bend on the lakeshore, drove the station wagon down there, and finally parked it near a large bush.

"Ok, family, time to stretch our legs," he proclaimed, while killing the engine.

Karen stared at him with a quizzing look. It was obvious he had surprised her; she knew how rigorous he was about his time plan.

"Can I allow Worf to get down, Dad?" Moreen asked, not pouting any more.

"Yes. This is exactly why we are having this surprise break. Have him walk a little while your mom and I check the itinerary on the road map," answered Derek.

"Did we get lost?" Dwight asked in a sarcastic tone.

"No, Dwight, we did not. Your father is right. Worf is too excited. Maybe he needs to relax a little, as you know he's not used to long trips in the car," intruded Karen. Was there a note of mockery in his wife's voice?

Moreen opened the rear door, leash in hand, to allow the animal to get out. However, the dog was faster. It jumped out of the opening, dodged the girl, and ran straight toward the waters, barking and growling at imaginary dangers.

"Moreen! Get him!" Derek shouted.

The last thing he wished for was being charged by some country cop for ignoring local animal laws.

What a day!

The girl sprinted after the retriever, complaining about her precious sneakers getting muddied in that marshy terrain. But then she froze in her tracks. The dog was no longer running; it had stopped close to the waterline, its head low to the ground, baring its teeth and snarling at something.

Oh my God! He's messing with a gator!

Then, he realized the animal was not growling at something in the water, but at something in the air, just above a mound of packed sand and mud.

The dog has gone nuts!

****

Karen Bigelow hated her husband. He was so full of himself, so secure in his little world made of certainties and order. A control freak. And an asshole, too. There was a time when she had loved that man, when she appreciated his tidy and neat world. However, that was a long time ago. Now, he was just boring, punctilious, obsessive, and compulsive. He had to spread his control over everything, including his family. The camping gear must be checked at least three times before departure— sleeping bags, tents, barbecue, and two coolers for fresh food, neatly arranged in the perfect Derek's Way. Fishing tackle, flashlights, camera, and sunscreen. A lot of sunscreen.

Growing up in the Girl Scouts had been helpful, and funny, but it had done nothing to prepare Karen for any eventuality in married life. Especially life as a banker's housewife. Derek was Assistant Manager, but he acted as if he was the bank manager himself. He took responsibilities for things he had no need to. The same in family life. He had to manage the whole lot. Moreen had to be watched closely; she was sixteen now, the right age to get an unwanted pregnancy. Dwight had to be checked for drugs. Even the dog had to be squared in Derek's Way. And now this trip.

She had told him how much she liked the idea of a chartered cruise—the right way to relax, after a year spent looking after the children, managing the household, preparing food, cleaning their clothes, and doing all those dull things. But no, he had insisted on the camping trip. That *'Funtastic Road Adventure'* he was planning, all by himself, for sure, for more than three months.

The bastard!

However, she got tired of fighting and she had complied. He'd won—although it was a pyrrhic victory. Karen had been having an affair with her younger neighbor for four months by now. At the start it had just been a sexual diversion, a way to punish her neat, tidy husband. With time, it had become something bigger. She had fallen in love with Hugh. Hugh King was a gym instructor, single, with a charming smile and a roguish attitude. Messy, unpredictable, and wild, he had brought a spot of chaos inside Karen's ordinate life.

And she loved it.

What had begun as an illicit tryst had slowly gained strength, growing to be a sincere passion between the two. Hugh was tired of the situation. He had told her a dozen times to leave her husband, but Karen was not ready—not for Derek, but for her children. It's a dangerous world out there, and if you don't look after the children, no one else will. Especially Derek. He might be a control freak, but he was also a jerk. She figured that once his perfectly ordered world had been shattered by separation, he would turn into some kind of larvae, something she knew was hidden inside that 'I-can-manage' shell. Without her, Moreen would slip away, her natural rebelliousness twisting into something darker or self-destructive. And, Dwight would become a bully and a petty thief. She had already surprised him stealing once. She had kept it secret from Derek, and Dwight had promised it would not happen again.

Derek couldn't stand that Justin Wythe, but he did not know the boy was having the right influence on their son, keeping him away from drugs and other dangerous things. Derek and his 'Perfectlicious World'. He knew nothing. Even his dog was going against him today.

Worf had been the best of dogs for much of his life. Obedient, respectful, submissive. The name he wore was a joke. Dwight had insisted on calling the puppy after a character from *Star Trek: The*

Next Generation, a *Klingon*. However, the dog had grown up nothing like an aggressive alien warrior; but rather, a docile, playful pal. Derek was so proud of having well trained the beast, but he ignored that the real master was Moreen. Worf respected the girl the most in the family.

Unfortunately not today.

The retriever kept baying like a maddened Chihuahua from the time they had entered that small rural town, and things had gotten worse when they came closer to the lake. Karen was afraid the beast had contracted something in the Everglades. She was wondering about this when Derek ran straight into the recreational area and stopped the car near a large orchid bush.

"Ok, family, time to stretch our legs," he'd proclaimed while switching off the engine.

What was he doing? Was he getting mad, too? When Derek had a schedule in mind, nothing, except maybe a natural disaster, would stray him away. He glanced at her with that stupid half-smile.

"Can I allow Worf to get down, Dad?" Moreen asked.

"Yes. This is the just why we are having this surprise break. Have him walk a little while your mom and I check the itinerary on the road map," answered the dork.

Check what? What is he talking about? He never allowed her to check anything, He was the absolute master of the family, he alone could steer the destiny of their station wagon.

"Did we get lost?" Dwight blurted out suddenly.

"No, Dwight, we did not. Your father is right. Worf is too excited. Maybe he needs to relax a little, as you know he's not used to long trips in the car," she said, regretting her sarcastic tone. She had told him that Worf could not be relied on to stay locked in for hours inside their fully packed car without whining, that the most logical choice was to let Hugh King, their 'handy' neighbor to take care of him, as the man had so willingly offered himself. In truth, it had been Karen's idea. After three days, he would call the Bigelows to tell them that the dog was whining and barking all day and he had received some complaints from neighbors, thus ending that pathetic camping trip.

But no. Derek had insisted on bringing the dog along. This was his *'Funtastic Road Adventure'*, carefully planned for the Bigelow Family's delight, dog included.

However, Worf had other plans of its own. Karen noticed the dog dodge her daughter and run past her toward the waterline, but said nothing. She just smiled to herself, happy to watch Derek's face as the beast slipped away from his neatly controlled world.

"Moreen! Get him!" Derek shouted.

His fucking Perfectlicious World was shattered to pieces by a maddened dog, which kept snarling at thin air.

And she loved it.

****

Moreen Bigelow was on the verge of gagging. It wasn't enough to be forced to go on a camping trip with the family, and Dwight's sticky friend. No. The dog had to crack, too. Worf had embarked on that behavior from the morning. It was clear something was going astray around here. Maybe, those stories about strange chemicals in the water were true. Or this place was haunted by one of those legendary 'Skunk Apes' she had heard about. The name referred to some creatures supposed to hide back in the darkest parts of the swamps, only rarely sneaking out of the marshes to prey on folks. Skunk apes were supposed to be large, shaggy, manlike creatures standing almost eight feet tall. They exuded a stench unlike any living creature, smelling like a combination of a compost pile and rotting cabbage, hence the name. Some said it was a relative of Bigfoot. Her imagination worked overtime. Worf could also be anxious because he felt something was wrong with the people there. What if they were weirdos—and one must be a weirdo to go and live in such a place—who fed on lost tourists, like those mutant guys of the hills she had seen in that scary movie?

Well, that was a bit over the top, but some faces around here—like that creep down at the Lakeview Motel—seemed to come out of a horror flick.

What's the frigging place's name? Prosperity Glades.

Yeah, there was nothing prosperous around here, just the mosquitoes that bit constantly at her legs, neck, and shoulders. How much she hated this dump!

She was supposed to be in New York right now, enjoying the sights and nightlife of the Big Apple with her best friend Janeesha. Oh, great! Who wants to go camping today? Kids, geeks, and old people. That was the right answer. And she was none of the above. Being the most popular girl in school, she deserved a way cooler vacation, not this pitiful mockery of a happy family trip.

Come on.

She knew things weren't so idyllic between Mom and Dad. Dad was a good father, but also a pain in the ass as a husband. So plain boring! Her mother was going to leave him, now or then. She felt sorry for her dad; however, she also understood her mother's plight. If things kept going on that way, she could really freak out and leave him, like Janeesha's mom had done one year before. Moreen had glimpsed her mom's gaze linger too long on Hugh King, the neighbor. That guy was one of the hottest guys in the whole 'hood. Moreen had secretly watched him performing gymnastics in his room. Her window faced Hugh's own. Unfortunately, she had also witnessed another kind of performance he'd had with a woman. She felt shocked, at first, replaced by embarrassment, and then, she felt unable to get her eyes off the scene. Obviously, she had never told anybody what she had seen. Besides, that was none of her business.

So, were Mom and Dad destined to split up?

Janeesha's were divorced and that had been a boon to her teen life. Her parents were locked in a contest on who was going to spoil her better. On the bad side, there was the fact Janeesha had to spend some time with one parent and some with the other, which forced her to live like a nomad.

Moreen sent away those thoughts while trying her trick to soothe Worf's conduct by whispering sweet words into his ear. The magic lasted two minutes, no more. Once they got closer to the lake, the beast began to bay again, aggressively pointing toward the dense aquatic vegetation, as though he sensed something off beam hiding over there.

Moreen shifted on her seat when one of her dad's fishing rods dislodged from the neatly packed gear behind her, stinging her left side. In doing so, she caught 'Justin Geek', as she called him, peek at her boobs again and cringed in disgust. She blatantly rolled her eyes, forcing him to shift his gaze away, blushing like a kiddo. Suddenly, her dad changed direction, driving the car toward some kind of rest area, or something like that.

"Okay, family, time to stretch our legs," he said, killing the engine.

Fantastic! Nice choice to have her new sneakers stained with filthy mud. However, it was also better than standing inside that cheerleader's trap with a fourteen-year-old jerk drooling at her tits.

"Can I allow Worf to get down, Dad?" she asked, watching Justin warily.

Try another peek, you dirty worm, and I'll feed your balls to the gators.

"Yes. This is just why we are having this surprise break. Have him walk a little while your mom and I check the itinerary on the road map," Dad said.

Itinerary? What itinerary? There was only one straight way to reach that damn Indian reservation.

"Did we get lost?" her brother asked.

"No, Dwight, we did not. Your father is right. Worf is too excited. Maybe he needs to relax a little, as you know he's not used to long trips in the car," answered her mom, causing Moreen to get immediately out of the car. She had perceived her sarcastic tone; a fight loomed between Mom and Dad, and she wanted to stay clear of that. She reached for the leash, went around the station wagon and opened the rear door. Worf jumped out of it like he had seen the Devil, rushing toward the waterline.

What the heck! Great! Now she had to get closer to the water.

"Moreen! Get him!" her daddy shouted.

"Damn! My shoes will be full of mud! I hate mud. You're going to pay for this, stupid dog!"

Pouting, she sprinted after the retriever, avoiding the wetter terrain, and and stood firmly on the drier parts of the recreational area. She sidestepped a large orchid bush and spotted the dog still running toward a mound of packed sand, or mud, until it halted its crazy run at less than a yard from the knoll, its head low to the ground, its teeth bared at some invisible thing in the air.

A shiver of fear ran along her spine. Something was clearly wrong here. Worf was not crazy, she knew it. He perceived a danger. Suddenly, the animal jumped in the air, as though trying to bite an unseen enemy, then landed on the mound, shook off some sand from its fur and turned its head toward Moreen, no longer growling. Whatever had been over there had fled the place. Bushy tail waving happily, Worf was now much more interested in the mound, with its long snout pushed into the ground, while pawing away some muck and sniffing the soil again.

"Here, Worf! Leave that stuff in peace, please..." Moreen muttered, still shocked by the previous events. Then, the dog began to dig with its front paws, frenetically trying to reach whatever had caught its interest belowground.

It found it. And when Moreen Bigelow saw what the retriever had unearthed, she screamed.

And gagged, too.

****

Humans can't sense everything. Worf had perceived the strong Essence of the place from the moment their station wagon had come into that site. There were aplenty of those things from the Beyond here, all over the area, floating around humans, items, houses, plants, and mostly above the waters. They came from a

181

hole, somewhere in the swamp, in the same way fleas were attracted by his blood. Fleas they were, of a different breed.

Worf knew he was smarter and faster than the humans he helped out. He could hear everything, everywhere. They could not. And he'd been trying to warn them since this morning, telling them in the only way he knew how that this was not a good spot to be. The adult male (they called it Dad, mostly) had been yelling at him to quiet down, but he could not.

Many of those things were harmless, tiny as motes, not a threat to the Family. However, some were bigger, like that one he had spotted hovering above a woman in that clearing full of mobile homes—the one that kept prodding her with its long shadowy appendages, for unknown reasons. It was not the first time Worf had seen one of its kind; he had glimpsed some in the big city, especially lingering near people who reeked of desperation and hopelessness. He had witnessed one of those things plunge itself inside one man, possessing him like a mad puppeteer. Once inside, it had forced him to walk in front of Mr. King's home, the human who lived in the house close to Worf's own, the same man who was very caring with 'Honey'—that was the name of the adult female of his family. The Shadow-Flea had used the tramp's body to wait and stare. Just stare at King's house. To be precise, the thing had used the body's eyes to gape at the house's front window. It had stood there for almost three hours, unmoving, his head inclined on a side. Then, the Shadow-thing had left him, returning to whatever place it had come from, leaving the poor host wondering why he had popped up there.

The thing had done this for five nights in a row, until Mr. King—or 'Do Me!' (That was the other name Worf had heard Honey call him when paying a visit)—had summoned the Pack. The Pack were humans who were called on by Families to be protected by threats. Dad called it 'Police'.

When two members of the Pack had come to take the tramp away, the Shadow-Flea had left its host, and had leaped inside one of them, causing him to continue its strange vigil. The other Pack member had tried to shake him out of that weird behavior; however, he gained only tiny responses from his partner, until he had slapped him on the face, causing the parasite to flee the host.

Back then, Worf had not growled to the thing; he was too curious. He had been studying the being. Besides, the Pack had not solved the problem. Worf had noticed that those creatures were prolific. Two weeks ago, nobody became aware of three weirdoes who had come to stare at King's home in the darkest hours of night...

Then, there were the Mockers. These shadow-beings appeared similar to those of Worf's species, but they would never beguile a smart dog. They looked like strays, pawing their way among refuse and mimicking 'real' dogs in every way. However, they were not dogs. Mockers were untrusting, and would most often flee when first encountered. If they felt cornered, or if their food supply was endangered, they would attack with a blind fury, causing some of the bad stories about stray dogs to circulate among humans.

Worf had seen many other types of Shadow-Creatures; however, they were usually harmless, less dangerous than a mouse. Here, in this marshy and green place full of weird odors and strange plants, there were zillions of them. Swarming around like a school of fishes, sticking from the ground like moles, slithering and coiling around people as snakes.

Worf had to warn his Family. There was no other way. He knew they could not see the creatures, but he could keep them at bay with his growls. One of the slithering things had tried to get into the car, eyeing 'Dwight', the younger male of the Family. It was an amorphous being, bristling with steel-like needles attached to syringe-looking growths filled with strange, dark fluids. Worf had been faster, with his barking and snarling to let it know how big and powerful he was.

This had gained him another rebuke from Dad, though it had achieved the desired effect on the thing, which had backed off from the boy. Things had gone better later, until they came close to the water. There, Worf had spotted something bigger, different,

183

and smarter. It floated just above the waterline, some kind of nebulous being, sporting two humanlike eyes. And those cruel eyes had stared back at him.

Worf had never been scared by the Shadow-Fleas, yet this one sent a shiver down his spine, and he had reacted, like all dogs do when threatened, by barking back at the menace. The Shadow-thing had ignored him, turning its eyes toward Moreen—his Alpha Female, the real leader of the Family, even if Dad thought he was—perceiving the affection Worf had for her. This had enraged the dog even more, increasing the fear that the thing was targeting his beloved mate. So he yowled and growled and did all he could to tip off the Family about the peril. Nevertheless, they had acted in reverse by halting the car and letting Moreen get closer to the thing.

"Okay, family, time to stretch our legs," Dad had said.

"Can I allow Worf to get down, Dad?"

That came from Moreen. Worf had grasped only his name, so he had turned with hope toward her.

"Yes. This is the just why we are having this surprise break. Have him walk a little while your mom and I check the itinerary on the road map," Dad had said.

Meanwhile the big thing had disappeared behind some large bushes, yet Worf could still feel its unseen presence. The Family was bickering among themselves about being lost or something, yet Worf was too focused on detecting the Shadow-Thing to pay attention to what they were saying.

It was still out there ... threatening Moreen. When the girl got out of the car, Worf's heart faltered. He had to act fast; he had to protect her. Worf avoided her gentle hands, dodged her clutches, and ran straight to the spot where he sensed the creature was.

Splashing in the mud and jumping from wet to dry ground, he zipped around a large orchid bush and sniffed the air. He inhaled it then—the smell of death. Something was rotting here. Worf raised his canine eyes and saw the big shadowy thing feeding on a series of worm-like beings, which were floating above a mound. The cloud-like being ignored him then left the place on its own accord, continuing its alien errand.

Worf relaxed when he saw the creature leaving, no longer a threat. However, some of the worm-like creatures still hovered above the mound feeding from the essence of decay coming from the rotting thing below the earth. Suddenly, he jumped in the air, trying to bite and scare off the things, which behaved like pigeons, scampering around and taking refuge in the waters. Then he landed on the mound, shaking off the sand from his fur and turning the head toward Moreen when he heard her coming.

"Here, Worf! Leave that stuff in peace, please..." said Moreen.

Worf happily waved his bushy tail as he focused on the mound and forgot about the Big Shadow Thing. He played about and sniffed the soil. Then, he began to dig and finally found the rotting thing. Swollen with pride, the golden retriever locked his jaws on the dead thing and unearthed parts of it, and then turned toward his human master expecting her to cuddle and pet him. However, the girl reacted in an unexpected way. She saw the charred human hand Worf was holding in his jaws and screamed in horror before running back to her family. The disappointed dog watched the girl run away, his head tilted to one side.

Afterward, he decided to unearth the whole body.

CHAPTER 24

DRIFTER GIRL

Frank Hall's BMW paraded the length of construction site, drawing stares from the workers at its elegant European design as they sniffed the smell of money and power it radiated.

Supervisor Carling rushed to the car. Mr. Hall rarely paid a visit to the lot, usually having Mrs. Thompson, his trusted icicle-like secretary, to deal with the hands. Having Mr. Hall himself inspecting the works rang a dead bell inside Carling's head. He noticed the man speaking into his cell phone, while Fisher, the chauffeur, carefully maneuvered among large dunes of slaked lime and concrete. Once the automobile braked to a halt, Paul Carling dashed to open at once the rear door, allowing Hall to dismount the vehicle.

"Good evening Mr. Hall," he said reverently.

Frank carried on with his conversation, merely waving a gesture of acknowledgment with his free hand, while striding direct to the manager's office. Paul followed him like a stray dog, only passing him to unlock the door and switch the lights on. Frank Hall snapped closed the cell, glanced distantly at the simple décor of the workplace, and adjusted his position on the visitor's chair in front of the manager's desk.

"Carling, I have a request for you," he started.

"Of course, sir. How can I help you?" Paul asked, seriously worried about his future. Frank Hall was reckoned as a demanding man, easily annoyed and bad tempered. Coming from the town's most prominent family, he had been raised to be a ruler among his peers.

"Just relax. I need some information concerning recently hired hands," he continued.

"Oh ... well, I mean ... yes, sir. I'm at your complete disposal on the subject. Is there any problem with the temps?" Carling asked.

"No. I just need to know if you freshly hired some drifter. Not a local, someone from out of town. I'm looking for a woman in particular."

"A woman? There ain't a lot of gals in this field of work, sir. In fact, we just hired one. An excellent worker, a master in carpentry, tell you. I was surprised when——"

Hall raised a hand to cut short his praises. "Hush, now! You're saying we do have a woman working here. Maybe she's the one I'm looking for. Can you tell me more about her?"

Paul Carling eyed him with suspicion. Hall had almost ruined his whole life years ago for chasing skirts. His wife had left him after that scandal regarding his frequentation of some prostitutes in Clewiston, he'd had to resign from the position of mayor for the same motives, and rumors of mobbing and sexual harassment on female staff at the Osceola Mall were often heard in town.

"Well, sir. Her name's Cheri Ridge. She comes from up north, I think. She's half Indian or something. Very good with her hands and a nimble climber, too. Showed up a week ago, looking for employment. Put her on test and found out she wasn't a joke. The girl is the real McCoy, no-nonsense, a silent and hard worker. I pay her daily..."

Again, Hall raised his hand. "Black-haired? Blue eyes and fair-skinned? Dresses like a cowgirl?"

Carling mused why the man was so curious about Ridge, to the point of acting like a damn detective out of a mystery novel. Something was fishy here. Hall seemed to know the girl, the description perfectly fitting Cheri. Still, Paul detected something sinister about the man's inquiries. He couldn't tell why, but he did not like it.

"No. I mean, she's got chocolate brown hair, and I do not think Ridge has blue eyes. They seem darker in hue to me. And, on her way of dress ... no, she's into baggy stuff. Far from being a country starlet, looks much more like a tomboy to me," said Carling.

Hall eyed him, sending tremors down his spine. "Are you sure, Carling?"

"Yes. She's a good worker, nothing more. About the eyes, I'm not sure. I do not spend my time staring at workers' faces," Paul answered defiantly, regretting it a second later.

Hall rose from the chair and went for the water cooler, poured some into a plastic cup, and quenched his thirst in the humid afternoon, made even more insupportable by the office's enclosed space.

"May I ask you why you are looking for this woman, sir?" Carling queried.

Hall ignored the question, finished his drink and turned his eyes again on the supervisor. "Do you know where this Ridge lives? I have to talk to this woman," he said.

"She rented a trailer down in South Glade, which one I cannot say. I never ask for such details from temporary hired hands. However, you can meet her here tomorrow morning. This is her day off, so she's not coming. Always on time. Pops up at six in the morning and goes away at three. Whatever she does after work, I do not know, and do not care."

"Okay. You were very helpful, Carling. Do not worry, it's nothing serious. It is possible this girl is a person I already met in Georgia. Listen, keep her working here if as you say she is very skilled. Yet, do not tell anyone I came looking for her. Is that clear?"

"Clear as water, sir."

"Good. It is of the utmost importance the girl doesn't feel hunted or threatened, since I intend no harm to her. This Cheri Ridge could be the daughter of one of my dearest friends. She messed with her family in Atlanta. Her father is still looking for her. So, please do not unnerve her."

An alarm sounded outside, signaling the end of the day's work.

"All right, sir. Do not worry," Paul said, thinking he was going to do the reverse. He liked the woman, and those stories about Hall gave him the creeps.

Frank threw the plastic cup into the gaping mouth of the garbage can, went for the door, and waved a hand without turning.

Once the boss was out of his office, Paul Carling loosened up on his chair, relief flooding him. He did not like that story. Besides, he knew Hall was lying. Cheri Ridge came from Tennessee, not Georgia, as Hall had stated. That phony yarn he had spun, about the young woman being the daughter of a friend of his, was the confirmation of his doubts.

Hall had some bad aims with Ridge, he could feel it, and he wasn't going to allow this.

Too bad he didn't know it was already too late.

CHAPTER 25

SPIRITS AND THOUGHT FORMS
(FROM AXEL'S HALL OF MEMORIES)

I woke up at noon. That night I had difficulties falling asleep as my mind fixated on that glimpsed image—the pale-faced woman. I had never seen her before, yet she looked familiar to me, in some weird way. She was the one who had killed Jay Fraser, the one who had tortured and butchered this Marvin Wilson; the one who was still out there. I was sure about that. She was hunting for more blood, on a personal revenge quest against a group of people who had somehow wronged her.

The last time the Rider had allowed me to see the face of a monster had been three years ago, when I stumbled upon one of the victims of the 'Face-Stealer', a.k.a. Lewis Perreira. Oh, nobody called him that way. That's why nobody ever suspected he was a serial killer.

To be more precise, nobody knew there was a serial killer hunting prostitutes in Prosperity County because I stopped him before his deeds hit the media.

****

I'm fond of kayaking around the marshy areas of the great lake, paddling along Okeechobee' shores, and penetrating its nooks and crannies, especially in northern Grassy Swamp, where I looked out for discarded stuff. I have a curious bend, I must admit.

Grassy Swamp proper is a vast, treacherous area, located around the Murchison River's delta. Made infamous by numerous accidents, which happened in its mires, the place has gained a 'cursed' reputation by the locals, who avoid it at all costs. It is also a gator's spawning ground. They can be seen lazily basking in the sun on wetland tree islands. Tree islands are small forests of trees and shrubs that have adapted to a wet environment. They provide an important home to the many mammals that live in the Everglades and are a site for wading and migratory bird rookeries. Tree islands generally are named after the trees that dominate them, with the most common being the bay, willow and cypress. The swamp is divided into numerous spots, some of these, having a story of their own. Like 'Suicide Point'.

According to local gossip, Prosperity's most desperate came to this spot over the years looking to end their lives. Most of the deaths had been ruled suicides, however, it seemed hardly so to me. Some of the victims were also impromptu treasure hunters, looking for rings, watches, or other valuables the suicides might have thrown in first. The town's oldsters told that the souls of these desperate people, being barred from entering Heaven because they sinned against the Lord by killing themselves, still haunt the place. They hold these robbers under the water for violating their unholy ground.

What I found back there in 2008 was not a specter's victim. It was the faceless body of a murdered woman, her skull skinned to the bone, like one of *Leatherface's* victims out of '*Texas Chainsaw Massacre*'.

She had been stuffed inside a large canister, one of those used by gas attendants and car repairers to store motor oils. Only, she had not been immersed into that stuff. The woman had been soaked in bleach; her skin, hair, and eyes appearing completely white. Naturally, I was tempted to call on the rangers or the sheriff; however, my Rider had ideas of its own.

It showed me the murderer's face, standing smiling under a neon sign that spelled, '*Wild Wild Wild*'.

I knew the place. It was a private gentlemen's club on the outskirts of Waynesford, a small community north of Prosperity, notorious for its ample choice of strip clubs, pleasure houses, and other sex-related venues. My uncle Angus had been a frequent customer of those places, before I put an end, once for all, to his disagreeable leisure.

Suffice it to say that I became interested in the guy. I started to actively hunt him down, gathering enough evidence to justify him ending on my Rider's list.

Later, after disposing of his body, I found five more canisters; each one holding a bleached and faceless surprise, like macabre Easter eggs. Another one, the freshest of the lot, I had found inside his garage.

Lewis Perreira was a mechanic, owner and manager of a large garage in Waynesford, with a passion for peeling off faces from hookers. A 'Hedonistic Lust Serial Killer'; that's how the FBI would classify him. Hedonistic lust killers are probably the grossest and most gruesome of all kinds of serial killers. Not all of them want to necessarily hurt or kill you; they simply want to wear your skin (like Ed Gein) or eat your heart or have sex with your severed head. It's just that your life gets in the way. Lust murderers often have an ideal victim type in mind with fetishistic elements, type of footwear or clothing worn, color or style of hair, body shape (a 'cheerleader type' or a 'slutty type'), and so on.

Perreira's were prostitutes.

Lust killers often need intimate skin-to-skin contact in their killing, and use a knife or strangulation to murder. Perreira lured his prey inside the garage, subsequently under the pretext of bondage games, strapped the unwary woman with duct tape, then strangled her with a chain. Necrophilia is a frequent aspect of lust killer homicides. In fact, Perreira felt the need to have sex only after his victim was dead. However, it was not that simple. He needed to bleach them out; only after they were white as chalk did he have sex with them. To attain this, he placed the victims inside some large oil canisters, filled them with bleach, and had them soak in the substance for a night. Afterward, he allowed himself to appease his sexual cravings.

Edmund Kemper, the 'Coed Killer' of California, who murdered ten victims and had sex with their corpses and various mutilated body parts, explained that the actual killing of his victims had little to do with his fantasies.

"I'm sorry to sound so cold about this," he said, "but what I needed to have was a particular experience with a person, and to possess them in the way I wanted to: I had to evict them from their human bodies."

Lust killers are often aware that their victim of choice is visible to police and may choose to travel to various jurisdictions in both their hunt for and disposal of victims.

That was not the case with Perreira.

He kept them with him for some time, then when he felt like his 'passion' had died off, he consigned the canister to the swamp, but not before removing the skin from their faces, a memento in eternal memory of his 'old flame'. He had nine such trophies inside a special box in his garage.

If someone would ask me why he did those awful things, I could not explain. I was not a detective, I did not look inside his head as a psychiatrist does, and I never searched for an explanation, something about his infancy or past traumas.

No. I accepted the facts. He was a monster. Just like me.

Maybe, he had an urging Rider, too. Maybe he had simply been plain crazy. It doesn't matter anymore. His hacked off body parts now rest inside one of those oil canisters in Grassy Swamp.

Until now, no one has ever found those canisters.

****

After my encounter with the Face-Stealer, the Rider had stopped. No more images, hints, fleeting ghostly sensations. Nothing.

My next victims—Tony Torrecone (a Mafia enforcer with a passion for rape), Pedro Valdemar (Drug dealer and a pedophile), Mariano Valente (another rapist), and the late Richard Solomon (the stalker)—I had found with some legwork and by illegal inquiries. Yet, the creature had deemed this 'Avenging Angel' as worthy of its needs. There was something special about her, something it craved. After so many years living with this invisible thing inside me, I still could not understand it.

Oh, I had done my research on the subject.

From Voodoo's Loa to certain Malaysian Spirits of Death, from Native American Spirits of the Other Side to the Kami of Japan— so far, I had not found a proper description for the being.

At the center of voodoo is the concept of the Loa. Linguistically speaking, Loa is a Congolese word meaning 'spirit.' During a voodoo ceremony, one, several, or many of the celebrants present become possessed by a Loa. The person so possessed is referred to as the 'cheval' or 'horse' of the Loa, and the possession, as being 'ridden' by it. Based on this, the Loa are sometimes referred to as 'the Horsemen'. While the horse is being ridden, he takes on the personality and characteristics of the Loa doing the riding. This transformation is independent of gender, age, and many other physical constraints. A young woman ridden by Legba, for example, would move and talk as an old, virtually crippled man, while an arthritic old man ridden by Ogoun would dance athletically and with abandon, seeming to be a young and energetic warrior. Therefore, it happens that, during possession, the Ridden often gains an incredible resistance to physical pain. There are many documented reports of possessed walking on hot coals and similar stunts, enduring the experience totally intact. Some Loa even grant special visions to their hosts.

However, I had never performed such a ceremony, and had never heard about voodoo practices until the age of sixteen.

More, the official creed declared that Loa rode their hosts only temporarily, never taking residence inside a single individual.

The concept of 'Spirits' is as old as man itself; the earliest human cultures believed in spirits, and that belief has lasted into the present. The first human cultures were animistic, seeing the power of spirit in everything around them. Invisible creatures were the cause of every mysterious phenomenon, from diseases and misfortune to the continuation of the natural cycles of the world, the movements of celestial bodies, the flow of rivers, the weather, and the migration of game animals.

Egyptian spirits were associated with either the celestial or the human realm, either powerful gods or human souls.

In addition to their extensive pantheon of anthropomorphic deities, the Greeks believed in many nature spirits. Many of these nature spirits were portrayed as feminine and highly desirable— dryads (spirits of trees), naiads (spirits of streams), and nereids (spirits of the ocean).

The Romans introduced the concept of the genius or 'guardian spirit', a spirit associated with a particular family or individual that provided guidance and assistance in exchange for veneration.

Ancient Hebrews believed in the existence of many different types of spirits, as their God told them, 'Thou shalt have no other gods before me'. Hosts of infinite angels served God and acted as agents and messengers of His will on Earth.

China's pagan religion was strongly animistic and devoted to understanding, communicating with, and pleasing a wide range of spirits, from powerful gods dwelling in heaven to spirits of the elements to beings like dragons, ghosts, and demons. Shamans known as 'Wu' acted as intermediaries between spirits and humanity. They offered sacrifices to propitiate the spirits and read omens to understand the spirits' intentions.

Shinto, the native Japanese religion, recognizes many different types of spirits, known as kami. Kami range in power from gods to minor spirits that oversee certain aspects of the material world, particularly natural formations.

Indian mythology includes ghosts, nature spirits, and demonic spirits like the rakshasa. Hindus believe in reincarnation, the perfection of the soul through a cycle of many different lives. Hindu tradition also describes avatars, that is, manifestations of divine spirits in the physical world.

Australian aboriginal tradition begins with the Dreamtime, the mythical time when heroes and spirits performed deeds of legend and the order of the world was laid down. Birth is seen as the incarnation of a Dreamtime spirit into the world, and that spirit is the person's totem throughout his life. Aboriginal shamans, known as karadji or mekigar, speak with the spirits to gain their aid for the tribe.

Like the Australian Koori, Africans often believe in a supreme creator that remains uninvolved in the affairs of the material world. Lesser spirits and gods carry out the high god's will. Mortals can communicate with the spirits through trance, and the spirits often communicate through possession, speaking through a mortal host.

Native American religious and spiritual beliefs vary from tribe to tribe, but there are some common elements. Nature spirits are the most common, particularly spirits of natural phenomena, animals, and totems. The spiritual world is often divided into three: an upper or sky world, a lower or underground world, and a middle world where humanity lives. A sacred tree unites these three worlds. Shamans travel up and down this cosmic axis to reach the spirit worlds and speak with the spirits living there.

The Celts created legends of faeries and related nature spirits. Originally, 'faeries' were referred to nature spirits and the Sidhe, figures somewhere between nature spirits and gods. They lived in a magical "otherworld" but could move and act in the physical world at will.

Early Muslims recognized many spirits, particularly angels serving Allah and the djinn, 'creatures of smokeless fire' created by Allah with the rest of the world. Muslim magicians believed spirits could be bound and commanded, particularly using the power of Solomon's Seal.

The Spiritualist movement of the late nineteenth century generated interest in spirits and established the modem séance ritual in popular culture. Mediums conducted rituals to contact the spirit world in parlors across Europe. While some scientists attempted to study the spiritualist movement, most considered it mere fakery and superstition. Today, vast numbers of Americans still believe in guardian angels.

Spirits can be divided in various categories; from 'Animating Forces', such as the Soul, to 'Higher Powers', such as Angels and Demons; from 'Guardians', such as Ancestor and Totem spirits, to

'Monsters', such as like Tolkien's Ring-Wraiths.

Spirits can be tied to Nature—such as the Animal Spirits of Native Americans, the Elementals of Ancient Greece, or the Kami of Japanese mythology. Alternatively, they can be Outsiders—such as the Angels, Demons, and Djinn.

However, I found most interesting the Tibetan concept of Thought Form.

The 'Tulpa' of Tibet is a 'Thought Form': an artificial spirit created by the power of the human mind. It can range in complexity from a simple emotional impression to a fully sentient and aware being, gaining nourishment from human belief.

Therefore, let's suppose that I created my Rider in the first place, in response to the threat of Russell Floyd, while I was at the most vulnerable, filled with panic and terror. It is logical to believe that I gave it substance and complexity, by feeding it with the same emotional resonance that sparked it to life. A simple conceptual mote turned into a monstrous self-aware being, able to ride me like a Loa, eternally bound like a summoned demon.

From Master to Servant.

Maybe, it found some of my victims tastier, somehow more nourishing than others. Maybe, some of them also hosted a similar being, not as developed and devious as mine, but interesting enough for it to feed upon.

These questions were crowding my mind while I mechanically prepared a hearty breakfast of scrambled eggs, sausages, and pancakes. Next, I spent some time surfing the web, checking the usual things—my Facebook account (still at 13 friends, no private messages, no requests…), e-mails (someone from Nigeria was asking for me to send him personal information, in order to share billions of dollars…), and a glance at the news. When I had enough of this stuff, it was time for me to get dressed up for work.

As always, I waved my hand to salute Charlie Woods, my diligent and hyperactive neighbor.

My, my, that man was always busy at something on his front lawn. Whether he was mowing the grounds or painting his low fence, he was always there. Some people seem to not have a life, they just keep going on and on, in an endless routine, broken only by the occasional twist of fate.

Suddenly, I realized that my own life of the last twenty years or more could be seen like that as well: wake up, get to work, return home, sleep.

Repeat cycle.

Except, I had an urge from time to time, some kind of need that completely absorbed my whole existence, turning me from the unsympathetic and lonely guy of the obituary, to a stealthy and remorseless night prowler. Yet, even those exciting moments began to feel phony, a surrogate of what real life must be. They were not mine, they belonged to the Rider.

Have you ever loved, Axel?

Did I?

No. I was unable to feel; feeling was something alien, something that everybody on Earth experienced, except me. Yet...

My mind rushed back to a precise memory of my past, a time before Kamp Koko and my unfortunate bond with this nameless thing using my body for its own dark purposes.

I had been happily running over a green hill, chasing something ... a butterfly, maybe. Yes, it was a large butterfly, and I was very young, my short legs barely able to hold a firm footing, staggering awkwardly left to right to keep pace with the colorful flying insect. I tumbled, tripping on my own foot; the impact had been so strong that my head reverberated when it hit the ground face first. I started to cry, more for the scare than for the pain. I was four ... three years old maybe, at the time.

And a voice, a sweet voice had called me, trying to calm me down, telling me that it was nothing, just a scratch. I raised my face, and there she was: my mother.

Yes, I had loved her. I loved my mom, like all the kids loved their own. I had not been different. I had feelings.

Have you lost them, Axel?

No! That was a lie! I had never lost my feelings; they had

subsided, pushed down into the deepest recesses of my being, isolated from the outside world, replaced by the egotistical needs of that unearthly creature.

It had betrayed me!

The Rider had offered me comfort and promised to send away the terror that was gripping me inside that dark half-submerged pipe. It had made a deal with me.

However, it had been a Devil's deal—it had removed the fear, but it also took away all my other emotions. It had twisted me into a parody of a human being, without purpose or wants.

But something was shifting inside me. I could no longer trust my Rider. The being had plans of its own, some of them I could even agree with, yet others…

This Avenging Angel, for example.

It needed her, was eager to feed on her flesh, so it urged me to find her as soon as possible by hammering the padded walls of my mind like a chained down lunatic in frenzy.

Yes, I would find the pale-faced avenger; nonetheless, I had no intention to kill her. Not this time.

No. Period.

I wished to talk with her, to try to understand what made her different from Richard Solomon and the others, and why was she so important that my Rider deigned to send a vision of her features like it had done for Face-Stealer and a few others.

I suspected all of them harbored something inside; a sibling or kindred of its species. If my Rider was a spirit made out of fright and hurt, the one inside Lewis Perreira had to have been similar, urging the man to torture, kill, and deface those hookers.

Maybe it craved those beings to grow, get more powerful in a cannibalistic way to increase its influence on me. Or who knew what.

All my doubts about the Rider were swept away the instant I entered the autopsy room. A surprise was waiting for me there, along with Abigail Zimmermann.

For on the main dissection slab rested Jay Fraser's charred

corpse.

They had found him!

CHAPTER 26

FALLING OUT OF EDEN

Somewhere, beyond a wall made of Reason and surrounded by a trench dug out of Ignorance, lies another world.

The Cherokee people called it 'The Other Side'; a world in itself, inhabited by spirits and the souls of the departed. They stated there was no clear demarcation between that world and our own, the world of 'This Side'.

A strong connection links these worlds, both unable to exist without the other, yet they must stay separate lest the natural order would fall into chaos, undoing what has been so perfectly crafted. These worlds are held apart with great strain and effort because they are so deeply attracted to each other, they would merge should the Wall not be there to separate them as membranes do in the living cell.

This 'Wall'—or Shade, or Veil—consists of such a thin barrier that it can be breached by both sides. Sometimes it is actively pierced by those in the know, but more often it simply creates rifts, or narrow cracks between the two worlds, which allow things to seep through. These verges do not come into being by chance or pure randomness; they are brought into existence by the continuative outpouring of emotional experience, be it positive or negative. It doesn't matter which, because that's what the Spirit World is made of: Emotional Essence.

In some way, it is the same world, reflecting the same events and objects, but on a different spiritual 'frequency'. The Spirit World reflects our counterpart like a mirror, yet a blemished one, for even at a first glance, the reflection is different. Everything is hazy here, shrouded in floating vapors; illumination from uncertain sources pierces its mists like lighthouses on the rocky shores of northern seas. The landscape appears similar. You can find trees and animals, yet they are vague and indistinct, as if sketchily

JEFFREY KOSH

drawn by a lazy artist. The plants are in the same place; however, they cast longer shadows and move on their own accord, not by the whim of inexistent winds. Creatures make their way through the vegetation, but something is different about them. They look weird, warped, and alien to the earthly equivalent, almost stylized or slightly abstract.

All the living things own intelligence equal to, but unlike, a human's. It is a world of concepts, ideas, and most of all, emotions. There's no subtlety here, no shades of gray. Everything is clearly defined by its Essence. This spiritual energy fuels every being, and it can be either gained from our world or boosted by consuming smaller creatures of the same resonance. Each act of consumption carries a weight, though. It changes the spirit's nature that does the consuming; creating something that is a mixture of both beings. Thus, spirits prefer to feed on prey that reinforces their own nature. For a Rage-Spirit to grow stronger while keeping its nature, it needs to feed on other Rage-Spirits.

However, some spirits can feed on 'prey spirits' of other, fitting kinds, and still increase their own nature. A Wolf-Spirit devouring a Rabbit-Spirit would save its lupine self, as feeding on rabbits is part of what it is to be a wolf.

Spirits feeding on negative emotions or events seek to promote the suffering that spawned them to prevent their own decay and to grow. A pain mote quickly dissolves if the injury that brought it to light heals. Therefore, it is in the interest of an awakened Pain-Spirit to keep promoting the existence of pain for as long as it can. The longer it manages to survive, the more likely it is that other spirits of a similar nature will form, giving the original being the opportunity to consume them and grow in power.

Nemesis was one of such creatures.

At first a single mote of green light, it had no purpose or sentience. Until it was attracted by a source of Essence—that is, a Nexus, a verge between the Spirit World and our Material World, a crack formed by strong, vital emotions of living creatures, tarnishing 'The Other Side' with echoes of past anguish.

202

Nemesis was lured by this Nexus, instinctively knowing it to be a safe place, a source of nourishment and a possibility to thrive and continue its existence.

However, Nemesis fell through it and ended in the other world. Nemesis was not scared because it was not made of such essence; it was a pain spirit, and it knew only pain.

Then, it noticed that when one of the animals was wounded, attacked, or fell ill, it produced a resonant essence, on which it could feed. And so, Nemesis prospered, feeding like a parasitic being, feeding like a remora—that fish which attaches itself under the mouth of a shark to feed off the by-products of its attacks. The more it fed, the more Nemesis grew. The more it grew, the more it gained awareness of self.

And with awareness came the 'Urge': a state of being in which all mature spirits seek out a single creature to settle in and use as a mount. So, it dove inside one of the wounded animals. It felt better, but didn't last, because once the beast died there was no more pain to feed on. Therefore, Nemesis plunged inside one of the predators, a large alligator. It worked, for a while, yet the spirit noticed that it was not different from its previous existence as a parasite; it had no meaning and purpose beyond feeding when the big predator produced the pain essence. It tried to jump back and forth from predator to prey, to better feed off the essence.

Still, there was no meaning, no purpose.

There must have been something more out there, something more akin to its urge, a spark of light amid the darkness of basic nourishment.

And one day, Humans returned to the Nexus.

In ages past, the verge known to the native Turtle Tribe as Niyohonteh—Hole of the Cannibals—had been the silent witness of many atrocities committed in the name of a goddess now forgotten. The Turtle Tribe, a population of displaced Arawak, had been wary of the 'Ridden' Sagoyaga Carib that claimed the land as their own, practicing raids on nearby villages to feed their unending thirst for blood and pain. However, both tribes had ceased to exist, erased from history by fate and change, and the Nexus had become silent, the raw resonance of agony and grief reduced, but still tainting the glade by the great lake. Like a knife stabbing through the fabric of both realities and pinning the two together in a single spot, the Nexus had anchored itself, surrounded by legends and myths, its continuative existence caused by the emotional echoes of distant wickedness.

With time, another tribe of dispossessed humans had come to find solace from their persecutors, and they too became tainted by the Nexus' resonance.

Nemesis felt they were different, for these beings produced all sorts of essence, as other mote-like spirits of joy, anger, mourning, and regret flocked around them like moths to a flame. Soon, they attracted larger creatures from the Spirit World, like Animal-Spirits, that began to commune with the sapient creatures, some temporarily riding them, gaining Essence from the act, then jumping out to return to their shadowy world.

Yet, Nemesis did not like the idea of returning to its world. Something unique existed here, barely noticed by its kin in the Endless Swamp.

It jumped inside one of the Humans, but was immediately bounced off by an invisible barrier.

It tried anew, yet the rebound happened again ... and again.

Next, it noticed one of the creatures standing alone, on the outskirts of the tribe, seething with rage, yet afraid of his own kind. This lonely being was emarginated by his clan, bullied by larger specimen, avoided by females, and despised by the elders. Nemesis found his Essence's aroma irresistible.

It plunged inside him. And it worked!

It also found something new. Nemesis could urge the being to produce pain; it could steer him as a rider steers a horse, tempt him into creating more suffering. More, the spirit could stay inside him indefinitely, as long as the creature resounded with the same Essence it was made of: fear and suffering.

When that Human created fear and pain from another of its

species, Nemesis felt the single thing it lacked.

For the first time in its existence, it felt something different.

Nemesis had found its purpose, out of Eden.

CHAPTER 27

BITTER COP

Vice Sheriff James Lane had been an honest man. Once.

That had been when he was a patrol cop on the streets of West Palm Beach, cruising the A1A with his partner, looking out for dealers and alley scum. He had seen all kinds of shit happening in the background of white sandy beaches and cheap cocktails, the back-scratching and favors between police officers and shady individuals, yet he had endured. He had seen colleagues on the take, collecting regular payments to look the other way from organized criminals running rackets of all kinds, especially prostitution, yet he had endured.

His partner, Jackie O'Leary, came from a long line of notable and honorable blues in New Jersey, never on the pad of anybody, never asking for free or discounted lunches—a model in honesty. Yet he had been killed. Not by criminals, nor by street-scum. He had been killed by his own friends, betrayed by his own family. Jackie paid with his life for being honest. Nothing was ever proved, but James knew he had been murdered because he had become a pain in the ass for all those on the take.

"Frank, let's face it. Who can trust a cop who don't take money?" Tom Keough said in the movie *Serpico*.

He still remembered the hidden smiles at the funeral, the whispers, and the satisfied occasional glances between some of the most corrupt guys dressed up in high uniform to commemorate a lost member of the family, while sheltering delight under their hats. Then, he had surprised his wife Adrienne sucking the rod of Larry Holbrook, also a colleague, and she had been doing this (and more than that) for seven months. After that, James had resigned, seeking a new life in a simpler world, a small place where old values still meant something.

He had not fought for divorce, allowing Adrienne to keep the house and half of the account, unwilling to waste time in lengthy law battles and eager to reach his 'Promised Land'.

That 'Promised Land' was named Prosperity Glades. At first, everything appeared diverse, with people respecting traffic lights, no major crime in progress, the Sunday mass, clean streets, and behaving kids.

Then, the darker side of this paradise had showed its ugly face. It had all been a lie. Prosperity was no different from West Palm Beach, only, people here were smarter in hiding their dirty deeds under a façade of 'Small-Town-USA' ideals.

Sheriffs were elected not for their skills, but because of their affiliation, friendships and memberships. After ten years of working for the Prosperity Glades Department, James Lane had finally lost his battle against corruption. He had been assimilated by it.

At some point in a routine check, James had intercepted Jay Fraser's car while he was doing one of his errands to deliver drugs to Warden Doyle. Jay had made an offer to cut him into this operation and let him go. He had accepted.

To Hell with Prosperity!

He started to inform Fraser about the patrol movements in the area, to warn him about bad nights to make deliveries, and covered all traces of the business. Lane had also made his personal investigation into the matter, discovering a larger world beyond the small one Fraser had presented to him. He had suspected Vince Lucci, owner of the Rainbow Glade private club, was the main supplier of drugs to the Aryan chapter in town, although he had never seen Jay Fraser there.

The Rainbow Glade was an exclusive nightclub favored by Prosperity's wealthiest, with a large dance floor and a strip-club on the side. A lot of deals and back rubbing happened within its darkened booths and private rooms.

For instance, District Attorney Travis Lieberman of Glades County had a penchant for private and intimate parties. He would come all the way from Moore Haven to indulge in a personalized cocktail of sex and stimulants. Obviously, no one knew about his habits or his career would see an abrupt halt—except Vince Lucci, who supplied him with everything he asked for, in exchange for certain favors.

He was just returning from the Rainbow Glade, where he had had an interesting conversation with Lucci. Driving along Pasadena Avenue, he enjoyed the pleasant smell the wind carried through the orchard trees, while his mind tried to analyze the situation. It was clear that a gang war was going on between the established Aryans and the newcomers, the Mexicans. The brutal murders of Fraser and Wilson, plus the destruction of the drug-cooking lab, were plain signals, an obvious message sent to the local dealers.

The truce had been broken, the Núñez brothers were playing hard, and like wild dogs, they had sensed their rivals' weakness and attacked from all sides. Maybe they had heard about Lucci's late fall down from glory, having been cut off from the major players in the state of Florida and emarginated to small-town-USA with only his name to bear, after the Colombo Family fiasco in Tampa. That was the way of the Underworld—an ecosystem of its own, full of big predators and hijackers, small marauders and tiny raptors.

Like the ocean, the underworld possesses its own ecology; there are bottom feeders, scavengers, opportunist hijackers, small and large predators. Bottom feeders, like pinchers and snatchers, live by taking the higher risk for a dime. Next came the scavenger, the scum who earned a slice by feeding on the needs. Then followed those who press themselves on weaker ones by forcing them to pay a percentage of their ill-gotten booty, like pimps and extorters. The big fish topped it all, getting fat on the work of others, creating extended, and branched, networks of pure vice.

Sometimes, these ravenous society parasites turned on one another, going to war like tribes of ancient times. And that was bad, really bad, especially in as small a town as Prosperity. Vince had sensed it, however, he wasn't yet ready to counter. Besides, the assault had not hit his organization openly, but indirectly; killing two Aryan brothers and destroying their drug factory was not a declaration of open war against the Gambino.

Nonetheless, the fact could not be completely ignored; something had to be done before things escalated into total gang hostilities.

James shuddered at the thought of it. The last time he had witnessed the result of such kind of conflict, everything had turned into blood and brains all over. He could still remember the pulp that was once the face of Charles Morales, his corpse riddled with bullet holes—each one plugged with a dollar bill and with the Mafia message spelling 'Mutt' in crimson letters.

Poor motherfucker!

When troublemakers were clipped by Mafiosi sometimes, symbolic items were left in or on the body to mark why he had been killed. Money stuffed into the dead guy's mouth or bullet wounds meant that he was too greedy for his own good. A rat, canary or even a man's tongue cut off meant that he was talking to the Feds. When a victim got his dick cut off and stuffed into his mouth it meant that he was fooling around with another male's woman, or was an informer.

And all this shit, all this woeful cocktail of violence and betrayal keeps going on for 'needs'. Need is the base of existence.

No need, no life.

We live in a carnivorous universe, always hungry for something. Junkies will sell themselves and rob their own mothers for a nickel purse; a lifelong friend will kill you cold over a debt of a thousand bucks. Making money is what it's all about; dead presidents come first, second and last.

Because of needs. Money pays needs, people supply needs, and gals sell themselves for needs. To be that heroine or own a fashionable dress, it doesn't count—it's just plain need.

Sometimes, you're forced into an artificial need—you get first dose for free, then you're into Hell itself. Sometimes, you willingly accept to live for a need, you crave for it. But, you can bet two out of three you've got no choice. You have a need. Watching it from the right angle, you'll notice that lines between the 'honest world' and the Underworld do blur. Nobody's really honest, not in a needful world.

Not even a cop.

CHAPTER 28

SWEET CROOK

Billy Gamble sat outside the *Happy Tandoori* Restaurant, facing Wear Street's ramshackle parking lot.

"Look, I don't like to come to you in this way, but I really need your help, Mr. Gamble," started Umesh Baska, the eating place's owner.

Billy was not really paying attention to the Indian's pleading as he watched for a battered old *Chevy*.

Seated next to him was Lawrence Bootes, a tall and hulky individual sporting blonde with Viking-like tresses and full beard. Bootes was the manager of a gun shop in West Bend, and also one of Gamble's in-training survivalists and Aryan wanna-be. Billy had selected him for his neo-nazi ideals and strong frame first and his militaristic dutiful attitude next.

"You see, my restaurant ... should be a classy place, you know yourself you've eaten here, but now it's going down the tube. My best customers don't want to come back, all because of this kid," Umesh droned on.

"The boy's got a temper, whaddya gonna do? He don't listen to nobody, he does what he wants," Lawrence chided, a sarcastic grin on his face while looking for his master's approval, as a faithful dog does after performing a requested trick. None came.

Gamble's eyes locked on the parking lot, witnessing the Banshee's serving staff's arrival one by one, yet no sign of the *Chevy*.

"I've heard people talking about this kid, how wild he is, how he's always waving a gun around, and I'm afraid he's gonna kill someone here. That's no good for my business," Umesh droned on. "Will you talk to him? I know he'll listen to you."

Billy turned toward the man, plucked out a cigarette—which Lawrence promptly lighted—and took a long drag. "What do you want from me? Why should I get involved in this beef of yours?"

The entrepreneur got silent, then mumbled something in his language but changed his mind when Gamble's stern eyes fixed on him. "Wait a minute, mister. I'm going to check something with Kabir, my brother, then I'll be back. Meanwhile, please, have something to drink. Make yourself at home."

"We're home, Umy! This is America, you know?" Lawrence broke in with sarcastic laughter, and again that 'good dog' glance to his master. Umesh rose from the chair and went inside.

"Are we going into the protection business, Bill?" Bootes asked his absentminded superior, who had returned his concentration to the parking lot.

Bill said nothing, then rose from his seat and stretched his arms and back. The sky darkened on the horizon and the usual daylight activity of West Bend was reversing into the wild nighttime buzz of strip joints and watering holes. Still no sign of the car.

A couple of junkies stuck out of an alley, like nocturnal animals coming out of their lair looking for their dietary needs. Billy watched them pass by with disgust on his face; yes, his business depended on them, but he had no respect for losers.

"What do you want to do to the gal, boss? I mean, are we going to have some fun with her, or just a reprimand?" Bootes asked.

"You just stick with me, Larry. Do not say a word or act without my mark, okay? This is your night, don't spoil it. The chick has nothing to do with your test, she's only the bait for larger prey," Bill answered back, then took another drag from the cig, while scrutinizing the other side of the road.

The tall man nodded. This was his night.

Billy Gamble had promised him this was going to be his initiation into the Aryans; he'd talked about kidnapping and a lesson to teach to a certain snooper, but had not said anything about the person's identity.

A waiter brought two cool glasses of beer at the table with a broad smile on his face. Bootes was thirsty, yet had no intention of touching the booze before his master gave permission. But Gamble kept facing the front lot, ignoring the beverages.

"Should we drink this stuff or not, boss?" Larry hazarded.

Without turning, Billy raised his right hand and signaled like a hunter directing hounds toward prey. Larry saw nothing at first, then noticed a white *Chevy* entering the parking lot and understood. That was their target. Immediately, he rushed to Billy's side, while the driver began to maneuver between a pair of rusted wrecks.

Umesh chose that moment to return, his balding pate shining under the neon lights, his brow sweaty in the night's humid air. "Look, I've got a proposal. Why don't you come in the place for twenty percent? You won't have to do anything, just let know the guy you've got an interest here..." he started, but was immediately silenced by Gamble.

"Listen Umy, I'm not into extortion, if that's what you mean. I've nothing to do with this kiddo and ain't goin' to turn this cesspit of yours into a spit and sawdust joint more than it is. I've got urgent business to deal with right now, but do not worry—I want this loathsome 'hood to be stripped off these worthless dregs as much as you do. I do not want a lousy percentage, just some favors, okay?"

Baska attempted a smile, which became a larger and sincere one when he noticed Billy's grimace. Then, the two goons crossed the road in the direction of the dirty junkyard that passed for a parking lot, while Kabir joined his brother from the main dining room.

"Has he accepted?" he asked, a glint of hope in his eyes.

Umesh kept smiling, then, turned toward his older brother. "No."

"And why on earth are you smiling? There's nothing to smile for ... the guy's going to wreck our business, he's..." Kabir started complaining, but was rapidly interrupted by his sibling.

"I didn't say he wasn't going to help us, I just said he didn't accept our proposal. Kabir! He's gonna do it for free!" he said, placing both hands on his relative's shoulders.

"So, it's real what they say," Kabir said. "He's a sweet crook."

****

Shannon Cooper was afraid. Her legs shook, her lower lip trembled and the weighty sensation of fear put pressure on her breathing. She was going to faint in moments.

A hand rose and slammed hard into her left cheek; water filled her eyes and blood from a crushed lip spattered down her chin. Her head staggered back due to the blow and she would have fallen if Larry's strong hands weren't clutching her arms.

They were inside Bootes' van.

The bastards had abducted her before she could reach her working place. Nobody raising a finger to help while she was lifted up like a rag doll and forcefully carried inside the vehicle's loading bay.

The place stank of dirty clothes and vibrant body odor. It was littered with old magazines (mostly about military gear and weapons), used Army fatigues, soiled uniforms, and some stacks of boxes.

"There was no need for that!" she cried. "I'm gonna do whatever you want, Billy! Just stop hurting me!"

The man lit a cig, and then moved closer, a grin on his face. She caught Larry's smile in anticipation, his eagerness for more violence. He liked rough treatment on chicks.

"Come on Shanny. It was just to wake you up, a rude awakening from that everlasting foggy state of yours," Gamble said.

She kept crying, and felt unable to lift her gaze for fear of meeting her tormentors'. Tires from a screeching car resounded outside the van, causing a jolt to her already twitchy nerves.

Billy grabbed her face, forced her to lock eyes with his own. He smiled sweetly, but she knew it was just a ruse. "Shanny,

Shanny, when you will learn? I'm not a bad man, you know? I can be as sweet as a little lamb. Ain't it so, Larry?"

Lawrence Bootes sheepishly nodded, sporting the same stupid grin on his face.

"Here. Listen Shanny, I'm not going to hurt you again unless you deserve it, in which case, be sure, I won't be so happy to do it. I don't like beating the crap out of people, honey. I just want your full attention and compliance," Gamble continued, caressing her face.

She nodded, at same time becoming aware that the lewd bastard holding her was pressing his groin against her ass, causing her to shiver at the thought.

"Are you going to behave, Shanny?" Billy asked.

Shannon nodded again, her tears drying around the corners of her mouth. Outside, someone had taken to kicking a wasted can around the lot, yet the felons ignored the sound, seeming unconcerned that someone could get curious about the light coming from below the van's rear doors. They kept their coolness, overconfident in their defiant sense of being untouchable.

"Good. That's the right way, baby!" Gamble exclaimed, giving off a grayish cloud of smoke on her face. She coughed, causing the man to laugh and Larry to join immediately in a parrot-like imitation of his master.

"Don't you like it? Oh, man, I forgot you're into marijuana, baby. Well, better's for you to get used to the lack of it, 'cause we're soon goin' to close the market," Billy said, turning away.

"What do you want from me, Billy?" Shannon murmured under her breath.

"Straight to the point, huh? Okay, I like this attitude. Besides, you're right, I'm wasting time gloating like a jerk. So, let's see. What do I want?" He faced her again, the cigarette stuck at the corner of his mouth, a sterner expression on his already dour features. "I want you to make a call, honey. Nothing less, nothing more. And I want you to be at your best, performing better than you usually do at that scum you call a job, am I clear?"

215

A call? What was he blathering about? The man was more dangerous than she thought; he was completely insane!

"What kind of performance? I do not work for hotlines," she said disdainfully, regretting it a moment later when Gamble hit her again with another slap. A softer one, luckily.

"What did I say? Respect, baby, respect. Full attention and compliance. Do it again and I'm going to break you a pinkie, okay?" Billy said, grabbing her short hair and pulling her head toward his grimace. She whined in pain, but nodded.

"Now listen, sweetheart, because I ain't going to explain it again. Do as I say and I'll not hurt you, I promise. Do not comply and I'm going to spend the whole night with you, *my way*. Do you remember *my way*?" Gamble released his hold.

Shannon nodded again, stars crossing her vision. She wished for this nightmare to end as soon as possible, yet couldn't make heads or tails of it.

"Larry, release the girl, please," Billy ordered.

She was finally free from those disgusting hands, at once taking her distance from the dirty goon. She rubbed on her aching arms.

"Promise you ain't goin' to rape me again, Billy," she said, unable to keep the fear from her tone.

"I promise," the man vowed, while Bootes looked on with disappointment.

****

Later, after Shannon had accomplished what Gamble had asked for, she went straight for the van's door, and received a shock when she felt his hand take hold of her jacket. "Now what?" she protested. "I've done my part, please, leggo!"

Billy said nothing; he just grabbed her and swiveled her into Larry's waiting arms. At once, the guy slammed her prone on the floor, while Gamble rushed in to hug her head in a vise-like grasp. She screamed in terror, hearing the too-familiar sound of a zip's tab being pulled down right behind her.

"You lousy bastard! You promised!" she cried out.

"No, Shanny. I promised that *I* wouldn't rape you this time. I didn't say Larry would not. You see, Shanny, I'm a man of honor; always keep my word. I'm sorry, but I promised my good friend here some good time, and, as I said, I always keep my word."

CHAPTER 29

NIGHT GOER

Spirits of objects or natural creatures always bore some resemblance to the things they reflected. Alligator-spirits were scaled and fangled, Plant-spirits had leaves and bark. Spirits of concepts, or emotions, had none. They often had a surreal, mythical, or frightful appearance.

Night Goer was one of them. In origin a simple mesh of barbed-wire looking entwines, paired to a couple of metallic raven-like wings, it had soon evolved into something greater, something generated by people's legends.

Sunnayi Edahi—that was the Cherokee name for it—was envisioned as a spirit of cannibalism, appearing as a stooped old woman dressed in tattered clothes, with a tangle of thorny hair on her head and long, razor-like nails. She spoke with the whispered sound of the wind into ravines, mixed with the cackle of a crone. They said she was a witch, able to assume animal forms and lure children to certain death. She could go about only under the cover of darkness, and hated the sun. She was powerful, yet could only come to 'This Side' if summoned by those in despair. She enjoyed playing with her food, feeding more on the terror generated before and after the kill than on the act of murder.

All these myths became true, shaping Night Goer into a spirit of pure revenge, a creature made of grudge, bitterness, and sorrow.

The rules of interaction between 'This Side' and the 'Other Side' were simple: anything powerful enough in one realm had a chance to affect the other. When something invested with emotional feelings and strong meaning happened in the 'Corporeal World', it gave life to a reaction in the 'Spirit World'; the strong beliefs, or fears, of the Corporeal World's inhabitants created the very monsters they envisioned.

That was the way the old Cherokee imagined her, forcing the

spirit to assume a form to better fit their legends. With time, it had been forgotten; relegated to secondary myths and fairytales. Few even believed it existed, sending the spirit into a torpid oblivion. And because of this, Night Goer had slept for centuries in its nook, awakening only to escape ambush from more active spirits. More modern ones.

It still bore scars from its last encounter with the Brood Mother. A deceitful spirit of eternal hunger, her endless gluttony drove the Gorger to devour everything she met on her path through the mouths of her drone-like spawns. Night Goer had been lucky the Mother was greatly reduced in power after her corporeal avatar had been relegated to the oceanic depths of the Atlantic. The grudging spirit had then lain dormant inside a forgotten cave located on Cherokee hallowed ground, a safe place because it was traditionally bound to a powerful being feared by all Indian tribes—the Windigo.

Windigo was known by many names, each tribe pronouncing it in different ways—from Weedigo to Weeghteko, from Wendigo to Winnebago. Nonetheless, they all carried the same meaning: Evil Cannibal Spirit. Windigo was the phantom of hunger, stalking lone humans in the wilds. Related to the Brood Mother, Windigo was always hungry, yet it was bound by countless legends and traditions, chaining it to the Spirit World's depths.

Night Goer was reawakened by the sudden rush of countless pain motes, soon followed by throbbing blood-red violence spirits. These swarms were feasting mightily, converting dark emotions into pure Essence, their natural fuel. Pain and despair were potent, collecting around everything like a septic infection, the reddish hue of raw violence seeping into the Spirit World like water oozing from the vault of a natural cave. Night Goer moved, pushing aside the lesser creatures, consuming some in the process—a meager meal compared to what it really needed.

Its curiosity was repaid, because there stood—lying down on the cavern's stony floor—a pain-wracked being, seething with rage that emanated from it in bright waves of emotional Essence. Night

219

Goer came closer, moved in the darkness. The being was a human woman. She had been violently assaulted by her peers—who had left her dying, like a pack of satisfied coyotes. Yet, the girl was strong in Essence; she kept fighting the pull of death by defiantly hanging on a will of revenge, as if that basic emotion could gift her with new life.

So, Night Goer had whispered in her ears, asking how much she craved for vengeance, how much she longed for it, what she was willing to do to get it. The woman had answered back, accepting the spirit's offer. Hastily, Night Goer had complied, joining her soul and riding her as she had done centuries before—finally finding purpose.

Night Goer had kept her promises and had led the Ridden in her search for vengeance, to bring pain and terror to her persecutors.

It pointed her in the right direction, never failing the woman in her pursuit for retribution.

****

That night, Sunnayi Edahi urged her again. In dreams, the girl clearly saw the Indian crone waiting for her near the end of a wooden bridge. She wore the ragged clothes of a violated woman and clutched the Shortening Staff in the left hand, while signaling for her to come closer. The dreaming girl hastened her pace, but failed to close the distance, because when she reached the spot in which the hag once stood, she found it empty. She glanced around and saw the crone farther ahead, scampering along the county road, until she turned southward, disappearing on a hidden off-road trail. Again, the girl increased the pace of her footsteps, breaking into a full dash to avoid losing sight of her guide. She found her lying by a cedar tree, smiling wickedly with her fang-like teeth. The crone's pointed a bony finger at a large structure surrounded by putrid marshy terrain. "Here we are, child," said Night Goer, her yellowish eyes probing the host's resolve.

"What is this place?" her Ridden asked.

"That is the Lair of the Devouring Worm; the Feeder of Windigo. Yvn'wini'giski Ama'yine'hi, the Water Cannibal," said Night Goer.

The Ridden turned her attention to the building, taking note of all its weaknesses and its assets, immediately developing a plan to stealthily infiltrate the fort and reach her objective, and then she realized the place could not really exist in 'This Side'.

"Is this a vision of a real place or am I watching its conceptual reflection in the 'Other Side'?" she questioned.

Night Goer faded away, turning into a seeping fog, then whispered into her Ridden's left ear. "Child, listen to me, this place is as real as your bundle's old tobacco, as sturdy as Uncle Johnny's dreamcatcher. Look for it; follow the road I showed you. Yet, do not falter, because this servant of Windigo surrounds himself with traps and followers. Be strong in your need and you will prevail."

The Ridden girl vainly searched for her guide, but it was nowhere to be seen, so she concentrated on her enemy's stronghold. Once she terminated her exploratory survey, the girl allowed herself to be lifted up by the strong gale that began to blow from the east, levitating over the swampy forest, letting it bring her back home...

In her trailer, Cheri Ridge opened her eyes, eager to start a new hunt.

CHAPTER 30

AMBUSH
(FROM AXEL'S HALL OF MEMORIES)

I had just finished my duty of re-examining Jay Fraser's charred residues when my cell phone rang.

What else? Is this town going astray?

Being a neatly person, I hastily retrieved the device from where I'd left it—perfectly aligned with all my personal items on the second shelf to the right, as always.

"Hello," I said, wondering who was calling me, after noticing the 'Unknown ID' message flashing on the display. You see, my personal list of memorized numbers can be enumerated on one hand's fingers, because the only people who really cared to call me were so few, and all in the business. Mostly cops and fellow examiners.

"Dr. Hyde?" a female voice spoke.

"Yes, that's me. May I know who am I talking to?" I replied. Clearly, she wasn't Morena Espinoza. I have an eidetic memory for anything—including voices—and this particular one I had never heard before.

"The name's not important, doc. What really matters is a simple question: why are you looking for me?" she asked.

I was immediately thrilled by that query.

Could it be?

The murderous cowgirl had found out I was actively hunting her, at the same time hiding her tracks from police.

Yet, how?

"Doc, I know you've been snooping around, inquiring about my latest encounter with that guy who's now residing in your workplace. And, if you're wondering how I gained your personal cell's number ... well, you ain't as smart as they say," she continued.

The 'real me' kicked-in, dispelling the humanlike masquerade I always wear to appear as one of you. Besides, I quickly guessed what she was implying.

"Stop playing games, please, and get to the point," I said in my best cold tone.

A pause, then she breathed hard on the phone, as if she was undergoing some kind of activity while talking with me.

"What's your need?" she asked.

"Are you going to ask me what's my favorite horror movie, too?" I answered back sarcastically, yet she didn't get it.

"You know what I mean, doc. Why are you hiding what you know about me from your police friends? Why are you doing it?"

Interesting question, I mused.

"I'm hiding nothing. I'm just doing my job. I work for law enforcement and—"

"Bullshit!" she interrupted. "Do not fool around with me, doc! You're an examiner, not a detective." Another pause. "Your duties do not include investigating on the field. More, you're clearly concealing evidence from cops, and I'm wondering why."

I was surprised by her direct ways; still there was something wrong about that, unfitting to the profile I had developed of the killer.

"This isn't something I'm going to discuss over a phone, miss."

"I was thinking the same. Why don't we meet, doctor?"

Again, that strange feeling that something was not right about her. Yet, I kept the conversation going.

"Are you sure about it? My mother taught me to be wary of people who don't give their name, you know?" I chided.

She hesitated, and in that I detected what was wrong—I sensed her fear. Although it was the first time I was listening to that woman's husky voice, I was able to determine that she was afraid. Oh, she was trying to hide it under her scorn, but my well-trained ears individuated that trembling note lying under a thick sheet of phony confidence.

"Yes," she finally said.

Too much reluctance in that simple statement. I was right.

"Please, state the place and timing," I declared, sounding like a Southerner duelist, which caused me to smile like a dork.

Sometimes I can be quite a moron—my-my!

She didn't get the risible part in my request, being too tense to even crack back; it was evident she was losing her initial sureness. "Do you know the small scenic area located at the end of Murchison Bridge on the county road?"

"Yep."

"Very good. Let's meet over there at..." Again that faltering, then she hastily added, "Let's have it tonight. Thirty-past-ten, can you make it?"

"Yup, no problemo," I affirmed, the last word coming out in my worst Spanish.

What the heck was happening to me? Where was all that euphoric jolliness coming from?

"Okay, so, see you then, Doctor," she said, ready to close conversation. However, I broke in before she ended the call. "One last thing, lady."

"Y...es?" She hesitated again, clearly surprised by my last request.

"I'm not used to blind dating, so, I was wondering … what kind of dress code will it require?"

A hard click was her response, signaling she had interrupted our jovial chat.

My-my, she was really lacking humor.

But I was having some! Lame, but still some. What the heck.

But it was not that what worried me at that moment.

Yes, people believed I had no sense of humor; but that wasn't true. You see, from the moment I'd realized I had not lost my feelings, I had decided to freely express a vast repertory of them, mostly in private.

No, what really worried me was the fact that the mysterious woman had not requested from me the usual stuff dangerous

criminals demand when someone is going to meet them.
That being: *Come alone and unarmed.*

****

At a quarter-past-ten, I parked my car in the scenic area. What is so *scenic* about that dingy and desolate clearing hosting a picnic area and a series of rusty swings I will never understand. It borders the Istee River, and is made up of packed mud and sawgrass; a normally hearty grass-like species that has formed thousands of acres of marshes in all the Everglades. Floating varieties of bladderwort, white water lily, spatterdock and maidencane dominate its waterscape, while patches of royal palm, bromeliads and ferns claim possession of the land. Sadly, the place has been completely ruined by human intrusion; you can notice it by the quantities of garbage and floating empty cans in the slow-moving river. The Park Rangers out of Brighton do their best to patrol the area, but they aren't there all time, so they can't cope with drunkards returning home after a brave night in Waynesford and stopping there to have one last round of canned booze before getting back home.

I scared a Great Blue Heron in the process of getting out of the car. The large bird squawked and flapped its wings, but was too lazy to fly away; it just opted for a walk in the shallow waters.

As I expected, no one was there waiting for me, not yet at least. I glanced over the area, mentally taking note of all its nooks and possible hiding spots, the only source of illumination coming from my car's headlights. I yawned, then stretched my legs and arms like a trucker after a long trip; it had been a very stressful and wearing day at the morgue.

Then, I kept pacing back and forth along the edge of the road, watching every incoming vehicle.

I returned to the car, killed the lights, and just stood there, relaxing in the dark, leaning on the hood.

Another cawing cry got my attention, this time coming near

the water's edge. There, I spotted a large bird, repeatedly trying to lift something with its beak. It was a crow, black as midnight, its lively eye reflecting lights from passing autos like glass fragments left on the macadam after a crash.

Stop thinking about death, stupid!

For the first time in my life, I surprised myself with a rebuke against my usual ghoulish thoughts.

It reflects light like a polished mirror – sounds *better, don't you agree?*

I shook off those conflicting voices from my head and returned my concentration to the bird. It was now using its beak to peck at the smaller thing, but I detected the last was alive and fighting back, resolutely snapping its little jaws.

It was a baby alligator. You know I have a fondness for those reptiles, sensing some kind of kinship with them: so simple, so effective. Still, I do not usually feel enough empathy to intervene in natural disputes. In the wilds, only the stronger survives.

Yet, something moved inside me, feeling different. A new kind of urge took hold, and I found myself waving my arms to scare away the attacking crow. The bird cawed, but fled away irritated. I rushed to the spot and looked down at the little creature, heart pounding loudly inside my chest, fearing it was too late. But the animal was alive; it just presented a tiny prick on its snout, made reddish by ruptured blood vessels.

I smiled.

Maybe you think I'm a jerk, or just as crazy as *Alice's Mad Hatter* for feeling relief at the survival of that puny version of a natural born killer, but I disagree. You see, it was not about the baby gator's health that I was pleased—yes, I was happy it was safe—but I was smiling because of my emotional response to another living creature. Until now, I had only felt anger and hate toward those monsters I had butchered and nothing for their victims. All these years I had not avenged their unfair deaths or wrecked lives, nor had I felt the need to.

Henry had got it right; I was only projecting my monster

outside in a protective manner.

It was not innocent people I was protecting.

It was me.

The ten-year old tyke who had suffered so much horror, so much fear at the hands of one of those monsters. Monsters who fed on fright, monsters who fed on the feeling of omnipotence they had on fair game.

Ten-year old Axel still hated them, experiencing a fit of rage every time I had the misfortune—or luck, depending how you see it—to meet one of those ravenous bullies. And all this hatred and fury had driven my life, both taking their toll on my other feelings, my humane emotions.

Still smiling, I grabbed the baby alligator by the nape, as you do when lifting a kitten from the ground, and then placed it into the Istee's muddy waters. I watched it disappear into the murkiness.

In that precise moment, I realized I was sated; no longer feeling the need for revenge, that endless seething rage incessantly burning inside my very soul from that summer of '78.

I'd been feeding the urge of something else for most of my life, something that had cajoled me—at first—then subdued my psyche, cowing me in a way to become not so different from those fear-eating bastards I despised so much.

I felt so euphoric about my inner digressions that only at the last second did I notice the man quietly approaching me from behind. Suddenly, a large arm appeared from nowhere to clench my throat in a strong vise-like grasp. Instinctively, I reacted by planting my right elbow inside my attacker's stomach and stomping my left foot on his. The man released the hold, yet he quickly recovered and pushed me on the ground, where I fell spread-eagled, face-first in the mud. I tried to rise up, but a second man rushed in, kicking me hard in the head. The blow was so violent that it sent me flying backward, my jaw dislocating on the impact. Stars blinded my vision and a throbbing pain exploded in my right temple, yet I would not give up so easily. Stubbornly, I tried to lift my body from the ground, yet I felt my strength falter and dizziness filled my brain.

Get back up, Axel! Fight!

The first attacker was again on me. He grabbed my head and knocked it hard on the ground, causing a deep cut into my brow, which kept bleeding profusely, sending hot blood into my already fogged eyes.

Then, he returned to take hold of my throat, clutching it tight—he was going to strangle me! My vision turned dark as I used my last energy to trash about, to flail my arms, in vain.

My world became dark.

It was, apparently, over.

CHAPTER 31

NEMESIS

Nemesis was worried. And worriment was new to it. It had never happened before and anything new could endanger its control of the host. How had it come to this? The Host was refusing to collaborate, to feed it what it needed. The spirit had been inside that human being for so many years and it had never experienced such defiance.

Was it possible that the time had come for a total takeover?

Nemesis hoped not. Such activity was never a good idea: it gave the spirit complete control of the host's body, but it didn't last much. The frail flesh would soon begin to show hints of an external influence and give away its convenient hiding place to others of its ilk.

Nemesis remembered too well what had happened in the past, when its breed openly rode the flesh and bone-beings. Spirits had walked among men as giants, and gods, revered and pampered by the Essence-producing creatures, but also attracting unwanted attention. There were bigger fish in Nemesis' pond and causing them to appear, lured by the aura of lesser spirits, was never a good idea.

More, Humans had a tendency to give new forms to spirits, shaping and weaving them into new things, willingly or otherwise. Legends were born out of ridden creatures, so their Essence would grow and mutate, becoming ever more attuned to the thoughts and beliefs of their shapers.

And so Windigo had been born, out of the inherent fear of loneliness and hunger, forever haunting desolate landscape, restless in its everlasting pursuit of unholy meals.

And the Haunter of the Moor had hunted among the young of the species, assuming new guises when her legend was transplanted in the metal and glass jungles of modern times.

Other beings, more ancient and primeval, simply attuned to new beliefs, adapted themselves in different cultures and tribes, and thus became forever imprinted in Humanity's racial memory.

What about the Seductress? At once known as Tlazolteotl; Eater of Filth, Aphrodite; Love Goddess, and Erzulie; the Passionate Woman, this creature had spawned thousands of lesser spirits, generating myths about Succubi, Sirens, and Harpies.

Or the Great Mother, who was known as Nuwa among the Chinese, Devi among the Hindu, and Freya in the Northlands. Worshipped and fed by her fertility cults, it had grown to such an extent that now it resembled nothing more than a gargantuan lump of throbbing flesh, covered with millions of craving mouths and ever-generating wombs.

Yet, there was a negative side to all that bliss and power. The same beliefs that gave might to a spirit could produce banes to it.

Shamans learned to fight 'evil spirits' with spells and fetishes, binding them to magical items or scattering their Essence through complex rituals forged out of the same Essence the spirits were made of. Many were the legends of Solomon and his entrapment of the Djinn, as well as those of trapped fiends in the bowels of the very earth.

Jabberwocky and Tommyknockers. Sprites and Fairies.

All were powerful, all bore weaknesses and banes. There were those who could not cross running water and those who could not stand the sight of a freshly plucked red rose. Thus, more myths were born, added to an infinite library of behavioral conducts, spiritual compulsions, and ritualistic bans.

So, the spirits had gone into hiding, preferring the subtle urging technique above the overt possession. Pairing with similar minded hosts allowed the spirit to fuel inner wants that were already present in the vessel's soul. Furthermore, the less humans knew about the urging spirit's nature, the less were they likely to create legends on it, to inscribe its Essence with dreaded bans and zeitgeists.

But Nemesis had overstepped with its late host. It had become so confident it had allowed him to realize the spirit was real, not a projection of his wounded subconscious. And Axel had begun to fight back—refusing to comply with its dark urges, not because he didn't like what it asked from him, but because, as all humans, he had a rebellious and independent nature.

A leashed llama thrashes and fights against the binding, but once free, it just sits close to its master. You can't show the leash to a llama.

Worse, the puny host had begun devising plans to get rid of his passenger by studying books and reaching out to knowledge hidden by the mists of time.

Soon, he would find the truth, or instinctively raise a wall between himself and his urging stowaway with the most dreaded tool available to human nature.

Will.

This could not be allowed, this had to be stopped. Now!

Nemesis was a simple being made of pain and fear, nothing more. Yet, it possessed some cunning, borne out of centuries of experience and survival.

No, this Ridden was not going to send it back from whence it belonged. No, this puny vessel was not forcing it out of its warm and cozy lair. He had to comply, in one way or the other. Nemesis would devise new ways. It would hide the leash from the thrashing llama, letting him believe he was free.

This was its home and nobody was going to kick it out of it.

CHAPTER 32

FEEDING ITS URGE
(FROM AXEL'S HALL OF MEMORIES)

No. It wasn't over. I woke up in a darkened room. It smelled of piss and trash, and the only light came from an opening in the ceiling I figured out to be a hatch. I immediately realized I'd been roped to some kind of seat with a straight back, yet no gagging muzzled my mouth. Whoever had captured me had no qualms about me crying for help.

And I didn't, because it was pointless. You see, if someone ties you up like a wild animal and leaves you the ability to scream it points only to one direction: nobody can hear you. Period.

My face and clothes were caked with drying mud (something that clearly upset me; as you know I hate getting dirty) and I could smell blood under my nostrils.

Hell, these guys had beaten me badly.

I concentrated on the sounds to try and get a better idea of the place.

First, I could hear the distinctive noises of the swamp. Bullfrogs humming, the cry of a heron—they all suggested I was close to Grassy Swamp. Even better, the sound of rushing water to my left suggested I wasn't far from the Istee.

Good. I wasn't so deep in the swamp to be unfamiliar with my surroundings.

Second, the occasional creaking and the easiness with which sounds penetrated the building told me it was entirely fashioned in wood.

Ah awareness, beloved awareness! How many times my passion for details had saved my ass from more dangerous monsters than me, I can't recall.

Boarding a plane? Take your time to memorize the closest emergency exit—it will not save you in a crash, but surely is helpful in case of forced landing (and quick exit); you will be there pulling the opening handle while others are still seated wondering about what to do.

Boat trip in the glades? Pay attention to every weird-looking tree or other natural feature; memorize a personal map while enjoying the outdoor experience. It comes in handy when a gator swallows your precious GPS.

Well, maybe I'm exaggerating, but I always like to get a clear picture of where I am. Bad things like these tend to happen to people like me.

Oh, and do not forget the most important rule for those living a dangerous life, as I do: proper outfitting. Never be caught unawares because you forgot that precious piece of equipment you so direly need right now, in the weirdest of circumstances.

When on the hunt, I always fill my kit with the right tools for the trade. Loose clothes are perfect for the wilds, but in a more urban environment I prefer close-fitting ones. Always carry a source of light with you and some kind of reasonably portable— and concealable—restraints; plastic fasteners are the best. And last but not least: blades. They are the means by which you carry out your business, your personal claws against a world of better equipped, or stronger, predators. I'm in love with big, large affairs, but these are useful only in your own killing ground, they are dangerous to carry, and police officers take it personally if they surprise you with a carving knife or a meat cleaver. No, when you can't bring prey to your lair, going out with innocent-looking tools is far better—because they are safer and more easily concealable.

Last thing to consider is the likelihood of a reversal of roles and becoming the bound prey, waiting for the unavoidable.

No. Fucking. Way.

Ponder this. Ninety percent of people would be roped or restrained with duct tape with hands behind their back, usually in a seated position, or lying on the side. Come on, how many times have you seen that scene on TV? Those guys tied with the silvery adhesive tape mumbling incomprehensible words under their gags are so trite. You can find them in every show.

Well, think about it, how could you escape from such a situation if not thanks to a sharp cutting device?

Do not expect to find it on the spot, because it is far easier for you to improvise a weapon later than escaping your bondages by rubbing your wrists against a sharp corner or jagged edge.

Criminals are clever; otherwise, they're dead criminals.

The best way is to always carry with you a lightweight, all-purpose piece of cutting metal.

But I'm sure you would remark that whoever stiffens you would also be smart enough to search inside every nook and cranny of your clothes. That's not always the case—most will simply pay a cursory inspection and get down to business in a rush to have you tied up as soon as possible.

I do not guarantee you'll succeed, but why not take the chance if you can?

That's why I tape a small switchblade just between the parting of my buttocks. It is not large enough to kill, but it can deliver a nasty surprise to eyes, genitals, and eardrums. And it can be used to cut bindings made of soft materials. If you're chained, tough luck. But, come on, we live in the twenty-first century, not in the middle ages. Who's going to chain you up as a slave? Guess it could happen, but it's rare.

And consider your personality—meaning how you appear in the eyes of your captor. Whoever kidnapped me knew I was a medical examiner not a *SPECTRE* agent—that fictional organization out of *James Bond* movies. Why would I glue a tiny switchblade to my butt?

I wriggled. Yes, it was still there! I took comfort upon feeling its icy presence on the fleshy part that I sat on. I fumbled with my hands to reach it, careful to not drop it in any way. Then, I switched out its little blade and let it eat away at the fibers of the rope. It would take a long time.

In the meanwhile, I finally heard my captors' voices, and I stretched an ear out in the hope of getting some clues about their identities and quantity.

They were at least three males, *that* was certain. One of them was named Billy and another they called Larry. The last one I couldn't make out clearly.

I had been lured in a trap.

But why?

Were they self-styled vigilantes who had, somehow, discovered my dark deeds? Or were they a legacy from a past victim of mine?

No. Stuff like that happens only in the movies.

Another approach was to consider them members of some kind of organized crime: gangs, Mafiosi, or small-time crooks.

I was afraid, yes, but I was also curious. It *had* to do with the recent murders. Besides, Jay Fraser and Marvin Wilson were allegedly Aryan Brotherhood associates. But what had I done to lead them to me?

Then I remembered.

Mark Scarlett.

Surely, the bartender had twittered about my weird inquiries on Fraser to his friends and they had settled to bring me on their turf and interrogate me. They needed to know—as much as I did—who was spoiling their secret game. So, they were going to squeeze the truth out of me.

Too bad I was clueless as well.

I kept biting at the cord with my little helper's blade. Faster.

****

Tears came out of my eyes once they faced the sudden change of illumination due to the improvised invasion of light. Question time had come.

"Muthafucker's awake," someone said from the threshold.

I tried to adjust my vision and focalize on the goons, but the light was too bright, blinding.

"Yeah, that's a big mutha, Larry," someone added. That

person stood behind a larger shape who was keeping his mouth shut, staring at me. He came closer and grabbed my chin, forcing me to gaze directly at his face, yet I could see nothing. The light came right from behind him and his features were darkened by shadows. "Can you hear me, dude?" he said, with a deep bass voice.

He was smelly, with a strong body odor—that kind of people I detest.

I nodded, pulling my face away from his offensive scent.

"Yeah straight, Boss, we didn't whoop his ass so hard," prattled again the one I mentally labeled as *Jolly-Golly* because of his old-style gang attitude.

"'Sides, he's a grown-up boy, isn't he, vato? I think the sucker's going to entertain us as a primo puta," commented the large guy named Larry, with a laugh.

"Stop that Brownie's slur immediately, fuckers! You know I can't stand it," barked the one who was obviously their boss, without turning to face them.

Brownie. What a weird term for Spanish-speaking people. I had heard many—Spick, Coyotes, or Hermies, among them—but I'd never got wind of *Brownie.*

Man, either I was getting old or this guy was a complete moron. I opted for the second choice.

He returned his attention to me. "Let's see. Tell me your name. Do you remember it?"

Although I couldn't see his eyes, I gazed straight into them. "You already know that," I said, chancing a simper.

"I want to hear it from your lips, dude."

"Okay, if that's what you fancy. Who am I to disappoint you? … My name's Hyde, Axel Hyde." My smirk turned into a real smile when I realized I had acted like James Bond. But he didn't get it. Too bad, it wasn't my lucky day. For once in my life, I was full of humor and no one was appreciating my puns.

Just the wrong audience.

"Good, Mr. Hyde, good! So you're of sound mind and you'll

understand everything I'm goin' to ask you," he said, smiling back.

I could finally discern his features. He was a white man, clean-shaven, with thin lips and a broken nose. Bushy blonde eyebrows surmounted slanted, fissure-like, green hued eyes. He wore his hair in a military cut and an old scar lined his right cheek from just below the orbit to the top corner of his perpetually smirking mouth. Fastened at his neck, gleamed a pair of dog tags.

My, my! Another of those army maniacs! Be proud, salute the flag, God bless America, and hide when they come to enlist you to defend Uncle Sam's interests in Afghanistan.

I was right; he was a moron.

"Tell me why you were looking for J.F., Mr. Hyde," he asked calmly.

"Jeans Factory? Oh yes, I know that brand, but I'm more into classical, you know? I don't see how—."

I never finished my sarcastic wordplay because the army fuck struck me so hard in the stomach he blew the air off my lungs. More so, it caused me to almost lose my grip on the switchblade. But I clenched it firmly inside my right fist, cutting the palm in the process.

"Yeah, teach him a lesson, Boss," Larry yelled, while Jolly-Golly just muttered an 'Ouch'.

I reeled in pain, mentally taking note to play longer with this bastard when my payback time would come.

"That's for not behaving, Mr. Hyde. I have some simple rules, you see? First: respect. Never cross me, never show scorn, never disobey my requests. Should you do that, you're goin' to regret it. Second: never piss me off. If I get pissed, you're goin' to regret it. Third: I'm the boss here, so you're goin' to do exactly as you're told, right?" he said, spelling out those regulations like an army training sergeant.

I nodded, and then tried to say something, but the lack of air in my pulmonary tract hindered it, and whatever came out was unintelligible.

"Take your time, Doc. Am not goin' to rush things up. Breathe deep and just say 'yes'," he smirked.

I regained control of my breathing and stared at him again, this time with a furious grin.

You're dead meat, guys. I can't allow you to live. Gimme an opportunity to break free and you'll get a taste of Doc. Hyde's famous medicine.

"Once again, tell me why you were looking for Jay?"

"Do you really want to know? Hell, why not? Haven't experienced sharing for quite some time. It is so damn refreshing and it makes you feel better when you can show your real self," I said.

"Just the answer. No bullshit, Doc. Do not make me hit you again," he stated.

"Okay," I nodded, "I was curious to know who had barbecued him and left his dirty ashes in my dumping ground," I said innocently.

A quizzical look crossed his face. "What do you mean?"

"Don't you feel it disrespectful when someone empties their car ashtray in your garden?"

"Hit him again! Whoop him up, Boss," smattered Jolly-Golly.

Army-Man ignored him. "Explain."

"Simple. I was having a wonderful night out, my usual— getting my prey, dicing it, placing it inside various carryalls, and disposing of the pieces at my dumping spot."

"What prey? What the fuck are you babbling about?"

A smile took shape on my face. "What kind of prey? Scum. I prey on scum. However, I'm an ecologist, you see, I like to recycle."

Jolly-Golly and Larry gazed at me with a stupid expression of disbelief, even more so than the usual ape-like gape they sported. Nonetheless, Billy displayed interest. "Are you saying you kill people? Why, doctor, you're an AME not a hit man. Let's presume I'll eat this – which I don't – but tell me, who you work for?" he said.

Working for? Interesting question. Most of my life, I had

believed I was doing it for myself, because of being different, because I was a monster spawned from another's dark exploits. However, lately I had a change of mind. Yes, I was working for someone—some *thing* to be more precise—that had kept feeding its alien needs until none of my humanity had been left. I had become like a 'Hit Man of the Netherworld': unquestioning, relentless in pursuit, dutiful and loyal.

Somehow, instinctively, Billy felt something was wrong with me, and he reacted the way a scared stray dog does when confronted by a perceived threat. He punched me again; this time aiming at my jaw, causing my head to snap back so hard I heard my neck crack. That was a bad one. I felt myself lose consciousness, so I stabbed my left palm with the tiny blade to avoid dropping it in case of knockout.

"Right! Kill the badass muthafucker! Beat him to a pulp!" Larry the Lapdog shouted in excitement. I could feel his arousal, how much he craved for me to be snuffed out by his master's hands. Hell, I was sure he was getting a boner.

Billy the Moron turned to face his puppies. "Get outta here. Ain't any need for an audience. Larry, take care of the artillery. G.T., get back to the sentry post. I want to handle this alone, is that clear?"

Both men turned tails with a pouting face, like a pair of kids who'd been sent to their rooms by their momma.

Then, Billy returned his hateful glare to me. "Okay, retard. Let's spell it clear one last time. I don't give a fuck if you enjoy your heavy work or not. I don't care if you're some kinda freak on the Mexicans' payroll or you're out on your own. I know you didn't kill J.F., or at least you weren't alone. There's a bitch inside the story and I want to know who the fuck she is. Now!"

He barked the last word trying to show up his sergeant-like attitude. Then, he palmed his fatigues and unsheathed a dagger-sized blade from his left leg's holster. It was a commando knife, one of those used by US privates in Vietnam; renowned for the deep cuts it inflicted, it was very useful for slitting somebody's throat.

He pointed it at me. "I swear I'm goin' to kill ya slowly, man. And I'm going to enjoy it every damn sec. You say you're into dicing, huh? Let's see if I can do even better. I'm going' to slice you up, a piece at a time," he said, grinning wickedly.

Grabbing my neck, he pressed the sharp edge of the knife against it to underline the meaning of his words. My vision turned blurry and my surroundings were replaced by the ghostly images of a young girl being raped and savagely beaten by him and Larry. Then other similar scenes of violence against other women, at different places and times, hit me worse than he'd done physically, causing me to retch in disgust.

That's when my Rider resurfaced, leaving its dark lair to get hold of my body, to eat away at that good-humored shell I had built so painstakingly to regain my long-lost humanity. It was going to send me back into that obscure dungeon of my soul.

'*Feed me,*' it whispered, not with articulated words, but with an empathic-like broadcast, like some unearthly radio signal coming from *Beyond*.

Billy pushed the blade harder, allowing it to bite my neck. I felt a thin stream of blood trail down toward my heaving chest.

"Tell me ... Who's this woman?" Billy whispered in my ear.

But, I wasn't listening.

'*Fight!*' urged its voice.

"NO!" I cried.

Billy was caught unawares by my loud reaction, understanding it to be a response to his request. Enraged, he retreated, plucked two fingers inside my nose, and placed the razor-like blade on the bridge. He intended to saw it away!

It was at that moment that I – or the Rider – decided to end the pantomime.

My tiny blade flashed and found its way into his right temple. Hot blood splashed on my face with a vengeance. The stab wasn't enough to kill him, of course – the blade was too short and thin to pierce his skull bone – but gave me enough time to grab the hand holding the knife and twist it to force him to lose his grip. Unfortunately, Billy was tough and combat-ready; he didn't panic and used his free arm to try and jab his elbow right into my nose. But I was already pushing up, using my body mass to unbalance him, so he only managed to hit my right cheekbone. I ignored the pain – or maybe the Rider shut off that part of my nervous system, I honestly don't know – and pushed forward to make him fall on his back.

It didn't work.

Billy planted both feet into the ground and opposed equal force, and we ended up looking like a couple of flamenco dancers. Or a pair of stags in deer rut. It was quite funny, but I soon got bored, so I let go of his right hand and quickly pulled the little switchblade out of his temple. Then I had it sink deep into his right thigh, just below the inguinal ligament, and pulled it out again. He ignored it, and immediately punched me in the face.

That was a hard blow.

I staggered backward, stunned, and he took that moment to kick me in the belly. The impact sent me sprawling in the chair, breathless; the switchblade flew in the air and disappeared in the shadows.

My, my, all that heavy work and I was back where I had started.

I lifted my head only to see the sole of his boot coming for a kiss. Lady boot was a starving lover; in fact her impetus cracked my lips and sent me – and the chair – to a joyful reunion with the floor.

"As I said," hissed Billy, "I'm gonna enjoy every sec of it."

From the ground, I laughed.

"You really ARE a sick fuck." I couldn't see him, but I knew he was sporting one of those stupid expressions on his face. All covered in sweat and blood, towering above me, but not understanding why I was laughing. After all, I don't think the guy was such an expert in anatomy.

He came around and kicked me hard again.

"STOP LAUGHING! YA HEAR ME?"

Another kick, this time into my spine, for I had turned to the other side to protect my stomach while I kept braying like the Joker.

"STOP!" – kick – "YOU!" – kick – "FUCKING! – kick – "Bast—"

He crashed to the floor and started breathing heavily.

"Wha …" He tried, but couldn't talk anymore.

I stopped laughing and lifted myself off the ground. Then I cracked a sympathetic smile to him. "You're dying, Billy, so just relax." I could see incredulity in his eyes, but at the same time he was starting to realize that something bad was really happening to him.

"I pierced your femoral artery, dude." I kneeled to look into his eyes. They were already glazing out and probably could not see me clearly. "Life isn't like in the movies; if that thing is slashed for good and you do not apply a tourniquet or any kind of pressure to stop the bleeding – or worse, like in your case, if you ignore your wound – you're a goner."

He passed out. Then, his lungs stopped pumping air. Around him, a dark pool of blood was quickly spreading wide and large.

I gave him one last look before going for the knife.

"Next time, do not mess with a pathologist, asshole."

CHAPTER 33

SUCKING

With quiet grace, a phantom-like figure slid behind Lawrence Bootes, clasped his mouth shut with a hand, and finally cut his throat open with a large blade. He died in less than a minute.

Cheri found herself charmed by the sight of the blood turning the man's white t-shirt into a red version of a Rorschach test. She felt nothing for this man; he was not the real target of her unquenchable fury. But she had no other choice than to kill all those that were standing between her and final victims. She felt no remorse, for she was far beyond that point.

Snapping out of her temporary but distracting fascination, the woman started to climb up a circular structure by the way of iron rungs that had been hammered into the wooden walls. She had placed the knife back into its sheath and was now freeing the hatchet from the sling that tied it to her belt. There was another man up there – so Night Goer had told her – and she had to get rid of him before going on with her true hunt.

Cheri knew that these were not Moon-Eyed People, but just pawns of the real monsters. Nonetheless they deserved to die just because they had allowed the evil spirits to poison their souls.

Once close to the top, Cheri froze.

Night Goer had been wrong: there were two persons up there. And one was a woman.

She pressed her body against the wall and listened carefully.

"Please, lemme go!" she heard the woman beg who was now seeming to be her captor. "P-L-E-A-S-E! What d'you want more?"

"Shut the fuck up, whore!" growled the man.

Cheri felt her fury grow. But she had to wait; she had to take in the whole situation first.

She listened as the man mulled around, apparently unsure of what to do. Then, she clearly heard the cocking of a gun's hammer.

The woman started to scream.

"SHUT THE FUCK UP, I SAID!"

And then the sound of flesh hitting flesh. Again. And again.

Silence fell; the woman had stopped crying, but Cheri's fine ears could still pick up her soft sobs.

"Tell ya what," said her torturer, "I'm really sick of standing guard here while Billy gets all the fun. I think I may deserve some of my own. Don't ya think so, Shannon?"

BILLY.

That was the man she was looking for. Night Goer had been right: he was here.

Night Goer had also said that the last man – Frank – would be there too at some point. And Cheri had no reason to doubt the spirit's words.

"Please, don't ..." The woman's voice was broken now. "You don't have to—"

Cheri heard the sound of a zipper being pulled down.

"Suck it and I promise I won't hurt you," said the man coldly. "Do anything stupid and I swear I'll clip you."

That was too much to bear for Cheri. Memories of her own abuse – her own humiliation – resurfaced and played as an old movie inside her head. Her body tensed, ready to pounce on the unwary man.

"Wait!" whispered Night Goer, *"If he fires the gun he'll put the others on alert."*

But Cheri wasn't listening. With a defiant cry she sprung out of the opening and swung her hatchet at the rapist. Instantly, she understood her mistake.

A yellow flash – soon followed by a loud thunder – exploded from the muzzle of a .357 Colt Python.

****

At the exact moment the bullet erupted from the man's gun, Night Goer perceived the presence of the Other. The spirit had felt it before; its tainted Essence was almost everywhere around this town. It was especially strong in that abandoned camp where Night Goer's host had killed the second person on their list of dead-men-walking. But now, it was right here; somewhere inside this building, the Other was feasting on death.

Night Goer had no idea of how the Other would react to an intrusion in what it certainly considered its territory. But there was no other choice: Cheri's rage toward those men was the only thing anchoring Night Goer to her; and the spirit absolutely needed his host to complete the pattern. That was the only way to provide Night Goer what it needed: a legend.

Then the ancient spirit would be free to create its own shell.

With that in mind, and wary of the Other's presence, Night Goer tried to regain control of its Ridden.

****

The first shot, fired in haste, missed Cheri by inches. The bullet buried itself into one of the roof's beams, spraying fragments of splintered wood into the night. Before the man could fire a second shot, Cheri let the hatchet fall to the floor and threw herself at him. She grabbed the hand holding the pistol. They started to fight: one to keep hold of the Python, the other to get it.

Behind them, the woman named Shannon was staring at the battle with bulging eyes.

"Cocksucker," the man grunted, spitting in Cheri's face. "Who the fuck are you?"

Cheri didn't answer; instead, she crashed the top of her head into the man's nose. The guy squealed like the pig he was as dark blood streamed down to his chin. Quickly, Cheri wrenched his hand, forced the gun's barrel into the man's open mouth, rammed it hard, and applied pressure to his forefinger, forcing him to pull the trigger.

"Suck this, motherfucker!"

BANG!

The Colt's bullet destroyed half of the goon's face before following its sibling into the wood.

CHAPTER 34

DRIVES

It had been a weary and tedious day. Going to South Glade Trailers Park and looking out for the Núñez brothers had proven fruitless. Charlie Escalera, their cousin, declared that the two of them were out of town, in Cape Coral, to attend to their ill mother. Their neighbors—those willing to talk, at least—had confirmed Escalera's statement. Then there was the boring paperwork to do at the office. To make matters worse, Agatha Kiley had a bad attack of her rare but severe back pains, so Morena had to spend her whole turn alone at the station house. The sheriff was in Moore Haven to check something about Fraser and Wilson at the Glades County Department. Lane was out all day, interviewing the Bigelows at the Lakeview Motel, then going to the Assistant District Attorney. Amber Willis was stationed down at the burned cabin to aid a couple of arson investigators from Palmdale. And this was Peter's day off, too.

To make things worse, there was the trouble with Dan Mantz. Ray Henderson—the *Happy Gator*'s barkeeper—had called in, reporting the darn boozer was again causing troubles with his customers. Everything had started when the boater had heard a couple of guys talking about 'Wild Bill' Hunter. Hunter had been the undisputed reigning champion at the annual Prosperity's Rodeo for five years in a row back in the eighties, and had become something of a local hero when he had won the Silver Buckle at the Brighton Country Fair in 1987. No one from Prosperity had ever come back with a prize at that competition. Wild Bill's fame had soon come to a crash when he had been surprised by Vice cops having his way with a thirteen-year old Haitian prostitute in Vero Beach, dripping acid from all pores. He had cut his own wrists in prison back in 1996. However, his stardom never completely faded away; some devotees still paid homage to his figure.

Dan Mantz wasn't among them. He hated that man almost unreasonably, the sole mention of his name sending him into an uncontrollable fury. No one knew why, and maybe not even he remembered the origin of that. Usually pacific—when sober—Mantz was the local boozer, and unfortunately, a large one. He could become mean after having three rounds or more, but limited it to rough behavior and a series of colorful, if obscene, swears and curses. People who knew him had learned to stay away and just let him steam off.

However, these two hombres came from Murchison Springs, a rural community beyond the Jackson reservoir made up mostly of cattle herders and cultivators. Dan Mantz had jumped into the conversation, blaming Hunter for some of the town's misfortunes, then referring to him as 'Wild Pervert Hunter', and causing the two fans to react harshly.

Bad move.

This had turned into a nasty argument, which had hastily tacked on ill winds.

Henderson had immediately called on Espinoza, knowing she was the only person Mantz had respect for in the whole county. She was certainly able to quell the approaching storm before it unleashed its galeforce winds. Yet, things hadn't gone as smoothly as the barkeeper might have expected.

When Morena had turned up, the two Murchison cowpokes had backed off from the silly fight, looking more like a pair of schoolmates in the Principal's office. But Mantz had not withdrawn. He had stood firmly in the middle of the room with a pool cue in his hands. Deputy Espinoza had tried to keep her exhaustion and irritation in check, but when he addressed her as *Agent Mierdoza*, she had lost her temper, kicked him hard in the stomach, and quickly handcuffed him.

He was now resting inside the station's drunk tank, snoring like a drowsy bear.

She was still brooding about her bad day when Peter Tipple came in through the station's front doors, almost startling her.

"What's up?" she inquired, puzzled.

Being off-duty, Peter wore civilian clothes, in this instance his preferred pair of *Wrangler* jeans (cowboys' favored brand) below a sleeveless, and faded, denim shirt. His inseparable chocolate Stetson hat and brown boots completed the country boy outfit. He was carrying a set of plastic bags stuffed with containers of various sizes in one hand, while concealing something behind his back with the other.

"I thought you were all alone down here, so I figured why not pay you a visit?" he said, smiling shyly, and then placed the bags on the front desk, awkwardly avoiding the assorted forms and stationery on the surface. He looked at her straight. "I believe you haven't had time for a meal break yet, huh?"

Morena smiled back, surprised yet pleased by that kind gesture. At the same time, she regretted his bad timing. She was about to leave as her shift was over. Agatha had just called in to remind her to switch off the lights, check the rooms, and the usual before Amber took service at four in the morning.

However, she opted to say nothing, and simply nodded. *Aw man, couldn't you just ask me out for dinner?*

Pete removed his hat—apologizing for his bad manners—and placed it on the nearby couch, involuntarily giving away the item he was trying to hide: a bunch of flowers, adorned by colored paper wrappings and strings, the kind you could only get at the *Greenery*, an expensive florist shop on Osceola Avenue. "Figured you'd be starving, huh?" Tipple said while pulling the steaming plastic containers and a large bottle of soda out of the bag.

"Well, actually yes, but I was about to leave. I have a hearty precooked meal waiting to be microwaved at my home," she answered, still wondering about those flowers.

Peter raised his gaze from the stuff, showing a hint of bafflement in his eyes.

"I'm joking, Pete," she stated hurriedly. "I appreciate your kindness."

His relieved smile brightened his face. He picked up the food bowls and cups, and then something seemed to hit him. He rolled his eyes and presented the flowers to her. "Here, these are for you," he said hesitantly, as if expecting one of her sarcastic cracks or worse, a scolding about 'sexism'.

However, none came. She smiled broadly and recovered the bunch from his hand. "For me?" she feigned surprise, allowing a soft chortle. "How's it? What have I done to deserve this gift?" She felt herself turn red. Peter took notice and smiled, then returned his attention to the dinnerware.

She lifted the bunch toward her nose and got a whiff of their aroma, closing her eyes when they caused old memories to surface in her mind. Adam-and-Eves were her favorite orchids when she was a young girl; she used to spend a lot of time in her grandma's garden in Calle Ocho, relaxing in the fragrances and the peace it offered, away from the chaotic gaudiness of her large family.

****

Doña Josefina Maria Soledad Huertas had been a Cuban expatriate of the first wave in 1960, when thousands of middle- to upper-income families fled Fidel Castro's newly established Communist regime, arriving in Miami on daily 'Freedom Flights' from Havana. Doña Josefina and her husband, Emilio Luis Espinoza, had immediately invested in the real estate business in the developing side of Calle Ocho, paying particular attention to coffeehouses and restaurants. She had always carried herself with an elegant—even snobbish—attitude, looking down at the 'Marielitos' of the second wave. In 1980, another influx of Cubans migrated to the United States; however, unlike their predecessors, many of them were poor and largely unskilled. In addition, it was soon learned that Castro had used the opportunity to empty his jails and sanitariums and get rid of thousands of violent felons, drug addicts, mentally disturbed, and other 'undesirables' by allowing them to embark at Mariel Harbor and land in Miami—hence the nickname Marielitos. When Carlos Esteban Espinoza, Morena's daddy and Josefina's middle son, had fallen in love with Ascencion Salteras, the daughter of escaped *campesinos* (peasants), a storm broke out in the Espinoza family. Josefina, a strong-willed and dominant figure in the family, had powerfully rejected the idea of mixing her blood with that of the Salteras. This had resulted in alienating Carlos, who decided to sever all ties with his folks.

Later, when Morena turned seven, the two families had reconciled, with Doña Josefina then being an old widow living alone in her large mansion. Morena suspected the peace had been signed because her father had fancied the idea of inheriting his mother's large fortunes, yet she could not forget her dad's sincere grief at her funeral. That grief and crying had turned into screams of rage later, when he found out there was no fortune to speak of, for Doña Josefina had completely dilapidated it by living above her standards for more than ten years. In fact, she'd been full of debt.

****

"Are you hungry or not?" Peter asked, sweeping away those old memories. Her attention returned to him and she could not avoid noticing how handsome he was. She nodded, then retrieved one of those glass vases Agatha used to decorate the front office and placed the clustered blooms inside it.

Thunder rumbled away as the couple had their dinner on the station house's front desk, signaling the coming of yet another tropical storm. Peter had bought that tasty assortment of morsels from the *Happy Gator*—a rich variety of burgers, fries, some salads and fragrant bread. He had also stopped at *Martha's*, a bakery shop in De Soto Avenue, to tempt Morena with one of those hyper caloric cakes the place was famed for.

They laughed and chatted together like a pair of old friends, yet Peter never mentioned the previous night's dalliance.

"Well, time for me to get out of this uniform," said Morena innocently, causing hilarity in Peter when he, obviously, took that as an interesting proposal. "I'd really like that!" he exclaimed.

Morena smirked, and then joined in his laughter. "No, seriously, Pete. My duty ended half an hour ago and no one is going to pay me overtime. I should go, and so should you," she said, while trying to regain her usual composure.

"Didn't you enjoy my company?" Peter asked, frowning.

She couldn't tell if he was acting for real or not. "I really loved it, Peter. It's just..." She hesitated. "Better for me to go."

Again, that baffled look on his face.

In a sudden gesture, he rose from his chair, grabbed her by the shoulders and kissed her passionately on her mouth. Taken by surprise, Morena's initial reaction was to resist his probing tongue, but she softened and allowed her body to respond. She rolled her tongue inside his palate. However, when Peter's craving hand reached down to caress her behind, Morena, feeling flushed, pushed him aside.

"Better for me to go," she repeated, panting—not with disdain, but with a hint of shame and shock.

She rushed upstairs to the changing room, took off her uniform and got into a set of those new clothes she had bought at the *Heights*, feeling embarrassment for provoking her colleague then retreating like a shy teenager. She buttoned the white lace top, pulled up her skimpy jean miniskirt, fastened it with a thick leather belt, and then slid inside a pair of soft and fashionable calf-length boots.

When she returned downstairs, Peter was still there, waiting for her. She averted her gaze, purposely looking for a nonexistent backpack—she had not brought it with her today, having opted for a more practical handbag that she'd placed inside the valuables locker downstairs, next to Amber's haversack.

"I offended you, didn't I?" Peter said in a low tone, as if feeling sorry for what he had done.

"No. It's not that, Pete," she said, this time raising her eyes toward his. "It's just ... Oh, I don't know. I feel so stupid!"

"You aren't," he protested.

"No, Peter, I *am* stupid. Look what I've done to you. You're a good man, you always behave sincerely and all these years, I never understood it. I know you liked me, yet I was too burned up by my past experiences, too bitter, to appreciate your genuine sweetness."

"We all make mistakes," he said, coming closer. "I made a lot myself. Just relax, don't worry. Yes, I liked you from the first time I saw you, but I never pressured you. I just tried to be kind, in my old-mannered way, if you like."

"And I mistook that as some kind of macho behavior. Besides, you look like someone used to female attention. You know you're handsome."

"Really? Well, I'm no Brad Pitt, but I'm not as ugly as Dan Mantz," he said, laughing and getting closer.

Morena instinctively took a step backward, just one.

"And look," he continued, parting the left side of his hair, revealing a deep scar. "I'm not so handsome." Then he pointed to his nose. "And here. The bridge was broken in a brawl at the County Fair five years ago. It never healed well."

Another step. Morena could see something new in his eyes, in the way he was looking at her, exploring all of her body.

Was it lust? Desire?

She giggled, then took another step backward. Yet she felt hot. She wanted him as much as he wanted her, and felt the drive to throw herself in his strong arms.

"Morena, I can't lie. I want you. I'm getting crazy about it. Last night, I was unable to sleep. My mind kept going to that kiss," he said in a deep voice.

"Well, it is better for us to forget about it. We're cops, we shouldn't be anything else. This kind of relationship can't last," she affirmed.

He was so close now, she could feel his body warmth and the spicy aroma of his aftershave cologne. It smelled good.

"I don't care," he said softly. "Who cares? I can't deny my attraction. Will it last? I don't know. Besides, I don't even know if I will die tomorrow or the day after tomorrow, you know?"

He reached out with both arms and grabbed her shoulders, pulled her closer, allowed her to feel his warm body against hers. She put up a fake struggle, but soon stopped it. She felt so good, so damn good.

He pushed her chin upward to have her eyes meet his gaze. Those steel-gray irises seemed to stare right at her soul, burning with sexual need like two hot metal dishes straight out of a blacksmith's furnace.

She reached up and kissed him again.

This time, it was different. They groped at each other with raw lust, their hot, burning mouths searching to ease the pressure of need. When his hands got down to grab her buttocks she didn't put up any opposition; on the contrary, she responded by pawing at his tight ass, pulling him closer. Aroused, Peter started to lick her neck, while she moaned softly at the passage of his turgid tongue on her responsive skin. He kissed, licked, and nipped, eliciting her moans as she grabbed him by the hair and guided him toward her breasts.

Soon, they were on the old couch, stroking each other, kissing and letting out their animal drives, not thinking about tomorrow, or yesterday, just about the now. She lay on her back, spread-eagled, while Peter pushed his bulge between her legs with singular intent.

She felt dazed, overcome by a lust she had not felt in years. She forgot about regulations, the statistical failure of cop's relationships, the fact that they were necking inside a police station. Yet something was desperately trying to draw her attention away from him; something inside her cop's mind kept crying for alertness.

Peter noticed her uneasiness, so he halted his moves to ask, "What's up?"

"Nothing," she said, panting, then reached down with her right hand to fondle his erection. "Just do me."

At that, Peter lost every restraint. He caught her by the hips, turned her sideways, and pulled down his jeans zipper in one fluid movement, releasing his stiff penis from the forced captivity of his pants. After pulling down her undies, he plunged it firmly inside her. He had his way with her in such a wild and unexpected manner, that Morena came shouting her unstrained pleasure in less than a minute, unable to have it last longer. Peter followed soon after, ramming against her back with violent strokes, and releasing a series of beastly grunts, which caused further waves of delight inside her.

As they wound down, they held each other on the couch. Peter caressed her face and she his back.

"I'm sorry for behaving like that," he started to say, but she hushed him up by placing a finger on his lips.

"I liked it," she said. He smiled and went back to caressing her.

Morena felt wonderful. She had never had such a passionate encounter in all of her life. Yes, it had been brief, almost a quickie, but it had been so full, so complete.

Yet, that small voice kept telling her something was amiss; she had forgotten something. But what? Had they left the front door unlocked? What if someone had come in and surprised them in that embarrassing circumstance? No, she remembered that Peter had locked it before their impromptu dinner on the front desk. The lights?

The fuck with those damn lights and Agatha Kiley, too!

No, it wasn't that. She felt that she had clearly forgotten something. Her mind returned to the last events, before having sex, to the conversation she'd had with him.

Still nothing.

She noticed he was ready to start again, turned toward him and kissed him, suggesting she was willing, too. This time they got undressed, but not completely, because this was a station house, their working place, and they could get both fired for that unusual, if not unconventional, behavior.

He allowed her to ride him and it lasted longer, as they took their time to enjoy the best out of the act. They moaned and groaned, filling the station with sounds it had likely never heard before.

Until they froze at another sound, the blood chilling inside their veins as the words carried to their ears from downstairs.

"WOULD YOU STOP SCREWING LIKE THE DIRTY ANIMALS YOU ARE? SOMEONE IS TRYING TO SLEEP DOWN HERE!"

And Morena remembered what she had forgotten.

That was the voice of Dan Mantz, no longer sleeping away the booze in the drunk tank.

CHAPTER 35

THE DARK ANGEL
(FROM AXEL'S HALL OF MEMORIES)

I heard the first shot while I was retrieving the army knife from Billy's dead hand. It had come from the upper floor. Now, that was interesting. Assuming that the only people present in this place where the now defunct Billy and his two goons, I wondered what the hell was going on. But staying there, in the dark, waiting for the two buffoons to show up was pointless, so I decided to go investigate the source of the gunshot. I opened the door and found myself in some kind of tight underground corridor. There were no other rooms; just a rough ladder that climbed to a hole in the ceiling. Stealthily, I made my way up, being careful to not poke my whole head out of it, but just the top, so that I could inspect the place for hidden dangers.

The square thing opened into a large room that I supposed to be the core of the survivalists' fort. The place was brightened by a weakly burning oil lamp, and contained some bunk beds, tables and some chests.

But the most interesting sight in the room was not the furniture.

It was the pair of glassy eyes that stared at me inches away. Those belonged to Lapdog Larry – Billy's loyal minion – who was now soaking in his own blood. Someone had slit his throat open and had left him there like a discarded soda can.

Except for a couple of disassembled hunting rifles and a *Beretta* (probably that was the *armory* Billy had referred to), plus some unspent cartridges and a pair of magazines, I couldn't see any gun that could have been used recently. I decided to climb out of the hole and check Larry's body for bullet wounds - even if I was sure I would find none.

It was at that moment that I heard the second shot. And the shout of a woman.

I moved toward the doorway that would lead me to where the scream had come from, balancing my weight so as to prevent the floor planks from creaking under my feet. As soon as I reached the threshold I instinctively retracted into the shadows to avoid being spotted by the dark clad figure that was now descending from the top of what looked like a crude military guard post. The newcomer stepped into the light and a gasp almost escaped my lips.

It was her: the Dark Angel!

Pale skin, black clothes, and silver jewelry.

Of course, I was tempted to reveal myself and talk to her, but after the last events I was no longer sure about anything. Could it be possible she was in league with these fuckers? No, I discarded that thought immediately. That hypothesis didn't fit with her modus operandi.

Still, I had to know what had happened up there before confronting her.

She scoured her surroundings like a wolf, and then she disappeared toward what I supposed to be the fort's entrance. At that point, I hazarded moving into the next corridor, but once there I found that she wasn't gone. Luckily, she was showing her back to me, while she sniffed the air life a predatory animal. I managed to skulk behind a metal locker just in time, for she soon turned on herself and scampered right into the room I had just come from. She was clearly looking for something – or someone – but she was acting weird, as if whatever she was trying to find could not be seen, but *felt* by means of unknown senses. The Angel danced from left to right; her legs slightly spread apart and bent, while she moved around the room as if she were blind. For a moment, I caught a glimpse of her eyes: they looked darker than the ones I had seen in my vision. They also looked … empty.

Then, she jumped down into the hole.

I had to be fast, so I hastily emerged from my hiding place and climbed the iron rungs up to the top.

There, I found the source of the scream: a woman had been hogtied to a chair. She was still alive, but it was clear that she had endured a lot of physical trauma, for her face was swollen and covered in blood. Somehow, under all that turgid tissue, she looked familiar.

I also found where the gunshot had come from – or more properly, where it had ended. What was left of Jolly Golly looked like a Picasso painting.

****

I was about to untie the girl when I saw the airboat docking with two guys onboard. I recognized the first one immediately: Vice Lane.

What the fuck was he doing here?

Identifying the second one took me more time, for he wasn't wearing his usual classy suit—but there was no mistaking him.

Frank Hall, one of the most powerful men in Prosperity Glades.

My, my! The plot was really thickening.

To be honest, I never liked the man: arrogant, classist, and shady. I suspected him of having connections in the underworld. However, he had never popped up on my list of playmates. For what I knew he wasn't a rapist or a pedo.

I watched them leave the boat and walk toward the fort. From here, I could see that the building I was in was a raw structure, mostly made of wood and patches of metal plates – probably discarded materials the fuckers had gathered from the swamp (I even recognized a piece of the door from Lewis Perreira's garage – how romantic) – laid out on a single floor, plus the underground room, and this observation tower.

"Who are you?" said the girl, suddenly.

"Me? I mean you no harm, stay sure; I'm a friend."

Was I? Everything was so messed up that I could not be sure of anything. It was all new to me: I wasn't some kind of superhero

259

rescuing endangered people, I was a monster. I mean, let's face it: out there, there'll be people that would surely give me a medal for what I was doing; people that had lost their kids, wives, friends at the hands of disgusting predators. But there were others that would send me straight to death row. And I knew I was no vigilante.

Edmund Kemper had said it: *what I needed to have, was a particular experience with a person, and to possess them in the way I wanted to: I had to evict them from their human bodies.* What I needed, what I did, was not related to a sense of justice, or duty. Like Kemper I felt the need to hunt a specific kind of prey. Yes, they were bad guys, but that was incidental. As incidental as me saving this girl's life.

Still, I felt something.

I really didn't want this girl to die. She was the girl I had seen being violated by Billy and his gang. I felt *angry* for the abuse she had suffered; and it was *my* anger, not the Rider's.

"Please, let me go," she said.

I heard the men getting closer; boots crunching sawgrass.

"Look, I promise to let you go, but first I want you to understand this: there are more bad men down there," I whispered. "Now, if we want to survive this I need you to stay silent and help me. Can you that?"

She nodded.

"Good."

I used the blade to cut the ropes and she was soon free.

"Shannon," she murmured.

"What?"

"My name. My name is Shannon."

"Nice to meet you, Shannon. Can you use a gun?"

"No."

"Well, I can't blame you; I'm a shitty shooter myself. Anyway—"

Down there, I heard Hall asking something to Lane. "Where's the welcome committee?"

"You tell me, I knew of the place, but it's the first time I come here," said the other.

Shit, they were almost at the fort.

"Well, it's quite weird. There's always someone on guard up there." Hall pointed in my direction, to the tower. "There! That must be Bootes."

Damn, he had seen me!

Luckily, in the dark, he had just managed to catch my silhouette, so he had assumed me to be this Bootes he was talking of. Good for me.

I decided to play along. I had no plan. Actually, I was feeling a bit confused for I couldn't focus on the two approaching men; I kept thinking about the Angel, but I had no intention to go into panic mode. I signaled for Shannon to stay silent, then straightened up and waved at them. I also switched on the big searchlight to brighten them and, at the same time, make it hard for them to see me clearly.

"Hey, Larry, it's me: Frank. And this one here is an old friend of Jay. I think you already know him. Vice Sheriff Lane," said Hall.

Larry Bootes is swimming in a pool of his blood, at the moment, I thought. Well, now I knew the full name of Lapdog Larry. Not that I gave a rusty possum fart about it.

"Shannon, get down and find a place to hide. We'll be like bears on a tree if we stay here," I uttered. "There's a locker down—"

"But what about Billy? And Larry?" she interrupted me.

"They're dead. Don't worry. There's no one else, except these two."

"And what about the woman? The strange woman?"

I had forgotten about the Dark Angel, or rather, I intentionally hadn't mentioned her. Well, I had no idea of her whereabouts, and it didn't matter at the moment.

"I dunno. I swear," I said, irritated. "We'll talk about this later, okay? I need to think."

I remembered the big gun stuck inside what was left of Jolly Golly's mouth. I bent and dislodged it, then I offered it to Shannon, but she refused to grab it, gagging. "Ain't gonna touch that. Sorry, but I can't"

"C'mon!" I insisted. "I know you said you have never used one, but it's not that complicated; you just have to point it and pull the trigger. Plus, I hope you won't need to."

Again I presented the revolver. And again she pulled back. This time she almost screamed. "Keep that thing away from me!"

"Okay, okay, calm down." Sheesh, I almost regretted freeing her. Holy shit, I was giving her a weapon to defend herself, not a kick in the ass!

Then I understood.

It was caked with blood, lumps of flesh, cartilage, and bone splinters.

I'm used to that stuff, but a lot of people can get squeamish around it.

I decided to give it a cleanup – using Jolly Golly's jacket as a rag – but there was no time. Something was going on downstairs. The two men had stopped advancing.

I peeked down and saw Hall standing just in front of the entrance, grabbing Lane's left arm.

"Why is the door open?" he shouted up at me, lifting his other hand to shield his eyes from the bright light. James Lane's right hand, instead, moved to his hip, looking for his gun.

Dammit. I couldn't answer; my voice would never sound like that of Lapdog Larry.

Hall's voice became colder. "I said: why is the main door open? Can you answer me or have you lost your tongue?" Now his hand went looking for something inside his camo jacket too. He was armed as well.

The hell with it! I switched off the searchlight and rushed down the tower. If I had to fight two armed men in this place I had to get an advantage. And, as I said, my Rider had always provided to that by enhancing my senses. Now, unless the two had a similar

262

thing inside – something I doubted – they'd have to rely on their flashlights.

I heard Shannon complain up there, but I ignored her.

It was show time. So I shut everything down inside my brain and went into reptile mode.

The light coming from the main room was not enough to brighten the small corridor going to the front entrance, so I took advantage of the shadows – as I had done before with the Angel – and lurked there, waiting for them to get inside. The front door had probably been left open by the strange woman when she had come in unnoticed by Billy's men. She was a perfect killing machine, using both stealth and guile to get her prey, employing all her natural charms and combat skills to get what she wanted – or needed.

Yes, I could not stop feeling admiration for her. At the same time, I was no fool. She was like a tiger: beautiful to look at, but you'd better stay out of the reach of her fangs and claws. I had to be careful; she was not my friend, and she was very likely to react violently to my presence.

What happened next proved me right.

Vice Sheriff Lane was the first one to cross the threshold.

And to die.

I saw his surprised expression when the blade flashed from the shadows and chopped his right ear away in a single stroke, then continued down to his shoulder, cleaving skin, muscles, ligaments, and finally, striking hard against the collarbone.

The Dark Angel had been here all the time; hiding in the dark and ready to pounce on the newcomers. Grabbing a hatchet with two hands she had lowered it hard into the cop. The man screamed in pain, and instinctively discharged a couple of rounds, blindly.

The first one missed her completely; it blew off a chunk of plaster and wood from the wall at the end of the corridor, inches away from me. The second one nearly found its mark. It scraped the woman's right hip, but didn't stop there; it went on and wedged itself into an old barrel.

The woman yelped, then screeched like a cat. The hatchet came back. It slammed against the door frame, where Lane had put his left hand in an effort to stand his ground. It sent splinters of wood and two fingers flying through the air.

Lane screamed again in agony, but it didn't last. His voice box collapsed when the blade cracked his jawbone. Instantly, he was on his knees.

The woman stood there; as an executioner getting ready for the job, she lifted both arms high in the air, then she split the cop's head in two halves.

Frank Hall, who had been just behind the vice sheriff, snapped out of his initial shock, lifted his own gun at the woman and fired a short burst. The three bullets went inside the dead body of Lane, for she had acted fast: like a trained killer, she had bent down and, by lifting it up above her head, she had used the cop's body as a shield.

I couldn't believe my own eyes.

Hall tried to fire again, but the Dark Angel was already on him: she grabbed his arm, then twisted it at an unnatural angle. A sharp *crack* told me she had broken it.

The gun landed into the mud while Hall howled like a dog hit by a speeding car. His deafening cry of pain was cut short by a powerful kick to his face that sent the man sprawling in the same boggy bed as his pistol.

Satisfied, the Angel reached down to check the man's breath. He must have still been alive because she decided it was not over: she grabbed him under his armpits and started to drag him inside the house.

Shannon chose that moment to call me.

"Hey, are you okay?" she shouted.

I was still in the dark end of the corridor, but when the Angel lifted her head in reaction to Shannon's voice, somehow she saw me.

Her face twisted into an animalistic snarl, and her green-blue eyes gleamed with rage. She let go of the man and rushed toward me, retrieving the hatchet from Lane's head while crossing the threshold.

She left me no choice: I had to fight for my own life.

CHAPTER 36

FACE TO FACE

Night Goer saw the Other's host. He was a large male specimen of his breed; much larger than its own Ridden. He also looked stronger and more resilient than Cheri.

However, the ancient spirit could *smell* his fear.

Yes, the human was afraid, and that was good. There was no sign of his Rider. It meant that whatever was riding him was not as powerful as Night Goer had imagined. Maybe this *enemy* was not able to claim completely its host; it could only urge it. Or it could be that the Rider was asleep.

But there was also a third, terrible possibility.

The *enemy* was so powerful that it possessed the ability to hide from Night Goer's senses.

While Cheri was busy checking the last of the Moon-Eyed People's life signs, Sunnayi Edahi decided to expand its *feelers* and look for subtle traces of its adversary. It knew that the human mount would provide a perfect ecosystem for lesser spirits: a possessed always attracted – or produced – a sizeable quantity of minor emotional entities. Simple, unintelligent motes, of course, but still useful for the residing Rider. Like a reef to a school of fish, a ridden being supplied both relative safety (a hiding place from other predators of the Shadow) and a nearby source of food generated by the attuned host's emotions.

But it found none.

There could be only one explanation: the Rider had fled the Ridden.

Emboldened by the revelation, Night Goer took complete control of its host, shrieked, and rode her into battle.

****

Nemesis knew that the Raven Mocker would employ insidious tricks to gain an advantage. Thus, instead of confronting it directly, it opted to lure it into a trap. It stepped out of the Material World and crossed into the Shadow.

The dark corridor immediately faded to reveal its spiritual counterpart: a black, murky river replaced the wooden planks, and the walls faded into a dense jungle of primordial vines and gnarled branches infested by tiny clouds of crimson pain motes. At the points where the withered roots of those colossal trees met the brackish water, larger – but still insignificant – amorphous clusters of despair spirits emanated a green phosphorescent light.

Nemesis, in its *Silent Hunter* form, slithered and quickly disappeared into the black waters, leaving them undisturbed, forming no ripples on its greasy surface. The air outside felt crisp, clean, but tense and pulsating at the same time. The *ground* surrounding the river looked like strips of torn flesh, as if the stream were a long gash on the earth's skin.

A sensation of '*being home*' overwhelmed the predator spirit, and it felt something similar to amusement at that. A part of it, the primal one, remembered with fondness the simple life before the fall. Everything was basic: hunting, feeding, hiding, sleeping, and awakening. It remembered being born of the Essence of the Alligator.

The evolved part, instead, only felt annoyance. It much preferred the Material World, with all its complex nuances and new emotions. The Alligator didn't care about the taste of scared meat. Food was food; nothing else. But the Evolved relished in the different flavors, it enjoyed the way food was enriched by the mixture of human emotions.

For many years, before finding the perfect mount in Axel, Nemesis had been forced into the role of an opportunistic predator and a scavenger. It had made its lair into a forgotten human relic; a tube of concrete that had been tainted with the Essence of dying children. Weakened by the sudden death of its last host, Nemesis had had no choice but to hide and revert to its basic primal nature.

The risk of being hunted and eaten by bigger spirits was too high at the time.

Axel had changed everything.

The human child had also found refuge into that place to escape a predator. And, like Nemesis, he had been engulfed by the mixed emotions of fear, rage, and helplessness. That attunement had made the joining smooth. Before Axel, Nemesis had been constrained to act in the ways of the Spirit-Thieves – creatures that it despised. Only the most desperate and lowliest would slam into a weak-willed host and shove aside the victim's personality to gain full control of their bodies. Yes, it had the advantage of ignoring the host's affinities, but the disadvantages were enormous. Complete control meant that Nemesis had to immediately master the ways of an unfit host. Its Ridden reeled and staggered like drunkards; except for autonomic muscular activity, movement of the stolen body required great amounts of energy. They were good for short hunts, but they quickly decayed, or worse, easily attracted unwanted attention. Thus, Nemesis used it sparingly. For example, if a group of unwary kids decided to explore Kamp Koko by night, in one of those weird dare things that humans loved so much, Nemesis would use that opportunity to possess the weak-willed one, and quickly kill the others to get sustenance. But once it was over, it was smart enough to drive its host completely insane, or have it commit suicide.

As a consequence, Nemesis preferred being an Urger, a spirit that had no direct control of its host, but that fueled pre-existing emotions and wants to gain mutual advantages. In short, it didn't like to drive, but loved to stay in the backseat and give directions.

This had allowed Nemesis to prosper and grow in power.

Of course, from time to time it had tested its Ridden's will, especially when there had been no way to explain to its host why it was important to hunt and kill a specific individual. Nemesis could not transmit to Axel the importance of feeding on similar Rider spirits. The host had never noticed that the man he had dubbed Face Stealer had no longer been a man, but one of the Claimed. In fact, the personality of the man once known as Lewis Perreira had completely merged with that of its Rider: *Empty Eyes*.

But Nemesis had known about it.

And now, in this particular moment, there was no time or need to explain that what was about to jump on him with murderous intent was not a woman, but the Claimed of the Raven Mocker. It was up to Nemesis to find a way to defeat a fully-fleshed spirit.

Camouflaged by motes of decay and tainted water, only its eyes pierced the shadow river's surface and looked for the approaching enemy – and prey. And in the phosphorescent light it saw the Raven Mocker take complete control of its Ridden.

Nemesis could see, under the pale skin of the host, the rotting feathers spreading, the bird-like skull opening its beak in a terrible shriek, the six red eyes glaring, and the iron talons ready to strike at Axel.

The Raven Mocker had not seen Nemesis. It had underestimated it.

And would soon pay with its own Essence for this.

****

Sunnayi Edahi felt its form expand through the host's body, and mold to the tender material flesh. It did not intend to warp the Ridden's form in an unnatural way, though, so it just allowed its spiritual matter to surface under the woman's skin. This would allow the body to gain some of Night Goer's abilities, the way it had done before when Cheri had to face the armed men, but without giving away its Shadow nature. Sure, there was no sign of the Other inside the prey, but that didn't mean it was not hiding somewhere. Claiming its Ridden was good for providing more strength and resilience its host's body, but at the same time would make Night Goer vulnerable to spiritual attacks.

Night Goer saw fear inside the human's eyes, and frenzied by its irresistible aroma, bent its host's legs, and she pounced on her prey like a famished harpy.

269

It was too late when it saw the black, spiky and fangled spirit creature erupt from the ground and dive into the Raven Mocker's Ridden's flesh.

****

Axel was doing his best to deflect the Raven Mocker's attacks. The Claimed kept swinging her hatchet, but Nemesis' host had so far dodged all of them. The Urger wondered why he was not using his knife to counterstrike. There had been a couple of instances where an opening would have allowed the man a clean hit to the woman's side, but he had just evaded the vicious blade and rolled away.

Yet there was no time to dwell on its host: Night Goer was now aware of Nemesis' invasion and was ready to fight back.

Quickly, the Urger moved upward, closing its razor-sharp jaws on one of Raven Mocker's wings. Once it felt the taste of the enemy's Essence – along with the satisfying crunch of broken bones – it locked its maws and pulled down. The Enemy reacted by trying to slash its eyes, but it soon found out that being in complete control of its host's body made that impossible. Nemesis had left the Raven Mocker no choice: it had to let go of its Ridden and fight Nemesis in the Shadow.

And that was exactly what Nemesis wanted.

****

I underestimated the Other! I thought it was a simple Rage spirit. No! The monstrosity is a hybrid! And this is its domain!

These were Sunnayi Edahi's last thoughts when it saw the large crocodilian-like form emerge from below. Its scales were not flat, like its material counterpart, but were instead shaped like iron spikes, jutting out of its huge, but flexuous body. Red eyes, hosting star-shaped pupils, rotated backward in the same way of those of an attacking shark, while its gigantic mouth opened to reveal three rows of sharp and wicked knives in place of teeth.

Night Goer felt the jaws lock on its legs, then was pulled out of its host and into the depths of the Shadow river, where it was swallowed at once.

CHAPTER 37

SHOWDOWN
(FROM AXEL'S HALL OF MEMORIES)

The Dark Angel was fast. Too fast, actually. She moved with a swiftness and a grace more akin to that of a feline than a human being. In fact, her blue glare on me made me think of a panther. Heck, even her black clothes and hair helped build up that mental image. Except …

Except panthers don't usually carry hatchets.

I really didn't want to fight her; I wanted to talk to her, understand what was urging her. But she didn't look like she was in for a group therapy session. No, she crouched like a leopard ready to pounce and then …

What the fuck?

She disappeared into the dark. I couldn't see her anymore. What was it? Could she turn invisible? Or had my *night vision* stopped working? I didn't know. However, I had no time to find out for I could still hear the rustling of her clothes.

As I said before, my creepy symbiosis has provided me with some kind of sensorial enhancement. It's not that I see in the dark like I'm wearing infrared goggles; no, it's just that my retina and pupils let in more light. In short, I usually have cat's eyes when my Rider is awake.

Had it gone dormant? Now? Well, thanks, you selfish bitch!

I had to act; I couldn't stay there like a piece of wood waiting to be chopped, so I moved a bit to my left, toward the door leading to the main room in order to be ready to tumble sideways. My hope was to avoid her first strike and gain more fighting space – and more visibility, as that room had a sputtering oil lamp.

Finally, I saw her pale face fading in from the dark as she crossed the wedge of orange light: her lips were stretched in a grin and her blue-green eyes …

Blue-green? Jeebus! They no longer were looking like pools of clear water, but they were now like pools of murky water!

And what about her skin? There was *something* moving underneath it; it was like tendrils of dark matter, or veins. And then that screech!

I was stunned by the vision of that mutation, but not enough to freeze on the spot. When she swung her hatchet at my neck, I squatted and the blade hit only empty air. There was a *swoosh* sound above my head and then the *thud* of my left fist hitting the flesh of her abdomen. I expected her to reel back from the impact, breathing heavily, but it didn't happen. It was like punching a bag full of concrete: she didn't flinch, but actually prepared for a second strike, this time by lifting the weapon upward to chop down straight at my skull.

Luckily, I rolled out of her reach by tumbling into the next room; the hatchet didn't find its mark, but managed to cut a strip of fabric off of my trousers' right hem. I kept tumbling until I was right under the central table, then swiftly moved behind it in order to put that wobbly piece of rotten furniture between me and my assailant. At that point I was just running on pure instinct, ignoring all the weird stuff that was happening to that woman. And this, probably, saved my life.

I saw her step into the room: her features looked different, more hawkish I'd say, and her eyes were now like pits of black tar. And she was so fast she seemed like she could actually fly. She vaulted across the room holding the hatchet high above her head with both hands. My reptile brain had me roll again to my right and the blade hit the floor exactly where I was a second ago, and wobbled from the impact. I pulled myself up as fast as I could. But she was faster.

I felt the metal carve its way into my hip and I hit the floor again, in pain. Blood started gushing out of the wound, but it didn't seem like I had suffered fatal damage, for my clothes had absorbed part of the impact and the blow had not struck any major artery.

The blade came down again.

Gritting my teeth, I rolled to the left, and the hatchet went deep into the dead chest of Lapdog Larry, making his body jerk.

I took that opportunity to spring up on my feet again, grab a metal box of ammunition (what where these guys up to here? Where they planning for WWIII?) and use it to shield myself from her next attack, for she had already dislodged the hatchet from the corpse and was once more coming at me.

The box sounded empty when the descending steel hit it hard. Sparks flew in front of my eyes as I desperately forced myself to keep hold of my improvised shield.

But I failed.

The box flew to the left, and went crashing against the wall with a loud *clang*.

Then she kicked me in the guts. I flew backward until I hit the edge of a shelf. Little glass jars – containing God knows what – and old magazines for gun enthusiasts invaded my field of vision as they showered down on me. The blow left me gasping for air. I knew I had to get away from there as soon as possible, but I needed time to catch my breath. Time I didn't have, because the Dark Angel was already lifting her blade for her final strike.

My vision turned blurry, and I could only discern her shape looming above me, surrounded by the dying orange light from the lamp.

Then, unexpectedly, the silhouette changed form: as when someone gives up after a long, tiring exercise, her arms came down, separately and in a weird way, and her legs gave in under her weight.

She crashed to the floor like a wet rag.

****

I lay there on the floor for some time, before I finally regained my strength. I was expecting her to be back on her feet at any moment, but it didn't happen. She didn't move and looked as if she were dead.

Another *WTF* entry in my daily dose of *WTF* moments. Not that I wasn't grateful for this one.

What had happened to her? One moment she had been full of homicidal rage and hellish stamina, and then she had collapsed as if an invisible puppeteer had suddenly cut the strings holding her up.

I crawled over to check on her, careful to not fall in an eventual trap. My rational mind kept telling me that made no sense: why opt for a ruse when you're having the upper hand? Still, the reptilian core of my brain kept me on guard.

She had fallen on her side; her left arm pinned under her own weight and the right one resting on her hip. Her beautiful lineaments were stretched into an expression of shock, though her eyes were now shut. The hatchet lay mere inches from her.

I immediately took hold of it.

Then I checked her pulse. It was there, regular and strong. I checked her breath. Same thing. She looked like she had fallen into a coma: alive, but inanimate.

I spotted a bundle of rope in the left corner, so I decided to not run risks and make my environment safer: I needed to tie the Dark Angel first, and then take care of Frank Hall.

The girl, I restrained to a chair. When I lifted her body from the ground I was surprised by her light weight; she was muscular, but not to the point of being bulky. Her skin, though made greasy by the mud and caked blood, smelled good and felt so warm to the touch.

My, my, I really liked her. Unfortunately, I was sure the attraction wasn't mutual. Anyway, that was not the place nor the time to develop a crush.

Hall, I hogtied to a table. A sturdier one, not that shitty thing that had barely shielded me from the Angel's attacks.

While I was busy making sure those two would no longer cause any harm, Shannon kept calling for me from upstairs. I reassured her that everything was okay a couple times, but she wouldn't stop. I really wanted for her to shut up. She was driving

275

my head in with all that yelling, and crying, and questioning …

I needed to focus.

What was I going to do now? Everything was such a mess.

Let's go in order. First: Frank Hall.

It was evident the man was part – if not the leader – of a criminal organization that had included Vice Sheriff Lane among its ranks. He was also responsible for something that had happened to the Dark Angel, but I still didn't know what. Of course, I could not allow him to live: a guy like that would make my life very complicated.

Second: Shannon.

I could let her go. I wanted to let her go. On the other hand, she had been witness to a lot of the shit that had happened here. Yes, all she knew was that I was a prisoner like her. Could she be trusted?

Last: my Dark Angel.

She was the main reason I was there. I wanted to know what was urging her; I wanted to know if she had a thing like mine inside her soul. I felt something for her, something stronger than I felt for Shannon. What, I couldn't say, at that moment. But it was like this: every time my eyes fell on her I could feel my stomach rumble and my cheeks warming up – exactly like when I had been spying on that Asian girl. I also experienced a hot sensation in my groin – and of that I felt ashamed. She was so beautiful …

I forced my eyes away from her and decided to go help Shannon out of her hiding place.

It was at that moment that the Rider spoke to me.

"Kill her," it pushed. *"You can't let her live …"*

I don't want to, I thought. *Why should I?*

"You'll do as I say. There's no time to waste—"

"NO!" I jumped at my own voice.

That prompted more worried questions from Shannon. "What now? Are you okay? Oh, God, what's happening? Answer me!"

"KILL HER! KILL THEM ALL!" The Rider's voice was stronger now; it roared like a caged beast and I could feel it

slamming against the walls of my ego, trying to grab the wheel and steer me toward its food. *"Oh, damn, are we getting squeamish, Axel? After all these years? After all the people YOU have killed?"* It underlined the fact that I wanted to kill as much as it did.

I tried to ignore it and moved toward the door, but before I could reach it my eyes spotted the large knife on the floor. It was gleaning in the feeble light. It was so beautiful, so charming.

"You want it, Axel, don't you?"

I was confused; my head was spinning and my arms were shaking.

"There, Axel," insisted the Rider, *"there, is the solution to everything: the blade. The blade that will keep away the fear. The blade that will keep the monsters away. Kill or be killed, remember?"*

It was right.

All these years, from the time it had rescued me from that musty pipe in Kamp Koko, the Rider had protected me, had made me feel safe. I was no longer scared of those sexual monsters out there. No, now *I* was the monster hunting them. And it needed to be done ...

"Take the knife. Take the knife and do it!"

My right hand touched the metal, then wrapped itself around the handle.

It felt good. It felt right.

(The face of Morena flashed inside my mind. She was smiling, like that day when I had walked her back home. I had enjoyed that night.)

"Kill her. You don't need her. Listen to me."

(Morena's face faded away and was replaced by that of my mother. I was again lying on my back, holding my knee and crying in pain, and her face was above me, upside-down. She was smiling too, and telling me everything was okay, that that was just a

scratch ...)

"Good boy; that's my boy. Take the knife, Axel. Everything's gonna be alright ..."

And then, I found myself standing in front of the now conscious Dark Angel. Except she didn't look any more like a dark angel. No, now she was just a girl; a confused and scared girl. Her eyes were wide open and were staring, worried, at something above my head. She was mumbling something, but I wasn't listening. I was listening to my mum – or the Rider – or both – telling me everything was fine and I should not be afraid.

I heard Shannon shout again, but I could not understand what she was saying. It didn't matter: soon everything would be over.

I lifted my head to follow the blue-green gaze of the girl. Up, up to ...

(The gentle smile of Abigail replaced that of my mother. She cared for me. I cared for her. Was she okay?)

... my joined hands holding the blade high.

My eyes returned to hers.

"You don't have to," she said.

Yes, she was right, I didn't have to.

"You NEED to," said the Rider.

"No, I don't need to. YOU need to," I blurted. "You only know this: fear, death, pain. I know more than that."

"Do you?" mocked the Rider. *"And what do you know more? There's nothing else inside you, Axel. You are made of the same things that make me."*

"Fight it," said the girl who had been the Dark Angel. "Show it you're stronger. Don't do like me. I thought Sunnayi Edahi was my savior, my protector, but I was wrong. It just wanted to use me. It wanted for me to be just a vessel for its own needs. But I can't feel it anymore. It's gone. It's finally gone!"

I hesitated. She *knew*! She understood what I was; she *felt* what was inside me!

278

"What is SHE to you? Nothing; she's nothing, you listen?" There was something different in the Rider's voice now, something new, something I had never heard before in its dark whispers …

"Fight it!" shouted the girl.

"Heeeelp!!!" howled Shannon from above.

"KILL HER!" cried the Rider.

What was she to me? What? Really. I barely knew her, and she had tried to kill me. She was no different from me; she was a monster …

"FIGHT IT!"

"H-E-E-E-L-P!"

"KILL HER!"

I closed my eyes. Darkness engulfed me. Then I saw my mom again, then Morena, then Abigail …

The shouts became distant until they faded into nothingness, replaced by the sound of chirping crickets; the musky smell of the survivalist's fort became that of wet grass after a thunderstorm.

"You have feelings," said my mother, kissing my forehead. "You can be as happy, sad, angry, and loving as anyone else."

"You don't need it," said Morena, kissing the knuckles of my right hand, and the green hill left place to a suburban street: yellowish light from a porch appliance, the smell of freshly-cut lawns.

"You are human," said Abigail, kissing my cheek. The smell of antiseptic, and that of her perfume now making themselves present as the street turned into my office at the morgue.

"I AM NOT JUST DEATH!" I shouted.

And my knife came down.

CHAPTER 38

CHERI'S TALE
(FROM AXEL'S HALL OF MEMORIES)

The blade cut her ropes, then clanked on the ground. There was no more need, no more urge. I felt weird, to the point of losing consciousness, but that lightheadedness didn't last: it was soon replaced by a new vigor, as if a weight had been removed from my shoulders after uncountable years. I straightened myself and looked at the girl. She was untangling herself from the restraints.

"You okay?" she said with that husky voice, now made even rougher by the stress her box had endured while shrieking like an eagle. "Are you in?"

For a moment I didn't understand what she meant, so I stood uncertain, gazing at my hands as if they belonged to someone else.

"Is it gone? Whatever was riding you … is it gone?" she clarified.

I lifted my head, slowly. My eyes met hers. There was no longer a shadow swimming in those blue-green irises; they looked clear … *human.*

"What do you think?" I said. "Is that possible?"

Her face contracted in a sad smile. "I don't know. But it's not here now; that's for sure. Otherwise, I'll be dead by now, right?"

I nodded.

"What's your name?" she asked. And it sounded so comical in that situation. We were surrounded by blood and dead – or restrained – people, we had just tried to kill one another while under the influence of things we barely understood, and she was there, asking for my name like we had just met in a bar. I couldn't refrain from snickering.

"What?" she said, then she looked around and understood.

"Axel," I murmured like a shy schoolboy. "My name is Axel. Look, I'm sorry for what I was—"

"Cheri," she interrupted, "I'm Cheri."

Then, she shocked me with something unexpected: she closed the distance, lifted a finger to my lips and with the other hand pushed me against her. "Hold me, please."

Without thoughts, without logic, I did exactly that: I held her tight, like my mother used to do when I was scared. I could feel her body shaking and saw streams of tears flowing down her cheeks. It was like years and years of repressed feelings had finally burst out of their prison.

I felt the same.

Memories of all my deeds – things that I had once found exciting and pleasant – flooded me in a red-lit horror. I was seeing them in a different way now, as if I were a phantom spectator watching, helpless, that macabre carnival of inhumane sadism. I saw flesh being torn, bones being crushed and cracked, and blood … blood everywhere.

And I wept. I wept like I had never wept before.

It started with silent tears, but soon turned into a pitched wailing that both surprised and scared me. I wept for young Axel; I cried loud for a wasted life and for those very lives I had taken. Honestly, I didn't feel remorse for stopping their own evil deeds; I was mourning the loss of my own inhumanity. The monsters I had killed deserved indeed to be stopped, for they would never cease feeding on the pain and fear they caused. But not in that way. By torturing and mutilating them I had been no different from them. In addition, I now realized even more how *that* Axel, that creature, had not been me, but just a vessel for the real monster inside my soul.

We stood there, crying and hugging as if we were the only survivors of a plane crash on a deserted island. As if we were the last humans on Earth. I didn't know what had happened to Cheri, but I knew that her life had somewhat been similar to mine.

It was she who interrupted our emotional moment. She slid out of my arms and sat on the ground, wiping away tears from her reddened eyes.

"I don't know if it's gone," she said. "I only know it doesn't control you. Yours is an Urging Spirit: it doesn't like to claim you fully, but it enjoys driving you, pushing you to do the things it likes."

I sat in front of her. "What about yours? Is it gone?"

"Yes." She offered me another smile. "Your spirit ate mine. My uncle told me that spirits need to eat other spirits to grow and become more powerful. And that's exactly what happened just now."

"Are you telling me that my Rider is even more powerful? Oh, God ..."

"Yes, but not more powerful than you." She took my hand. "Axel, whatever that thing is, it can't control you. You pushed it down – or aside, or out – and you just showed that your will is stronger than the spirit's."

"How can I get rid of it?"

"You have already started on that path. I don't know what happened to you, or how you attracted or contracted this thing. But I bet this is the first time you didn't follow its urges. I couldn't do that. I had made a pact: I offered myself to Night Goer."

It was getting even more confusing now. She had accepted that thing inside her, same as I had done at Kamp Koko, but she was now glad it was gone. "But you look relieved to be free of it. To me, it looks like you weren't happy with that thing inside you," I queried.

"Let me tell you my story," she said. "Then, if you want, you can tell me yours."

****

After her show at the Dancing Coyote, Cheri Ridge had decided to not go back home. She had been afraid that those monsters that had kept harassing her at the club would follow her there. She had felt unsafe. Living in a secluded area of Manchester could cause that effect when five horny and drunk men had been eyeing you in an ill-meaning and scary way during your nightly performance. After her uncle's death, she had felt alone in the world, but never as weak and as scared as that night. There was something different in the eyes of those men that had frightened her; they shone with the light of the Moon-Eyed People.

Uncle Johnny had warned her about monsters like these. These spirits were attracted to men with lust inside their hearts, rode their bodies as puppeteers, and urged them to commit the foulest of acts to quench their eternal lecherousness.

So she had opted for spending the night in the wilds, in the tribe's holy grounds, atop the grassy knoll of the Old Stone Fort, and for chanting prayers to the Good Spirits to help her hide in the eyes of the Ada'wehi. A legend said that the Fort had been built by the Ada'wehi themselves to find refuge from the burning light. However, Uncle Johnny had told her otherwise: he had said that it had been built by the Yuchi tribe to stand watch against the coming of those evil spirits.

Still, the Moon-Eyed People had come and taken her.

And no one had been there to help.

She had fought hard, but they were too many, and in the end she had become their toy.

"Hold her down, Billy! It's my turn now," she remembered Marvin protest when he had noticed Billy Gamble had released his grip of her.

"It's over, Marv. Don't you see she's more dead than alive? Are you such a freak you'd fuck dead people, too?" Gamble had snapped.

"She's still alive. And I have the right to—" Wilson had rebuked, but his sentence had been cut short by the sudden scream that had come out of Cheri's martyrized body. Pain was everywhere and she could no longer see; everything was covered in a dark crimson layer.

"Make it stop! Silence her ferchrissake! She's going to attract attention," the guy named Ray Lombardi had said.

Billy had grabbed her again by the throat and had slapped her hard, but she hadn't stopped howling and whelping like a wounded animal.

In the distance, she had heard Marvin Wilson complain to Jay Fraser. "This is unfair, man. This is unfair."

"Kill her, Billy; let's finish this," Frank Hall had replied, in a cold tone that had shut Marvin up for good.

Frank Hall had been the first of the lot. He had considered it his *privilege* as the head of this roving pack of vacationing men. They had come up to Tennessee for a formal meeting with one of the most powerful Aryan Brotherhood leaders. Being a member of the gang, Billy Gamble was the key contact. Jay Fraser was Billy's chapter mate, while Ray and Marvin were the latest additions to the ongoing project in Prosperity Glades.

Cheri had been witness to their dealings at the *Dancing Coyote*: one more reason for her to be silenced. But deep inside, Cheri knew that their shenanigans had nothing to do with it. No, it was just their lifestyle: like devious hyenas they used their pack to get what they wanted; together, they felt powerful and strong. Unstoppable. Each one of them was a gear in the murderous self-satisfactory animal-machine they had built.

Frank Hall was the mind, and his connections and status – if not his money – granted him the power to do as he pleased. If he wanted something, he took it.

Billy Gamble was the heart: pumping blood into the frenzied limbs of the beast.

Jay Fraser, Ray Lombardi, and Marvin Wilson were simply the limbs, claws, and fangs of it. They did as told by the brain and heart, never questioning the morality of their actions; excited and dumbed down by the drug that was Frank Hall.

Cheri had known that she was just the last of a long list of people that had been used, ravaged, and killed for their own entertainment. Or their needs. She had known from the moment she had locked eyes with their leader's that there would be no way out should they catch her. She had imagined them feeding on the pain they caused; like emotional vampires, they enjoyed the feeling of power and the terror they caused in their victims more than the physical acts. People like them were everywhere, hidden under masks of nine-to-five jobs, concealed by layers of faked humanity, and shielded by hundred-dollar suits. They had spouses, children, friends, and people they loved. But in truth, they only had each other. As a pack, they felt alive; without it, they were dead.

"Are you joking, man?" she had heard Wilson protest. "Do you really want to kill this bitch? Come on! She's just a whore, who's gonna believe her? She will never report."

But no one had said a word.

Then, Billie Gamble had strangled her.

Or so he had believed.

Later, after the five monsters had left her for dead, hiding her body inside one of the natural caves, Cheri had returned to her senses. But the wounds and traumas she had endured were too deep. She was dying.

And then the Spirit of Vengeance, the Night Goer, had come out of the dark. It had offered her a way out of death. It had offered her revenge. And left with no other choice, she had accepted. She had accepted even if that meant betraying Uncle Johnny, even if that meant renouncing to everything she had believed in.

Since that day, Cheri Ridge had been no more. She had become a simulacrum of herself: a walking vessel for that ancient spirit and nothing more. Led by the Night Goer, she had been put on a trail to get back at those men who had violated her.

Localizing them took two years.

The first one, Ray Lombardi, she had taken down in the outskirts of Prosperity Glades. After offering him a hitch to town, she had strangled him with a nylon cord. He had been lucky that she could not afford to play with him longer. She had dumped his naked body in a ditch, then had continued on her path to the Nexus. Night Goer had sensed it as soon as they had got closer to that Floridian hamlet. Deep in the swamps, the walls between This Side and the Other Side were thinner.

To the Raven Mocker it had not been a coincidence that the

Pack, as it called it, had come from this spot.

For they were indeed Moon-Eyed People …

****

Cheri's tale was interrupted by the cold voice of Frank Hall. He had come to and was now struggling with his own bonds.

"Hey! You two, let me go! You don't know who you're fucking with!"

Yes, I knew who I was fucking with. I knew the kind of monster he was. It didn't matter if he had been the willing or unwilling host of inhuman spirits like me. I knew he had enjoyed every single moment of his own *games*.

Were there really Moon-Eyed People inside those bastards? I don't know. And I don't care. The point is, as I have learned, that we are not innocent pawns to these creatures. We attract them when our own soul is tainted with hate, rage, and dark desires. They don't just jump into us randomly. Yes, they can beguile us; they can make us believe that there is no other way. But in the end the choice is always ours.

I had chosen not to kill anymore; and it had been *my* choice. This had sent the Rider back to its dark corner of my interior dungeon with its tail between its legs.

Cheri had never had this chance. She had been in pain and dying. At that moment it had been very hard to make a rational choice. Of course, her preservation instinct had prevailed.

But these fucks?

No, surely they had never doubted their own wants. They had liked what they had done and they had never shown traces of a supernatural presence inside their tarnished bodies. They were human monsters; if they were inside them, those things were nothing less than symbiotic spirits enjoying the free meals and rides.

"Let me go at once! Understood?"

I took the knife. Cheri took the hatchet.

"W-a-a-i-t! I can … give you whatever you want," he said.
"You don't have what we want," I said.
"Killing me ain't gonna help you, and—"
Then, he recognized Cheri Ridge and finally understood.

EPILOGUE

GOODBYE

So, my story's over, buddy. You know everything about this weird man who talks to dead people. Well, to be true, there have been other interesting moments in my life, but none as intense as last week. They have changed my life forever.

I had seen strange, scary things in the past—myself being one of them—but I had never seen a woman being completely taken over by something. Except in the movies.

Now I know you're wondering about what happened to Hall, Shannon, and Cheri. And I'm gonna tell you, don't worry.

But first let me tell you what's going to happen next.

You will be my last autopsy here. I've resigned. I've hoarded enough money in all these years to afford a year-long hiatus. I want a new life. Besides, I deserve it. The real Axel Hyde does, I mean, for I never truly lived; I just simulated my existence. I was still that ten-year-old boy trapped in a grown man's body, only, I didn't know it.

Cheri Ridge will bring me to the Old Stone Fort. She believes that by performing the right ritual there I can get rid of the Rider forever. It won't be easy, but it's worth a try. She said something I do not understand, but I know she means the best for me. She said that, at worst, we can feed the Rider to the Windigo.

I like her, you know?

Oh, I understand you might not be of the same opinion, given the circumstances, but I assure you that now that she is free of that Raven Mocker-thing she is a nice and sunny person.

I really wish to become more for her than just a friend.

As for what happened to Frank Hall …

Well, he's alive. You see, I was about to cut him up, but Cheri had this brilliant idea …

First, we went to get Shannon. The poor girl had been there all that time and she had no idea if she had to embrace us as her saviors or to fear us. We told her that those bad guys, those men that had hurt her, were all dead. Except Hall. We told her that we knew the former mayor had been helping Gamble's gang, but we had no proof to show to the police. We confessed having killed those bastards, but again, we could not prove our legitimate defense.

So, we asked her to lie.

We told her what to do and to not mention us at all.

She agreed, and this is what happened next.

Before leaving the place I gave Shannon a cellular phone. It belonged to Hall. Then, Cheri and I left the swamp and went to my house. Once there, we took care of each other's wounds, took turns in the shower, and finally collapsed (she on my bed, I on my couch).

In the meantime, Shannon had called the sheriff's office. Twenty minutes later, Andrews, Espinoza, and Tipple had showed up. Along with pissed off firemen. Tipple had called an ambulance for Shannon, and Morena had listened to her tale. Shannon had told her that Gamble, Bootes, and George Talbot (G.T.) had kidnapped her for a special party at the fort. Later, Hall and Lane had showed up and some kind of argument had turned sour. She couldn't say what, because at the time she was in the underground room, tied to a chair. She had heard a big mess coming from upstairs and then she had smelled fire. In panic, she had managed to free herself from the bounds and to reach the upper floor. There, she had discovered that the whole place was burning and that there were dead bodies around. Alarmed, she had fought her way out of the blazing inferno and that was when she had stumbled upon Frank Hall. He was half-naked and completely covered in blood. The man looked like crazy; he was holding a hatchet, his eyes bulged out of his sockets, and he was also making strange sounds with his mouth. Shannon had found herself stuck between a rock and a hard place as the building around her was starting to crumble down and the madman outside kept swinging the blade at her.

289

Luckily, the demented guy had passed out, and Shannon had proceeded to tie him to a tree and use his cellular phone to call 911.

Then she had discovered the reason for his unnatural speech: half of his tongue was missing.

She had told the cops she didn't know what the hell had happened there and the only thing she wanted was to be away from that place as soon as possible.

Sheriff Andrews and his squad were still at Fort Independence this morning, and they spent the whole day gathering clues and pieces to understand what had really happened. They're still banging heads against what's left of the structure. I was called late to go and try to identify the charred stiffs there. I have already sent my report to Abigail. Of course I have easily identified Billy Gamble, Lawrence Bootes, and James Lane. I'm keeping G.T. for my successor to work on. You know, the face of that guy is practically inexistent.

I have also sent her my resignation letter, explaining that I really need to live more and stay away from death for some time. Naturally, I've emphasized how our chats had helped me understand that I'm still young and there's more out there for me. Maybe a family. I've said to not consider this a goodbye, because I will surely be back to check on her. I will also provide her with my new address once I'll decide to set roots somewhere.

I can't wait to go to Tennessee with Cheri.

But now, back to my last act, buddy.

Here's what I've found: you were strangled by an unknown assailant who left you naked on the side of the highway. He—or she—used a nylon rope to kill you. Maybe you were robbed or maybe not. I do not care, Mr. Ray Lombardi.

Yes, I know you were one of those bastards, and I didn't need help from my Rider this time. Cheri told me she had killed a Mr. Lombardi on the highway with a nylon cord. And those signs around your neck tell me exactly who you were, you sick fuck.

It has been a pleasure, Ray.

Farewell and fuck off.

EPITAPH

A NEW MAN

SIX MONTHS LATER

Jerry Meeks was a completely different man. Yes, he had always been angry at the world, but now he knew that not the whole world had to be blamed: just parts of it. Just those bastards with nice jobs, pretty suburban homes, flashy new cars, and cable TV. While he was confined to a dreary shack, a stinky one-room apartment, a clunker, some broadcasted junk and an overcharged Internet connection.

And now he knew why.

It was all a conspiracy: all those shitty undeserving bastards that kept him away from money and respect. All those condescending bastards that smiled at him only to talk bad behind his back.

Like Sheriff Andrews. The motherfucker loved to bully him, didn't he? He felt so strong with hit big hat, his gun, and his shiny star. But Jerry knew the truth: behind that armor – manufactured by the Government – there was an old and weak man. Yes, Andrews was afraid of Jerry's superior intellect.

And Jerry was going to show him.

After all, his new friend, the one he had seen in dreams, at first, and in the mirror next, had promised Jerry he was going to have all the power he wanted. As long as he kept giving it what it wanted. All Jerry had to do was to grow some balls and be more daring. It was like dreaming of fishing the big ones while settling down for Black Crappies.

And so Jerry had dared.

He had started by playing simple break-in games, just to test his skills and ingenuity. Innocent stuff; he never hurt anyone, he just enjoyed the feeling of being inside their precious suburban homes without them knowing. Once, he had even invaded Andrews' home, when he was away in Clewinston, and had defecated on the man's pretty bed.

Then, two weeks ago, there had been the accident, the game changer.

An arrogant woman from upstate New York, en route to better places than Prosperity Glades had stopped by his Fish and Tackle shack just when it was closing time. She was in need of directions and Jerry had really tried to be kind and helpful, to the point of inviting her out for dinner. But the bitch had looked at him as if she were looking at some disgusting thing she had suddenly found under the sole of her ritzy shoe. When he had tried to use his gentleman's manners she had started to laugh. Jerry had hated that laugh so much.

She was still laughing, back in the shack, except no sound came out of her mouth as the thousands of tiny fish hooks tugged her skin up into a permanent grin. This, after he had strangled her.

Jerry had tried to keep her there, but had to concede that the smell was becoming too difficult to mask. Even with all those disposable air-fresheners dangling from the ceiling. So, he had hacked her to pieces and had given her flesh to the alligators.

Yes, Jerry felt different.

And so did Nemesis.

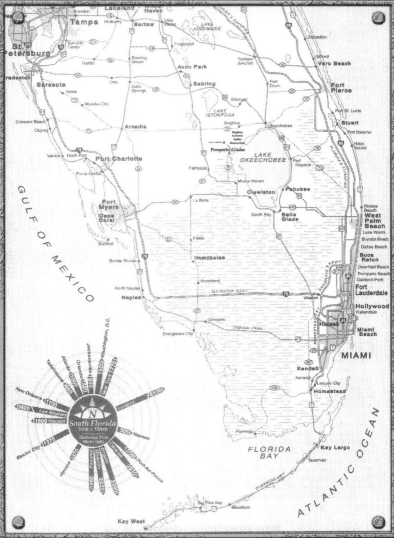

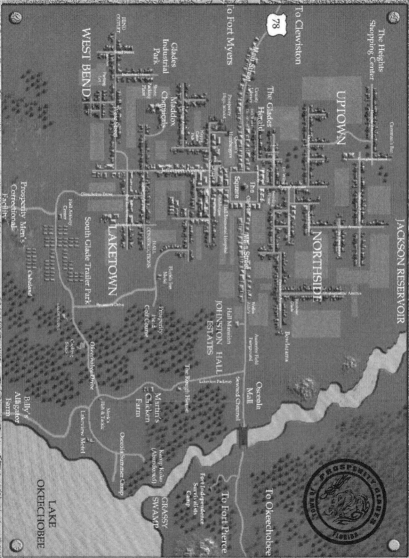

AXEL J HYDE
YOUR FRIENDLY NEIGHBOR

JEFFREY KOSH
FEEDING
THE URGE
REMASTERED

CHERI RIDGE
THE DARK ANGEL

JEFFREY KOSH
FEEDING
THE URGE
REMASTERED

MORENA ESPINOZA
YOUR NEW COP IN TOWN

JEFFREY KOSH

FEEDING
THE URGE
REMASTERED

PETER TIPPLE
COUNTRY COP

JEFFREY KOSH

FEEDING
THE URGE
REMASTERED

JEFFREY KOSH

FEEDING
THE **URGE**
REMASTERED

NEMESIS
THE SILENT HUNTER

JEFFREY KOSH

FEEDING
THE **URGE**
REMASTERED

NIGHT GOER
THE RAVEN MOCKER

Do You Want More Stories From
PROSPERITY GLADES?

Spirits, by their nature, are formless beings; in a way they are just memes. Each spirit represents something about human nature and wishes.

Spirits are wishes made into flesh - or almost flesh.

A thought form can range in complexity from a simple emotional impression to a fully sentient and aware being, and in power from a minor servitor entity to a god.

And they wear masks.

In Prosperity Glades all spirits wear a mask: the Veiled Queen, Nemesis, the Smiling Monster, the Dying Road, the Cloaked Man, and the Smokeless Fire. These tales are all about masks, spirits, and thought forms. All take place in Prosperity Glades, because there's a weak spot between our world and the spiritual one, right in the middle of Grassy Swamp.

And spirits - and thought forms - do thrive there.

Jeffrey Kosh invites you to return once again to that weird town in the heart of Florida's Everglades; where primal forces have a hold on human desires. Yet beware, once there ... avoid making wishes. They can come true and take form.

CHECK OUT THE OMP WEBSITE FOR
A COMPLETE LIST OF OUR TITLES

WWW.OPTIMUSMAXIMUSPUBLISHING.COM

BOOKS ARE AVAILABLE IN BOTH PRINT
AND ELECTRONIC FORMATS

BALLYMOOR, IRELAND, 1891

Patrick Conroy, a young American student of medicine in Dublin, decides to take a break from the hustle and bustle of the big city and spend a month in the quietude of the wild and beautiful Glencree valley, County Wicklow. However, surrounded by local legends and myths, he is soon dragged into an ancient mystery that has haunted the village of Ballymoor for centuries. Set on the background of the tumultuous years preceding the War of Independence, and colored by Irish folklore, the Haunter of the Moor is a ghost story written in the style of Victorian Gothic novels.

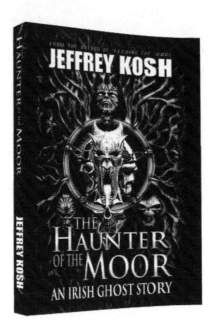

RICKY FLEET
HELLSPAWN
SERIES

10.35 AM, September 14th 2015. Portsmouth, England.

A global particle physics experiment releases a pulse of unknown energy with catastrophic results. The sanctity of the grave has been sundered and a million graveyards expel their tenants from eternal slumber.

The world is unaware of the impending apocalypse, Governments crumble and armies are scattered to the wind under the onslaught of the dead.

Kurt Taylor, a self-employed plumber, witnesses the start of the horrifying outbreak. Desperate to reach his family before they fall victim to the ever growing horde of shambling corruption, he flees the scene.

In a society with few guns, how can people hope to survive the endless waves of zombies that seek to consume every living thing? With ingenuity, planning and everyday materials, the group forge their way and strike back at the Hellspawn legions.

Rescues are mounted, but not all survivors are benevolent, the evil that is in all men has been given free rein in this new, dead world. With both the living and dead to contend with, the Taylor family's battle for survival is just beginning.

Book 1 in the Hellspawn series.

Kurt Taylor and his family have battled the living and the dead and now find themselves on the run, their home reduced to ashes. With unimaginable horror lying in wait around every corner, the onset of winter and the plunging temperatures only add more danger to their precarious existence. They decide to forge ahead and try to reach the protection of others who have hopefully survived the zombie apocalypse. If this fails, their only choice would be to try and reach an impregnable fortress, a sanctuary that has stood for a thousand years.

Standing between them and salvation are the villages and cities of the damned, a path that will test their spirit and resilience unlike anything they have faced before. More companions are rescued from the jaws of death and join them in their perilous journey. Mysterious attacks befall the group and it becomes clear the dead aren't the only things that lurk in the darkness.

Tempers fray and personalities clash. The group starts to fracture and Kurt is forced to commit acts that cause him to question his own morality. Can they survive the horror of their new existence? Will they want to?

The Hellspawn saga continues.

To Fight Evil with Evil

England, 1392.
As the Black Death quickly spreads through the kingdom, the little hamlet of Blythe's Hollow suffers under the yoke of a sadistic Lord. Desperate, the villagers decide to seek out the magical help of a local witch, causing the wrath of the Church. Torture and murder befall on those accused of being in league with the Devil, adding more sorrow to the beset folk of Blythe's Hollow. Yet, one man will rise against the tyranny; a man willing to learn Black Magick to fight back.

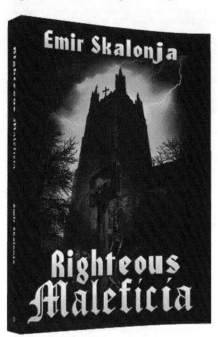

A modern dark urban fantasy, telling of two powerful families who uphold a secret duty to protect humanity from a threat it doesn't know exists.

Though sharing a common enemy, the two families form a long-standing rivalry due to their methods and ultimate goals.

Forces are coalescing in a prominent Central European city criminal sex-trafficking, a serial murderer with a savage bent, and other, less tangible influences.

Within a prestigious, private university, Lilja, a young librarian charged with protecting a very special book, finds herself suddenly ensconced in this dark, strange world. Originally from Finland, she has her own reason for why she left her home, but she finds the city to be anything but a haven from dangers and secrets.

Book One in a planned series.

Meet Mason Ezekiel Barnes, former NFL tackle turned successful author of the naughty ninja adventure series Mia Killjoy. Mason is obsessed with winning a Pulitzer and is thwarted by his fellow author and nemesis, the twerpy little gnome Conrad Bancroft.

Perk Noir is full of comedic relief, pop culture, NFL, jazz, a little touch of romance, and flashbacks of Lightning and his family during both the first half of the 20th century and later during the Civil Rights movement. Mason and Shelly and their adventures is a fun filled thrill ride that will appeal to all readers, there is something for everyone at the Perk.

Two hunters pursue the same prey.

Fate has forged the slayer, Trey Thomas and the Sandrian vampire, Adalius, two natural enemies, into an uneasy alliance against an evil more powerful than either have ever faced. Only together do they stand a chance of defeating Anna; if they don't destroy each other first.

As they pursue Anna, the apprehensive Lycan watch as a confrontation looms on the horizon between vampires, the New Bloods and the Old Guard, which threatens to plunge the vampire world into civil war and trigger an all-out supernatural conflict which in the end could destroy them all.

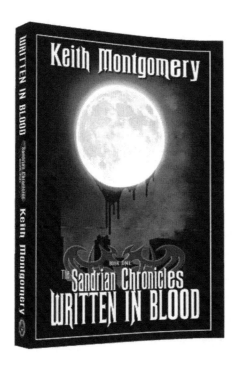

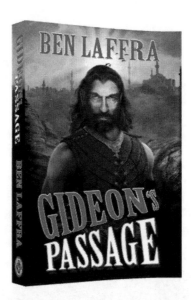

Killing is the sole province of the religious fanatics, an axiom as true today as it was some five hundred years ago; and no nation, region or person is immune.

Europe had clawed its way out of the Middle Ages with the dawning of the renaissance, only to be plunged once more into darkness, as the dogs of war circled to destroy its resurgence during the 16th century. The Islamic successor to the Roman Byzantines, the Ottoman Caliphate, flexed its muscles to conquer much of Western Asia, North Africa and South-Eastern Europe. Christian Europe shuddered when the once invincible bastion of the Knight's at Rhodes were defeated; and now trembled as the Ottoman army rattled the very gates of Vienna. No Christian army, it seemed, could withstand the ferocity of the Azabs, the Akıncı, the Sipahis, the Janissaries, and ruthless Iayalar's of the all-conquering Islamic hordes.

This then is the cauldron into which Gideon de Boyne is unwittingly thrust with his small army of dedicated Christian warriors. On the hostile island of Crete, at the doorstep of the Ottoman Empire, Gideon must face not only the overwhelming force of Muslim warriors but his own inner conflicts of the futility of war and his very Christian beliefs.

Will he succeed and come out of it unscathed?

Collected tales of Madness and Terror

Maximus SHOCK

An OMP Magazine

MAXIMUS
SHOCK
0

Complete
Collection

16 Mind-Shocking Tales!

RICKY FLEET   JEFFREY KOSH   EMIR SKALONJA

KEITH MONTGOMERY   SCOTT CARRUBA   CHRIS GARSON

LORRAINE VERSINI   MAURA ATKINSON BUTLER   MATT HAY

LEON BROWN   WK POMEROY

EDITED BY
CHRISTINA HARGIS SMITH

41731393R00177

Made in the USA
Middletown, DE
21 March 2017